Ladies of the Fire

ENDORSEMENTS

The ladies of the fire are not just friends, they will become your friends. They will speak to your heart's memory of current friends and friends gone by. Trust me, when you are done with this book, you'll find yourself looking for them in your "contacts." Oh ... and did I mention ... their story is both delightful and heart-palpitating!

—**Eva Marie Everson**, bestselling, award-winning author & speaker, *The Ornament Keeper*

Both heart-touching and heart-pounding. In *Ladies of the Fire,* Robin Luftig delivers a fabulous story of friendship, love, and finding purpose. This one leaves me smile-sighing.

—**Rhonda Rhea**, TV personality, humor columnist, and author, *Turtles in the Road* and *Off-Script & Over-Caffeinated*

Ladies of Fire began as an interesting story, then almost immediately, turned into an intriguing one. Adding to my reading pleasure is that this author, in her debut novel, provides a cast of compelling characters, entertainment, mystery, and matters of the heart. Robin Luftig has developed a thought-provoking story of struggle, friendship, and faith. I look forward to more from her.

—**Yvonne Lehman**, author of fifty-nine novels and sixteen nonfiction books in the Divine Moments series. (*Hearts that Survive—A Novel of the Titanic*, Abingdon)

LADIES OF THE FIRE

Robin Luftig

PUBLISHING THE POSITIVE

ELK LAKE PUBLISHING INC
Plymouth, Massachusetts

Cover and Interior Design: Derinda Babcock

Editor(s): Judy Hagey, Deb Haggerty

Author Represented By: Cyle Young Literary Elite

PUBLISHED BY: Elk Lake Publishing, Inc., 35 Dogwood Drive, Plymouth, MA 02360, 2020

Library Cataloging Data

Names: Luftig, Robin (Robin Luftig)

Ladies of the Fire / Robin Luftig

354 p. 23cm × 15cm (9in × 6 in.)

Identifiers: ISBN-13: 978-1-951970-91-8 (paperback) | 978-1-951970-92-5 (trade paperback) | 978-1-951970-93-2 (e-book)

Key Words: Friendship, family, Vietnam-era, mystery/suspense, female protagonists, women's fiction, Christian

LCCN: 2020942839 Fiction

DEDICATION

To Deidre and Joni,
You will always be the ladies of the fire.

acknowledgments

I thank my good friends, Joni Motolla and Deidre Bevan who inspired and challenged me to finish this book.

Thanks to Eva Marie Everson and Word Weavers International who reminded me over and over that I was a good writer each time I was ready to quit.

To my husband Lew for understanding me every step of the way.

Thanks to Derinda Babcock for the cover design. A big thank you to Deb Haggerty and Elk Lake Publications for believing in the story.

And a final thanks to my Lord and Savior, Jesus Christ. Without him, I am nothing.

prologue

Ever has it been, that love knows not its own depth,
until the hour of separation.

—Kahlil Gibran

Lily-Rose Pembrick brushed the ashes to the outside of the firepit then piled dried kindling atop crumpled newspaper. Overhead, the sun hung low in the early autumn sky and the cool air whirled through the dried leaves.

This would be their last fire together. Private. For celebrating—and mourning.

It had to be enough to carry them until—she didn't know when exactly. Nonetheless, the evening had to be as close to perfect as possible.

She wiped the day's dust off the three metal shell chairs around the pit. The well-packed ground beneath each one stood clean of grass from months of foot tapping. Answers to life's questions were seldom found with calm feet.

She returned to the house and retrieved paper cups and plates—much like those she and Sugar and Fiona had at their first fire. Holding them—gripping them—she took another shaky breath and raised one brow. Her life had changed here. How would she find the words to tell them how her heart ached from the thought of missing them?

"Lordy, nothin' slips by you. I thought you might light the fire early." Sugar Bowersox rounded the hedge, carrying a plate of cookies covered with plastic wrap. Strands of wavy blonde hair poked out from under a red paisley bandanna while large hoop earrings framed her face with a Bohemian flair. A tall, leggy woman—a bit of tomboy, a touch of elegance—that was Sugar.

But red-rimmed eyes betrayed her cheerful voice.

"No sad faces tonight," Lily-Rose warned.

"Don't know if I can. This is it, ain't it," Sugar said, more of a statement than a question.

"You can—you have to, Sug. How are we going to get through the evening if you go blubbery or look all hangdog sad? We agreed, remember?"

"You're right." Sugar flopped in her chair and began a nervous rock. "At least I brought some cookies I made today. Between everything else goin' on." Sugar offered the plate.

"Excellent. I hoped you would. Seems appropriate, right?"

"I almost had to wrestle the girls for 'em."

Lily-Rose knew Sugar's sass was an attempt to brighten the mood.

"Do you think she'll make it?" Sugar continued.

"Yep."

"She's pretty busy. Ever since she decided—"

"This is important to her too. Give her some time. She'll be here."

Lily-Rose scuffed a matchstick against the firebricks and a puff of acrid sulfur filled the air. Moments later, small flickers of flame crackled, licking the wood as they seized the kindling for their own.

"Always chases the chill away. Every time," Lily-Rose said.

Momentary silence hung around them as they sat in front of the fire. A star-lit sky closed in and put the day to bed ushering in the cool evening. Soon enough, the birds stopped singing. Cicadas picked up their own hymnals. Squirrels rustled through the leaves while the sky's deep blue hue replaced the day's yellow light.

Sugar sighed. "What if we're the only ones at our farewell fire? What if—"

"For the love of everything holy, Sug, stop fretting. She'll be here." Even as she spoke, Lily-Rose kept her doubts to herself. "She gave her word."

"She gave her word for what?"

Lily-Rose and Sugar turned in time to see Fiona Kasey emerge from around the corner of Lily-Rose's house. Fiona. Always the picture of perfection. She wore bellbottom jeans, a poor boy sweater and carried a canvas bag. Coming closer, light from the fire's flames illuminated her ebony skin, blue eyes, and long sleek black hair. Though casually dressed, she exuded beauty and poise.

"There you are. Never doubted you for a second, Fiona," Sugar said, giving Lily-Rose an embarrassed sideways glance.

"Didn't you hear my car pull in the drive? I'd done some errands for Mrs. Ferguson and needed to put things away and change clothes. Can't stomp through the grass in heels. And these were cooling in the fridge."

She placed her bag on the ground, the contents offering a rattle. Reaching in with both hands she pulled out two bottles of sangria with a flair.

"Red? Or white?" she asked. "Miss Fergie set these aside for us. She figured we could use them."

"Depends on the type of cookies Sugar brought." Lily-Rose winked.

"Oatmeal-raisin, but of course," Sugar uncovered the cookie plate.

Lily-Rose distributed the cups and paper plates while Fiona opened, then shared, the bottle of red. The fire's crackle filled the still air. She looked from one friend to another, memorizing their faces—their mannerisms. She didn't want to waste a moment. She smiled, listening to the banter between her friends.

"Weeds," Sugar said with her self-appointed mother-knows-best voice. "You don't have to pretend you're somthin' you ain't. You can drink this fruity wine from paper cups just as good as fancy crystal. In fact, out here paper's better than that delicate stuff. No fear of breakin' it, and besides, you can burn the stuff after you're done."

"If you'd get out more than just to the food court," Fiona shot back, her eyes dancing, "you'd see there's nothing wrong wanting more in life than what's served on paper or Styrofoam, you crazy woman. And get with it. I let you call me by my childhood nickname. That tells you I'm not snobby."

From the beginning, Fiona and Sugar had found a cadence of lobbing sarcastic barbs at one another to ease away awkward silence. But tonight's finality brought a tension that fun jabs failed to ease.

"Ladies, hold a truce for one night, okay?" Lily-Rose put her palms to her temples.

"She started it," Fiona quipped.

"Nuh-uh," Sugar shot back.

"Enough. Anyone listening would think you two hated each other. Stop flipping out like that."

"Saww-ree," Sugar said in a little girl voice, but reverted to momma bear in an instant. "But I'm right. I can't help it if my opinion on good upbringin' is better than hers."

Sugar and Fiona's gaze met. They acted like adversaries, but in truth, adored each other. They were an inside to the other's outside—opposing, yet always connected.

Sugar gave in first. "Fiona, I'm sorry. Recent events have made me extra sensitive." She leaned forward in her chair, resting her forearms on her knees. "You're both like my own kin. I can't imagine life without you in it. She turned and looked at Lily-Rose. "Truth be told, you're closer to me than some of my own people. You know I'd take a bullet for either one of y'uns, right?"

What was meant to be a flippant comment hung heavy between them. Sugar finally spoke. "Sorry. Just an expression."

"Yeah, I know." Lily-Rose let out a sigh.

The burning wood crackled as the crickets chirped and cicadas droned.

"I'm sorry too," Fiona reached for Sugar's hand. "Your friendship kept me on this side of sane these last few months. Love you, you silly wabbit."

"Ain't's nuthin'. You made the right decision, sweetie. No worries."

Fiona winced and dropped Sugar's hand. "What do you mean, ain't nothing? I try to show my appreciation—and we all know that goes against my grain—and you shut me down."

Lily-Rose closed her eyes and reminded herself how their devotion to one another had not simply withstood two years of challenges—their relationship had taken on the strength of steel.

"What a tragedy at the festival, right?" Fiona changed the subject in almost a whisper. "I still can't believe it. Wish I could have been here when everything came down, but I was in Cleveland." She looked from Sugar to Lily-Rose, then at her drink. "Sorry, you guys."

"It was like I had an out-of-body experience." Sugar rested back in her chair.

"The police and the last of the news crews left here a bit ago," Lily-Rose replied. "They'll probably come back. Off and on for a few weeks I bet. So let's not rehash everything just yet, okay? How about focusing on each other—and the fire."

All three women sat in silence, sipping and nibbling, the evening dew thickening the night.

Fiona spoke first. "To think, Sug, we didn't give one another the time of day until Lily-Rose moved in and started her fires." She tilted her head and grinned. "Lily-Rose, I blame you for this southern discomfort in my life."

Lily-Rose smiled. How had two women with backgrounds and goals so diverse come to mean everything to her, each having a part in bringing light back to her shadow of a life again?

"Nobody else is stopping by tonight?" Lily-Rose asked, omitting the names of players they all knew.

"Not from my house," Sugar said. "Dungar wanted a change of scenery for tonight and offered to take the girls to the drive-in. *Willy Wonka & the Chocolate Factory*'s playing there until school starts. I made sure they put their pj's on before they left—the girls, not Dungar. This way they can go straight to bed when they get home. I even packed snacks and drinks for 'em—the girls and their daddy." She snickered. "I hope he parks by the bathrooms." She paused then added, "And Granny's getting together with her bowling league buddies tonight. So she'll be gone most the evening."

"I'm good," Fiona offered. She didn't elaborate; she seldom did.

"My two spent the day with some friends. They wanted a break after everything that happened. They'll be home in the morning. So, I'm good too," Lily-Rose said.

"What about—" Sugar asked.

"Nope. Just us. It's only fitting we close the fire the same way we started," Lily-Rose said.

"Or will—" Sugar motioned toward Fiona.

"No, I said I'm good. All good." Fiona said and then muttered, "Land sakes, how many times do I need to say 'good' to you space cadets tonight? Lily-Rose, pass that sangria back."

Again, they watched embers escape the flames and reach

the sky, silence crackling between them.

Lily-Rose leaned over to stir the fire. "Can you believe how we've changed? You two helped me find strength again."

"Where we came from to where we are now," Fiona added.

"Our lives were touch-and-go for a while ... but we made it," Sugar said.

"What do we do now?" Fiona whimpered out of character.

Lily-Rose's gaze went from Fiona to Sugar, trying to capture the vision of them in the firelight. Seeing them for who they were. Taking in what each of them brought to their friendship. She smiled.

"I couldn't have planned this any better if I'd tried. You guys remember how this started?"

"Sure do," Fiona cackled. "Who knew you'd be a phoenix rising out of the ashes?"

Sugar frowned, "I swear, Fiona. "Y'uns need to pay attention. What's travelin' to Arizona have to do with us now?"

"I'm a Pembrick. We always rise to the occasion." Lily-Rose laughed easily, even as she quietly thanked God for putting her on the path to Applegate, Ohio, two years earlier ...

chapter 1

May 1969

A person often meets his destiny on the road he took
to avoid it.

—Jean de La Fontaine, French poet

Today's the day she would bury her husband.

Lily-Rose sat under the awning on a padded chair—the
special chair—reserved for a mourning spouse. Unusually cool
and tormenting May winds whipped between the headstones
in Lincoln's Wyuka Cemetery, drawing her long and unruly
auburn hair from her hat. The Pembrick mausoleum stood in
prominence with other mausoleums bearing the well-known
Lancaster county names—the same names that marked streets
in the historic Nebraska city. Butler. Kennard. Miller and
Paine.

Lily-Rose had attended many a funeral in her thirty-five
years, but she still couldn't recall the proper etiquette. Should
the grieving widow stand or stay seated when the minister
approached? She lifted a quivering gloved hand to Mark
Backus, pastor-in-training, as he approached, hoping he would
help her navigate the proper decorum.

"Uh, Mrs. Pembrick, ma'am," Pastor Backus accepted her
offered hand and motioned her to stay seated. He cleared his
throat, seeming to search for the appropriate words. "It's hard
to explain such an unforeseen death for someone in the prime

of life. Edward still had so much to offer. Who can fathom the will of God?"

Lily-Rose's gaze stayed unfocused and she offered no response.

"Edward's life shined as a beacon in the community," he continued. "I hope you find solace, knowing that many people loved and admired him."

With still no reply, he straightened his back, raked his fingers through his hair, and muttered. "Father, help me here."

Lily-Rose looked in the direction of the man of God, veiled confusion clouding her view. "Your platitudes sound hollow."

The pastor startled at her raw and unfiltered comment. He tried again. "Er, uh—don't worry about a thing, Lily-Rose. This will only take a few moments. We'll have you home in a jiffy."

Her tone remained flat as she finally made eye contact with the pastor. She raised an eyebrow. "Really? Don't worry about a thing? And just what am I supposed to do with my life when I get home … in a jiffy?"

Lily-Rose looked down again and rubbed her fingers over her lap, pressing imaginary wrinkles from her suit. Even in her foggy state, she regretted her words hit so hard. Maybe Pastor Backus didn't mind being here, but she hated it. She shifted in her chair and tried to bridle her words.

"I'm sorry, pastor. I must've left my manners at home. Momma'd give me a good talkin' to for how I'm acting. Forgive me," her voice cracked, "but no words are gonna make this better for me."

She shifted again, trying to get comfortable in her seat. Her clothes, though elegant to fit her station, were not fit for the occasion. While her short black boots hugged her ankles and offered a respite from the wind, her one-of-a-kind Jacques Heim suit did little to keep her warm.

She had picked this outfit from her closet in honor of her husband. Even though Edward enjoyed Lily-Rose's casual preferences in attire, the sight of her in this designer's clothing always made him smile. "If it's good enough for Sophia Loren, it's good enough for my Lily-Rose," he'd say. But truth be told, she would have traded anything to be in a pair of jeans, a cable knit sweater, and her favorite high-top Converse tennis shoes and away from here, where she was surrounded by Lincoln's hoity-toity society.

Anywhere but here.

The psychotropic medication prescribed by the family doctor had set her head in the clouds. He had guaranteed their ability to carry her through the funeral—and a bit after. He promised no harm. No foul. Maybe that's why her words to the pastor were so biting and out of character.

She refocused her thoughts on the present and spoke softly to the hapless man before her. "It's not getting any warmer, pastor. Let's move this show along."

Local news crews lurked outside the cemetery, just as they had parked at the gate of Lily-Rose's home, waiting for the money shot—the first picture of the young, rags-to-riches grieving widow about to gain control of millions. In the days since the accident, she had agreed to let a few of Edward's associates into her gated protective bubble. She had turned to his team for support but was met with either empty words or callous comments.

"Lily-Rose, darling, I feel just awful about Edward," or "Lily-Rose, everything's all cool. Considering your age and piles of money in the bank, you won't have any problems finding another dude for your ankle biters."

The comfort she so desperately needed came from her children. Lily-Rose's son Delaney—nicknamed Del—now sat on his own padded chair and huddled against her, staving off the elements. She treasured his presence. The smell of his hair. The emotional connection they shared since his birth. Her baby. He buried the left shoulder of his slight twelve-year-old frame into her side. She wished there was more to offer him than just the comfort of her presence. His blue eyes—his father's eyes—that once danced with laughter, now puffy and pooling with tears. His freckled nose—her nose—shone red from crying.

His words after the accident still haunted her. "I'm sorry, Mom. It's my fault Dad's dead."

No, she had told him, but she knew the accident would live rent-free in her son's heart the rest of his life. Not because of him, but because of that. Edward had fallen from a tree in their backyard while retrieving a snagged Frisbee. An accident, pure and simple. One slip. Now her kids had only the memory of a father.

Ironically, she and Edward had chosen to live in a gated community to keep their family safe. Still, heartache managed to find them. Edward was dead. As she watched the expression of guilt wash her son's face, Lily-Rose ached, even in her drugged state.

Mary, Lily-Rose's sixteen-year-old daughter, sat like a block of ice at her left in another chair of honor. Her auburn hair and beauty mirrored her mother's. Straight bangs fringed her porcelain skin. Her strong jaw—that defiant mannerism that caused so many fights between them—was apparent. Even grieving, she cared little about propriety and insisted on wearing the most with-it style. The collar of her Nehru maxi-dress peered out of her muskrat fur peacoat.

Lily-Rose winced at the thought of her daughter's pouts and flinches when she reached out for her. Probably because Mary blamed her for Edward's death. Not surprising. Mary seemed to blame her for everything these days. Nothing came easy to the relationship between this stay-at-home mother and her teenage daughter. As they waited by Edward's final resting place, the memory of Mary's words and the pain that came with them at the accident site rushed back.

"If I'd been there," Mary screamed, "this never would've happened. I climbed that tree a million times. It's your fault Dad's dead. I hate you. I wish *you* were dead."

As hours passed that horrid day, Mary's anger lessened as she worked through the shock of her dad being gone.

"Mom," Mary said the day after her tantrum. "I'm sorry 'bout what I said when Dad fell." She walked to where Lily-Rose sat and curled onto her mother's lap, the way only a child who knew all the sweet spots could. Lily-Rose embraced a reprieve from emptiness with her daughter in her arms as their heads nuzzled.

"Mommy," Mary said, voice breaking. "I'm still pretty ticked off at you."

"I'm angry, too, sweetie," she said, knowing her daughter's anger wasn't truly on her.

Mary's snuggling filled Lily-Rose's lap. Silence hung in the air. Lily-Rose inhaled the sweet smell of Mary's shampoo.

"I could've fixed it."

"I know it's hard, girlie, but please don't dwell on the whys of this too long. You'll just find grief and sorrow there."

Moments passed. Mary stayed cuddled in her mother's lap. "Mommy?"

"Yes, dear?"

"Who's going to teach me to drive a stick?"

Lily-Rose smiled. The picture of Mary grinding gears in the driveway brought a moment of joy to her.

"How 'bout me? Would that be so terrible?"

"S'pose not."

More silence.

"Mommy?"

"Yes, Mary." Lily-Rose stroked her daughter's hair.

"When I get married, who's gonna walk me down the aisle?"

"I don't know, baby. Do you plan on getting married any time soon?"

"Huh. No."

Lily-Rose kissed the top of Mary's head then leaned her cheek against it, savoring the moment. "Well, that's a relief. Maybe we can find the answer to that question when we get closer to your big day. What do you say?"

"I s'pose.

More time passed. Lily-Rose fingered the tiny tangles in Mary's hair in silence.

"Mom?"

"Yes, Mary."

"I'm still ticked."

"Yeah, I know, Mare. I'm still ticked too."

Lily-Rose's awareness of that day's finality returned to her. Yes, she was angry. And sad. And scared. And alone.

Lily-Rose's skin began to crawl as she looked around and spied Christopher Pembrick, Edward's brother, seated behind her, staring at her. She smiled. Lily-Rose had overheard comments from several of her husband's colleagues that Christopher might make an appearance from Saint Lucia with his latest conquest to attend the funeral. Sure enough, he had.

He hadn't seen much of the family in years. He'd worked alongside Edward at Pembrick Transportation when necessary, but seldom spent time with Lily-Rose and the kids. She marveled over how the kids adored their uncle even though he rarely saw them. Yet she understood. When Christopher let someone into his life, the effects were inspiring.

She remembered. But that was years—a lifetime—ago.

Maybe this could be a healing opportunity for Christopher.

For all of them. With Edward gone, maybe Christopher would find peace with the remaining Pembrick family.

Christopher sat scrunched in his seat with his coat collar flipped up, staving off the wind's assault. His beard stubble gave away the fact he probably hadn't decided to attend until the last minute. He hadn't removed his aviator sunglasses, but Lily-Rose could only guess they hid the evidence of an alcohol-filled all-nighter.

A tanned, long-legged woman who didn't seem much older than Mary tried to wrap herself around his arm.

As Lily-Rose turned to face forward she heard the woman's whine. "Christopher, the wind's cold." Her gum cracked between the words and emitted the faint scent of peppermint. "When can we go back to the island?"

"Shh. We talked about this on the way here, Melody, and you promised to be quiet." He exhaled deeply. "My head's killing me."

"My name's Melanie, remember—Melanee, not Melodee."

"Right. After I put some business behind me, we can leave and pick up where we left off."

"But I'm cold."

He tilted his head toward her and talked quietly, but Lily-Rose still heard the exchange. "Haven't I taken care of my ol' lady up till now? The sand, the shopping"—he paused—"and the nights? Relax, be your gorgeous self and know every man here envies me."

"You think I'm gorgeous, Christopher?" Still snapping.

"Yeah, yeah, sure, baby. I promise we'll take the Pembrick plane back when I'm done. Maybe you could wear one of the groovy little numbers I bought for you. Wear for a bit, anyway."

Shocked by such talk at her husband's funeral, Lily-Rose turned to glare at her brother-in-law in time to hear, "Okay, Christopher, whatever you say."

"Thanks, honey. You won't regret it. I promise."

Christopher noticed Lily-Rose's frown and pulled his glasses down the bridge of his nose to meet it.

She softened. This was for Edward. "Nice to see you, Christopher. Thanks for coming."

"Yeah, no problem. It's been awhile since we last spoke. You look good—considering. Sorry for your loss."

"Edward's death is your loss too. You, me, and the kids are all that's left now."

"And Pembrick Transportation. Don't forget we still have that."

Del and Mary turned at the sound of Christopher's voice. "Hey, Unc-a-bunk."

Christopher offered a genuine smile to the kids. "Hey," was all he said. With that, the kids turned back.

Christopher leaned in for a more private conversation with Lily-Rose. "Excuse me for sayin', but you're still smokin' hot. Edward was one lucky guy. First you, then the family business. He had everything a man could want. The perfect life ... until last week. So much for perfection, right? I mean really, he went and got dead."

Lily-Rose gasped and whipped around, wishing she had never initiated their conversation.

The sharp wind carried Christopher's voice to her again. "Don't worry, Melissa. We'll be in Saint Lucia before you can blink. Meeting with the attorney won't take long."

"My name's Melanie, not Melissa. 'Member—Melanee."

"Sure, honey, whatever you say."

"Thank you for coming to honor the life of Edward Cooper Pembrick," Pastor Backus's voice faded into the background. Lily-Rose bit the inside of her cheek to distract herself from crying. She needed to be strong for Mary and Del. She needed to show Christopher he couldn't shake her. She needed to prove to herself that what Edward had said all along was true. She would be worthy to be a Pembrick.

chapter 2

If you can look into the seeds of time, and say
which grain will grow and which will not, speak
then unto me.

—William Shakespeare

Kid Karn had wasted no time moving his father's personal touches out of his office and bringing in his own flare. He removed William G. Gaul's classic piece, *The Pow-Wow*, and replaced it with a piece Kazuo Shiraga had painted with his feet. He also gave away his father's treasured Frederic Remington sculpture, *The Broncho Buster*, and brought in a bronze bust of Ulyanov Lenin. He successfully removed all paternal memories from Pembrick Transportation except a portrait the PT's senior executives gifted him of his father after the old man's death.

The king is dead. Long live the king.

Kevin Karn Jr., corporate attorney for Pembrick Transportation, paced through the office making sure the setting gave him the greatest advantage of power over Christopher and Lily-Rose Pembrick when they arrived. Kevin knew his not-so-loving clients referred to him as Kid. But he'd take the insults—because the salary was incredible. But he hadn't signed on to be legal counsel to freaked-out people the likes of Christopher and Lily-Rose. Especially the former. A nut—zero to sixty. If the money hadn't been so easy up to now, he'd have been gone long ago.

Bringing them to the office before regular business hours

the day after Memorial Day had been brilliant. The move was worth paying Janice, his lovely assistant, double time for that extra hour. He couldn't wait to show them he controlled their time as well as their money. Let them know off the bat who was in charge.

He shifted one chair an inch to the left. Not too close to the other or to him or his desk. He had learned the importance of staging from his father, who'd been known as Counselor, the previous legal representative of PT. His father had left huge shoes to fill. But Kid wanted nothing to do with his father's shoes. What he wanted was the easy money and prestige that working for this transportation empire afforded. So far, so good.

He looked around the room making sure everything was perfect. He smiled as his gaze landed on his father's portrait. "Watch and learn how modern lawyering's done, ol' man. I'm going to own them. Make Christopher cry like a baby. And he won't even see it comin'."

Kid steeled his emotions as Janice led Lily-Rose and Christopher through the mahogany doors and into his office. He flipped on his charm and greeted Christopher with a firm handshake. But Lily-Rose's grasp met his like a fish that had been out of water too long.

"Lily-Rose," he said, adding a lilt to the end of her name, hoping she'd feel safe around him. "You okay? You look a bit … distracted." If truth be told, she resembled a character from *Night of the Living Dead*.

When she didn't answer, Kid continued. "Please. Sit here. Christopher, you too." He walked them to their seats then went to the front of his desk and picked up the ivory cigarette box, offering Lily-Rose a choice imported Indian-blend smoke. "Want a cig? These are the finest money can buy."

"No. Thank you. I think the medications they put me

on are working their way out of my system now. It's been a rough week, but I should be okay. I'll follow today's meeting, I promise. If I have any questions, I'll raise my hand."

"Fine, fine," Kid moved back around his desk. On his way, he glanced again at the picture of his father and gave him a nod. He cleared his throat and began a prepared speech. "Lily-Rose and Christopher, I'm sorry for your loss. When William and Sandra Pembrick died nine years ago, my father felt the loss too. As you know, he was dedicated to your family. I watched him take immense pride in making sure he honored your parents' last wishes. I—"

"Yeah, yeah. Thanks for the sashay down memory lane, Kid." Christopher stood, reached across Kid's desk for the ivory box and pulled out a cigarette. "And, yes. I'd like a cig, not that you asked me. Now … let's review the abridged version of the story, shall we?"

He swept the brass desk lighter into his free hand, taking ownership of Kid's space. He lit the cigarette, took a deep drag, and exhaled three smoke rings toward Kid before returning to his chair, which he leaned onto its back legs.

Kid squinted through the shroud of smoke. But he held his tongue. Today's entertainment had just launched, and he sure wasn't going to let this Pembrick upstart steal his thunder.

All in good time. All in good time.

"As you recall," Christopher began, "the last time we were here, your dad read Mother and Dad's will to Edward and me. They had tried to placate me with a generous allowance, but bottom line, they bequeathed everything to Edward. I threatened to take him to court, but to keep our squabble out of the papers, he offered me half the company if I took time to learn the business." He harrumphed. "That was a laugh. I already knew the business inside and out. But I was fine playing along with Ed's new rules. Anything for Pembrick

Transportation."

Pausing, Christopher surveyed the room as if he owned it, then flicked ashes on the floor, leaving Kid to bristle under the audacity. "So, days later I sat here while your ol' man, Big Brother, and I drew up an agreement saying that perfect Edward would split the company fifty-fifty." One brow shot up. "Yep, I remember it like it was yesterday."

He paused. Winked in Lily-Rose's direction. "You with me on this, sweetheart? I haven't lost you, have I?"

Lily-Rose stared at Christopher, her eyes shining like empty glasses, still saying nothing.

"I guess I'll take that as a yes." Christopher dropped the chair back to its front legs with a thud, then stood and strutted toward Kid's desk.

"Now let's move on to today's business. Where do I sign? There's a plane for me to catch and I don't know how long I can keep Merissa holding on."

Kid's hands shook from excitement. He lived for moments like this—moments to shine. What he had been waiting for. Satisfaction at its finest. He planned to savor every second.

"Hold up there, Christopher. We're not there yet."

All motion in the room halted. Christopher and Lily-Rose stared at Kid. He straightened his tie. Pulled his cuffed sleeves tight under his suitcoat as he stood and stared Christopher in the eye. Who owned the room? He did. And he would enjoy reminding Christopher of that fact. You're the king of the mountain, Kid. Never forget that. The guys downtown would get an earful over drinks tonight. They'd hear all about how he took the wind out of the sails of the spoiled and indulged Christopher Pembrick.

"We should read Edward's last will and testament first," Kid said, meeting Christopher's gaze and seeing the veins in his neck instantly bulge.

Christopher paused, returned to his chair, easing into the seat, and crossing his legs. Kid knew he was plotting his next move and looked forward to it. He smiled. Kid looked from Christopher to Lily-Rose, cleared his throat, and began.

"I, Edward Cooper Pembrick, a resident of the county of Lancaster and the city of Lincoln, state of Nebraska, being of lawful age and of sound and disposing mind and memory, do make, publish and declare this to be my last will and testament and do hereby revoke all former wills and codicils made by me—"

Christopher uncrossed his legs and slid up on the chair as he pounded the chair's armrests. "Hey, no way, man. What's going on? What's this about revoking all former wills and codicils?" He snuffed out his cigarette on the arm of his chair and flicked the butt over his shoulder, leering at Kid who stared at the place in the carpet where the cigarette had landed. "What are you trying to pull off? Where's the agreement I signed with Edward?"

Kid winced. Okay. This wasn't at all how he envisioned the conversation going. Granted, he hadn't had much practice with crazy, but he at least recognized a nutcase when it stood in front of him. His fingers danced nervously on the desk. His mind raced. His throat tightened. He needed to find an existence somewhere between being a bootlicker to the Pembrick family and chasing after ambulances.

"I'm waiting."

Kid's hands continued to shake. Conversations between him and his father flashed in his mind. Conversations of kowtowing to the Pembricks, each time renewing his determination to never be an errand boy like his old man.

Kid looked at Lily-Rose. He could tell by her tilted head and furrowed brow that he would need to speak in such a manner that his words would register. He played with his pen, buying time. "Funny thing, Chris—Mr. Pembrick. Funny-odd that is, not funny ha-ha. I can read the document you and your brother had my father craft after I finished Edward's will if you like. But I hope you recall the small but significant stipulation everyone agreed to. You needed to have studied the business—"

"I did study the business," Christopher jumped out of his chair and slammed his fists on Kid's desk as he leaned in. He reached for another cigarette and grabbed the desk lighter. "I went to every board meeting. I followed Edward around like his lackey. The humiliation from jumping through all those hoops almost finished me off, but I did it. 'Christopher, do this, Christopher, do that.' I did what was asked of me—and more. I did what was necessary because of Pembrick Transportation."

Christopher lit the cigarette and took a long hard drag. He then exploded with an exasperated, "Aargh" as he threw the lighter toward Kid. The startled attorney ducked as it whizzed past and bounced off the back wall. He continued to stare at Kid as the air thickened with smoke.

Composing himself, Christopher inhaled a deep breath and walked to his chair and sat again. "My shrink says I have anger issues." He closed his eyes, clearly preparing himself for Kid's next move.

Lily-Rose continued sitting in her seat. Not a peep. She hadn't moved an inch since she arrived.

Kid leaned down and picked up the lighter and placed it back on his desk. Never had he been more thankful than this moment that his mahogany partition offered enough distance to hold Christopher at bay while he enjoyed the adrenaline—and the rush from fear—shooting through his body. Who knew this would be such a ride? Who had the power now, Chris, ol' boy?

"You were to study the business for ten years," Kid noted.

"It's only been nine since you signed the agreement, meaning you haven't met your obligation to complete the arrangement."

Lily-Rose shifted in her chair. "What are you saying, Mr. Karn?" The cloud began to lift from her eyes.

Before Kid could answer, Christopher turned, staring at Edward's widow. "It means, dear sister-in-law, I've been a chump once again to believe any Pembrick would ever consider me a part of this family." Christopher stood once more and paced the floor before stomping back to his chair. He kicked it over, then returned to his pacing. His face went red. His eyes blackened.

For years, Kid had listened to his father's stories about Christopher's stunts and had become bored by the tales of juvenile escapades. Now the stories took on flesh right before him, in living color. He'd need to stay focused if he was going to have the appearance of showing respect and appreciation to the Pembricks. His dad always pushed that respect-and-appreciation thing.

"The Pembricks are fine, hard-working people, son," he'd said. "I've made a solid living with them, and they never asked me to bend the law for them—not once. They owe you nothing, yet from the beginning they've encouraged you to consider taking my place at PT after I retire. You should at least show some respect and appreciation."

"Respect and appreciation, hah. They'll be lucky to have me. Greenbacks talk, nothing else. You're a fool, old man. I plan to ride the Pembrick cash cow all the way to the bank. Maybe even milk them dry. Hey, cow … milk. See what I did there?"

Now he sat front and center witnessing Christopher's short jaunt into insanity. Where did respect and appreciation fit in here? The man before him made his father's stories sound tame, and he wished he had called security to be ready, just in case the business got out of control. He reached for the loaded derringer taped under his middle desk drawer.

Christopher's tone continued to rise as he ricocheted from one side of the office to the other. "I'm such a sucker. I shoulda seen this coming. This has been the story of my life. Edward this. Edward that. The way they acted you'da sworn they only had one son. They could have made up for the way they treated me when they died. But no. First Mother and Dad embarrassed me by saddling me with an allowance. Then they all but kicked me to the curb when they gave PT to Edward."

He booted the toppled chair again, sending it against the wall of bookshelves. "And to seal my fate, my jive-turkey brother puts the final nail in my coffin by dying a few months prior to the agreement's maturation. This is unreal."

"Mr. Pembrick, sir," Kid's shirt collar tightened, his illusion of power waning. "I'm sure we can work something out. You'll keep your allowance. Nothing's going to change there. Let's figure—"

"What? Figure something out? Enough is enough. I am their son, whether they ever accepted that or not. Me, I tell you. I'm their last heir. The company goes to me."

Lily-Rose cleared her throat and finally joined the conversation. "Mr. Karn, let me give PT to him. I don't even know anything about the transportation business. Christopher'd be better at the job than I anyway."

"Sorry, quite impossible, Lily-Rose—Mrs. Pembrick, ma'am. My father was a thorough lawyer. I've studied this paperwork. He made sure to safeguard PT in trusts for you and your children. For Christopher to gain control, you'd all need to—"

The room went still. Lily-Rose's gaze stayed on the attorney, and Christopher stopped pacing in front of Kid's desk.

"Finish your thought, Kid." Christopher leaned in again,

staring at the flustered attorney. "They'd all need to—what?"

"Well, uh—" He cleared his throat and pulled at his collar. "Die. Dead—I mean—Lily-Rose and her children would all need to be dead. They're the legal heirs. But if they weren't around, Pembrick Transportation and its holdings would automatically go to you. Mr. Pembrick. Sir."

"Seriously," Lily-Rose said. "I don't need to die. Is all this necessary, Mr. Karn? I mean, really. I'm fine with PT going to him."

Christopher's gaze locked on Lily-Rose, yet his attention was elsewhere. "I hear dying's all the rage now. Everybody's doing it." Slowly, deliberately, he set the chair right and lowered himself into the seat. His eyes still held a dark cast, but his demeanor cooled. Calmer yet more frightening than before. Unnatural. He sat motionless for a moment as if collecting his thoughts. Finally, in a controlled and polite voice, he addressed the attorney. "Do you need anything more from me, Mr. Karn?" He pulled his aviator sunglasses from his breast pocket and put them on. "If we're done here, I do have a plane to catch." He pulled the shades down the bridge of his nose and peered at Lily-Rose. "Or better yet, some new plans to attend to. You never know when the next Pembrick funeral will take place."

Plans to attend to? Next Pembrick funeral? Man-o-man, Pops. You said Christopher could be trouble, but what he exhibited here went beyond that. The boy was a real fruitcake.

Kid had been in some dark and nefarious situations before and had perceived the seedier side of life, but he never thought evil was real. Now he couldn't be so sure. Had he just witnessed Christopher threaten to kill Lily-Rose and her kids? This most definitely hadn't gone according to plans.

"I'm sure we can work something out, Mr. Pembrick. If you give me some time, maybe I can find something—a payment plan, perhaps? You must be right. I undoubtedly missed something."

Christopher spoke through clenched teeth. "If you think I'm going to let you hold all the marbles and give me payments on what's rightfully mine, you're trippin' man. You're already the administrator of the PT fortune, right?"

Kid cleared his throat. "Yes, but only until the paperwork is finalized, but someone—"

"I'm that someone who should be managing this company— not her, you twit."

Kid's gaze darted from Christopher, then to Lily-Rose, who sat wide-eyed and her mouth opened to speak, but had remained mute. Finally, she broke the silence. "Come on, Christopher, cool down. Please. We can work something out. Like Mr. Karn said, maybe he needs to look through the paperwork some more. Different possibilities. He'll find something, I'm sure of it. I bet—"

Kid held his breath as Christopher's glare—devoid of any apparent emotion—moved from him and focused on Lily-Rose.

"I'll be interested in what you'd bet. Wager. Risk." Standing, he huffed then paused. "Now, if the two of you will excuse me."

Christopher nodded to them, then left. Lily-Rose and Kid sat frozen as they looked at each other

"Well, that didn't go too badly." Kid finally settled back into his chair. He tried to hide the tremor in his hands as he reached for the lighter he'd picked up from the floor and a cigarette. He cleared his throat. "Over the next few days I'll do what I can to find loopholes in the trust." Bringing a touch of formality to his voice, he continued. "But I gotta say, Mrs. Pembrick, I doubt I'll find anything new."

Lily-Rose's brows furrowed as she tilted her head and looked at him. "But you told Christopher there might be something you missed."

"Didn't you see him? No offense, but your brother-in-law's whacked. He scared me half to death. I'da said anything to make him happy. I thought he was gonna kill me a couple of times. Did you see what he did to my Persian rug and mahogany chair? They're burned. Ruined. Just like that. Sure glad he stayed on his side of the desk. And you saw him come at me, right? He almost grabbed me by the neck. You saw it, right?" Kid knew he exaggerated, but wanted his words to sink in. He wasn't altogether sure the woman sitting before him would remember most of the meeting.

Lily-Rose stood and collected her wrap and purse. She stared at the floor a moment before she headed for the door. Her brows furrowed. Kid could tell she was trying to comprehend all that had transpired.

When she reached the door, she turned. "Thank you for your time, Mr. Karn. Let me know if I can be of any assistance." With that, she left his office.

This was nuts. Nosiree. He didn't sign on for this. The attorney paused and looked again at his father's portrait, swearing he heard his voice. "You'll know soon enough, son. Lawyers learn what they're made of when they get burned by the flames of legal fires. What you decide to work for always comes down to a choice—either character or cash. It's almost impossible to have both. If you haven't learned that being a man of character is more important than anything else, nothing you've ever learned has value."

Oh, sure. His father insisted on haunting his thoughts now?

"Janice," he called to his assistant through the half-opened door. "Clear the rest of my day, will ya? I gotta get out of here." Then, to himself, "I'm sensing a three-martini lunch in my future."

chapter 3

Anger, resentment, and jealousy doesn't change the
heart of another—it only changes yours.

—Shannon L. Alder

Lily-Rose left the lawyer's office, reeling from the ordeal
with Kid and Christopher. Kid said it'd be a simple meeting—
just sign a few documents. That's all. However, the get-together
turned out to be much more. Seeing Christopher lose control
like he did reminded her of years gone past. But this time,
he went further than he'd ever gone before. His words, "I'll
be interested in what you'd bet," had brought her out of her
medicinal fog and left her shaking. What had he meant? Seeing
him act out wasn't new, but there had been nothing like today.
First outraged, then eerily calm. She couldn't shake how his
eyes looked. Dark and hateful.

Her heart began to race as Lily-Rose entered the almost-
empty parking garage. She struggled catching her breath as
her legs carried her without direction. The intensity batted
around in Karn's office had brought her back to reality but
left her feeling like a limp dishcloth. She focused ahead. There
was her car. Her way of escape from the craziness she had just
experienced.

When she reached the vehicle, she leaned against it,
wishing the day away. No, not the day, but the past two weeks.
A nightmare had taken over her life and left her helpless. Lily-
Rose closed her eyes, trying to collect her thoughts until tears

slipped down her cheeks.

An airy whisper escaped her lips. "Edward, what am I gonna do?" Her husband had always taken care of the planning. He handled all Pembrick business matters. And that had been fine with her. But now he was gone, and Lily-Rose needed to clear her mind and be ready for PT—and Christopher.

"Lost in thought?"

Lily-Rose's head jerked, and her eyes flew open. Christopher stepped out of the shadows, thin lips blowing a thick cloud of smoke toward her. "Gotta be careful. You never know who you'll see in a parking garage." He offered a cryptic smile. "Or who might see you."

"Stop it, Christopher. You're freaking me out." She collected her wits, then added, "What are you doing here, anyway? I thought you had a plane to catch."

He moved closer, cigarette smoke following him. His eyes, dark and penetrating, bore into her until a shudder ran up her spine, then down again.

"Change in plans, darlin'. I decided to send my playmate ahead. Looks like I'm sticking around for a while."

Lily-Rose dropped her gaze, hoping to break whatever hold he had on her. "There's really no need. Mr. Karn is looking—"

Christopher stooped down, tilted his head, and looked at Lily-Rose's face. "Look at me." Lily-Rose met his eyes. "Let's at least be honest with one another. You and I both know Karn won't find anything. It's over, Lily-Rose." She started to protest but he held his hand up to stop her. "I stood by and watched Edward take everything. He took Pembrick Transportation from me. He took all the love and attention my parents offered. He took—" Christopher paused and looked deep into her eyes. A sweetness—tenderness—reflected over his face. "Everything."

Memories from happier times they had shared in college

flashed in her mind. Christopher's head tilting back in laughter. The times they quizzed one another over coffee. Playful jabs and jokes. A lifetime ago. "I'm sorry it has to be like this. But we'll clear this up. I promise. Give me some time. I know this isn't what you expected. But Kid said—"

Christopher stiffened. His tone became harsh. The memories gone. "Kid's a weasel. We both saw his face. He would've said anything to get me out of there without ripping his head off. No, there's no way to avoid trouble. Real shame too. I really liked your brood. I just don't see any options left for me." Christopher's gaze never strayed from Lily-Rose as he pressed his back against the car and took a deep drag off his cigarette. Exhaling, he leaned in close again to her. "You know I travel in some—shall we say—hardcore circles." He shrugged his right shoulder. "I do favors for people. People do favors for me. I'll stress—as part of my favor—that you and the kids aren't to suffer."

Let me wake from this terrible nightmare.

Lily-Rose's attention focused. Hearing Christopher talk about causing harm to her family shook her from what was left of her stupor. "Stop talking crazy, Christopher. You're scaring me."

He cocked his head and said as if working out details in his mind, "Of course, it'll have to look like an accident."

Her eyes widened. "Don't say that. Someone will overhear and take you seriously." She breathed out. Had to focus. Had to. "Christopher, the kids love you. You're important to all of us. We can work this out."

But Christopher continued as if never hearing a word. "It'll be a shame about your kids. A real pity. They're cute." He exhaled. "But Karn and his ol' man leave me no choice." He pushed himself away from the car and returned his focus on Lily-Rose. "It can't happen right away." His eyes darkened and the muscles in his jaw rippled. "But I swear. On Edward's grave. Pembrick Transportation and everything that goes with it will be mine."

"Christopher. We've known one another for too long for problems like this." Her hands trembled as she reached for his arm. Panic set in. "What you're talking about isn't the answer. Let me work with Mr. Karn. We can figure this out. I just need time. I—"

"I gave Edward time." He pulled away from Lily-Rose's touch and pointed his finger in her face as his voice rose. "And my patience cost me ten—no, nine—years of waiting for what should have been mine all along. I'm the one who had the heart for the family business, not Edward. But being Dad and Mother's favorite, he got control anyway." His penetrating stare caused Lily-Rose to turn away. "No. No more waiting."

"And don't think you can get the fuzz to help. How do you think Dad got me out of all those—what'd he called them—delicate situations over the years?"

His rant stopped abruptly as he smiled, reached out and picked a piece of lint off her jacket. "Drive carefully, sister-in-law. Wouldn't want anything to happen to you."

Christopher turned, flicked his cigarette toward a distant car and walked away.

Lily-Rose hurried into the car and locked it. Her fingers continued to shake as she fumbled in her purse for her keys. Keeping an eye out for anything abnormal, she finally engaged the key in the ignition, revved the motor, backed out of her spot, and zipped out of the parking garage. She first watched for ongoing traffic then kept an eye on her rearview mirror, expecting one of Christopher's friends to come careening out of nowhere and ram into her.

Of course, it'll have to look like an accident. And it can't happen right away.

She shuddered recounting Christopher's words.

There's no way to avoid the inevitable.

I'll stress to my associates that you and the kids aren't to suffer.

His face. Those eyes. His hatred. There was no doubt he meant every word he said.

How had the struggle between brothers gotten to this point? Christopher had truly gone over the edge. That was the same look—that crazy person look—she saw on her mother's face before the county people took her away. Was Christopher capable of doing something he would later regret? Something they'd all regret? Lily-Rose and her children had become the rightful heirs of Pembrick Transportation when Edward died. Had all-consuming greed twisted her brother-in-law's mind to justify doing whatever necessary to take that from them? Could that mean killing them? Was he that sick? She had to think. It was just her now. She had to take any necessary steps to keep the kids safe. There had to be a way.

She looked in the rearview mirror and whispered, "I wish we could just disappear. Go where nobody'd find us ever again."

Wait. That's it!

As Lily-Rose continued home, she started putting plans together. She looked at her reflection in the mirror again. "We don't have a choice."

chapter 4

Only trust someone who can see these three things
in you: the sorrow behind your smile, the love
behind your anger, and the reason behind your
silence.

—Unknown

Lily-Rose breathed a sigh of relief as she drove into her
gated property and up to the house. Safe. For now, anyway.
But not for long. There was precious little time to think. Only
a little more to act. No time to put the car in the garage. She
took the circle in front of the house and stopped at the front
door. She barely had seconds to waste.

Lily-Rose walked through the front door and shouted,
"Kids! Pack a couple bags. We're going on a trip."

"Where?" Del asked, trotting into the foyer to meet her.

"It's a surprise," she said, giving him a quick hug. "Grab
clothes for a week or two. That should get us started." She
looked over his shoulder. "Where's Mary?"

Del pointed toward his sister's bedroom.

Lily-Rose muttered looking at her wristwatch, "Still in bed?
It's almost ten o'clock." She headed to her daughter's room,
"Mary, get up."

As she opened the door, a voice groaned from under the
covers. "Can't you knock, Mom? I'm sleeping. Besides, school's
out, 'member? Summer break."

No time for sparring this morning. Lily-Rose had work to

do. And fast. "We're going on a trip. If you want a shower, better get a move on. We're heading out within the hour."

Del peered from the doorway. "Geez, Ma. What's the rush?"

Lily-Rose gave him another deliberate hug. "We have things to do. That's all, sweetie. Now skedaddle and pack your things. Once you finish, make sure your sister gets up."

"I heard that," Mary snapped, as she peeked from the covers. She stretched, then dropped her feet to the floor.

"Good. Maybe that will motivate you. Wheels up in sixty."

Lily-Rose's mind was clear now, focused on survival. She went to Edward's home office—and stopped after opening the door. This was the first time she had allowed herself to enter it after the accident. Being there took her breath away. This was Edward's sanctuary. Where he read. Planned. Dreamed. And this was where he came from to pull Del's Frisbee from the tree.

A light woody scent of cigar smoke lingered from only a few nights past. He kept his not-so-well-hidden Cubans in a humidor on the credenza, occasionally enjoying one with a glass of eighteen-year old scotch. Lily-Rose always scolded him, but he'd flash his "all men need at least one vice" smile. He had determined years ago that a good scotch and cigar were going to be his.

Oh, how she missed him.

First edition books filled the dark mahogany bookshelves that lined a portion of the room. Artwork worth millions covered the open walls. No contemporary artists like Warhol or Picasso for Edward. He admired the old masters. His prized piece, van Gogh's *The Town Hall at Auvers*, hung behind his desk. Lily-Rose marveled over their beauty as well. But they needed to be left. For now. As would the supple leather furniture and thick Persian rug he commissioned that rested under the desk. Family pictures from trips all over the world stared back at her from every table. Her heart ached. How could they leave this?

But now was not the time for sentimentality. This was about keeping her family alive.

She strode to a nondescript wall-mounted framed print. Tilting it on its invisible hinges revealed Edward's safe. He kept thousands of dollars here. He called the bounty their "just in case" stash. Lily-Rose and Edward seldom fought, but when they did, the fights more times than not had something to do with his cash reserve. "I can't feel safe having so much money around, Edward. If thieves find out we have so much cash, who knows what they'd do to get it?"

Edward would smile and give her a bearhug. "Nobody knows the money's here except us, honey. Not even Dad. Besides, you never need it"—he'd pick her up and swing her around—"'til you need it. We have enough here to get us through any rough patch, plus a bit more. This is important to me. Let me do this one thing, please?"

Her thoughts returned to the present. "Is this the rough patch you envisioned, Edward?" she whispered, then shook her head. Focus, girl. Focus on priorities. She grabbed the bundles of bills. Everything else had to be left behind.

The kids, a few personal things, and cash. That's all she needed to get out of Lincoln. Fast.

Wait. She ran back to the safe and grabbed their passports. If Christopher convinced the authorities to search their house, they'd find the safe open and passports gone. Maybe that would throw him off her trail.

Yes. This really was about survival.

Next was her bedroom. Lily-Rose pulled a duffle bag from the closet then rifled past her designer outfits for jeans, T-shirts, and sweatshirts. She selected a few of her favorite family pictures from the dresser and wrapped each of them in pieces of clothing.

This would have to do. She turned to leave and spied one of Edward's undershirts on the floor by his side of the bed. She stopped, picked it up, and pulled the worn shirt to her face. She could still smell him—his scent—and ached for him once again. She stuffed the shirt into her bag and headed for the door, never looking back.

Within an hour, Lily-Rose stood by the open car trunk and called for her daughter. "Mary. Let's go." She turned to her son. "Del, can you please get your sister?" But the words were no sooner out of her mouth than Mary emerged from the house.

"Finally," he said.

She put her bag in the trunk with a grunt and rolled her eyes at her mother. "What? You're acting like there's a fire. Be cool, Mom. And why do I have to go anyway? Can't I stay with one of my friends until you get back?"

"Because I'm not sure when that will be."

One answer was seldom good enough for Mary. Lily-Rose braced herself for more of Mary's teenage interrogation.

"Where we going? Jennifer's party is this Saturday. We'll be back by then, right?"

Lily-Rose needed to get on the road. "I'm not sure, sweetheart. Let's see how things go."

Mary still hadn't finished. "But what's so impor—"

"Mary. Get in the car. Now."

With a few bags apiece, they left their home. Their next stop was Tier One Bank.

It was late morning when they pulled up to the bank. They all got out of the car. Lily-Rose peered around, looking for any sign of trouble, as she guided the kids inside. "I'm stopping in to see Mr. Johnson. Please stay in the lobby and don't move, you understand? Don't go chatting up tellers, asking for suckers." She paused and pointed as Mary and Del each claimed a leather chair inside the bank's entrance. "Magazines are right there on the table. Just stay put and I'll be back as quickly as I can. Remember, don't talk to anyone."

Satisfied the kids were secured, Lily-Rose headed toward the administration offices after she watched Del and Mary scour through the variety of *Look* and *Time* magazines then plop back in their spots.

"Hello, Mrs. Pembrick. Again, I'm sorry for your loss." Gaylord Johnson, president of Tier One Bank said to Lily-Rose after his secretary led her into his office. He came from behind his desk and took her hand. "Please, have a seat. What can I do for you?" he asked as he returned to his chair.

Mr. Johnson, a mild-mannered sort of man, had been more than Edward's financial mentor after his father died. He had become a close family friend. Some evenings he and Edward spent hours talking politics and finance. Now would be the test to see just how good a friend and confidante he really was.

"Thanks, Mr. Johnson. I'd like to withdraw our—I mean my—funds. Today. All of them."

"All of it?" His eyes bulged as he stared at her. His dark hair framed his pale face. He left his chair and walked over to sit in the one next to hers. "Are you unhappy with how we handle your funds?"

"No—I don't mean everything. Just cash. I want all the cash."

"Did I do anything wrong, Lily-Rose? I always tried to honor your husband and his wishes." Lily-Rose was surprised how Mr. Johnson's face lost even more color by the second as they chatted. She envisioned wheels turning in his mind as he thought of explanations to give the Tier One stockholders of why she had withdrawn so much money.

Lily-Rose took a deep breath and decided to risk it all.

"You're fine, really. You've gone above and beyond your responsibilities. You've been a good friend to all of us."

She paused, checking his response. With Mr. Johnson still following her every word, she continued. "It's Christopher. He doesn't seem to be doing too well since the reading of the will. I think life would be better if I take the children and leave town. Hopefully, he'll calm down, but right now he's pretty upset about not receiving Pembrick Transportation from Edward's estate."

"No further explanation necessary." Mr. Johnson stood and reached out, squeezing her shoulder. "I understand. And your traveling plans are safe with me. Stay here and I'll be right back."

Lily-Rose knew there was no love lost between Mr. Johnson and Christopher. He had managed the Pembrick fortune for years and had probably heard the stories about Edward's parents bailing Christopher out of jail. Or paying off someone. Or covering for one indiscretion after another. Likewise, Christopher didn't have much use for Mr. Johnson. Christopher's mantra had been "the person holding our family's money should dress like the money he has access to." Instead, Mr. Johnson's shirt collars and cuffs were a bit threadbare—a condition Christopher would never allow for his own.

Mr. Johnson and Christopher were as different as night and day. Lily-Rose hoped she could trust that difference.

A few minutes later, Mr. Johnson returned and gave her a satchel stuffed with more money than she ever handled at one time. He also handed her the receipt and six envelopes.

"Do you know where you're going?" Johnson asked.

"Not yet. And probably just as well. It's safer if I make a clean break."

Johnson nodded. "I couldn't take out all your funds but pulled out all that was possible." He gestured toward the envelopes. "Sometimes cash isn't enough. I gave you six copies of your latest bank statement plus letters of authentication from Tier One just in case you need a bit extra. Let me know, and I can wire funds to you as you need them. I'll do the transaction myself and make sure nobody's the wiser. Just keep me informed as to where you are."

Lily-Rose stuffed the envelopes into her purse, then closed it. "Thank you, Mr. Johnson. I'll be in touch." Lily-Rose stood and adjusted her purse strap over her shoulder, tucking it close to her body with her elbow and grabbed the satchel with her other hand.

"If you need anything, Lily-Rose, do not hesitate to call. While there were times easier than others, working with your family has always been an honor. It will be my pleasure to assist you in any way I can. You've all suffered so much heartache."

She reached up, kissed him on the cheek, and left his office.

chapter 5

Because of the LORD's great love we are not consumed, for his compassions never fail.

—Lamentations 3:22

Lily-Rose left the bank, then made two more stops. One for a quick carryout lunch and another on the outskirts of town at a car dealership to make a quick trade. By two o'clock, they were rambling along in their new pre-owned Vista Cruiser. Lily-Rose hadn't thought ahead to where they'd go, but their destination had to be far enough away that her face wouldn't be seen on local news. Somewhere they could blend in.

The weather broke the day after Edward's funeral, bringing sunshine and a warm breeze. They rolled down their windows as they left the dealership. She made a right turn into traffic—she hated turning left—and headed east. Besides, that meant there'd be no sun glare in her eyes if she'd turn right.

Baby steps in making decisions. At least it was a start.

As she took NE-2 out of town, the image of sun streaks glistening off the Nebraska State Capital dome bid her farewell in the rearview mirror. She hated leaving her city behind. But for now she needed to leave her beloved Lincoln and home. Through their marriage they experienced so many firsts there. First home. Then their kids. So much love shared.

Memories. Keep them for later. Now's the time to focus forward.

Survival mode. She could do it. Knew she could do it. She'd

done it before. Marrying Edward had washed all that from her life, but the how-to returned in a flurry. She only needed to take one step at a time. Drive one mile at a time. Take the lesser used roads.

Get through one hour without crying. And then another, and another, until …

Edward. She missed him. Lord, how she missed him.

Later. Cry later.

Or cry out of sheer frustration listening to her kids' squabble. Mary commandeered not only the front passenger seat, but the eight-track player and radio as well.

Del didn't relinquish without a fight. "Mom, make her stop changing stations all the time. Makes my head hurt."

Why did she even try. "Mary, stop changing stations like that. Pick an eight-track—something you both like—and play that for a while."

"But they're all boring," Mary repeated, as if they hadn't heard. "Bor-ing."

"Mom." Del rifled through his bag he had kept close, not ready to lose the fight. "I have Simon and Garfunkel. The Beatles. CCR. More Beatles. Come on, Mom. Make her stop."

Not willing to lose, Mary went for the jugular. "You're such a mommy's boy."

"Mom."

"That's it. I'm pulling over." Lily-Rose was done playing.

When the car stopped, orders began. "Mary, get in the back with Del."

"But Mom—"

"You heard me." Once Mary changed seats, Lily-Rose continued.

"Both of you. Look at me." They scowled. "You know the drill. Now hold hands."

Del protested, "Ew, gross, Mom."

Momma Bear plowed forward. "Del, right hand. Mary, left. You'll sit like that until I say you're done."

Lily-Rose turned around and bit her lip. She hated yelling at them. Before putting the car in gear, she looked in her rearview mirror in time to see Del lick his palm before offering his slimy hand to Mary.

"Mom!"

Lily-Rose stifled a giggle.

"Remember, don't let go until I say so. Now, my turn to control the radio." She turned the knob and found a station that played songs from the 1950s. "These are real singers. Connie Francis. Frank Sinatra. Ricky Nelson."

Mary interrupted. "That guy on TV? I'd watch that show after school sometimes."

"That's the one. Did you know his career began when he was eight years old? The Adventures of Ozzie and Harriet started as a radio show."

"That guy on TV." Del wrinkled his nose and whined, making fun of his sister.

Lily-Rose refused to engage. "No letting go, you two." She pulled back onto the road listening to Nelson's "Poor Little Fool."

Time passed, and the two were finally allowed to let go of one another. They all settled into their rhythm of the trip.

Lily-Rose turned her attention to the other drivers on the road. By the time they reached deep into Iowa, her imagination ran wild as she passed cars along the way. Were the drivers going to after-work meetings? First dates? Maybe just on their way home for dinner.

Home. Not her and her family. They were running for their lives.

Outside Bloomington, Lily-Rose looked for another car dealership to swap vehicles again. Honest Abe's car lot looked perfect.

"Kids, stay still. I'll be back in a minute."

Mary shared her displeasure. "Mom, I gotta stand up. I can't feel my legs."

Del chimed in. "Me too, Mom. And no offense, but if we get back on the road, it's okay if Mary sits in the front and picks the music. I'd rather hear static instead of your stuff." He looked around and added, "Where are we, anyway?

"Somewhere in the middle of Iowa, I think."

Del and Mary exchanged glances. Mary spoke. Her tone steady. "Mom, what's going on? Where you taking us? We've never done anything like this before. Where we going?"

Del followed up. "Yeah, Mom. Where we going?"

"Let me take care of the car, and I'll get right back, okay? If you need to stretch your legs just make sure you stick together and stay close. Understand? Close to the car."

After a few moments of chatting with Honest Abe, Lily-Rose handed over the registration of the Vista Cruiser they arrived in and became the newest owner of a used Chevy Impala station wagon. She considered registering it under her maiden name, Lily-Rose Delaney, but she needed to have a clean start. No lying. But Honest Abe'd been all too willing to accept an extra payment to stay quiet about the transaction.

Mary and Del moved their belongings from one vehicle to the other. "Mom"—Mary wrinkled her nose—"Smells funny in here."

"Smokers, I guess. When we stop for gas, we'll pick up an air freshener. Don't forget anything in the other car."

Once finished, they were on their way.

"What was that all about, Mom?" Del asked.

It was after seven o'clock. Snacks and sodas picked up along the way had taken them only so far. They all needed real food. And Lily-Rose needed to open up to her kids about their future. "Let's find a place to eat where we can chat."

They drove in silence then spotted an all-night diner, pulled into a parking spot, and folded out of the car. With cash in her pocket, Lily-Rose and the kids entered Sloppy Joe's Diner. The clientele looked like regulars and were peppered throughout the booths. Lily-Rose found the most secluded corner available.

The kids acted hungry—and for more than just food.

Once their plates and drinks were delivered and ketchup passed, Lily-Rose began. "I never thought I'd lose your father so soon. This has been difficult, but I think we need to pull together. Heal our family. We all need it."

"But why buy two different cars?" Mary slurped her soda.

"Guys with cameras were all around the house. You saw how they hounded us at the funeral."

"Then why not just hire more security?" Mary was like a dog after a bone while Del found interest in eating his fries.

Lily-Rose answered in her I'm-the-mom-and-know-what's-best voice. "I needed time away. And I needed you with me. Maybe get a new start. Now. Let's finish eating and get back on the road."

They finished their dinner, climbed into the station wagon, and continued east. Mary and Del, still both in the back seat this time, waffled between arguing and sulking. Soon enough, however, boredom took over. By eleven o'clock, both kids were sound asleep.

Lily-Rose drove in silence. Her thoughts drifted to Edward. She longed to hear his voice. He'd give her the answers, for sure. Fix all her problems. He always had. From convincing Luigi's Pizzeria to add double pepperoni onto their pizza to refereeing arguments between Mary and her.

She hoped her choices of stepping out and taking charge—trusting what Edward had called a person's "Knower"—would have made him proud.

"Lily-Rose," he would say, tapping his chest. "Mother taught me and Christopher about our Knowers. 'Your Knower always knows. You can trust it,' she'd say." His Knower seldom let him down.

He'd take her in his arms and swing her around. "Didn't my Knower know you'd be a perfect wife for me? Yep. Never doubt the Knower."

But Edward was dead.

The adrenaline rush that kept Lily-Rose moving forward had waned and a continual flow of coffee burned in her belly. They'd been driving for nearly eight hours since dinner and crossed into another time zone. Exhaustion crept over her like slow-flowing lava—quiet, but deadly. She needed to stop soon.

Lily-Rose turned off the thruway onto a two-lane business route in hopes of finding a place to lay up for the night. A few hours' sleep and they'd be moving along again. She rolled to a stop and looked left. When she turned right, she spied a sign directing her to a town called Applegate.

"Hmm, Applegate." Name sounded wholesome. Safe. Her brow rose. "Seems a good enough place as any to catch some sleep, don't you think?" she whispered to her sleeping children.

Nothing like Lincoln. The business route maneuvered her through a downtown—and nearly out of—Applegate. The quaint community was faintly reminiscent of places from long ago she was hard-pressed to remember. Memories of her mother before darkness took over had always been faint, but seeing small shops side-by-side on old-fashioned downtown streets stirred a warm feeling in her heart.

It only took moments for her to reach the outskirts of town. She turned around, intending to go back to the highway and look for a different town. That's when she came upon a hand-painted sign, the wood scarred and lettering faded, that read Applegate Motel. An arrow, barely perceivable, pointed her through a grove of trees and toward a gravel driveway. Following its direction and slowly maneuvering the double gravel paths aside sod, Lily-Rose heard the crunch of stones as she rolled forward. A light squeak of a fallen branch dusting her car joined the night sounds as she passed. At the end, a mom-and-pop strip motel stretched in lonely solitude. At the closest end of the row of ticky-tacky rooms, an overhead light illuminated a door labeled Office, followed by two windows, then two doors flanked by green shell-back metal chairs, the pattern repeating alongside the building.

Lily-Rose parked outside the office door. She looked back and saw Mary and Del flopping over one another, Del with a bit of drool reflecting the lights from outside and Mary with her hair a mess and hanging over her face. Both offering that deep sleep sound that always brought her comfort. She put a few dollars in her pocket then pulled the keys from the ignition. She'd see about getting a room for the night.

Cool evening air greeted her as she opened the car door and sprinted for the building. A whiff of stale smoke met her as she entered the office. Dingy, fake wood paneling covered the walls. An amber light shown from under a ruffled shaded lamp that sat on the end of a chipped laminate counter. Newspaper racks stood stuffed with local and regional papers, their edges tattered and curled. A faded eyeglass donation drop-off box covered with dust rested atop an industrial spool that had been converted into a table. A kitty-cat wall clock with dancing eyes offered a rhythm of too late, too late as the time read past three o'clock. Lily-Rose tapped the table bell hard enough to produce a small sound, then picked up the local paper trying to look calm as she waited for someone to emerge from somewhere. Eventually, a disheveled, white-haired man, entered from behind a curtain that separated the office from a secluded sanctuary behind.

"Can I help you?"

"I'm looking for a room for me and my two kids. One room with two beds would be fine if you have it." This was her first time making traveling decisions. Edward had always taken care of securing accommodations. The last time they traveled they had a three-bedroom suite. That style of traveling wouldn't happen again any time soon.

"Don't want no trouble. Everyone legal? Don't take checks either. Only deal in cash."

Why did this man put her on edge? "Wha? Yes, everyone's legal. We're just traveling through. And I have cash. Sir."

"Yeah, well, I see all kinds of stuff. Angry husbands, spiteful wives. Terrible stuff." He stifled a yawn. "Like I said, don't want no trouble."

"No trouble here. We just need a place for the night. We'll be leaving in the morning."

He looked at the kitty clock. "It is morning."

"Yeah, well, you're right about that." She stifled her own yawn, "I mean we'll be leaving later today. After I get some sleep."

"Have to charge you for a full day, ya know. No matter what time you sign in after six. Don't want no trouble, understand? Checkout's no later than noon sharp."

"Yes, sir, no trouble."

Lily-Rose paid the man and watched him take a key off a pegged board behind the counter. The key's green plastic fob read Applegate Motel Room C in white letters, large and worn. The other side had a note, Drop in Any Mailbox We Guarantee Postage. Smiling, she could never imagine losing such a monstrosity of a key. Return postage was probably close to her night's rent. Still, she slipped the key and newspaper into her jacket pocket and hurried back to the car.

Shadows seemed more alive after she left the office.

A screech of an owl made her turn to look for the culprit. Shadows. Noises. Hopefully, these strange sounds wouldn't stop them from getting a good night's sleep.

She returned to the car then moved them in front of Door C and coaxed the kids awake just enough to get them inside.

Door C needed a push to open, and creaked as they walked into their oasis for the night. The stench of mildew and stale air greeted them. Two beds each covered with worn blankets and flattened pillows all but filled the room. A small orange Naugahyde chair sat shoved in the corner ready to accept flopped jackets and bags. A scratched nightstand stood between the two beds holding a rotary telephone and the only clock in the room. An echo of dripping water came from what she hoped was the adjacent bathroom. Lily-Rose cracked open the room's only window seeking some sort of reprieve from the stench. She refused to consider the condition of the sheets. Tonight, what she didn't know wouldn't kill her.

Del stumbled to the bed farthest from the room's door and collapsed on it setting the springs in motion. Mary climbed onto the other and found sleep once again; neither of them offering comments or concerns.

Safe. For now.

chapter 6

Two roads diverged in a yellow wood,
And sorry I could not travel both

—Robert Frost

Lily-Rose was bone weary yet too electrified from the journey to sleep. Remembering the local newspaper from earlier, she pulled it from her jacket and went into the bathroom. The latch clicked as the door closed. She groped for the pull chain to turn on the light above the sink, lowered herself to the edge of the tub, and reviewed her crinkled copy of the local news. Flipping through the pages to the hum of the burning light, she saw articles on bake sales, baby showers, and retirement parties. A small ad in the real estate section caught her eye—House for Sale: Quaint cottage on Norwood Street. Safest street in town. Priced ready to sell. Immediate availability. Contact me anytime, Connie Hastings. A phone number beneath the ad quickened something deep inside Lily-Rose.

Her Knower.

"Safest street, huh? Wouldn't that be nice," Lily-Rose whispered and smiled skeptically at the thought. She closed the paper, turned off the light, and returned to Mary's bed, hoping not to disturb too many springs. She did everything possible to get comfortable without touching the stiff bedspread. They would be back on the road in a few hours, thank the good Lord, and leave this room with its smells and stiff covers behind.

Her mind raced, wondering what the safest street in town looked like.

"Stop it," she chided herself. "You need sleep."

Yet her mind zeroed in on that street. On that house.

Sitting up and rubbing her face. Contact me anytime reverberated in her mind.

Lily-Rose sighed and carefully climbed out of bed, grabbed the paper, and went back to the bathroom. She clicked the light on again and turned to the page and reread the ad. "Quaint. I like quaint. Safest street in town. Well, there's no guarantees on that now, is there. Immediate availability and priced to sell." What did that mean?

She grabbed a cup from the window ledge, ripped the plastic wrap off and poured herself a drink of tap water. She paused and looked at her reflection in the cracked mirror over the sink. There were new lines around her eyes. Had she aged over the past few days? She could use a break.

Anytime, huh? That's what it said. She could test that, right? What would the realtor do? Threaten to kill her? Stand in line, lady.

Lily-Rose tiptoed to the bedroom and took the rotary phone from the nightstand, then pulled at the cord, thankful that it stretched back to the bathroom. Closing the door again, she returned to the side of the tub. She read the ad once more, then dialed the number listed for Connie Hastings. The call connected after one ring.

"Answering service. Can I help you?"

Startled, Lily-Rose replied. "Ah, yes, ma'am. I'm calling for Connie Hastings."

"This is a service, ma'am. I can take a message for her."

"Oh." Disappointment niggled at her.

"Can you speak up? I can barely hear you."

Holding the phone base against her hip and its handset

between her shoulder and side of her face, Lily-Rose stood and stepped back to the bathroom door. She peeked at the kids and, seeing them lost in sleep, raised her voice a bit more than a whisper. "Can you let her—Connie Hastings—know I saw her ad in the paper. I'd like to see the property on Norwood Street tomorrow morning, as early as possible?"

"That'd be pretty early. Connie calls in for her messages before she gets Earl ready for work. Are you talkin' 'bout the old Hamilton place?"

"I don't know. I just saw an ad in the paper."

"Probably the place. It's been empty for a while. Cute house. Great location. Safest street in town."

Lily-Rose sighed and stole a look at the clock on the nightstand. Almost four o'clock. She needed sleep, but also needed to see this house. Her Knower told her so.

"Do you think Mrs. Hastings would be able to show me the house at eight?" Though tired, she found the operator to be as frustrating as her small-town personality was delightful.

"Oh, sure. Earl doesn't need to be ta' work till nine."

"Good. Can you have her meet me there?"

"Sure thing. What's your name, dear?"

Her name. She had told herself she wanted a clean start with no lying. But this could prove to be harder than she anticipated. Maybe she should give her a phony name, an alias, in case Christopher found out. No, how could he trace her due to looking at a house in the middle of Ohio? Survival doesn't mean being paranoid, does it?

"Hello, you still there? What's your name?"

"Pembrick. My name's Mrs. Pembrick." There. Done. Take that, Christopher. I need to be smart, not crazy.

"Will do. You're not from 'round here are you?" she asked, followed by, "I can tell. Do you know how to get there?"

"Not really."

The voice on the other end of the phone gave her directions from the motel, then quipped, "Thanks for callin'."

Lily-Rose stood, turned off the light and climbed back onto the bed. She set the alarm and drifted off to sleep, dreaming of Edward. Disjointed thoughts wrapped in laughter. Since the accident, he had never been far from her thoughts—not a day passed that hadn't brought him to mind—but he hadn't been in her dreams until now. Streams of images lingered in her mind, filling her with equal parts of sadness and joy.

A part of her had died when Edward fell. He would hate that she felt that way, but it was true. Her life was all but over in the space of a single heartbeat. The future stolen. Seeing him again—if only in her dreams—filled her heart. If only for a moment.

The alarm sounded at seven-thirty. Lily-Rose startled, grabbing the clock before the clanging woke the kids. Trying to focus, she struggled to remember the where, what, and why of her location. Then—Edward's death. Christopher's threats. A motel in Applegate, Ohio.

Lily-Rose went to the bathroom and splashed water on her face, brushed her teeth, and pulled her hair into a quick ponytail. She wrote a note to the kids with paper and pen from the nightstand in case they woke. "Be back soon. Went for breakfast. Love, Mom" and propped the message in front of the clock. She opened the door just enough to scoot out before letting all the cool morning air in the room. Getting her bearings, she allowed the stillness of the new day to welcome her. A thin layer of frost sparkled from the morning's light. Funny, the motel didn't look as dingy in the morning as it had looked the night before.

Maybe that was a good sign.

She made sure to follow the directions the service gave her which sent her through downtown again. Sunlight—and a few hours' sleep—offered a stark contrast to her memory of the town. Clean streets flanked with small trees sparkled from the morning dew. Store windows held a variety of wares. Music instruments. Sporting goods. Kitchen appliances. And the street held its own charm. Cars parked diagonally in front of the bakery, patrons walking in and out with morning purchases.

Adorable.

Farther still, she found Norwood Street. Pulling into the driveway, Lily-Rose put the car in park and stepped out, looking around. The neighborhood sparkled from the early sunlight shining on the crystal dew. All the homes along the street looked well kept. Spring flowers welcoming the warmth. Early spring mowing left yards lined, showing the eagerness for a new season. All the attention to detail reflected a depth of established love. Brick houses as well as shingled homes in yards with a combination of oak and maple trees emanated individuality and pride. She smiled, imagining seeing pixie dust flying in the air keeping this the safest street in town.

Returning her attention to the cottage, she focused on the property description and its surroundings that brought her here—small, cute, and immediate availability.

Lily-Rose walked up the drive for a better look at the house. The white-sided cottage showed a bit of neglect—not as pristine as the other homes. Faded green shutters bordered the multi-paned windows. Overgrown shrubbery everywhere. A maple tree dominated the front yard with two flowering crab trees dotting the corners by the house. Plump buds sprinkled in the trees' branches promised beautiful colors—probably white and pink. A sweet scent wafted through the air.

Glorious.

She rounded the house to see a small side yard. Nothing special. From there she saw a backyard where a patch of overgrowth stood on one side and an oak tree filled the other.

A small white shed stood in the back corner of the lot probably holding underused yard tools. Everything in the yard needed dire attention.

She turned back to the house and pressed her nose against the window peering at sparsely furnished rooms needing a little TLC. "Why were you left like this? You radiate character."

"I hope you haven't been waiting too long, Mrs. Pembrick. I'm Connie Hastings." First a voice, then the woman appeared, cup of coffee in hand. A middle-aged woman with a mop of gray hair sent a crooked smile her way, showing lines through makeup that had been applied with too heavy a hand. The missing top button of her shirtdress threw off the match all the way to the bottom, and the belt cinch around her waist had missed its loops. "Ready for a quick lookie-lookie inside?"

"Thanks for meeting me so early." Lily-Rose offered Connie her hand.

"Not a problem, honey." Connie turned on her heel, signaling Lily-Rose to follow. "There been offers on this place, but none of the buyers could wait till the estate got settled. Too much lawyer spattin' to close the sale."

Once inside, Lily-Rose trailed her fingers along the walls as they walked from room to room. Several areas of plaster begged for patching from years of neglect. Excess layers of paint diminished the integrity of baseboards and crown moldings. What looked like original carpet showed wear and matting, reminding her of the hotel where, hopefully, her children still slept.

Nothing like their Lincoln house. No gated community or five-car garage. This was a fraction of the size and had none of the luxuries. But she knew it was here. Beauty. Waiting to be recovered. What would her kids think? Didn't matter. They needed to be safe. That was her priority.

"The bones of this structure are good," Connie rambled.

"They built this house after the war. The plaster's still intact with not many cracks and the roof's solid—been replaced once. Comes as is. The furniture, curtains, sad as they are, and even kitchen odds and ends. It's a complete package. A real ready-to-move-in home."

Connie walked closer to Lily-Rose and locked arms with her, leaning in as a best friend would to share a secret. "I know this place needs work, honey. If you make an offer close to the asking price, I'm pretty sure that'll start a point for negotiations. The owners want to be done with it."

Really? The thought of making an offer never occurred to her. Could she do that?

Lily-Rose smiled and slipped her arms from Connie's grasp to continue meandering through the house. She paused in the kitchen and looked out the window. "I always liked a window over the kitchen sink," she said matter-of-factly.

From the sink she could see the driveway leading into the garage. A rusted basketball hoop hung over the garage door; its net long gone. Had kids lived here before? Or maybe grandparents?

Lily-Rose turned her attention to the house again. From the kitchen she walked through the living room, down the hall, past the bathroom and to each of the three bedrooms. She noticed a louvered section on the ceiling in the hallway. "What's that?"

"Why, that's an attic fan. Pushes all the hot air out of the house through the attic 'n pulls the cooler air through the opened windows. All the rage when they built houses back then."

Was she crazy to entertain living here? Her intention was to be far enough away to not be seen on the nightly news. She was half a day and close to a thousand miles from Lincoln, standing in a house on the safest street in town, praying it was far enough—and safe enough—to protect her and her children. Applegate checked all the boxes. What more did she need?

"I don't mean to rush you," Connie said, pulling Lily-Rose from her thoughts. "But I have to get back and make sure my Earl gets up in time for work. Can I tell the owners you're thinkin' about making an offer?"

"No need," Lily-Rose replied, distracted by entertaining herself with thoughts of living here. Her Knower sensed tenderness had, once upon a time, flourished under this roof. Maybe the house could share some of that tenderness with her and her kids. It had offered her a hug when she had entered. She was certain of that.

"I'll take it. I'll get the cash to your office later this morning. Can I get the keys from you then?"

"Ca—cash?" Connie stuttered, dropping her almost empty cup of coffee. "Ah, sorry." She pulled a tissue from her sleeve and wiped up the spill then looked back at Lily-Rose. "You might want to take a moment, honey. This is a major decision."

But Lily-Rose didn't waiver, even as Connie continued. "Don't get me wrong. I'm eager to make a sale. It's just—holy moly—I never had anyone make such an important decision— I-don't-know, so, so quickly. And no dickering? In all my years, I've never sold a house this fast. You sure? If ya are, I guess I can make sure to get the utilities turned back on before the day's over."

They shook hands, confirming the asking price and sealing the purchase.

"I'll be by your office later to sign the papers," Lily-Rose walked to her car. With a quick wave, she left Connie standing in the driveway and drove back toward the motel.

The purchase was either a brilliant—or completely foolish— move, but Lily-Rose let out a whoop while driving the streets of town—her town. Driving back the way she came earned a stop at the bakery on Main Street. She parked on the opposite side and crossed at the light. No sense jinxing a perfectly good day by jaywalking.

Lily-Rose opened the bakery door, and the bell attached at the top jingled. In front of her sat glass case after glass case of delicious pastries—sticky buns, jellyrolls, donuts in every color and flavor imaginable. She walked to the register and waited until the person ahead of her finished their order. When her turn came, the lady behind the counter greeted her. "What can I get for you, dearie?"

"May I have three—no, six glazed donuts, please? And do you sell milk too?"

"Milk's in the Frigidaire behind you."

By the time Lily-Rose returned with three one-cup cartons, her donuts were ready. The order totaled and bagged, she handed the lady her money. "Thank you. I can't wait to get into these. And my kids will enjoy them too. Thanks again."

Lily-Rose caught herself smiling as she walked out the door. She felt better in that moment than she'd felt in days.

Her return trip to the Applegate Motel gave her time to organize her thoughts before talking with the kids. Maybe it wouldn't be what she told them, but how she said it. They had a new home now. She would tell the kids about it and the changes that would be coming their way.

Lily-Rose peeked in and smiled before slipping in the room. Her two darlings were in the same positions as they were earlier. She placed the donuts and milk on the chair and removing her shoes, she slid under the covers by Mary and felt the tension slip from her body.

There would probably be pushbacks—especially from her daughter. But even with the possible flurry of drama, Lily-Rose had a good feeling about buying the house and living in

Applegate. Christopher would never think of looking for them here.

Norwood Street, the safest street in town, would be a good place to start making new memories. Goodness knew, they needed them.

chapter 7

Even if happiness forgets you a little bit,
never completely forget about it.

—Jacques Prévert, French Poet

"You did what?" Mary shot out of bed and looked around. Clearly, donuts and milk hadn't eased the situation like Lily-Rose had hoped.

"If you think I'm stayin' in this godforsaken … where are we, anyway? On the edge of the world? You're … you're … you're a crazy woman."

Lily-Rose winced with each of Mary's shrills. "Shh. Don't wake Del."

"Mother. I don't believe—you've really gone loco. I'm gonna call Jimmy and have him come get me."

"What's goin' on?" Del sat up in the bed, blurry-eyed and looking confused.

"You're not calling Jimmy. Here, Del. Have a donut." Lily-Rose gave her son a hand towel to put his donut and carton of milk on. She turned her attention back to Mary. "We talked about this last night. We're getting a fresh start, and that means no contact for a while with people in Lincoln. This change won't be forever. I promise. But for now, you must trust me on this."

"You've kidnapped us, Mom. Un-be-lievable. I hate you, you know that? Where's the phone. I'm calling the police."

"What'd I miss?" Del wiped glaze from the corner of his

mouth.

"First off," Lily-Rose said, "I haven't gone loco. And you're my children—I already have custody of you, Mary. So, no, I didn't kidnap you."

Mary flopped back onto the bed, folded her arms across her chest and began bouncing her foot, sending the springs singing.

"Secondly, to get a clean break from Lincoln, that means no contact. We must disappear for a while. That's why I bought two different cars. And buying a house here fits too. These changes are for our own good. We will go back to Lincoln as soon as we can. We will reconnect with our friends and reclaim what we left behind. But not for a while."

Looking them in the eye. "Can you trust me on this?"

"We're buying a house?" Del asked, after taking a swig of milk.

"But Mom," Mary whined. "Where are we?"

"We're in Applegate, Ohio, sweetie. It's a cute little town. I drove through it quickly this morning. There's a grocery store, a library, and oh, I didn't see it, but I think there might be a college here. And I found the cutest house for us, you guys. The realtor said our new place was on the safest street in the world."

"The world. Really, Mom?" Mary stared at her.

"Well, maybe not the world, but at least in town." Lily-Rose forced a smile. "I can't wait for you to see it."

Lily-Rose sat beside a sulking Mary. Del propped himself on an elbow and leaned into them. He held out the box of donuts for them to claim their breakfast, then joined the conversation. "Jeepers, you guys. What's going on? I go to sleep in the car. And this morning Mom's gone and bought a house for us in—this Appleseed place?"

"That's Applegate, dear," Lily-Rose said.

"Okay, yeah, Applegate. Can we start from the beginning? Please?"

Lily-Rose took a deep breath and told them both about the house, the town, her drive through the area, and her hope to start afresh.

"We can do this. I know we can. All I'm asking is for you to give this place—Applegate—and this house a chance. If it doesn't work, then we'll move on."

"Back to Lincoln?" Mary pushed.

"Sorry, Mare. We'll move on to another little town if this one doesn't work out." Lily-Rose reached out and put her hand over Mary's. "All I'm asking is for you to give this a try."

They finished their breakfast in silence. Afterward, they took turns showering and preparing for the new day. When they were ready to go, Lily-Rose grabbed her duffle bag of cash and the three drove through town in silence.

"Kids, isn't this town cool?"

"Adorable," Mary drolled.

Lily-Rose's latest trip through Applegate gave her another opportunity to check out the downtown area. She spied more businesses—a drug store, small theater, diner, a five and dime—stores for almost every need. Finally, she reached Applegate Realty.

"Okay kids, can you sit tight for a few moments? I have some business to take care of here."

Mary stared out the window. "Sure."

After she grabbed her purse and satchel, Lily-Rose entered the realtor's office and saw Connie talking to a husky, middle-aged, balding man.

"Hi, Mrs. Pembrick," Connie greeted her. "Joel, here she is. I told you she'd be in."

"Please, call me Lily-Rose." She stretched out her hand to the man.

"You the little lady buyin' the Hamilton place with cash?" Joel sucked on a toothpick while drinking coffee.

Lily-Rose stared at Joel and tilted her head. How does he not swallow that toothpick along with his coffee?

She cleared her throat. "I'm here to buy the house on Norwood Street, if that's the Hamilton place you're talking about. Is anyone else interested in buying it?"

"Oh, lands, no," he laughed. "You payin' cash? Connie said you were gonna. I bet her five dollars you'd back out. Nobody buys a house with cash."

"Well, I do have the money—if you want it," Lily-Rose answered. "But I also have a recent statement from my bank in Nebraska and a letter of authentication. If you'd rather, we can use that. They said they'd wire the money if I needed the transfer."

Lily-Rose reached into the satchel's side pocket for the letter and handed it to Connie. Looking the letter over, her eyes bugged when she saw the bottom line of the statement, showing Lily-Rose's financial assets. "If we contact this fella, Mr. Johnson, he'll vouch for you?"

"Yes. He's the president of the bank. He gave me those papers yesterday, in case I needed them. If you want, I can give you cash instead—if getting a wire is a problem."

"Ya know, Connie," Joel said, putting his cup down and moving his toothpick from side to side. "If it's all the same, let's take the cash. I'll never see that much money at one time again in my life. You've seen those TV shows where people roll around in it? I won't do that, but this'll be about the closest I ever get." He turned back to Lily-Rose. "Cash'll be fine."

"I think you're right, Joel. But I want to contact the bank first, just to make sure everything is on the up and up. You understand don'tcha, honey?"

"Completely. I'd probably do the same thing. Ask for Mr.

Johnson. Like I said, he's the bank president. He'll be happy to answer any of your questions." Lily-Rose looked at the clock on the counter and tried to choose her words carefully, knowing she was working on little sleep. She continued. "I was hoping my children and I could get into the house today. Would that be a problem?"

Joel continued twirling the toothpick from one side of his mouth to the other as Connie looked on. "I don't see any problem, Connie. For cryin' out loud, she's gonna give us a boatload of money for a house we haven't had luck in selling. Don't bother her banker friend."

Joel took the toothpick out of his mouth and slipped the tiny sliver of wood into his shirt pocket.

"Ma'am, you got yourself a house. Let's count out the cash and close this deal. I s'pose you're also good to give the keys to. And if you ain't, we know where to find ya."

Without realizing, Lily-Rose had been holding her breath, waiting for Joel to give his approval. Receiving his go-ahead, she pulled the satchel off her shoulder and placed it on a side table. Opening the bag in a way to not expose its entire contents, Lily-Rose began pulling out bundles of cash. "Uh, let me see" she paused, looking at the wads of bills, "the twenties are wrapped in violet bans, the fifties in brown and the one hundred dollars are wrapped in yellow ones."

Connie stared then cleared her throat. "Those stacks stand up so nice and purdy. Joel. Look at all those colors. Have. You. Ever?"

"No, can't say that I have." Joel continued to stretch his neck in the direction of the satchel as if trying to see how deep the piles of bills were.

After Lily-Rose finished doling out the stacks, she double-checked, making sure they equaled the right amount. "Could I have a receipt please? And the keys? The kids are waiting, and

I'm in a hurry to show them the place."

Connie stopped staring at the money and turned her attention back to Lily-Rose. "You sure can, sweetie. I can't wait to tell Earl about this one. Good heavens. A story, for sure. If you can sign these papers here, we'll be all done."

After a few signatures, the sale was official. The old Hamilton place had officially become the new Pembrick home.

Back at the car the kids were just as she had left them. Were they being compliant or were they in shock? She wasn't sure. She started the car and pointed it in the direction of Norwood Street, then to their new house.

CHAPTER 8

Man cannot discover new oceans unless he has the
courage to lose sight of the shore.

—Andre Gide

At first glance, the house didn't seem as magical as it had earlier. Had the drying dew taken the sparkle from the trees? Had she made a mistake? She pulled in the drive, turned off the car, and let out a deep breath. "Here's our new home, kids. What do you think?"

Silence. No bickering. No yelling. This wasn't good.

"Awesome driveway, Mom. Paved and everything. I can see why you'd leave civilization for it."

"Work with me, Mary," Lily-Rose warned, preparing for battle—and another stop for donuts if necessary.

"Okay, sorry," her daughter said. After a moment she added, "Honestly, Mom, don't you think everything looks a little rough on the outside. Do we have to go in?"

Lily-Rose held her breath. This was the moment of truth. Would they see what she saw her first time in the house, or would they want her to turn the car toward the freeway and head off to another place?

"You're right. The yard's a mess and the house needs some work, but nothing we can't do if we chip in together, right? Some cleaning and a splash or two of paint will make a vast improvement."

Getting out of the car, Lily-Rose noticed Del eyeing the

basketball hoop over the garage door. "Ah, man, I didn't bring my basketball."

This was promising. "We'll get you a new one. No problem."

They entered the house through the breezeway in silence. Once inside, Mary was first to speak. "Hmm. Can we see our rooms?"

"Sure. You guys figure out who gets what."

Mary looked around the kitchen, only to find an open flow from one room to another. She kept looking for a door. "Where's Cook stay? I don't see any suites for the help."

Lily-Rose took a breath. "There's not going to be a cook, or a housekeeper. It's just us."

"Are we gonna starve? Who's going to take care of us?" Poor Del.

"We're going to take care of ourselves. We'll cook—I can, you know—and pick up after ourselves. We'll make our beds in the morning and make sure the kitchen is cleaned by the end of the day."

Mary and Del looked at one another, speechless.

"Don't worry, we won't die. For now, go check out your rooms."

Mary and Del headed down the hallway. After a few moments they returned, Mary leading the chattering, "Can we pick out our own color—"

"Yeah, the colors back there are awful, Mom—"

"Majorly gross. The grossest—"

"Yeah, the grossest, Mom."

"Oh, Mom." Mary grabbed Lily-Rose's arm as she pivoted from one subject to another. "We've got beds and dressers already, but do you think we could Mod podge them? Cindy, you know her, back in Lincoln, she did her dresser and nightstand and they looked groovy.

Del would not be outdone. "Can I get posters? Maybe

a poster of Pete Maravich from Louisiana State? He's really good." He started jumping up and down, holding on to Lily-Rose's other arm. "Ooh, ooh. Or maybe Pete Rose? He plays baseball with Cincinnati. That's not too far, right? Maybe I could even get him to sign it."

Lily-Rose laughed. "One thing at a time, you guys." They stopped pulling on her arms and she reached for her purse and pulled out some paper and a pen. "Make a list of the things you both need." Mary grabbed the pen and paper then ran back to her bedroom, Del in tow.

They had never worked within a budget before. How would this work? Lily-Rose shook her head and smiled. She then pulled out an old envelope and pen and began making her own notes. Bucket, rags, and a broom topped the list. Heading toward the bedrooms she heard Mary and Del talking.

"Blue. What do ya think of blue?" Del asked his sister.

"Blue'd be okay. That's considered a boy's color, I guess. I want hot pink with green. Big flowers everywhere."

"Ew," Del made gagging sounds.

"Stop it, brat. What do you know about decorating? My ideas will be perfect. Mom," she bellowed, not knowing how close her mother stood. "When can we go to the paint store?"

Lily-Rose raised a brow. Had it really been that easy?

Moments later they left the house to forage through Applegate. Towels, kitchen necessities, sheets and blankets were all checked off the list. They returned home only to empty the car and head out again. This time they drove to the Applegate Motel for their belongings. Lily-Rose pulled in at three o'clock and watched as the manager slid a note under the door of Room C.

"Hi. Sorry we're late. We're leaving now."

"Gonna have to charge you for another day. I told you checkout's at noon."

"I'm really sorry, but I didn't realize I'd be buying a house here. I had to go in town to see the realtor and make arrangements."

"Bought a house, huh? Where 'bouts?" Lily-Rose didn't know if he was checking the validity of her story or genuinely interested.

"Norwood Street."

"The cottage there? Lots of lawyerin' been over that place. Connie's been working a long time tryin' to move it. Good to know that place is gonna have folks livin' there again."

He reached down and secured the corner of the invoice with the tip of his finger, pulled it from under the door, folded, then slipped the paper in his pocket. "If you're gonna be a neighbor, and as nobody's knockin' down the door to rent your room, I guess I can let the extra hours slide." He held out his hand. "Name's Foster."

She took his hand and smiled. "Thanks, Mr. Foster."

After loading the car with their belongings, they found their way to the local grocery store, bought the essentials, then headed back home.

The strain of the last few days worked its way from her lower back to the rambling of her thoughts. After putting the food away, she posed a question. "How 'bout we find a burger joint and call it a day? I'm exhausted and don't think I could cook a meal after all we've done."

"You're gonna let us eat hamburgers? I like this place already," Del answered.

Heading into town, they followed signs to the Applegate College campus and Al's Burgers 'n More. Lily-Rose maneuvered passed the roller-skating carhops and toward the parking spots for those eating inside. After they went in, Del grabbed the nearest booth while his mom and sister went to the counter and placed their order. He used his time selecting songs from the booth jukebox and waited for his mother to bring back change from their order.

"Three songs for a quarter, Mare. They have some good ones here. 'Hey Jude,' 'Born to Be Wild.' Looky here, Mom. 'MacArthur Park.' You like that one. I get first pick, then Mare, you get the next. You can have the last one. Okay, Mom?"

After they took their spots in the booth, Mary divided their fries, burgers, and shakes. She paused, then looked at Lily-Rose. "Mom, I get it that you don't want to tell us everything about why we left home. But you have to tell us more than what you said yesterday. If we're supposed to trust you, you need to trust us too. It's hard to feel like we're a team when you keep us in the dark like you're doin'."

Ouch. Mary had saved these conversations for Edward. He always knew the right things to say when their family faced a crisis. Now the hard conversations were on Lily-Rose—and she would need to maneuver them all on her own. Make something up or tell the truth? She didn't want to scare them, but Mary was right. They needed to trust one another.

Edward. What should she do? Be honest or protect their innocence a bit longer?

Lily-Rose swallowed, took a breath, and leaned forward, looking into their waiting faces, offering no incrimination. She knew they would believe anything she said. She also knew that she was creating the foundation of their lives together—at this moment.

Would her relationship with her children be built on truth? She took a deep breath.

"It's about Unc-a-bunk and the family business. He wants Pembrick Transportation and is pretty upset he didn't get PT after Daddy died. Our lawyer's working out a way for him to have it. But until that happens, we best steer clear of anyone or anything related to Lincoln for a while."

Del wiped ketchup off his chin. "Why don't you just give him what he wants, Mom?"

"I want him to have the business, but your father and counsel wrapped the company up tight to protect our interests. Looks like the logistics will take some time. Legal's looking into getting Christopher what he wants. But we can't contact anyone from back home. Just not yet anyway."

"Even Jimmy?" Mary's eyes brimmed with tears.

"Sorry, sweetie. Even Jimmy." Lily-Rose placed a hand on her daughter's arm. "But it's not forever. When I get the word from Mr. Karn that everything's safe, we'll see about going back."

"Safe? Do you mean we're not safe?" Del asked.

Lily-Rose watched their faces and realized maybe back-peddling some of the information would be best. "Of course, we're safe. We're going to live on Norwood Street in Applegate, Ohio, the safest place in the world, right?"

"Mom, you're so corny." Mary rolled her eyes. "But we get it. No contact with Lincoln friends, at least for now."

Lily-Rose tried her best to stifle a yawn. She started to gather and crumble the waxed papers and stack the empty baskets from their fries. "Let's go home, okay, kids? I'm exhausted."

Home.

Leaving Al's Burgers 'n More, they drove back through town then toward Norwood Street. Turning in the drive she looked at her new home. There it was. Just as she'd left it. She pulled into the garage and they each loaded their arms with items left in the car from earlier in the day.

"Looks like we're home, kids." A sense of comfort wrapped about Lily-Rose as they walked in the door. Her Knower had been right.

The kids each grabbed the bags with their newly purchased transistor radios and set out for bed. Tomorrow would be a new day. The purchases could wait and be sorted out then. Before the sun set, both kids were sound asleep, in their clothes and sprawled on top of their beds.

They had survived the day. Tomorrow would be another struggle. This house had been empty for far too long. The walls needed to be wiped down and patched. Floors and windows washed too. She needed to see if any of the curtains or bedding could be saved. Later she'd see about refinishing the floors and stripping the trim.

While the list in her mind grew, Lily-Rose knew she needed sleep. But along with chores, her mind raced with thoughts on what-ifs and how-comes. What if she'd made the biggest mistake of her life moving her kids across country and buying a house that needed more work than they knew how to do? And how come she thought Christopher wouldn't find them here? If he did, they'd be dead for sure.

Thoughts bounced around in her mind like a charged pinball machine. She hadn't slept well in days and unfortunately, didn't see tonight being any different.

She needed a distraction. After climbing out of bed, she put her boots and sweater back on and wandered outside. Maybe taking in the evening sky might give her a moment of much-needed peace.

Nebraska skies were some of the most beautiful in the country. But Lily-Rose gasped as she walked out and turned to the west. The blues, pinks, and lavenders surrounding the setting sun of the spring sky took her breath.

Her throat tightened as tears washed her face. "Aww, Edward, you're missing the most beautiful close of our first full day in Ohio." She watched as the sky changed from the blues, pinks, and lavenders to oranges and reds. Then darkness. Lily-Rose's soul felt, what—unworthy? No, that wasn't it. Small. The beauty of the evening sky made her want to weep. Now the colors were gone, just as so many other things in her life. All gone.

Meandering through the backyard at dusk, Lily-Rose nonchalantly kicked through the overgrown lawn. This was nothing compared to their grounds in Lincoln, but she wagered nobody ever died here either. She walked back to the garage to turn on the outside lights. Fumbling with the light switches, Lily-Rose finally found the one that controlled the spotlight over the backyard. When she returned to her adventure, the toe of her boot found something hard. Bending down, she found what seemed to be a masonry something. She kicked the dried leaves and overgrown grasses away, then pulled through with her hand until the overgrowth gave way and offered Lily-Rose a closer look.

A firepit?

She stood and with hands on her hips studied the spot. Kicking away more long grass and leaves, she walked off what seemed to be a radius of the round bricked pad measuring approximately six feet. In the center was a stone pit itself looking about four feet wide. Dusting off her hands, she put them on her hips again.

This looked promising. She ventured to the shed and found some split wood, a stack of crinkled newspapers, and a can of matches. After a few trips between the shed and the pit, she had gathered enough supplies for a fire.

"Okay, Papa. Let's see if I remember what you taught me." Lily-Rose made sure all the dried grass was pulled away then arranged the kindling over a few pieces of crinkled newspaper. She then lit the paper just as Papa showed her how when she was younger.

"Like riding a bicycle." Once the fire was settled, she pulled a chair from the shed and pulled it to the edge of the pad. She then went back into the house and searched through the linen closet and found an old blanket the owners left. Then, she ventured to the garage and turned off the spotlight over the backyard. Once outside again, she took the corners of the blanket and shook out the mustiness and dust. Satisfied, she wrapped herself in its warmth and sat on the chair. She snuggled in front of the crackling blaze, allowing the yellow flickering flames to mesmerize her. The only sound accompanying the fire was the distant thunk of a falling branch and the evening songs of night warblers. All else in the world lay quiet.

CHAPTER 9

Change your thoughts and you change your world.

—Norman Vincent Peale

"Relax your mind, deary. I know you can grasp economics. Take a deep breath. Relax." Miss Fergie shuffled behind Fiona Kasey and toward the stove as Fiona sat at the kitchen table studying.

Fiona pulled her long ebony hair to the side, rubbed her temples, then leaned back in her chair. "I don't know. This might be the class that beats me." She moved her hands over her eyes and let out a sigh. "I can't seem to get it."

"Sit in the chair correctly, dear." Fiona smiled and straightened her back. Miss Fergie picked up where she had left off. "I've watched you make sense of all sorts of numbers and theories. Just keep trying." Miss Fergie took her green Fire King cup off the shelf, dropped a spoonful of Sanka granules into it, then added hot water from the kettle. She stirred the elixir, sending that coffee-like smell into the kitchen. She set her steaming cup of black brew on the table and pulled out the chair across from Fiona. After lowering herself onto the seat, she waited until Fiona looked her way. Miss Fergie smiled. "I don't know why, but God made your brain like a sponge. Lord knows I don't know supply and demand from the man in the moon. But you're different." She reached over and squeezed Fiona's arm. "And here you are, working on your master's. Relax. Don't let any of those theories derail you. You can do this." She patted her arm. "But time to put the books away. It's Sunday night and dinner's ready. Miss Fergie knows best."

Yes, Miss Fergie did know best. She always had a sense about life. And Fiona thanked God every day that Miss Fergie had a sense about her. As a full-time live-in domestic companion and part-time student at Applegate College, Fiona's place in Mrs. Ferguson's—lovingly referred to as Miss Fergie's—life was difficult to explain. This silver-haired, slightly hunched-over widow had been Fiona's champion for as long as she could remember. The first white woman who ever touched her. Dined with her. Even took her to a movie theater matinee to see *Song of the South* before the movie was retired. They received stares when they left the theater singing "Zip-a-Dee-Doo-Dah," but Miss Fergie said to pay no attention. "Small people, small minds."

Yes, her sense was Miss Fergie knew best. Even when Fiona couldn't quite understand what she meant.

Like when Miss Fergie invited her to move in after she graduated from high school and started working at the local five and dime. Fiona had worked there two years when her friends started getting married and beginning families. Marriage or babies didn't interest Fiona, and the job was good enough, but Miss Fergie wanted more for her.

"If you're gonna stay single, you'll need a job where you use your mind, not your back. And that kind takes an education."

"But I don't have the money for college. Besides, who'd hire a black woman for a job other than what I'm doin' now?"

That had been the only time Fiona heard anger in Miss Fergie's voice. "Fiona Pearl Kasey. You are more than the color of your skin. But if you don't get an education and take care of your future, you won't convince anyone any different. Do you hear me?"

"But—"

"No buts. Let me get my bag, and we'll go to the admissions office right now."

Eight years had passed. Fiona quit her job at the store and moved in with Miss Fergie, began classes part-time, and never looked back.

Her duties as a companion were light. She cleaned the small but stately three-bedroom house and cooked their meals. For her efforts, she was given a robust wage, college tuition, a beautiful bedroom and private bath, the use of Miss Fergie's car, and all the freedom to come and go as she pleased.

The only time required of Fiona was Sunday evenings when the tables turned, and Miss Fergie made dinner for her. Meals that included different types of foods from Miss Fergie's past. Creamed chipped beef gravy over toast or Spam and eggs were often her go-to choices. Or when the weather turned chilly, she'd make rivel soup from her Pennsylvania Dutch grandmother's recipe kept tucked at the back of a Betty Crocker cookbook. They'd eat together and watch all Miss Fergie's favorite television shows, chatting during commercials.

While Fiona had been studying, Miss Fergie had created a feast of liverwurst spread on white bread with coleslaw and pickles on the side.

Fiona finished off the last of her soda-pop, put the glass in the sink, and closed her books. Sliding them out of the way on the side counter, she smiled. "It's like you're moving me on, Miss Fergie. Is there something you're trying to tell me?"

Following their weekly tradition, she headed to the living room to watch *Mutual of Omaha's Wild Kingdom*, followed by *The Wonderful World of Disney*, jumping over to *The Ed Sullivan Show*, and finishing the evening with *Bonanza*.

Miss Fergie put Fiona's plate on the TV stand next to her and her own plate on the coffee table. "Lands, my dear, no. I enjoy your company. But I'm not going to be here forever, and you'll need to be able to take care of yourself. I thank God for dear Mr. Ferguson. How he married me and saved me from my station. I'd be scrubbing floors for a livin' still if we hadn't fell in love the way we did." She took a sip of her Sanka, then continued. "I want more for you than that. Land sakes, for being such a smart woman, it took me years to convince you to apply for college."

"You've always taken good care of me, even when I was little."

Miss Fergie snickered. "Remember that Wendy Ward class I signed you up for?" She sat straight and recited the class's motto. "'Proper etiquette is as essential as proper knowledge.'"

Fiona wiped the crumbs from the corners of her mouth with her napkin. "Man, I was young then. But I still remember what she drilled into us. 'Sit straight. Stand tall. And don't be afraid to look people in the eye when you talk to them. It's strength you show when you take pride in who you are.'"

Miss Fergie turned her attention to the television. "The show's starting, dear," signaling a pause to their conversation. When a Marlin Perkins commercial for life insurance interrupted the show, Miss Fergie returned to their earlier conversation. "You're smart enough to have people work for you, not the other way around. I don't want to see you settle for another domestic position. Another pickle with your sandwich, dear?"

"No, thank you." Fiona picked the crisp dill spear off her plate and took a bite. "I don't know why you ever took such an interest in me, Miss Fergie."

"Let's just say I see someone in your eyes." She paused. "Someone from long ago." Miss Fergie sat still for a moment then refocused on their conversation. "I'm no fool and I don't want you to be one either. We both know you're going to have to work twice as hard as the white girls at school to get ahead."

She shook her head. "That's not the way the Lord meant life to be." But added a smile. "Sometimes He needs a bit of help, that's all."

"But—"

"Besides, God never blessed Raymond and me with a daughter. Only my sweet James. And he's been gone more years than I had him." Miss Fergie stopped talking and took a bite of slaw. After chewing and clearing her throat, she continued. "Just me now. Me and the house is all there's left."

"I'm not complaining, but ever since I was a little girl—"

"Shh, baby girl. Commercial's over. Look at those tigers Marlin Perkins is hunting. Can you believe it? Lordy, those colors. I'm so glad Mr. Jenkins downtown talked me into buying a color set this time. It's just like we're there."

Fiona smiled. She loved her charge and their relationship. The drill was always the same. She'd have to hold her thought until the next break in the story line. But Miss Fergie surprised her while they watched Jim Fowler finally catch and cage the wild cats.

"Hon, I'm sorry, but can you run to Al's for me and pick up some French fries? I know this is my night to cook … and you don't like going out after dark … but I've got a taste in my mouth for some of those greasy-salty pieces of potatoes they make. They'd go right along fine with my sandwich."

Fiona took a deep breath, then smiled. "Sure thing." She'd do anything for Miss Fergie. Even drive at night. "I'll be back before Ed introduces his 'really big shew'."

"Mr. Sullivan, dear," Miss Fergie corrected.

She smiled. "Yes, ma'am."

Fiona drove to Burgers 'n More, picked up an order of fries, and headed home. Making her way down Norwood Street she noticed lights on next door in the old Hamilton place and scowled. The house had been empty for so long it seemed odd seeing glows from previously dark windows. Fiona wrinkled her nose and muttered under her breath. "My luck, they'll have a backyard filled with chickens and goats who will inevitably wander through the neighborhood." As soon as the words left her lips, she chided herself for being a snob. After all, Wendy Ward's training wouldn't allow it. Just then, she saw a young woman with wavy red hair curled up in a chair by herself washed in the glow from a fire in front of her.

"Looks harmless enough," Fiona said to nobody. "Who knows how many kids she has in the house. I better not see any broken-down refrigerators or cars on cinderblocks in the yard." And they'd better not bug Miss Fergie.

Drat. She chided herself again and remembered her training. She sighed as she turned into her driveway, knowing she needed to work on her attitude. Who knew? That redheaded lady might be … nice.

chapter 10

Perhaps it takes courage to raise children …

—Unknown

"If I have to come up there one more time, there's going to be trouble. Now go to sleep. I'll make sure Daddy sees the pictures you colored for him when he comes home. Now goodnight." Sugar Bowersox hated yelling at the girls at bedtime—any time really. They always joined forces and gained strength when she did. But this time they'd gotten on her last nerve. She had tried to make bedtime different tonight. Keep her wits about her. But it always seemed to take five fits of yelling to get them to settle down for the night when she did handle everything on her own. Stories and final drinks of water. Fix their covers. Check for monsters in the closet. This was definitely a two-person operation. Unfortunately, tonight turned out to be just another night—like the one before and even before that.

Her husband's position as Athletic Director at Applegate College paid the bills and helped them get ahead financially but did little to build their family relationship. They'd purchased a four-bedroom colonial home and were able to get rid of their college-day's furnishings and buy pieces they liked, not just what they could afford. Sugar had been thrilled when they arrived in Applegate, but slowly understood the price that went along with the mortgage. Their family dynamics suffered. The girls rarely saw their father. And Sugar, her husband.

Earlier that day, Dungar had walked in the back door,

wearing an apologetic grin, while Sugar placed the last part of their supper on the table. "I did my best to get home for dinner, Sug, really." He walked around the table, greeting each girl with a hug before sitting at his regular place. "But at least I can eat with you and the girls tonight. That's good, right?"

Sugar forced a smile. Again.

Within minutes, he had finished his plateful of food plus seconds. He gulped his water as he pushed back his chair from the table and started offering goodbye hugs to the girls before leaving. His almost-nightly ritual. "Members of the SDS organized another protest against the Vietnam War for tonight. All administrators living in town are required to be on campus to help keep an eye on things. That means I'll have my hands full watching my boys. Seems these protesters love recruiting athletes." He paused after hugging his last daughter. "Sorry I won't be able to help with baths tonight. Can Granny give you a hand?"

"No, tonight's bowling." Sugar's mother had moved in with them to help, but lately she was gone more than available to offer support.

Sugar followed Dungar to the door to receive her own hug. She held on to her husband a bit longer than normal. She whispered in his ear. "Am I such a bad wife that you can't stand to be home? Maybe it's because I'm a bad mommy. I swear, Dungar, sometimes it's all I can do to get these preschoolers ready for dinner, let alone bedtime. That's it, isn't it? I'm a bad mom."

Dungar pulled back and looked deep into her green eyes. He took a deep breath and gently brought her close and kissed the top of her head. "First, I love you. I know you put up with my impossible schedule. I try to get home when I can, but this hasn't turned out to be a nine-to-five job. None of this is your fault. I swear."

He smoothed her hair as he caressed it with his cheek. He whispered, "And you're a great mommy. The girls and I are lucky to have you. Nobody could put up with us like you do." He pulled his face away and looked into her eyes, reaching down, and brushing a trace of a child's milk lips from her face, "Don't forget. There's three of them to your one. If the girls ever figure out those odds, we're both goners."

He kissed her cheek. "Let's talk this weekend and see when we can set some time aside for just the two of us. Okay? You're the best," he hollered over his shoulder as he headed out the door. "See you later. Don't wait up."

After the girls finished eating, she herded them upstairs for their bath. Scooping them up and settling them all in the tub, she lathered legs, scrubbed markered knees, and washed the food from their faces and hair. The girls giggled and splashed, seemingly enjoying the nightly routine Sugar endured.

With the girls finally settled in bed, the mommy day was over, and Sugar was ready to tackle the rest of her chores. But not before she snagged a cookie from the Bugs Bunny ceramic cookie jar. Then another. One now and the other to enjoy later with a cup of tea. Tea always tasted better with a cookie.

Sugar leaned against the counter, savored the first cookie, and looked at her mess of a kitchen. Dishes, pots and pans. Crumbs all over the floor—and socks. What were socks doing in the corner? She was too tired to figure out the puzzle. And she had too much to do to care.

If she'd sweep the floor first before finishing the dishes instead of doing the dishes first maybe that'd add variety to her life. She leaned on her broom handle and huffed. "Some think people who talk to themselves are crazy. Giving jabs to myself is plum loco."

By the time she picked up all the dirty clothes strewn about, swept and mopped the floor, moved the chairs back into place, and loaded the dishwasher, she was ready to tackle the pots that had soaked sufficiently to make the scrubbing easier. "This is the way life's supposed to be," she said to an empty room. "Pots not needing too much effort to clean."

Sugar had another day done and the only things to show for her efforts were clean kids and clean pots draining in the sink rack. She placed the last pot on the drainer and paused, looked out of the window over the sink at nothing particular as she had so many evenings before. But tonight activity stirred across her side yard. From her window she noticed a glow from a fire in the backyard of the old Hamilton place. She leaned forward, trying to see more. Pressing closer to the window, she focused her attention. It was a woman. And suddenly the woman looked in Sugar's direction. Horrified, Sugar ducked away from the sink and window.

For a few moments, she sat on the floor thinking about the lady she saw. She looked harmless enough, from what her quick glance told her, anyway. Not too old. About her age. Maybe a bit more. And pretty. All cozy in front of her fire. Wrapped in a blanket. Out there all alone. She stayed on the floor, hoping her new neighbor hadn't seen her. After a moment, she peered out the window again.

The lady hadn't moved—maybe she hadn't seen Sugar. That'd be a relief. No sense starting off on the wrong foot, having fire lady thinking she was a Peeping Tom.

No, wait. Peeping Toms look in windows, not out. Nonetheless, Sugar didn't want to scare her off. Maybe she had the fire by herself because her family had gone off to do important things in their lives too.

Should she welcome the new neighbor? Maybe take her cookies?

Nah.

Sugar didn't have the strength to tackle one more thing

tonight. Maybe tomorrow. She dried her hands with a towel hanging on the refrigerator door, then slathered them with Pacquin's hand cream. Her day was officially over. Time to head upstairs and go to bed. Alone.

Again.

CHAPTER 11

In the end, it's not the years in your life that count.
It's the life in your years.

—Abraham Lincoln

"Old people drink tea, Mr. Bird," Bob Biddle said as he poured hot water over a reused teabag. "Guess this makes it official—I'm old."

Biddle wrapped his hands around the warm cup then sauntered to the perch where his African grey parrot swayed back and forth. Mr. Bird had been his good friend. He shared judgment with only words and phrases Biddle had taught him. Mr. Bird's support, though a bit convoluted, had been enough to carry him through the past nine years.

He put his cup of tea on the closest stack of boxes then reached for the cracker tin atop a nearby bookshelf. Mr. Bird's swaying quickened. "You know what's coming, don't you fella?" Biddle pulled a saltine from the tin and offered a piece to Mr. Bird. The parrot gently accepted the treat with his claw, lifted it to his beak and began eating.

Biddle watched as Mr. Bird's tongue worked the cracker around. Crumbs fell to the floor. No worries. The floor was covered with papers to catch the bird droppings and food particles.

"Crackers, a bit of fruit, and a perch by a window. That's all you need, isn't it?" He stood close and stroked the top of Bird's head.

Fortunately, Mr. Bird's needs were few, because Biddle had little to offer. They lived in a tiny apartment consisting of a living room-kitchen combination and a bedroom. The bathroom was an oversized shower stall with a sink on one side, a toilet on the other and a floor drain in the middle. He kept the toilet paper within reach on a shelf just outside the bathroom door when he showered so it wouldn't get wet.

Boxes and stacks of papers lined the walls of the rest of his oasis. All orderly, but most unneeded. Reminders of a life left behind. A life he threw away looking for more.

If not for that terrible accident all those years ago, everything would be different. But his life had fallen apart that night. He lost his career, self-esteem, and ultimately his family because one domino kept knocking over the next. Until there were none left. And it all happened in a moment.

First misery, then old age crept in. Hadn't he played ball with Johnny in the backyard of the family home just a few years ago? Sunlight streamed in between the leaves onto that beautiful lawn. While lawncare did demand his time for feeding, trimming, and watering, looking back now, the work somehow didn't seem so terrible. He remembered how he and his son mowed the grass together. He kept his steps small so his son could walk along, feeling a part of the task.

Funny, he hadn't thought of cutting grass with Johnny for years. Maybe his mind was putting things in place. Pulling thoughts from one file and putting them in another. Making room for new, fresh ones. About what, he had no idea.

The death process does funny things to a person. Memories return and the illusion of control flees. And there was no doubt. He was dying. That's what the doctor said, anyway. Illness had found him resting with his loneliness and old age.

When he got married, he thought he had all the time in the world to build his law practice. Once he made a name for himself, his family would be set. Then it'd be smooth sailing.

Biddle had worked tirelessly beyond his typical schedule, including evenings and weekends, trying to get ahead. How had he not noticed the change in his family? Biddle's wife stopped waiting up. Johnny stopped leaving notes. Little by little, his marriage and family had moved on without him. Surprise rocked him when his wife told him they were leaving. He begged her to stay—hang in there just a bit longer.

She did stay—but with one stipulation. He had six months to either land the big account or get the poisonous hunger for position and prestige out of his life so there would be room for their family. He set out to hook the biggest fish in the Lincoln sea—William and Sandra Pembrick and Pembrick Transportation. He orchestrated impromptu dinners with mutual friends, gifts, and run-in's at different places where the Pembricks were known to frequent, trying to build a relationship with them and win them over. Finally, Sandra agreed she and her husband would entertain the notion of testing his legal prowess.

The Pembricks gave him one duty of responsibility—a test of his legal maneuverability—to see if his skills would make it beneficial to end their relationship with Kevin Karn, the company's current legal counsel. Biddle spent hours poring over legal briefs, making sure every move he chose for them would be legal and binding.

Finally, Biddle gave them his discoveries. Days later William invited him to have dinner with them both at The Cedars, an upscale restaurant where business deals were often made over a filet mignon and a glass of Bordeaux. After the post-dinner coffee had been poured, William turned the conversation to business.

"Biddle, I have to give it to you. Great work. Karn could have probably done this, but to be honest, your tenacity, persistence, and dedication to getting a job done was what sold my wife and me on you."

Biddle didn't know what to do. Should he agree? No, too arrogant. Maybe fawn manufactured humility? No, that wouldn't match the picture he had painted for them of who he was.

William continued. "If you still want the job as vice president-general counsel, it's yours. Come by my office in the morning, and you can sign all the appropriate paperwork to make this official."

William stood and offered Biddle a signed draft letter of offer, then watched as the lawyer slipped the folded paper carefully in his breast pocket. He reached out to shake Biddle's hand.

Biddle did his best to present a cool front, while on the inside he danced a jig. He wanted to throw his arms around him, but instead shook William's hand like a pump handle.

William laughed. "Welcome aboard, Biddle, welcome aboard. I'll break the news to Karn once all the i's are dotted and t's are crossed."

"Thank you, sir, Mr. Pembrick, sir. I promise I won't let you down."

William reached into his breast pocket and pulled out an envelope. "And to cover your time"—he handed the packet to Biddle—"here's some cash for your efforts handling such a ... delicate ... situation." Williams gripped Biddle's forearm and looked him in the eyes as he reached for the money. A friendly gesture to stress his point. "If it's all the same, I'd like to keep this matter quiet. Sandra and I made a terrible mistake with the previous one. Hopefully, this new last will and testament will undo all that. We want our sins to go away, never to be thought of again. You understand."

The "you understand" came through as a statement, not

a question. Funny how money can do that to a conversation.

"Completely, sir."

Biddle all but danced his way to his car in the parking lot. He had done it. Landed on easy street. Beat the system. Life would be different from now on. He rolled down the windows and turned the radio on in the car as Sly and the Family Stone's "Dance to the Music" began to play. He turned up the volume and followed along while tapping the beat on the steering wheel. "Ba ba ba bump bumb, Ba ba ba bump bumb."

Reaching home, his watch told him his bedtime passed. He turned the key as quietly as he could, stepped over the creaky floorboard, and maneuvered his way to the liquor cabinet. He poured himself a celebratory scotch from the bottle hidden in the back and sauntered to the couch.

Relaxing in the dark room, he considered what to do first. Should he move the family to an exclusive neighborhood? She might like that. Or get Johnny in a private school? No more public stuff for his boy. He'd take care of them. They'd live in the lap of luxury now.

Biddle kicked off his shoes and stretched. Maybe they'd travel. He always wanted to see the world. Go as a family. Never have to work holidays again. Ever.

After spending time basking in his upcoming fortunes, he finished the scotch, picked up his shoes and headed for bed. Tiptoeing down the hall, he entered their bedroom.

She laid there sleeping, looking as beautiful as the day they met. He wouldn't bother her now. He'd hold off telling her until breakfast—when they could dance in the kitchen with Johnny. As a family. Everything would be okay from here on in. He had dodged a bullet, but the gamble paid off. He'd put his career in a good place. When his head hit the pillow he couldn't wait to drift to sleep. He anticipated good dreams. Great dreams. How could he not? Life would be just as he always wanted.

How shocking it was, then, when he woke to the radio's morning show discussing the tragedy the evening before.

"Two of Lincoln's finest family business leaders died due to a car accident after leaving The Cedars last night. The car of William and Sandra Pembrick, founders of Pembrick Transportation, was found crashed into a tree on the side of Mercantile Lane. Preliminary reports say Mr. Pembrick may have swerved and lost control. We'll have more information as the day goes on. In other news ..."

Biddle rubbed his eyes and tried to shake off sleep.

No!

He frantically dressed and went to the kitchen. There his wife sat sipping her coffee.

"You were out late last night."

"I gotta go. There's been an accident—"

She held her cup mid sip. "Oh, no. You okay, Bob?"

"I—I think. I don't know for sure." He grabbed his jacket off the hook. "I need to go. I'll be back soon." Before any more was said, he went out the door and headed to PT headquarters.

"Welcome to Pembrick Transportation. Can I help you?" the receptionist asked, holding a tissue to her eye.

"Good morning, my name is Robert Biddle. Bob Biddle. Mr. Pembrick told me to come in and sign some papers today. They were legal contracts. Who would I speak to about that?"

The receptionist picked up the phone receiver. "One moment, please. I'll contact Mr. Karn. He's the vice president-general counsel."

"No, no. He won't have 'em." Biddle's voice was louder than he wanted. Words falling out over one another. "Maybe the forms are on Pembrick's desk. Is there any way I can go in there and see? There's a contract—we had dinner last night and discussed it."

The receptionist paused, receiver in hand. "I'm sorry, what did you say your name was again?"

"Bob. I mean, Robert Biddle."

"That's right, you said that before." She scanned her appointment book then looked up.

"I'm sorry. I don't see your name on the list. We're all a bit off today." The receptionist dabbed at her eye again. "Last night, there was a terrible accident—"

"I heard about it on the news this morning."

"So you can understand why everyone in the office is out of joint."

Biddle leaned over the desk toward her. "I understand, miss, but you don't understand my predicament." The receptionist pushed her chair back, expanding her space.

Just then, a security officer approached the front desk. "Sally, you need any help here?"

"No, Brett, Mr. Biddle was just saying he had some papers that Mr. Pembrick had promised to sign."

The guard stepped between Biddle and the front desk, forcing him to step back. "Sorry, pal, there's no more signatures coming from WP. Sally here can get Edward Pembrick, that's the son, or Mr. Karn, head of legal for you—"

"No, neither of them will do. They don't know about this."

"Really?" the guard looked Biddle over. "I can't imagine Pops Pembrick not including either his son or attorney in any business dealings." He paused, still eyeing Biddle. As if sizing up the situation, he spoke again, this time his voice deepened as he addressed Biddle. "Sir, if you don't want to talk with counsel or Edward Pembrick, I'm going to have to ask you to leave the premises. If you have any questions, you can call for Mr. Karn."

With a firm grab to his arm, Biddle was escorted out the front doors.

CHAPTER 12

Memories are the key not to the past, but to the future.

—Corrie ten Boom

Nine years had elapsed. Biddle closed his eyes as he remembered the exchange as if it were yesterday. The irony of the events never ceased to amaze him—how the trajectory of his life changed with two heartbeats—those of William and Sandra Pembrick.

Something had snapped inside Bob Biddle the day he was escorted out of Pembrick Transportation. He had been a fool. Instead of mourning Pembrick Transportation's loss, he internalized the death of William and Sandra Pembrick as a personal attack on his world.

He hadn't meant to neglect his private practice. If life had treated him better, none of this would have happened.

Within a few weeks of the accident, Biddle was financially ruined. His practice folded and his office doors were locked due to nonpayment. His car was repossessed. And adding to his chagrin, his wife held true to her word and kicked him out of their home. That's when he moved into his pathetic little apartment.

Nine long years ago.

Since then, he stayed in his cocoon. His food was delivered. He even cut his own hair. He occasionally ventured to the laundry room in the basement to wash his clothes.

He had become a recluse—he and Mr. Bird. His connection to the world came only through the newspaper and television or the superficial conversations from neighboring tenants. Any communication he needed to do was done via mail. Society held no value to him. His meager pension and the savings his wife allowed him from the divorce staved off the outside world. Since that fatal crash nine years ago, he was alone. And he preferred it that way. If he hadn't taken his yearly bus ride and visit to the city mission, the doctor would have never given him the bad news.

Biddle stroked the crown of his companion and cleared his throat. "Mr. Bird, seems I better get someone in here to dust. The air seems thicker than usual." He coughed again, this time catching the racking in his handkerchief.

That's when he first saw blood. Reddish brown. The first sign of death.

He stumbled to his chair then leaned back and closed his eyes. Maybe this would bring an end to his torment.

Biddle pushed his handkerchief into his frayed pocket, stood up and headed toward the sink counter. He grabbed his spoon from the rest and pressed the soaked tea bag against the inside of his cup, squeezing out all color then tossed the bag into the trash. He pulled a wrinkled apple slice from the fridge and ripped off a bite for the swaying parrot. Biddle began coughing again and put his cup down as he gasped for air. He wiped his mouth again, this time with a paper towel. More speckles of blood. Redder this time.

No, not long now.

Settling at the dinette table, he opened the local paper and was greeted with the headlines, Funeral Today for Lincoln's Royalty. Scanning the article, he read all the details of the Pembrick family and their rise to fortune. He didn't feel a bit remorseful for not being sad over Edward's death. On the contrary, he fought the fury growing from his depths and regained his composure. Edward had everything—the Golden Child.

Wrapped in frustration and melancholy, he began refolding the paper and was getting ready to put it in the pile for the bird cage but stopped when a picture of the family at the funeral caught his eye. He saw who he guessed was Edward's wife Lily-Rose and her children, huddled together facing the beginning of life without their leader. Then he saw Christopher, sitting behind Lily-Rose. As always, Christopher had been delegated to a back row.

For the first time in years, lucidity grabbed Bob Biddle, washing over him. Seeing the lost look on Christopher's face—even behind sunglasses—brought clarity to him. Bitterness, envy, and selfishness had ruled his life. Nine years ago he experienced the loss of a dream and fell apart because of it. One look at that picture showed him fragility of life and how even the wealthiest of families could fall apart like a house of cards at any time. He had experienced that frailty himself. How could he forget? Everything he had felt was right there staring back at him. But looking at the newspaper picture, Bob Biddle also saw a flicker—a possibility—of redemption.

He walked over to the swaying bird and stroked its head. "Maybe I can fix this, Mr. Bird. I may be a dying old man, but if I hurry, I might be able to make a difference."

He hoped he'd have enough time to right his wrongs—and enough energy to stop a terrible injustice that happened years ago.

CHAPTER 13

If tears could build a stairway, and memories a lane,
I'd walk right up to Heaven And bring you home
again.

—Unknown

Lily-Rose dreamed of Edward.

Since the accident, many of her dreams had been drug-induced flashes and feelings. But this was different. This time everything seemed real. Down to the scent of his skin. The look on his face. How he stared into her eyes. Everything was there.

He didn't speak at first. He didn't offer reassurance that he was at peace, nor did he seem tormented. Instead, in her dream, he stood before her. The light surrounding him was so bright it was difficult to look at him, yet impossible to turn away.

She wanted to reach out to him but somehow knew if she'd move, he would disappear. She couldn't bear to lose him again even if he was only an apparition.

Lily-Rose didn't speak, unsure of what she could or should say. In her dream, emotion filled her eyes with tears as she covered her mouth for fear of crying out. That's when he leaned in and took her in his arms, held her close, and stroked the back of her head, offering comfort. As they stood there, his scent filled her nostrils.

"Shh," he finally said.

Lily-Rose clung to him, unwilling to let him go. Over and over he cooed gentle words of love.

When the lump in her throat eased, she looked up at him and their eyes met. It felt as though he was alive, and they needed to catch up after a long absence. There was so much she wanted to tell him, so much she wanted him to ask.

He brushed the hair from her forehead and kissed her there ever so gently. "You have amazing courage, and you've chosen well," he whispered, his eyes warm with love. "I'm sorry for everything. In time, you'll know joy again."

She stared up at him, not able to speak. How could he say that? She hadn't been courageous at all. She'd run. She'd taken the kids and left town. She wanted to argue. Stress her inadequacies. And yet she didn't. Wouldn't. She feared he would leave if she questioned him and she wanted the dream to last. Peaceful feelings had once again filled her heart—a heart that had carried such a heavy burden over the past few weeks. For a moment—this moment—her broken heart felt just a little lighter.

She finally spoke. "I don't think I can do this without you. Christopher's threatened me, Edward. I'm afraid. That's why I ran."

"You can make it, and you will. Your need for right will take you further than I ever could. Continue to trust your Knower." He smiled and tweaked her nose. "In fact, I know that you'll have a long, full life." Edward bent his head toward hers and lightly brushed her lips with his own. Pulling back, he continued. "And you will feel joy and peace. You will even feel love again. Find comfort in knowing that much of the good waiting for you will come from your decision to buy your new home."

Lily-Rose frowned. She knew it was a dream, yet everything seemed so vivid. "But—"

"This house is my gift to you," Edward continued. "Don't doubt, my love. God will show you."

And then he was gone.

Lily-Rose sat up. "Edward, come back. Please." She held her breath as reality settled. She was alone.

She laid back into the pillow, exhaled, then rolled over and buried her face into it. Sobs racked her body. He had been there. With her again. Touched her. Kissed her lips.

But now he was gone.

The pain ripped through her heart as it had when he died. Moments passed, and her crying slowly waned. She sat up again and pushed her back into the headboard. Edward had been there. She knew it. And he had given her a message. Lily-Rose reached to the nightstand and turned on the light. She needed to be alert. Gather her thoughts. Remember every word spoken.

"A gift? Was that you? Were those your arms I felt around me when I walked in this house? I'll never doubt your love, Koochie. Never."

Lily-Rose held her chest as she felt the continued quickening of her heart. She closed her eyes, and purposefully tried to slow her breathing, even holding her breath for a moment, struggling to get a handle on what just happened.

Sitting there, she rubbed her eyes with the heels of her palms and forced herself to focus. After a long sigh, she got out of bed and, forgetting her slippers, walked across the cold hardwood floor to the kitchen for a glass of water. After pulling a tumbler from the cupboard, she paused and closed her eyes and took a deep cleansing breath. Her tears had been real. His words had been real. The dream had been real.

After pouring tap water into her glass, she took a sip then held the glass to her cheek to feel the coolness. Drink in hand, she headed back to bed. There, sipping her water in the dark,

Lily-Rose tried to add impressions from Edward to match his words. Lily-Rose whispered to her dead husband. "You've never lied to me, Edward. Don't start lying now."

Against Lily-Rose's will, her dream faded as she fell back to sleep.

chapter 14

With the new day comes new strength and new thoughts.

—Eleanor Roosevelt

Lily-Rose's mind stirred from a deep-sleep fog as pitter-patter stole across the hardwood floor. Then clarity washed over her. Edward was gone. Life started over today—a life without him on Norwood Street.

"Hey, Mom." Mary took the lead as they flopped on their mother's bed. "We want to go exploring. Can I have the keys?"

"Yeah, Mom. Explore," Del followed.

Lily-Rose caught her breath. She couldn't allow them out of her sight. Never again. Christopher could be out there. Watching. Ready to make good his promise. No, this was quite impossible. Then again, she shouldn't scare her children. She had to be cool. Collected.

She propped herself up on an elbow and rubbed her eyes. "You feel confident driving in a new town, honey?"

"Sure. Piece of cake—"

"Yeah, Mom, like cake. Chocolate cake. Confetti cake." Del bounced with each word.

"Stop, Del, or I'm not taking you with me."

"No fair."

Lily-Rose dropped back to the mattress that had a lot to learn about true comfort, ignoring the bickering. "Okay." She yawned and cat-arched her back in a stretch. "Make sure to take your license. And grab some change from my purse in case you get lost. This way you can call the police station if you need to. They'll come and get me."

"Mother. I'm not a child."

"You're right," Lily-Rose said. For a moment she wrestled with the thought of not letting them leave her sight. Ever again. But she willed the feelings to pass. "Might as well get more money from my wallet while you're there. Say, ten dollars?"

"Is that all?"

"I imagine life's different here than in Lincoln, Mary. Let's keep it simple, okay?"

Both kids headed for the door, but Lily-Rose stopped them. "Kiss first, 'member?" Life seemed too fragile since Edward died. Why couldn't she just hold them close and never let go? No, that would never do. The thought left again. If Mary's confidence had returned, and she was ready to drive in a strange town with no supervision, Lily-Rose needed to trust her daughter.

Mary smiled and returned and gave her mother a kiss on the cheek. Del, however took a leap and landed back onto Lily-Rose's bed, bringing along a bear hug and sloppy smooches. Lily-Rose laughed as she pulled him close, returning the hug and nuzzling his neck.

"Agh, gross, Del," Mary moaned. "Let's get out of here."

Mary called, "I put the percolator on for you. We'll be back after a while."

"Thank you."

"See ya," she returned before the door slammed shut.

Lily-Rose cocooned herself into the blankets for a moment, clinging to the pillow just as she clung to her daughter's words. "We'll be back."

They had to be back. What's the point of living if they didn't? If they didn't make it back, she'd have failed—completely failed. Failed them. Failed Edward. Failed the Pembrick name. They were the reason her heart continued beating.

Lily-Rose uncurled, climbed out of bed, and headed to the pile of shopping bags in the kitchen. She rifled through them and found what she needed—new robe, bathmat and towels, soap and shampoo. The process would soon become rote again, but for now, each task took explicit effort. She headed for the bathroom and readied for a shower.

Warm water rained over her body as she stood behind the plastic curtain—plastic, so unlike what she'd stood behind only a few days ago. A gasp from deep within her chest caught her unaware, her body's need to release the torrent of emotion taking over once again. Lily-Rose swallowed hard to contain her emotions, but finally gave her body over to the racking sobs. She grabbed a washcloth left over from one of the kids' showers, still wet and clinging to the scent of soap—held it to her mouth to muffle the sound. Although she couldn't imagine from whom.

Minutes later, the spray turned from hot to tepid, then cold. She turned off the water, shuddered and stepped out of the tub. She grabbed her towels, wrapped one around her body and the other her wet hair. Her reflection in the mirror showed a pathetically twisted face. Puffy eyes. Swollen lips. She looked away, then sat on the edge of the tub and focused on the new day. Anything but the loss of her best friend.

Edward.

The scent of brewed coffee seeped around the closed door. She sighed. Stood. Put on her robe. She padded into the kitchen to find the percolator hard at work. The blip-blip of coffee shooting through into the glass top reminded her of normalcy. And memories of Edward.

Edward.

Lily-Rose found a cup, blew out the dust before rinsing

and filling it with coffee. She rifled through the newly stocked cupboards and found the English muffins and orange marmalade. She whispered a soft thank you, Hamiltons, as she used the left-behind toaster, browned her goodies, and sat at the table to enjoy her first Norwood Street home-cooked meal.

Finished, she licked melted marmalade from her fingers, stood, spied a pad of paper and pen on the counter and brought them back to the kitchen table. She needed a list of items to start their lives over.

Getting records and stereos for both Mary and Del was a must. Maybe stop by the telephone office and see about extra phone jacks for their rooms too. She couldn't expect the kids to start new lives while not having at least some of the amenities they were used to. They had lost almost everything. Replacing what she could was important. Today, she'd at least set the appointment for someone to come to the house to install more jacks as well as get an unlisted phone number plus the extra phones.

Lily-Rose paused from list-making and smiled as she looked around the kitchen. How serendipitous to find several basic household items were left behind by the Hamiltons. Bedding. Pillows. A smattering of furniture and appliances. All items necessary to get them started—at least through their first night. But it would take more than the left-behinds to turn the cottage into their new home. They needed some Pembrick personal touches. Later, she'd pull out the framed photos from her duffle bag and place them around the house. That would get her started. She went back to her list. Paint supplies she scribbled as a foreign smile slipped from her lips. Time to start the cottage's transformation.

Lily-Rose walked to the bedroom. She combed out her damp hair and tied a red bandanna around her head, then put on what needed to pass for work clothes. While going through her bag, she found Edward's shirt and pressed it to her face. She took a deep breath then set her jaw. Now was the time. Time to face life without Edward. And time to put some Pembrick flair into their new home.

She put Edward's shirt away for safekeeping. She then went to the back door … squared her shoulders … then pushed it open. When she stepped outside, the sun's rays warmed her skin as the cool spring air hit her face. She looked around, this time with a more critical eye than she had when with realtor Connie Hastings. Instead of fairy dust, she now saw a yard that had been overlooked and neglected, both akin to how she had been treated as a child.

She walked to the shed to see what tools were available. Two yard rakes, one garden rake, a shovel and spade, and a smattering of hand tools and gloves lined the shed's small shelf. She pulled out a pair of gloves and a rake, then headed for the yard's farthest back corner. She would start at the firepit and move from there. She raked and pulled dead debris and stacked everything into a pile. As the stack grew, the wind whipped through, stealing leaves. The wind. Lily-Rose dug her fists into the dip of her waist. She hadn't anticipated it'd be a problem.

"I have a tarp you can borrow if you want. Might help."

Lily-Rose turned to the direction of the voice.

"Over here," the voice said again. "Other side of the bushes. You can maybe toss it on top of the pile as you go—the tarp I mean—then bag 'em before they get away from you."

Lily-Rose squinted and peered through the overgrown hedges where a woman stood staring back.

"Hi, my name's Sugar. Sugar Bowersox. Me and my family live here, this side of the bushes. Glad to have someone move in the old Hamilton place." Her chin jutted up. "Looks like you and your husband have your hands full, gettin' everything cleared, I mean."

"I'm Lily-Rose. Lily-Rose Pembrick." She walked around the hedge, pulling her glove off on her way, then stuck out her hand. "No husband anymore. He died. Just me and my kids." The easy-going tone and the no husband anymore startled her. The words came easier than she imagined they would.

"Oh. Sorry. None of my business." Sugar stammered, clearly not as comfortable as she first projected. "Well, if you want to borrow the tarp, you can. Like I said. Could hold 'em down for a bit to make baggin' easier. You can also borrow the hedge trimmers if you want. Those bushes may need some attention too."

Lily-Rose looked over the row of overgrown hedges as she lifted and rubbed her forearm across her brow.

Sugar kicked at the ground. "Lands sake, listen to me. I'm pointing out more work for you to do. I'm sorry. They look fine. Really do."

A month ago, Lily-Rose would have shunned such a forward person. But her new neighbor—this Sugar person— clearly had no idea of the Pembrick drama she had left behind. Nor did she seem to want anything from her. Maybe she was just being friendly. Lily-Rose smiled. She had forgotten what neighboring was like in a small-town community.

"Thank you, Sugar. I think the tarp would be a great help."

"Mommy, where are you?" a voice from Sugar's house rang out. Sugar glanced over her shoulder but continued talking with Lily-Rose. "Good. I thought you might. I already pulled the thing from the garage and drug it to the driveway. Feel free to come over and get it." She looked back again at her house. "Duty calls. I need to get in there. Nice to meet you, Lily-Rose."

"You too, Sugar."

As fast as Sugar appeared, she vanished. Lily-Rose walked over to the tarp, grabbed two of its corners, and dragged it to her yard, pleased that she had met at least one friendly face on Norwood Street.

After working most of the morning, her back ached. She stretched as the crunching of car wheels pulling into the driveway brought a relief she hadn't been aware she needed. Mary and Del had returned home.

Del bolted from around the corner of the house talking all the way. "Mom, Applegate is cool. What's for lunch? I'm starving."

Lily-Rose straightened and leaned against the rake. "Cool, you say." She smiled. "What'd you guys see?"

Del gave a quick hug. "Lots of stuff. We found a store that sold comic books—and they carry the latest Batman and Justice League. Just like back home."

"We also found a plaza full of little shops," Mary offered as she rounded the corner. Then, with a hint of a whine, "But we didn't go in. I only had ten dollars, remember?"

Lily-Rose chose to ignore the line. "Sounds like a productive morning." She chided herself for being so fearful earlier. Her kids stood with their eyes wide and faces red with excitement. Her fear could have stolen their experience. "Let me clean up here, and we can go back out. I also want to see the school. I imagine the year's over for them, too, but maybe someone will be there for us to talk with. It'd be great if we were able to go ahead and get you signed up for next year." She paused and thought of her list. "After that, we can see about picking up other odds and ends. Like more clothes, maybe even a television or a couple stereos. Did you happen to see an appliance store when you were out?"

Mary's words spilled out. "Not far from the plaza. Maybe we can go in this time?"

"Cool," Del said. "Thanks, Mom." They both turned and ran into the house. Mary stopped. Turned.

"Don't worry about Unc-a-bunk, Mom. He'll never find us here. Del and I will do our part, I promise."

Lily-Rose had leaned over to pull a leaf trapped by her shoelaces but stood straight at the words. So young, yet so wise, her daughter. "You're sweet, but it's my job to make sure we're okay. It's your jobs to be kids." Lily-Rose's tone lightened. "Now, let's skedaddle."

chapter 15

Only those who risk going too far can possibly find out how far they can go.

—T.S Eliot

With their quick lunch finished and kitchen cleaned, Lily-Rose and her kids backed out of the driveway with a left-behind outdated phonebook in hand. They located a map of Applegate on the blue pages between the white and yellow pages. The directions took them to the edge of town where they turned off the main road onto a pot-holed side street. They came to a wooden sign with tall faded red letters, Applegate Junior High School, Home of the Applegate Rough Riders.

"Look there. Look there." Del pointed.

They followed the drive to a two-story brick building. As they got closer the cornerstone's Established 1902 came into sight.

Mary stared. "Are you kidding? Established in 1902? Gross."

Lily-Rose stared too. The state-of-the-art private school Mary and Del had attended in Lincoln was set in a secluded area surrounded by acres of private grounds and fences. Here their new school sat between a bus garage and a field of winter wheat.

They turned in at the gravel driveway between the garage and school, stopped and stared at the building.

"It's not fancy, but I guess it's okay," Mary offered.

"That's the spirit, Mare." Lily-Rose rolled the car past the school and into the sparsely occupied parking lot, stopping by the sports fields. For several moments they sat in stunned silence, then got out of the car and headed toward the fields to see if there was any activity there.

"Can I help you?"

They turned to a man behind the voice that had startled Lily-Rose enough she'd almost yelped.

"I'm Cole Matheson, the school's coach."

"Hello, I'm Lily-Rose Pembrick"—she stuck out her hand—"and these are Mary and Del. We just moved to the area and wanted to see the schools. I hope we're not causing any trouble."

"No, not at all. Hi, Mary, nice to meet you. Del, with those long legs of yours, you look like you could be a football star—wide receiver. Am I right?"

The young coach reached out to shake Del's hand, which sent a myriad of emotions across his face. A simple gesture that knocked Lily-Rose off guard in a pleasing sort of way. Welcomed. Accepted. Valued.

"Yeah, kind of," Del muttered.

How had she missed this? Her son was an almost man in need of another man to offer validation.

"What grades are you two going into?" Cole assumed the stance of a coach-on-the-sidelines—feet braced apart, knees locked, arms crossed.

Del's voice lowered in pitch. "I'm going into seventh. Mary, she's gonna be a junior."

"Is any office staff here today?" Lily-Rose asked. "We'd hoped to get a tour of the school if possible."

The coach nodded as he dropped his arms and turned slightly. "You might catch them if you hurry. The staff's just as excited as the kids to be done when the year's over. I just came from the office. They're still wrapping up the year." He turned his attention back to the kids. "And you're in luck. This school houses both junior high and high school." He glanced at his watch. "If you want, I can show you around after practice. We could wait for your husband if you'd like."

"No, that's fine. But thanks anyway. We'll see if we can catch them inside."

"No problem." He looked back to the field. "Sorry, I have to get ready for practice." Cole gave a two-finger salute and trotted toward the track. He turned, walked backward, and hollered, his voice dying out the farther he went. "Maybe I'll see you guys around town sometime?" He pointed at Del. "We'd would love to have you try out. What's your favorite event? Cross country? The 440? Keep them in mind, okay?"

"Okay, thanks, Mr. Matheson. I—I mean Coach."

"Let's go," Lily-Rose said. They made their way to the administration office where, just as the coach had said, only two staff members remained. Lily-Rose hurried to fill out the paperwork to register Mary and Del for next year's classes, not wanting to keep the staff any longer than necessary. Finished, she thanked them, then led the kids back to the car.

"Mom, I'm hungry," Del said. "Could we hit Burgers 'n More again?"

"But we just—" She stopped. No. She should be glad his appetite had returned. She'd monitor what they ate later. Lily-Rose checked her watch. "I guess it's not too early for another bite. But then, we're off to check out the plaza, okay?"

Inside Al's, they discovered a group of teenagers, who had already staked out what appeared to be the cool booths. Like their seating choice, the three boys and two girls wore the latest in cool—jeans cutoffs and T-shirts. Lily-Rose noted that the girls' hair was only a tad longer than the fellas—something Edward had railed against time and again. "A boy ought to look like a boy," he'd mumble, then wink.

Lily-Rose, Mary, and Del headed to the other side of the seating area. When Mary's chin rose and back straightened, Lily-Rose glanced over her shoulder, noting that the cool-booth kids studied her daughter, something Mary was obviously innately aware of.

"You want to go over and say hi?" Lily-Rose asked.

"Mo-ther. It's not done that way."

Lily-Rose bit back a smile, then pulled the list from her pocket as they slid into their own booth. "All right. First stop is the phone company to see about setting a time to have extra phone jacks put in." She looked up. "But just like in Lincoln, there will be phone rules. Understand?"

"Yeah, no long-distance calls and no contact with Lincoln friends. We remember," Del piped in. "Right, Mare?"

"I remember," Mary sighed.

"And after the phone company, we'll head back to the plaza you told me about." A perfect opportunity to get items they needed while spending time together becoming familiar with Applegate.

They quickly finished their sandwiches and started their adventure. After their stop at the phone company, they headed for the plaza, parking at the far end to visit the stores and see what Applegate had to offer.

They worked their way down the line. Their trip proved productive and Lily-Rose carried their packages like a packed mule bringing gold home from the mines. Their path eventually brought them in front of an ice cream store. Knowing her son could be easily persuaded with sweets, she said, "I feel the need for a chocolate sundae. How 'bout you guys?"

"You bet."

They went in and ordered, then sat at the counter with their ice cream treats. Lily-Rose looked up when the bells over the door jingled in time to see the same kids from Al's Burgers n' More saunter in and sit at a table nearby. "Looks like we have company."

Mary looked up and smiled at the crowd. Smiles returned, along with a couple raised chins and subtle waves. Mary commented to her family. "Can I go over? They want to meet me. Can I?"

"But how—"

"Oh, Mo-ther."

"That's twice today you've given me an 'Oh Mo-ther.' We must be back on track, right Del?"

Del managed to look up from his chocolate swirls. "Uh-huh."

"Go ahead, Mary, but stay close. We don't know any of those kids."

"Oh, Mo-th—" Mary's eyes twinkled as she stood. "Sounds good."

"After Del and I finish, we'll meet you back here in an hour, okay?"

"Thanks, Mom."

In a moment, Mary walked over to the group. Lily-Rose focused on spooning her ice cream, but her ears tuned to the words at the nearby table.

"Hey," Mary offered. "I'm Mary."

"I'm Donna. Donna Masters. This is Skeeter, Randy, Vance, and Cindy. You visiting?"

"Nah, we just moved here."

"Oh, yeah? From where?"

Lily-Rose held her breath. Would her daughter give away too much information?

"Nebraska."

Lily-Rose exhaled. Good job, Mary. She took a bite of ice cream. What would Edward say about their daughter's new friends? She smiled. He would have probably given them the evil eye for good measure.

Skeeter jumped in. "Far out. Dude, I mean really, that's far out."

Lily-Rose frowned. Something about that kid. And she could hear Edward now. "I'm not so sure I like that Skeeter fella," he'd say. "His jokes are lame."

But the kids all smiled, then scooted in to make room for Mary. Soon heads were nodding, and kids were laughing as they continued their teen-speak, covering the same topics as the ones Lily-Rose had overheard between Mary and her friends back home. Satisfied her daughter was safe, Lily-Rose returned her attention to Del as he finished his sundae.

"Ready for more shopping?"

"You bet." He wiped the last bit of ice cream off his chin with his fingers.

Lily-Rose and Del visited the balance of the stores, then carried their bundles back to the car, window-shopping at the stores they chose not to enter. Lily-Rose made a mental note to pay more attention to Del's interests. She had to have the eyes of two parents now.

She noticed a savings and loan in the plaza and resolved to come back later and deposit her satchel of money there for safekeeping. If, indeed, it would be ... should Christopher's goons be sniffing on her trail, a bank account might enable them to find her. But this was a risk worth taking. Keeping all that cash at home held its own risks.

Del suddenly stopped walking and faced her.

"Mom, do you think you're happy? I mean, as happy as you thought you'd be when you were my age?"

His question startled her. "Where'd this come from? Besides, sweetie, it's not polite to ask people questions like that."

"Like what?"

"Like are you as happy as you thought you'd be." She guided

him over to a bench, sat, and patted the empty space beside her.

He continued his line of questioning, "But you're my mom."

Lily-Rose laughed. "Especially your mom."

He looked confused. "I don't understand."

It appeared her son was ready for a life lesson. "Because asking someone if they're happy is offering them a one-way ticket to Depressionville. A person needs to determine early on whether to be happy or not. Seek out peace or not. Circumstances might influence how a person feels but shouldn't be allowed to dictate them." She brushed his hair away from his eyes. "I've been struggling a lot since your dad died." Lily-Rose collected her thoughts and did her best to control her tears. This had to get easier. "And I imagine I will continue to struggle for a long time. But that doesn't mean I'm not happy. I'm just sad and miss your dad. Does that answer your question?"

"Not really. But is this gonna be one of the things I'll understand when I get older?"

Lily-Rose leaned in and Del gave her a hug—a bit longer than usual. "Maybe, sweetie. But know for sure that I'm happy. I may have lost your dad, but I still have two awesome kids who remind me of him every day. And that's a great thing." She tilted her head and looked into his eyes. "But I'll make a point of showing you more, so you won't need to ask. Deal?"

chapter 16

The greatest legacy one can pass on to one's children is not material things accumulated in one's life, but rather a legacy of character and faith.

—Billy Graham

Lily-Rose and Del returned to the ice cream store to find Mary laughing with her new friends. She stood after she spotted them, waved goodbye, and then joined her mother and brother on their way back to the car. Mary's walk had the old bounce back again, and her voice held a lilt.

One of her kids laughing again. Baby steps.

They passed a woman with a child's playpen on the sidewalk in front of the pet store and were mesmerized by a flurry of black and white four-legged fluff balls wrestling and romping over one another.

"Puppies," Del exclaimed.

"Del—I don't think," Lily-Rose stammered, but she was too late.

He ran to the pen and pulled a soft and cuddly mutt from the litter. He sat giggling on the sidewalk as the wiggling puppy stretched up to lick his face.

"Mom," Mary smiled, "a dog would be great company. Look at his paws. I bet he won't get too big. And look at Del. It's like he found his new best friend."

She could not say no. Lily-Rose couldn't deny that Del's face, crinkled from laughing, had returned to how it looked weeks earlier. She nodded toward the pet store.

"Guess I need to step inside for pet supplies before heading home." She handed over the bags to Mary. "Can you guys take these to the car? I'll meet you there when I'm done here."

Besides, she couldn't deny it—the puppy was adorable.

"What should we name him?" Lily-Rose asked after returning to the car, chewy toys and dog food in hand.

"Scout." Del said immediately. "He's gonna have a nose to seek clues. I can tell."

"How's that?" Mary asked.

Del giggled as the puppy climbed all over him. "'Cause he won't sit still. And his nose is in the air, tryin' to sniff us. Scout, stop wiggling."

The puppy looked at Del, cocked his head to one side, then the other.

"See, he understands what I just said."

On the way home, Lily-Rose stopped at the pizzeria and grabbed the night's dinner. She kept the food close while the kids and Scout stayed in the car's back seat, all packed in and around newfound treasures. After arriving home, Del and Scout bounded out into the front yard, both rolling and playing. Mary helped Lily-Rose bring the food and purchases in the house.

Once the car was unloaded, they sat at the table for dinner. Scout stayed at Del's side as the kids devoured the pizza, laughing over their discoveries in Applegate.

"I can't believe I got a dog. I've always wanted one."

"And I got new friends and their phone numbers," Mary said. "Now I just need a phone."

"They'll be here tomorrow to install the jacks and hook our line up."

"Great. That'll give me time to work on setting up my room the way I want. Can I have my new friends over then?"

Lily-Rose's heart smiled. This girl was a ball of energy.

After dinner, Del and Scout went outside to play. Scraping of furniture against floorboards broke through the music from Mary's room, which meant she made good on making the space her own. Within an hour, Del and Scout came in and settled for bed. Soon, the noises from Mary's room stilled. Lily-Rose peeked in on both. Everyone was sound asleep—even Scout, curled up at the foot of Del's bed. All exhausted from the day. As exhausted, she pondered, as she was.

With both kids down for the evening, Lily-Rose stepped outside to listen to the quiet. A soft breeze worked through her hair as she faced west. Only a tinge of horizon remained visible. She walked back to the firepit as she had the night before. This time she paused, looking through the shadows to a tidy yard, congratulating herself. She pulled her wrap tight, then grabbed pieces of wood from the stack she'd made earlier and began another fire.

Automatic. Life here had already shifted into automatic.

"Would you like some company? I brought some goodies."

Lily-Rose turned as Sugar skirted the hedgerow with a plate of cookies in her hand.

Lily-Rose smiled. "Hi, Sugar. If those taste as good as they look, you can stay as long as you like."

"I hope you don't mind I invited myself over. I thought that maybe cookies might soften your mood iffen you weren't too sure 'bout me. The kids are sleepin' and Dungar's at work again. If they wake up ..." She turned, stuck her hip out and showed a walkie-talkie sticking out of her pants pocket. "I've got ears on 'em."

"I'd love the company. Besides, fires are meant to be shared."

"Does that welcome extend to another neighbor?"

Lily-Rose and Sugar peered into the darkness as a woman walked toward the fire from the other side of Lily-Rose's cottage. She carried a wine bottle loosely in one hand, and it swung in rhythm to her hips.

"Fiona Kasey," she said by way of introduction, "I live in the green house." She nodded backward, indicating the house on the other side of Lily-Rose's home. "I saw you and your fire last night. My night with Miss Fergie—I mean, Mrs. Ferguson. Then I noticed you again. Tonight, I mean. Thought I'd come by. Introduce myself. Be a bit neighborly." She lifted the bottle in her hand. "Miss Fergie said not to come empty handed. Said some Lambrusco might help ease introductions."

Fiona's choppy sentences were a challenge to follow.

"Welcome, both of you." Lily-Rose stood. "Tell you what. Why don't you two get a couple of chairs from the shed. I'll be right back with some plates and glasses."

With paper plates, paper cups, and napkins in hand, Lily-Rose returned to the fire where the three women shared wine and cookies as the flames crackled and the moon rose in the sky.

The evening was quiet. Not much conversation. A word here, a few more there. But Lily-Rose appreciated having people around her who weren't staring or asking inappropriate questions about her or her family.

"This is just like when I was a kid," Sugar said. "I grew up in the hills of Kentucky. Didn't have much, but Papa said the sky was free for all who'd look at it. Not too many things purtier than an early summer sky at night."

Fiona stared at the fire, sipped her drink, then chimed in. "I wasn't allowed out at night."

"Is that a fact." Sugar took a bite of cookie. "Why in the world not? The night's great. After a day in the sun, the nighttime breeze'll give you goosebumps."

Fiona continued to stare at the fire. "It's different when your skin's the color of mine. I had to be in at dark. No ifs, ands, or buts about it. They even had a fit when my brothers, Lionel and Marcus, were out, but they had friends on the basketball team that took care of 'em. But girls? My parents said girls were different." She finished her cookie and picked up a stick to poke at the fire, "It's taken me years, and to be honest, I'm not all that thrilled to leave the house at night even now."

"I hope you're okay with coming over here," Lily-Rose said. "I remember hearing some of the same things from kids when I lived with different families growing up."

Fiona studied Lily-Rose. "Doesn't sound like life was so easy for you, either."

"I got by. The last family was the best. That's where I learned to make a fire."

"Glory be"—Sugar grabbed another cookie—"whoda thunk I'd have the knowin's about somethin' you'uns ain't got."

Fiona and Lily-Rose looked at Sugar. Then at each other. After a moment they burst out laughing. Lily-Rose said, "Sugar, do you mind sayin' that again? Maybe a bit slower this time?"

Sugar hmphed a sigh. "Sorry. Dungar says I go mountain when I get excited. I promise to speak slower next time. Truly."

Just then a car pulled into Sugar's driveway. She stood and reached for the empty plate. "Dungar's home. Time for me to go."

"What's a Dungar?" Fiona asked.

"Dungar's my husband. That's his nickname 'cause he wore dungarees when we was growing up." Sugar looked back at the ladies. "Thanks, Lily-Rose. I had a great time."

"I should leave too," Fiona added as she stood, tossing her empty cup into the fire. "It's been a gas. I haven't played like this in months. And at dark, no less."

"Thanks for coming over. Let's do this again, okay?"

After the ladies left, Lily-Rose put the fire to bed. With her belly satisfied from wine and cookies, she returned inside, brushed her teeth, and washed her face before crawling under her covers, anticipating dreams of her beloved Edward.

Instead, memories of her time in the parking garage with Christopher needled her mind.

She didn't want to waste dreamtime—and possible visits from Edward—on Christopher's vengeance toward her and her family. And she surely didn't want to be distracted trying to figure out how to deal with the ugliness her brother-in-law threatened if she and the kids were found out.

God help her.

Chapter 17

Out of suffering have emerged the strongest souls;
the most massive characters are seared with scars.

—Kahlil Gibran

"Another Canadian Club. Neat this time."

The bartender looked up from sweeping the floor of the near-empty bar and wiped his hands on his pants. He leaned the broom against the back counter where the reflection of liquor bottles danced under the low florescent lighting. "Sure, pal. Be right there."

Frequenting out-of-the-way hole-in-the-wall bars in the Lincoln area when he wanted to get his drunk on was like breathing to Christopher. He sought out drinking establishments where people wouldn't know him. Judge him. If other patrons were there, they were more than likely there to get drunk themselves.

He studied the cigarette between his nicotine-stained fingers, then lifted it to his lips for one last deep drag, closed his eyes and inhaled deeply, stopped. Held his breath for a moment. Then exhaled slowly, curving his lips and tongue to create three perfect smoke rings.

"Hey, you're pretty good at that." The bartender placed a drink in front of Christopher on a clean napkin and picked up the empty glass and soggy scraps of paper from the previous drink in the same motion. How many other empty glasses had been removed earlier, Christopher couldn't say.

"Yeah, well," Christopher snuffed out the cigarette in a dirty ashtray the bartender had emptied and wiped clean only minutes before, then searched his coat pockets for an unopened pack. "We all have to be good at something."

The bartender placed a fresh bowl of pretzels on the bar, then plucked a few out before popping one into his mouth. "When a guy comes in here and drinks like you're doin'," he said around his chewing, "it's almost always about a woman. And I don't mean their momma."

Christopher chuckled. "You been at this awhile, huh?"

The barkeep leaned his tattooed forearms on the bar. "Long enough to know when someone is drinking to get drunk instead of enjoying themselves. The Canadian Club was my first clue. I'd say you look"—he stared at Christopher a moment—"more like a Macallan 18 man to me."

Christopher smiled then took another sip. "That's what I have at home."

The bartender walked to the cash register and reached up to ding, ding, ding the bell, the sound echoing between Christopher's ears. "I told you. I'm good at what I do."

"You can stop that any time now." He nodded toward the bell. His head ached, and the evening was still early.

"Sorry, man," the bartender said, though, to Christopher's way of seeing, the man only half meant it.

Christopher leaned in. "What's your name? I don't want to share my secrets with a fella when I don't even know his name."

"Call me Bud."

Christopher sat back. "Okay, bartender Bud. Fine name. Bud."

Christopher put his drink on the table, patted his pants pockets, then shirt pocket where he found a fresh pack of cigarettes. He tapped it against his palm three times before peeling the cellophane off the pack. He opened the foil on one side of the end and ripped it off clean. Pulling out a single cigarette, he tapped the filtered end again on the counter a few times before putting it to his lips.

On the opposite side of the bar, Bud methodically poured himself a cola, looking like he was getting ready for a story. Odds were, Bud had been down this road before.

"I was a goner, Bud. She was beautiful. A face that begged to be touched. And the craziest red hair you ever saw. On top of that, she was so smart. Boy, was she ever smart."

"Yeah?"

Christopher struggled to sit straight. A low backache had started hours ago from being in a chair not meant for comfort. "I fell hard the moment I saw her. She'd moved here from back east. We both attended college in town." He leaned in, confiding to his new friend. "You know what was best, Bud? I can call you Bud, right?" He nodded. "Yeah, I fell hard for her."

"Did she come from lots of money?"

"Nah, good one." He put out his cigarette. "I'm the one with the money. Ya know what the best part about her was, Bud? I can call you Bud, right?" Christopher glanced around then whispered. "She didn't think she was pretty at all. She kept to herself, kinda shy, ya know?" He pulled back and nodded smugly, as if he had just uncovered a well-kept secret. Again, he tried to straighten. His muscles pulled, this time up to his shoulder blades. "Her roomies called her lily-white Lily-Rose. But that didn't matter. I was gonna be her friend. And I was. She told me all sorts of things. Like how she came from nothin'. No money. She didn't know her dad, and her mom was taken away when she was a kid. Spent most of her life livin' with people she barely knew." He shook his head. "Bad stuff. Real bad stuff."

Christopher lifted the glass to his lips, slurped a bit of the golden spirits, paused, and stared ahead at his reflection in the mirror behind the bar—one he hardly recognized from the young man who had fallen in love with the girl who would become his sister-in-law. After a moment he shook his head. "I told her I needed help studying. But I just wanted to be near her. Talk to her. She was somethin', ya know."

He lit another cigarette, and one side of his mouth curled in a smile.

"I remember this one time when she laughed so hard, she accidentally snorted. We both belly-laughed over that. I thought we'd be tossed from the coffee shop." His eyes found Bud's through a haze. "We were in a coffee shop, ya know? The one on the edge of campus. We always met there."

"Sounds like you remember everything about this gal from all those years ago."

Christopher fell silent. Took three good sips of his drink before looking over as Bud gulped the last bit of his soda and glanced at his watch. Christopher knew the tells. Almost closing time.

"So I guess everything went south on ya, right?"

"I didn't know he knew her too. You can imagine my surprise when my brother brought her home to meet the family." He laughed. "Can ya believe that, Bud? Me and my brother fell in love with the same girl." Christopher downed the scotch and pushed his glass and napkin toward Bud. "I'll take another one."

"Bummer, dude. That's cold." Bud stuffed the napkin into the empty glass and headed for the coffee machine by the register. "Time to switch to coffee. I'll start a fresh pot."

"You're probably right." Christopher lit another cigarette then noticed the one burning in the ashtray. He scrunched the shorter one out and picked up the new one.

"To be honest, and because you're my friend, Bud."

Christopher's words began to drag. "Wasn't their fault, really. Lily-Rose and I never even shared our last names. It was a game we played. Keep our friendship light, she said. Something about not being distracted by a committed relationship. Just be friends. Study partners. I thought the whole setup was perfect. I wanted to keep her in the dark about my ol' man's money. Have her like me for me, ya know?"

"Yeah, I get it." Bud frowned as he switched the coffeepot on. "Lily-Rose. Wait, you don't mean to tell me you're talking about Lily-Rose Pembrick, are ya? That rich widow? Her husband just died recently. I saw her picture in the paper. What a looker. Far out hair. Her dead husband—that your brother?"

"I'm just as good as my brother."

"Dude, sure ya are, sure ya are." Bud stepped to the far side of the bar and retrieved two coffee mugs.

"I hated my life before I met her, but I dealt with it, ya know? My brother had everything I ever wanted. Good looks, parents' love and attention—everything. Then I met Lily-Rose. I thought she'd be someone I could have for myself." The intoxicating aroma of coffee reached his nostrils, inviting him, but he tossed the used napkin on the floor and lifted his empty glass up to his lips to drain any leftover booze. "But Edward had to take her too. I bet the two of them laughed about me behind my back."

Bud placed a cup of coffee before him. "Coffee. Black."

Christopher brought the mug to his lips, the steam curling around his face. He took a sip. Swallowed. "Strong," he said.

"I think this evening calls for strong," Bud chuckled.

Christopher took another sip before setting the cup down, his hand twitching from the weight of it. He reached for a pretzel and tipped the bowl over sending twisted snacks along the polished bar. Yep, he'd feel this bender tomorrow. "Lily-Rose and Edward. I bet they laughed it up." He snorted. "Until he died, that is."

"Dude, that's a bit harsh, don't you think? You said yourself they didn't know."

Fury burned behind Christopher's eyes. He stood, lost his balance, then reached out and swiped his arm over the bar. Ashtrays and menu stands flung to the other side and his coffee spilled, forming a black river toward a stack of napkins. "He should have known."

"That's it." Bud pulled a bat from behind the bar and held it as if he were standing at home plate. "You've had enough and so have I. Get outta here, ya drunk. And don't come back, hear?"

Christopher stepped back, kicked over the bar stool and staggered toward the door. "You can't kick me out," he mumbled.

"Wanna bet?"

"You can't kick me out," he said again, weaving as his knees nearly buckled. "'Cause I'm leaving on my own."

Bud trailed him, keeping the end of the bat between Christopher's shoulder blades. "Yeah, you do that."

Christopher opened the door and staggered to where streetlamps sent halos into air that threatened rain. Behind him, the door locked. Hearing the click, Christopher leaned against the doorframe. "Looks like I can take this joint off my list," he muttered before sauntering to his car. He opened the door on the third try, then climbed in behind the wheel. After shutting the door, he attempted to shove the key into the ignition several times before giving up and throwing all the keys on the floorboard. "Forget it," he said, then leaned over on the seat, staying there until the world faded to black.

chapter 18

Late Summer 1969

Isn't it funny how day by day nothing changes but
when you look back everything is different.

—C. S. Lewis

"I know you say it's music, but does it have to be so loud?"
Lily-Rose rubbed her temples, trying to ease the pounding
behind her eyes. Mary had assured her that the reverberations
from her room were, in fact, sounds she enjoyed. Lily-Rose
wasn't sure why.

When Mary didn't answer, she took a deep breath and
headed for her daughter's bedroom.

She rapped on the door twice before walking in on the three
young girls who'd been holed up for longer than she thought
she could stand. Especially with their ... music.

"Hello?" The girls lay stretched out on their backs across
the bed, staring at the ceiling as sounds from stereo bounced
around the room—oblivious. Except for the tapping of feet
in air, none of the girls moved. Lily-Rose tried to get their
attention again. "Mary? Donna? Cindy?"

No response.

"Sweetheart, what are you listening to?" Lily-Rose said as if
these were her first words.

"It's cutting edge, Mom. Rotten Eggs' newest album."

"Is Rotten Eggs the name of the group or the sound?" She

scrunched her brow. "Kinda nasty, don't you think?" Clearly, she stood alone here. "Can't music just be pretty?"

Mary finally spoke. "Mother. Pretty's overrated, don't you think?"

Lily-Rose remained in the doorway for a moment, stymied. "I don't know. Do you at least think they're good?

Mary sighed, her eyes never leaving the ceiling. Clearly annoyed with her mother. "Not really. But, aren't they cool?"

Lily-Rose started to ask another question then thought better of it. Any question she'd ask couldn't match her daughter's train of thought. Instead, she stepped back into the hallway and left the door ajar. How could Edward—who listened to Bach's *French Suite II in C minor*—spawn a child who preferred this racket? She followed the hall to the kitchen and headed to the backyard for some peace and quiet. While this postage-stamp-sized yard couldn't compare to the grounds at their previous home, the backyard on Norwood Street held her heart more than the groomed landscape in Lincoln ever did.

She walked by the bed of red and white petunias she and the kids had planted a few months earlier. The flowers had flourished and even welcomed the occasional trimming to promote more blooms. The intense Ohio sun and her newly found green thumb had coaxed magnificent colors from the posies. The last time she cared for petunias was—well, she couldn't remember when. Nor could she remember the family she lived with nor the town. Yet the memories of how to care for the precious flowers came back when she needed it.

Lily-Rose sauntered to the oak tree and settled on the bench she'd found the morning she and the kids spent at a local Saturday flea market. Life had settled into simple here. Shared chores and laughter. A good place to raise a family— away from threats and worry. So different than Lincoln.

She leaned back and welcomed the warm breeze in her hair and allowed herself to think about the life and home she had months earlier. It wasn't so much the property and possessions, but her history there. Family history. Birthday parties. Grilling at the pool.

And Edward.

Her heart still ached over her loss. But she was determined to make new memories here. Applegate memories, she called them. She whispered to her dead husband. "You'd love life on Norwood Street, Koochie."

Just then Scout came bounding around the house straight for her, jumping into her lap and licking her face.

"Heel, Scout, heel. Aw, come on fella ... heel. Please?" Del rounded the corner behind his dog, Scout's leash in his hand, his chest rising and falling.

Lily-Rose laughed, returning to reality. "Looks like you have more work to do, son."

Del flopped on the ground at her feet and caught his breath as Scout continued to show Lily-Rose favor. "We were fine until a cat walked by and broke his concentration."

Lily-Rose's laugh continued as she stretched her head back, putting distance between her face and Scout's wet tongue. She finally coaxed him off her lap. "Concentration? Oh, yes, I'm sure it was the cat. Maybe next time you can take treats along. Help him concentrate. Rewards are the key."

Lily-Rose scooched over and patted the spot beside her, giving Del room to sit. He climbed onto the bench and leaned into her. She hugged him close and kissed the top of his head. They snuggled without saying a word. Lily-Rose started her check-in conversation.

"How ya doing, sweetie?"

"Hmm, pretty okay, I guess."

Lily-Rose pulled back enough to look down into Del's face.

"That answer doesn't build confidence in me."

Del looked away. "It's kind of hard here without Dad. I'm trying to be happy. Like you said." He shrugged. 'But I don't really have anyone for me. I mean, you're here and all." He looked back at her. "I miss the guy stuff Dad and I used to do." He wrinkled his nose. "There's always girls around. No boys. Just me and Scout. Most the time, though, he doesn't count." Del peered up. "Dad use to say I'd like having Mary's friends around when I got older." He leaned back into her. "I guess I'm just not older yet."

Lily-Rose's eyes felt warm as she tried to blink the tears away. If she could only scoop him into her arms like she had when he was a baby. But that was no longer an option. He wasn't a baby now. He'd faced more tragedy at his young age than she ever imagined a person could.

She looked straight ahead, remembering Edward's instructions on talking with their son, "Lily-Rose, women talk face-to-face, but men talk shoulder-to-shoulder."

Scout finally settled at her feet, resting his nose in her lap. She stroked the top of his head. "Yeah, I can see that'd be a problem." She kept her gaze straight ahead. "How do you suggest we deal with it?"

"Make Dad not dead."

She closed her eyes. "Oh, sweetheart … if only I could." Lily-Rose watched as Scout nudged Del's leg, trying to get his attention.

"Tell you what. Why don't I head over to your new school and see if we can find out about what sports are available. That nice man Coach Matheson said you looked like a natural for football or track. What did he say, wide receiver, right? He said something about cross country too."

Del sighed and continued to look away. "I don't want to be your project, Mom."

"My project? Where in the world did you get an idea like that?"

Lily-Rose knelt in front of her son. She knew what Edward had said, but this time she wanted—she needed—her son to look into her eyes and see the truth and devotion waiting for him there.

She gripped his hands and held them to her chin. "You are my heart, baby boy. Do you hear me? I would take a bullet for you or your sister. Any time or day of the week. You are not a project. You are my son. And I will love you until time starts over."

Tears welled in Del's eyes, and he swiped his arm across his face.

"Thanks, Mom."

Del reached out and hugged his mother's neck for a long moment, wiping his face on her shoulder and sniffing away his runny nose. He then let go just as fast as he had held on. "Scout, let's go. We have trainin' to do." He turned to his mom. "We'll be back for dinner."

"Don't forget to grab some treats," Lily-Rose called after him. They disappeared around the corner of the house as fast as they had come in.

The following morning Lily-Rose woke before the kids and headed to the school, hoping to catch Coach Matheson there. When she drove through the empty parking lot closest to the sports fields, she saw the coach painting the outside of the baseball dugout.

She parked and walked toward the field. "Coach Matheson," she called. "Good morning."

The coach turned toward her, then leaned down and turned

off the transistor radio.

"Good morning to you," he smiled as she got closer. "I wasn't sure if I heard new lyrics to the song or someone was calling me." He cleaned his hands off on a painter's rag as she approached, then took off his baseball cap and wiped sweat from his brow with the shirt on his upper arm.

She hadn't noticed before how he towered over her. To be honest, she hadn't noticed much about him at all on the day they'd first met. Maybe she had been distracted by her grief and fear—her worry and stress—that kept her from seeing him fully back then. Or, maybe it was the sun springing up just past the horizon that gave him a tan—richer than she remembered—and bleached out his sandy-blond hair she clearly hadn't noticed. His brown eyes seemed to dance when he smiled—again, something she couldn't recall from May. And, in all honesty, the way he filled out the Applegate Roughrider T-shirt distracted her, just for a moment.

Lily-Rose chided herself. Married women don't think like that. But she also quietly quipped that Sugar and Fiona would have a fit about right now if they could hear her thoughts.

"I don't know if you remember me—"

"I remember you. You're the lady who bought the Hamilton place. A son and a daughter, right? Sorry, but I can't recall your names."

"Pembrick. I'm Lily—"

"Rose. Lily-Rose … I remember now. And your kids had Irish names as well, right? It's coming back to me. So, Mrs. Pembrick, how can I help you?"

A shudder ran through her, both uncomfortable and welcomed. She took a breath. This was for Del. She would deal with uncomfortable conversations if that meant helping her son.

"I need help, Coach—"

"Cole. Please call me Cole. Especially if I can help you."

"Okay ... Cole. I should tell you I wasn't completely honest when we met. There's no husband. I mean there was a husband, but he died. That's why I need your help." She crossed her arms and tried to relax her stance. "It's my son, Del. He's in a rough place right now, missing his father and living in a new town and all. You mentioned some sports the last time we were here. Do you think there's room for him on one of your teams?"

"What's he into?"

Lily-Rose stared at Cole as tears formed. She blinked several times. Tears—she hadn't expected tears.

"I don't know anymore." She sniffled, then walked to a nearby bench to sit. "Ever since Edward died, he's shut himself away from me." She pulled a tissue from her purse. "I must be a terrible mother that I don't even know what he likes."

Cole shuffled toward her, repositioning his baseball cap.

"Somehow, I doubt that, Mrs. Pembrick." He sat at the opposite end of the bench, his elbows resting on his knees, the paint rag hanging loosely from his right hand.

"Lily-Rose, you can call me Lily-Rose." She hoped he didn't think her forward, but she needed a friend right now—most especially one who would help with her son.

"Lily-Rose it is then. But honestly ... Lily-Rose ... Del's entering a strange place for a young man. And there's not a lot you can do to protect him, from puberty, that is. But I see your predicament. New house and school. All without a father."

Cole wiped his rag over his hands and the already-dried paint, either stalling or thinking; Lily-Rose couldn't tell which.

"Let me think about Del and see what I can come up with. Maybe a couple days. How's that sound?"

"That sounds great. Cole. Thanks for this."

"My pleasure. Lily-Rose."

chapter 19

The best thing about the future is that it comes one day at a time.

—Abraham Lincoln

Cole watched as Lily-Rose walked away. And he continued to watch as she drove out of the parking lot and out of sight. Once she was gone, he turned his radio back on and continued painting, humming along with The Grass Roots.

After the morning at school, Cole returned home for a quick lunch of bologna sandwich and chips. He pulled the files labeled Track/Field and Football from his desk and tossed them on the table. He then walked to the refrigerator and pulled out the plastic pitcher of iced tea. Taking off its top, he took a giant drink straight from the jug, then poured a glass and walked back to the table. He sat, and after saying a quick grace, he opened the football file first and took a bite of his sandwich. Reviewing the previous year's information, he nodded his head. Last season had not been stellar, but his team had the beginnings of real talent.

Del Pembrick. He sipped his tea, munched on the chips, and leaned back into his chair. If he remembered correctly, Del had long legs. He'd seen that immediately when they met. Adding him to the roster might bring a boost to the team as well as help the boy get through this rough patch. A win-win, for sure.

He grabbed his keys. He had a full day of errands to do.

He caught his reflection in the mirror as he headed for the door, then looked again, raking his fingers through his hair and tilting his head to the left, then the right. Maybe he'd get a haircut before he stopped at the Hamilton—the Pembrick place. No sense looking like a bum. He headed out the door, with a spring in his step and whistling a tune.

~

Two days later, Cole stopped by the Pembrick house to see Del. He smiled as he neared the house and saw the young boy with his dog playing in the front yard.

Recognition registered on Del's face, and he called out, "Hey, Coach. What brings you here?" as he ran to the car that now idled in the driveway.

"Hi, Del." Cole shut off the engine, then got out of his car and adjusted his ball cap. He bent down to pet the dog. "Nice dog," he said. "What's his name?"

"Scout."

Cole straightened, directing his attention back to the boy. "I saw your mom a couple days ago, and she said you might be interested in playing football this fall. I remember chatting about it with you a few months back. Still interested?"

"I guess so. Sure."

Cole offered a crooked grin and mussed Del's hair. "You need to be more convincing than that."

Del laughed and shouted in his best military voice. "Yes, sir."

Cole gave Del a jab in the shoulder. "All right then. That's better." He turned back and reached through the car window to pull out the school's football schedule. "Here's a copy of the schedule for you and your mom. We start practice in a couple weeks. Every morning except Sundays. Seven o'clock sharp.

Think you can do that?"

"Yes, sir." Del's smile grew.

Just then Lily-Rose came out the front door. "Hi. I wondered who—"

"Mrs. Pembrick," Cole said, careful not to appear too casual in front of his young student.

"Lily-Rose, please."

"Mom, look," Del handed her the schedule. "The coach invited me to start practicing with the team."

"Yeah," Cole said as he took off his cap. "Looks like I have a new football player for the Applegate Rough Riders. That is, if it's okay with you."

Del looked at his mom. "You have to get me to practice at seven in the morning, Mom. Is that okay?"

"That's pretty early. You sure you want to do this?"

"I'm sure." He turned to Cole and offered his hand to shake. "Thanks, Coach. I won't let you down. Come on, Scout. Let's go." Del ran off, leaving his mother and coach standing in the driveway.

"Yes, thanks, Coach." Lily-Rose smiled and turned to walk away.

Cole stopped her. "Lily-Rose." He fidgeted with his cap. "Once practice starts, if you ever want to know how Del's doing, let me know. I can keep you up to date on how things are going and stuff. His schedule. If I see anything bothering him. And stuff."

Cole looked at his shoes. And stuff? He sounded like one of the middle school boys.

"Thank you," she said, seemingly nonplussed by his awkwardness.

He met her gaze. "I mean, if you want, we could talk about your kids—especially Del. I can fill you in on what his schedule will be like and you can tell me about him. What motivates him. Bothers him."

Cole looked at his shoes again.

"Or you could tell me about yourself. I'd like that too."

"Oh. Well, I don't know, Cole. I—"

"Sorry, I didn't mean to—"

"No, you're fine. I guess it's time to learn how to be a parent by myself." She paused. "I would like to talk about Del, though. I'm really concerned about him. I'm lost when it comes to understanding what boys need."

Lily-Rose stood in the driveway with Cole, seemingly trying to figure out what to do next.

"Well. No sense in waiting 'til practice starts," Lily-Rose said. "Want to meet tonight? At Al's?"

Cole startled. "Sure. Great. Want me to pick you up?"

"No, I'll meet you there. See you … say … eight o'clock?"

Lily-Rose remained in the driveway while Cole opened his car door and slid in, never moving as he adjusted his cap into place. "Thanks, Lily-Rose."

❧

When Lily-Rose arrived at Al's Burgers n More at two after eight, she saw Cole sitting in a booth by the window.

This is about Del, nothing else. And if it gets too weird, you can just leave. Take a deep breath. You can do this.

When Lily-Rose walked in, Cole stood and waved her over. The smell of French fry grease filled the air and made her stomach growl. As nervous as Lily-Rose felt, she was also ready to order a basket full of salty delectables. They went to the counter and ordered. Cole carried their tray back, and Lily-Rose began dividing their food.

Cole smiled.

Lily-Rose caught herself. "Sorry. It's a Mom thing." She

took her fries and drink from the tray. "I'll leave yours. Sorry."

Cole continued to smile. He reached for his portion of the snack. "Thanks for coming out. What are Mary and Del doing tonight?"

"They're hanging out with friends. I told them I'd be gone for just a bit."

"Thanks for coming out," he repeated.

"Thanks for caring about my son."

Cole and Lily-Rose talked about Del's habits and likes. They talked about his fears and his heartache since his father's death. Cole turned the subject to Lily-Rose.

"How are you doing?"

"I have my moments," Lily-Rose said. She grabbed a fry, dunked it in the ketchup, and stared out the window. "Some days are better than others. I'm not too keen on talking about myself. Not really ready. Hope you understand."

"Sure, I get it. That's cool."

"But what about you?" She tried to deflect the attention away from herself. "I'd really like to hear about you. What makes a guy want to be a coach?"

Cole laughed and grabbed a fry for himself.

"I didn't start out wanting to be a coach. I started out wanting to be a preacher. Kinda my destiny. Not because my father, Charles Matheson—"

"Wait. Is your dad the Charles Matheson with His Holy Hands Ministries? I've heard of that. It's everywhere."

"Yes, that's my dad. He talks about Jesus in churches, on radio, and even on television sometimes. That's good for him. He really likes the spectacle and all." He shrugged. "But that isn't me."

Lily-Rose nodded. This guy is pretty interesting.

"People have different ideas of what being a pastor really means. Some think it's to only speak in church on Sundays.

Others think leading a church is about helping those in the congregation build a new garage or helping someone fix their car. Or some even think it's about getting a family member out of jail. You ask twelve people what a pastor's supposed to do and you'll get fifteen answers."

Cole fiddled with his cap sitting on the window ledge.

"To me, it's about being what God wants you to be in that moment for the people who are around you—for that moment. My parents saw preaching different from me. They started out dirt poor in ministry, but they had a real gift in connecting with people. First, they had their church, then the radio program. Word started getting out, and it wasn't long until they were on dozens of stations and in front of thousands of people every week."

Lily-Rose leaned in listening. "That sounds fascinating. But not what you wanted?"

"Not really. Because of the Matheson name, I never knew if people liked me because of me or because of who I was." He fiddled with his hat again. "Like when I was in college and met Sarah. We fell in love, and she told me she was excited about going into the ministry with me. Said she would be serving in a 'dynasty for the Lord.' Dad was thrilled. He thought Sarah would help ground me into his ministry. Second generation, so to speak."

"I understand all about family responsibilities." Lily-Rose nibbled on another fry.

"Sarah will fit right into our lifestyle," Cole said pretending to be his father. "She's beautiful and sings like a bird. She isn't afraid of speaking to crowds, either. I've seen her work a room. She's perfect for you."

"At least your dad wanted the best for you."

Cole paused and slowly shook his head.

"Dad wanted what was best for him. He wanted me to take

on his ministry, but like I said, we saw preaching differently. I'd feel more like an Elmer Gantry than a Billy Graham. Television and radio flash aren't for me. Don't get me wrong, Father's been able to serve the Lord by standing in front of thousands. It's just not my cup of tea. He wanted someone who would be perfect to carry on His Holy Hands Ministries for him. But I knew God had a different plan for me."

Lily-Rose watched as Cole became animated when he talked about finding fulfillment in his life.

"I wanted more—something more personal with God." He showed his hands as tipping scales. "Father wanted big. I wanted intimate. Needless to say, we fought a lot."

"What happened to Sarah?"

Cole looked out the window, as if looking to a different time and place.

"I'm sorry, Cole. I'm intruding. I was just so wrapped up in your story—"

"No, that's fine," he said, returning to their conversation.

"She agreed with Dad. She felt the pull of fame that wrapped His Holy Hands Ministries. She assumed when I said I was going into the ministry that meant filling my dad's shoes. I told her I wanted a different path than my parents. More of a grassroots type, working with people up close and personal, you know. Where churches are filled with people who love God and their neighbors. Where they know they can rely on both and be thankful for the slim resources they have. I wanted to see God work in an area whereby Pop's standards look a bit bleak. I wanted to see the hand of God move when people had little."

Lily-Rose sat transfixed on Cole's story. "Cole, I never heard anyone talk about preaching like this. You must really love what you do."

He smiled. "Yes, ma'am. I do." After a sigh, he added, "but

Sarah didn't share my passion. Oh, she was good with serving God, but she wanted to serve while living in a nice house and having nice things. We soon went our separate ways. My heart was broken for quite a while, but everything turned out for the best."

"I understand wanting different—wanting better—than what your family offers." Lily-Rose settled back into her booth across from Cole. *This man knows what it's like to make life choices too.*

"Then you came to Applegate?" Lily-Rose washed down the last bites of fries with her cherry cola.

"Yeah. When I met with Applegate's Mercy and Grace Community Church hiring committee, I told them they were not getting a younger version of my father. They were relieved. They were a bit embarrassed over the salary they wanted to offer. But they also had the parsonage for me. And there's Harriet—what an organizer. She's a lifesaver for me."

"So how'd coaching get into the mix?"

Cole's face broke out in a smile. "I love kids. The pain they go through these days is unreal. I want to help them anyway I can. I was a fair athlete in school, so I thought I'd give coaching a try. It's fun. Gives me extra money. And helps me keep my pulse on what's happening in Applegate."

"I'm glad." Lily-Rose said.

"I'm glad you're glad."

She looked down at her hands then back up at Cole. "Cole, this is about Del. That's all. You're a great guy and I really like you. I'm psyched you're up for being there for my son. I think you have just what he needs. But—"

"I get it, Lily-Rose. You're not ready for anything else."

"That's the thing. I'm married. I have a husband. The problem is he's dead. But the relationship is still very much alive. Do you understand?"

Cole took his hat off the windowsill and placed it on his head with an awkward adjustment.

"Of course. I get it. Your heart's still married. That only makes sense."

"I didn't want you to get the wrong idea."

Cole looked—really looked—at Lily-Rose's face.

"You fascinate me, Lily-Rose. I'd be lying if I said anything different. But I'll honor your wishes. How about maybe I touch base every now and then? Other than a cup of coffee or soda sometimes, I promise to keep everything professional." He adjusted his hat toward the back of his head. "Now then, want to tell me about Mary?"

She smiled and shared all the wonders that go with raising a daughter as they finished their fries.

CHAPTER 20

You never really understand a person until you
consider things from his point of view—until you
climb into his skin and walk around in it.

—Atticus Finch, *To Kill a Mockingbird*

Lily-Rose and the kids settled into a rhythm of their new
life as late summer transitioned into fall, bringing with it
the anticipation of a new school year. The days were mostly
predictable, yet surprises showed now and then. With the
help of his football team and Scout, Del emerged from his veil
of grief. Mary's trips to Al's Burgers 'n More scored a gaggle
of friends. Several times a week, kids came by and swept her
away. Like today when Lily-Rose returned from taking Del to
practice. She and Mary met as she headed out the door. Lily-
Rose stopped her daughter.

"I'd like to get to know these new friends of yours sometime.
Why can't you stay here? I'll make cookies and lemonade for
everyone."

"Oh, Mother, we just hang out." Which had become Mary's
go-to comment.

"That's all well and good, but I still want to get to know
them." Her eyes widened. "I know what we can do. Let's have
a party. With punch and cake. Maybe some pizzas. And I can
pick up some games. How about Twister or Uno?"

Mary stared at her mother, then offered, "I'll mention it."

"Let's plan for this Saturday. If you tell them today, they

can let their parents know in advance. Then their families can plan accordingly."

Mary inched toward the door. "Mom, my friends don't plan. They just do. Makes them cool, right?"

"Yeah. Right." Lily-Rose pressed. "I still want to get to know them better. Cindy and Donna have been over, but I'm still not too sure about the fellas—what are their names again? Maybe I can even meet their parents."

Mary gave her mother a sideways look. "Skeeter, Randy, and Vance. Remember?" She hesitated, her hand on the doorknob. "But what if they recognize you, Mom. The parents, I mean?"

Lily-Rose hadn't thought of that. She mulled Mary's question a moment. "If they do, we'll face the music then. It's not like I'm a convict on the run. Our family's been out of the Nebraska limelight for months now. There's probably bigger fish to fry than us. Anyway, yours and Del's safety is more important than fearing what ifs. Tell them the party's this Saturday. I'll have everything ready at 7:00."

With a "We'll see," Mary ran out to meet her friends.

Lily-Rose made a pot of coffee, poured a cup, then strolled out her back door to the bench. As she sipped the steamy brew, she surveyed the sanctuary she and the kids had created during the summer. The leaves that had showed their new-green flair now offered deeper colors, readying for the upcoming orange, reds, and yellows. The spring petunia beds had been enjoyed— but cleared—for the planting of autumn bulbs. The addition of tulips, irises and daffodils would guarantee the promise of beauty pushing through the frozen ground next year. And the rich deep tones of burgundy and clean white geraniums would also add color in her oasis through the next fall.

She studied the back of the house. They had tackled painting it together, she doing the ladder work while the kids painted the trimmed and lower siding. At first, they balked, but later seemed to enjoy seeing the fruits of their labor. Lily-Rose even taught herself how to re-glaze the loose panes of glass in the windows and repair the awnings. Sitting there, she looked down at her hands and saw calluses once again, just as they had looked when she was a teen. Lessons she learned while doing chores at some of the foster homes she had lived in. Calluses or not, she found satisfaction viewing their accomplishments.

Lily-Rose finished her coffee and returned to the house. She grabbed her mail and began looking through the flyers when she noticed three envelopes addressed to Richard Bowersox. After finishing looking through everything, Lily-Rose grabbed the letters, then headed to Sugar's back door. Not only could she deliver the mail, but this gave her the perfect excuse to drop by and chat a moment. Sugar was the only parent she knew in Applegate. She felt good to have a sounding board for kid issues next door in case she needed one. Life seemed to be getting better for them, but that could change in a moment. She had already lived through one of those moments where life couldn't return to how it had been.

⁂

Sugar was in bed when she heard a crash from the kitchen and voices that were typically angelic rising to a feverous pitch. "Mommy. It's her fault. She made me do it."

"Mom, she's messing with my things. Make her stop."

"Ouch. Stop pulling my—Ma-mee. She's hurting me."

That's when a knock on the back door invaded Sugar's world. Perfect. She rolled to her side and pulled the covers over her head. No, not today. She had spent the last hour or so crying, and if she'd look in the mirror, she knew she'd find swollen eyes and a splotchy face. She needed to be alone for a bit. She couldn't bear to speak to anyone right now. She had watched Dungar get ready and leave before the sun came up—again. The thought of putting on a smile to the world was impossible.

Impossible.

She continued to listen. The knocking stopped. The yelling stopped. That couldn't be good. She sighed then propped herself on an elbow and strained to hear what was happening in the kitchen. A lady's muffled voice was all she could make out. Then silence again. She let herself fall back onto the pillows, landing on her side, and staring at the wall.

Moments later, eldest daughter Keara came into the bedroom followed by the younger Addison and Lucy. They all ventured to the wall-side of the bed so they could see their momma's face. Keara reached over the covers and tried to pry open Sugar's exposed eye. "Momma, you wake?"

Sugar smelled the sweet aroma of her daughter's breath as she allowed her eyelid to move to her daughter's prodding. "I am now."

Addison laid her cheek on the bed in front of Sugar's face. Sugar pulled her head back a bit to focus. Lucy held her arms up to Keara who helped her climb onto the bed.

"Did I hear someone downstairs?" She rolled onto her back and put the back of her hand against her forehead pausing. "I thought I told you not to open the door."

Keara answered in a breathy voice. "Sorry, Momma. But it's that new lady next door. The one with the dog? Said she has some mail for you."

Addison piped in. "And she said we should come get you."

She didn't need this. Not today. Probably any other day. Lily-Rose. What would she think? She was nice the few times they chatted over the hedge.

Not today.

"Sounds like you had quite the conversation. 'The one with

the dog.' What else did she say?"

"Mmm, not much. Said he doesn't eat garbage and have stinky breath like Buster."

Sugar frowned. "How does she know Buster? Wa-wait. And how do you know Buster eats garbage?"

It was Keara's turn to frown. "'Cause he stinks." She nudged her mother's shoulder. "Come on, Momma … you comin' down?"

Sugar took a breath and then threw back the covers. "I'm coming, I'm coming." She pulled on some shorts and kept her nighttime tank on, finger-combed her hair and pulled it back into a ponytail. She hoped the neighbor lady—this Lily-Rose woman—would understand she had little to offer today.

She walked down the stairs, careful not to step on any stuffed animals or dollies. The steps ended in the dining room, and she automatically sidestepped the table and chairs. She had planned to make her way to the kitchen and then on to the back door. She paused when she saw the kitchen as the girls left it. Counters covered with dirty dishes, cereal boxes, and half-emptied cookie packages. Milk-filled bowls, cereal and cookie crumbs obscured the table. Pots and pans all pulled out and loosely stacked in piles on the floor.

Lily-Rose stood by the door, mail in hand and eyes questioning. "I don't mean to intrude" she held out some envelopes. "These were in my mail but are addressed to a Richard Bowersox at this address. That's Dungar, right?"

"Thanks." Sugar accepted them and looked at the pieces. "Yep, Dungar's all right." She tossed the mail to the counter, one piece landing safely while the rest fell to the floor.

Lily-Rose stood and stared for a moment. "Um. I hope I didn't scare the girls. I made them open the door when I came up. They said they weren't allowed, but I heard a crash—" She looked around. "What was that, by the way?"

159

Sugar shrugged. "Who can say. Girls." Two girls peeked around the corner and a third toddled over. "This is Mrs. Pembrick. She lives next door—"

Keara stepped closer to Sugar, cupped her mouth, and whispered loudly. "We know, Momma. We let her in, 'member?" Addison and Lucy offered slow nods. "I told her you were layin' down, but she wanted to see you anyway."

Sugar stared at Lily-Rose. "Oh, that's right."

Lily-Rose stepped closer and placed a hand on her arm. "Sugar. Are you okay?"

Sugar's tone was expressionless. "Right as rain. Girls, what made that crash?"

Lucy and Addison looked up at Keara. "We was just playin'. We made a tower of pots for our castle. The monster knocked over the tower—"

"I'm no monster. I was gonna save the princess." Addison defended herself.

Lily-Rose stooped to face the girls. "Well, at least nobody was hurt, right? Did you save the princess?"

The girls nodded slowly. Keara spoke. "My friend has a dog. He's messy and has bad breath. He likes to lick my face, but I say, 'Stay down, Buster. You're not supposed to lick my face. You eat garbage.' Why doesn't your dog eat garbage?"

Lily-Rose smiled. "Just lucky, I guess." She looked at Sugar and caught her wiping her eyes with the back of her hand. She returned to her conversation. "Girls, do you have picture books?"

They nodded in unison.

She looked at Sugar then back at the girls. "Why don't you find some stories about dogs. They don't have to be stinky. If it's okay with your mother, I'll come in after I have a chance to talk with her and see what you've found. Can you do that?"

"Sure. Let's go, sissies." Keara led the way out of the kitchen with Addison and Lucy following. "Let's get doggie books, 'kay?"

CHAPTER 21

What lies behind us and what lies before us are tiny matters compared to what lies within us.

—Ralph Waldo Emerson

Lily-Rose stood and returned her attention to Sugar, reaching for her hands. "Are you all right? Is there anything I can do?"

"No, ma'am." Sugar picked up the mail that had fallen on the floor, placed the letters on the table and hiccupped between tears. "I'm not all right, but there's nothing you can do."

"Let me be the judge of that. How 'bout I make some tea or coffee. We can talk. The girls will be busy for a while."

Sugar wasn't happy this new woman was taking control in her kitchen, but she didn't have the strength to fight her way out of the funk she was in. Pathetic. Just pathetic. She pointed to a cabinet in the corner as she slumped in a chair at the table. Lily-Rose grabbed a dish cloth, wet it, and gave the table a quick wipe. She then went to the cabinet and brought two cups for them, then filled the tea pot with water. In no time the kettle was singing, and hot water steeped the tea bags Lily-Rose had readied for them.

"I'm not always this way," Sugar sniffled. "Today started out bad and went downhill from there. Dungar's only here to eat and sleep, then he's back to work. The four of us—my daughters and me—have been cooped up here by ourselves, and ... and ..." Between hiccups Sugar began to cry again.

Lily-Rose pulled her chair across from Sugar's then reached for Sugar's hands and held them. After moments of silence, she asked, "What do you need right now, at this very moment? If I could give you thirty minutes to do whatever you most need, what would that be?"

That was simple. "I want Dungar home."

Lily-Rose slowly shook her head. "I can't help with that request. What can you do in thirty minutes to feel better?"

"Second? What would I want next to that? Right now?" Sugar scratched her head. "I'd like to take a hot shower and not worry about the girls. A shower would feel real good."

Lily-Rose smiled. "Perfect. That's sounds doable." She stood. "I'll find the girls and check out their dog books. You get a nice hot shower. Take your time. I'll be here."

Sugar looked at Lily-Rose with tear-rimmed eyes. "Thank you." She rose from her chair and started for the dining room, rounded the table, and headed for the stairs. As she hit the upstairs landing, she heard Lily-Rose's voice. "Little ladies, I'm ready for dog stories. What do you have for me?"

Maybe having Lily-Rose as a neighbor wouldn't be so bad after all.

She went to the bathroom and turned on the shower. Steamy air filled the room. She climbed in and let the hot water wash over her. After letting the heat assault her, she backed it down and enjoyed how the tepid water hit her face and ran through her hair. She slathered soap over her arms and legs, then grabbed the back scrubber and covered the bristles with soap. She worked the lathered brush all over her back, enjoying the time she took for herself.

About a half hour later, Sugar went back to the kitchen looking like a new person. She'd traded her sweats for a pair of pressed jeans and a peasant blouse. Her hair washed, dried, and pulled back. She even had a touch of makeup on.

As she walked back down the stairs, she heard Lily-Rose barking, howling, and growling. And the girls were belly-laughing. Beautiful music, for sure. When she walked into the kitchen she saw Lily-Rose in a chair pushed away from the table with Addison on one knee, Lucy on the other and Keara backed in between her legs making it possible for all three to have a chance to see the book Lily-Rose was holding.

In that moment, she knew this woman would be her friend forever.

She smiled. "Thanks. I'm sorry you found me in such a meltdown moment. I haven't slept much, and the girls seem more needy than usual."

Lily-Rose looked into Sugar's eyes. "No problem. We all have moments we'd rather not show to anyone." She turned her attention back to the girls. "Thanks for sharing your books with me. How about I talk to your momma now. Can I do that?"

Sugar smiled. "Tell Mrs. Pembrick thank you for reading to you."

"Thank you, Mrs. Pembrick," the three girls offered together in a sing-song fashion.

"Now, can you take the books to the other room? It's my turn to spend some time with this nice lady. Can you do that for me?"

Lily-Rose bent down and gave each girl a hug as they gathered their books and headed to their playroom.

"Come on, sissies, let's go. We'll be back later, okay?" Just as they had done earlier, Keara led her younger sisters as they hopped their way from the kitchen.

Lily-Rose turned back to Sugar. "I'm not an expert on the subject, but sounds like you're grieving to me. I get it. I had my share of that, for sure."

"Sorry, Lily-Rose. I'm just thinkin' about myself. I'm not a widow like you. I still have a husband. He's just not here when I want him, for me and the girls."

Talking to Lily-Rose came naturally. How did she reach into her heart so easily? As if reading her mind, Lily-Rose looked into her eyes and smiled.

"How about you and I take care of the kitchen, and I'll tell you about my own meltdown moments?" As the girls played and the women cleaned the kitchen, Sugar heard the story of Edward's death and how Lily-Rose landed in Applegate, determined to leave unpleasantries behind and start a new life.

"Oh, Lily-Rose," Sugar's eyes widened. "I'm so sorry."

Lily-Rose swished the sponge in the soapy water, rang out its excess, and returned to wiping down more counters as she answered. "Yeah, I'm sorry too. But for now, I'm going to get up in the morning and do what needs to be done. After the day, I'm gonna go to bed and be ready to start the whole process over the next day."

"But what are you going to do?" Sugar pressed, happy to be focused on someone's problems other than her own.

"Focus on the kids, I guess. I don't know if they're doing okay or not." She paused and looked out the window over the sink. "They don't open up much. But Del's into football now. That seems to help. And Mary's got some friends. That should help her too. I just need to be diligent. Watching for—I don't know what." Lily-Rose turned and looked at Sugar. "What should I watch for? Mary and I had what I've heard is the typical mother-daughter relationship back in Nebraska. But we'd always get back together by the end of the day. Now, there's something—an edge—from the moment we wake up until bedtime. We all miss Edward. The grieving isn't as bad as it was, but he's not here. That leaves a big void. I just wish I knew what to do."

Sugar swept the last of the crumbs into the dustpan, then

leaned on her broom. "I'm a terrible person for only thinking about my stuff."

Lily-Rose stopped cleaning and looked at her new friend. "You are far from being a terrible person, Sugar. You're amazing. I admire you for all you do to hold your family together."

"I'm still trying to get my head around who I am these days. Like you said, I'll try to remember to do the next right thing for myself. Oh, I'll still focus on Dungar, the girls and Gran." She tilted her head. "But I promise, I won't forget to look in the mirror every once in a while to see how I'm doin' too."

Lily-Rose caught sight of the clock on the wall. "Look at the time. I've got to get Del from practice and pull lunch together for my troops." As she stood, she reached for Sugar's hand. "If you can, join me tonight. I hope to have a fire. The weather's supposed to be clear. A perfect night for it."

"I'd like that. I'll bring the walkie-talkie just like before." Lily-Rose sensed Sugar's wheels turning, setting her plan into action.

"Absolutely," added Lily-Rose.

chapter 22

There is a time for everything, and a season for
every activity under the heavens.

—Ecclesiastes 3:1

Lily-Rose picked up Del and pulled up to the driveway just
as Mary's friends were leaving from dropping her off. She and
the kids shared a lunch of leftover macaroni and cheese with
hot dogs.

"Football practice is getting easier," Del said between bites.
"But those sprints are killers."

"That's amazing." Lily-Rose marveled at the boy-man her
son was becoming.

"Coach is still trying to figure out my position." He took
a gulp of milk. "Hope it's a receiver. But could be a running
back. We'll see." Del wrinkled his nose. "That one would hurt
more, though."

"Still glad you joined?" Mary added.

"You bet. And I'm meeting some cool guys too."

"That's great, honey." Lily-Rose watched her son beam. She
turned to her daughter. "Any news on the party?"

Del, still hunched over his plate, looked up. "What party?"

"Yeah," Mary said with a slight shrug. "They said that'd be
cool."

"Mom, can I ask some of my friends to come too? That
would be so cool."

Mary stared at Lily-Rose. "Mother, this isn't going to be a

kiddy party, is it?"

"Ahh, c'mon, Mom," Del said over his sister's protest. "We won't bug 'em. I promise. They can have the house. We'll hang out in the backyard. Or the garage if it's raining. Please Mom, pleeease?"

Lily-Rose looked at her daughter. Mary returned the look then leaned in over her plate and stared at Del. "You make sure your pipsqueak friends stay away from us or I'll … I'll …

Del laughed. "No problem. Who'd want to hang out with you guys anyway." He came around the table to Lily-Rose and wrapped her in a tight hug, the kind he used to give. The kind she missed. "Thanks, Mom. I can't wait to call the guys."

"Keep it to five friends, okay? You'll have five, and Mary will have five. That'll be manageable here. Especially if the weather doesn't cooperate. Can you do that?"

"No problem. C'mon, Scout," he said to the dog who'd been curled at his feet, before he whisked his plate to the sink. "Let's figure out what we want to do this Saturday."

Lily-Rose chuckled to herself hoping that Scout wouldn't ask to bring five of his friends over as well.

※

Another day safely behind her and a backyard fire. In no time, the flames of the well-tended kindling began licking over the wood in the pit. She enjoyed the tranquility of these evening fires. A time to relax and shake off the day's stress.

She heard Fiona before she saw her walking toward the fire. "I pride myself in being a with-it woman. But I'm embarrassed to tell you I locked myself out of my house. I can see Miss Fergie through the window, asleep in front of the television. If I knock, I'll scare her." She chuckled. "She's too old to scare."

"Oh, Fiona. You startled me. The fire's mesmerizing." She

pointed to an empty chair, inviting Fiona to sit. She continued. "Locked yourself out, that's terrible. What can I do?"

"Could I use your phone to call the police? I'd call Miss Fergie, but I don't know if she'd even hear the phone with the television blaring so loud. I hope the police can get me in without waking her." Fiona flopped onto one of the two empty chairs and threw one of her legs over the arm and started kicking her foot. "At least I have my purse with me. I can show them my driver's license. Prove I live here."

"Absolutely."

Lily-Rose led Fiona through the back door and to the phone in the kitchen. Once the quick call was finished, Fiona headed back to her house and stood in her driveway until an Applegate police cruiser arrived. Two policemen got out and talked with Fiona. She gave them something that they both looked over, then together walked back to the cruiser. Fiona waited. After several minutes, they left the cruiser and walked to the back door with Fiona. Moments later the cruiser backed away from Fiona's house and went on their way. Fiona came out the back door, changed from her pantsuit into jeans and a T-shirt. She strolled toward Lily-Rose, two bottles of cola in hand.

"Today was a train wreck. I've been looking forward to coming home all day. Then I realized I locked myself out. The perfect end of a terrible day." She flopped again in one of the chairs. "Thanks for coming to my rescue." Fiona offered Lily-Rose one of the bottles. "For your efforts?"

Lily-Rose took the drink. "Thanks, but I didn't do much."

"You came to my rescue. Let me use your phone. You offered what I needed."

Lily-Rose put her bottle by her chair and brought two pieces of wood to the fire. "What took the police so long? Seemed they could have had you in lots sooner than they did."

Fiona stretched a bit. "That's what happens. Black person tryin' to get in a house like Miss Fergie's at night." She sipped her cola. "Like I said. That's just what happens."

Lily-Rose had no words for such ignorance. Oh, she knew these things happened, but that didn't mean she liked it. Or understood it. Especially not with someone like Fiona. Finally, she sighed and smiled. "Stay and enjoy the fire with me. Always seems to make everything better."

As the two women sat by the flames, Fiona fidgeted, as if trying to find some comfort beyond the soothing heat.

Lily-Rose looked at Fiona. "Was that upsetting? That thing with the police?"

"Being black, you learn to live with it. I knew I had to be smart, that's all. At least it was Earl and Harold. They've known me for years, so that helped. But they still needed to check me out, just to be sure. That's the way it's done." She changed the subject as she leaned against the back of her chair. "This is the first time I've stopped to relax since the last time I sat here at your fire." She coughed out a laugh. "I'm not quite sure how relaxing fits into my world."

Lily-Rose smiled as the fire's reflection danced across Fiona's face. "I imagine relaxing fits just fine, given the chance. I like having you come by. I enjoy my fires, but they're nicer shared."

Fiona fiddled with her bottle. "I never had much time to make friends. When kids were learning how to do that sort of thing, I kept to myself. Kinda shy that way. If it wasn't for Miss Fergie, I'da stayed in my own world forever."

"I understand being preoccupied with your surroundings. Was that way for me too. For a long time."

Fiona stopped fidgeting. "Really?"

"My start in life was a bit bumpy too," Lily-Rose stood and grabbed the stick she kept for stirring the embers. "If the Henderson's—the last family I lived with—hadn't stepped up and given me love and encouragement, I don't know where I'd be."

Fiona nodded. "Not living with your own people and being beholding to strangers. That's rough."

Lily-Rose finished poking the fire and placed the stick beside her chair. "What was rough was the mess they pulled me from. But they help put a hunger in my belly to press on. Change the direction my life was headed."

Both ladies quietly stared at the fire.

"How did you do it? The family thing, I mean. If Miss Fergie hadn't been there for me, I don't know where I'd be. She keeps me focused on doin' what's right for me. Making sure I look out for me." She tapped her knee each time she spoke. "But I still see my people sometimes. When seeing them fits, that is."

The fire continued crackling while Lily-Rose spoke. "I just did what I needed to do. I was lucky to have people helping me along the way. Then Edward made life easy. He was everything to me." She paused, still staring at the fire. "But he died. The kids and I are finding our own way now."

"Wow, Lily-Rose, I had no idea. Sorry." Fiona paused as to gather her thoughts. "Watching a fire really brings the world into focus, doesn't it?"

"Sure does."

"Mom assured me once I got married, I'd stop all my foolishness about wanting to be seen as my own person." She huffed. "She called me a bra-burning feminist. Like that was a bad thing. All I wanted was the opportunity to be seen. Marriage and kids didn't seem to fit. No offense."

"None taken."

"Thanks." Fiona finished her cola. "If there's ever a guy for me—he'll have to meet some pretty high standards, that's all. Until then, I'll keep listening to Miss Fergie and finishing my master's."

The conversation paused as a lone mockingbird sang from a nearby tree. Fiona started again. "Mom and Dad wanted me to be a secretary for some businessman or something like that. They didn't want me to be distracted by getting an education. 'Weeds,' they'd say—that was my nickname because my legs were so long and skinny—'don't bother spending money on an education you'll leave behind once you get married and have babies.' So, I worked super hard and paid for my own education.

"My brothers—I got two—they were different. Mom and Dad pushed them to excel—in sports, that is, so they could make their lives better. 'Find your groove on the basketball court and you'll write your own ticket to any college you want.' And that's what they did."

"What are they doing now?"

"Chasing their careers. One's in Detroit. Another's in Philadelphia. I'm happy for them, really. But they had my parents' blessing to follow their dreams while I was expected to stay here—help them as they age. Be the good daughter."

"Did you find any compromise? You know, between your dreams and being a good daughter?"

Fiona reached over, picked up the stick by Lily-Rose's chair and stirred the embers, then added more wood. Once the flames grabbed the offering, she sighed and settled in her chair. "School's got me busy, but I'm ready to move on to the next adventure. Try my hand maybe with an accounting firm in Cleveland. If they can handle me."

Lily-Rose offered a stunned look. "Are you hard to handle?"

Fiona paused. "Lily-Rose, if I seem to spaz with a bit of dry humor, don't take what I do or say personally."

Lily-Rose arched her brow. "What do you mean?"

"I come across snarky sometimes. But it's just how I talk.

People don't understand that I'm not literal when I say things. I'm only literal in my studies. Maybe I release tension through snarkiness. I don't know. But I'm working on what I say and how I say things. In fact, I have a course on that subject this semester. Something called interpersonal relationships."

"I'll keep that in mind."

The fire crackled, and the mockingbird continued its song, then a noise came from the hedges and Sugar appeared, washed in firelight.

"Is it too late for me to join ya?"

"Not at all. C'mon over."

Lily-Rose settled in her chair and listened to her friends and the fire. Watching the embers float from the flame filled her with a calm she'd never known. She truly cherished her time on Norwood Street and the ladies of the fire.

chapter 23

Bitterness does more harm to the vessel in which it is stored, than the vessel on which it is poured.

—unknown

Nights were always the worst.

Christopher woke with a start. Another nightmare. Sweat pressed his hair against his forehead. He sat up. Looked at the clock. Three thirty. The middle of the night.

He reached for a cigarette then thought better of it.

"Last thing I need … set myself on fire," he muttered.

The dreams had gotten worse since Edward's death, and the medication the doctor prescribed did nothing to stop them. His own self-medication did nothing either. And the meeting in Karn's office cemented the loss and speculations that played over and over in his mind.

Tonight's nightmare had seemed so vivid, as though he'd lived it just yesterday. Edward stood tall, looking down at Christopher in that sanctimonious way he had.

Christopher leaned into the pillows and closed his eyes, memories of a time long ago flooding back.

"Go back home, Chris, you can't come this time."

Christopher followed behind Eddie and his friends as they went to the basketball court. "Ah, come on, Eddie. I just want to spend time with you guys. I won't get in the way, I promise. Mother said if I was ever going to get on the basketball team next year, I needed to learn how you do things. Jeepers, Eddie.

I promise I won't get in the way. Promise. I can be the relief player when someone needs a break. I can even make sure everyone has water and towels. Please, Eddie, Pleeease."

"Leave him," one of Edward's friends said. "He's only a freshman."

"Yeah, a dorky freshman," another replied. "He'll ruin your image before you go to college if he sticks around. I say lose him in the dust."

Edward turned to his friends, hands open. "He's my kid brother, guys. What am I s'pose to do? Besides, I kinda owe him. He got me through last year. I'da flunked out for sure if he hadn't tutored me. All the coaches were begging me for one more year's win."

Edward's friends relented. "Come on, hurry up, Chris. You can do the water and towel thing if you want. But stay out of the way, got it?"

Christopher rolled to his side. He hated to admit to himself, but he'd do anything back then to spend time with Edward. Even listening to the biting and insulting comments from his friends. He didn't care. He adored his big brother. He even accepted being the lesser of the two when it came to sports, personality, and good looks. Besides, Christopher had his own area of superiority—education and business.

He rolled to his other side, scrunched his pillow, and looked out the floor to ceiling window into the night. He thought of Mrs. Riggins, his third-grade teacher. When had he last thought of her? Her attentiveness. She had offered such kindness to him even as Christopher understood his place in the family.

"Mrs. Riggins, I'm okay. I've never been as good as Eddie when it came to sports. I wish I was. But I know someone will need to run Pembrick Transportation one day. That'll be me. I want to do what Dad does. He's strong and smart. And I want to have a mother for my kids just like Mother."

"You sound so grown up," Mrs. Riggins said with a smile as she mussed his hair. "What makes your mother special?"

"The way she loves Edward, of course. That's special."

She knelt to be eye-to-eye with Christopher. "I don't understand, Chris. What do you mean? Don't you mean she loves both her boys—that's why she's so special?"

"Nah, it's not her fault. I'm not like Eddie. He's her favorite. Makes sense. She dotes on him and even has Cook make his special dinner of pot roast and mashed potatoes. She's a good mother."

Christopher sat up and raked his fingers through his hair. He stood and went to the bathroom for a drink of water, hoping to wash away the torment.

Trying to sleep was the worst. Controlling his thoughts was hard enough when he was awake. But days were far better than fighting the memories that flooded his dreams. Of Edward. Always of Edward. He was dead now, but still considered first.

"I should have stayed in Saint Lucia with Marabelle," Christopher muttered at the sink. He leaned over the counter and stared into the mirror, first one side of his face then the other. With no provocation, he asked his reflection, "Why couldn't Mother and Dad love you like they did Edward?" He shook his head, then hung it like a puppy who had played too hard. They couldn't help it. Everybody loved Edward.

He looked at the clock and saw there were still hours until sunlight offered a new day, so he went back to bed, hoping for a reprieve from the torment and a few hours of much-needed sleep. It seemed only moments had passed when his penthouse door opened and Carlotta, his housekeeper, entered. Soon, the aroma of coffee found its way into his bedroom.

He called out. "Thanks, Carlotta, but I won't be needing anything today. You can go home."

"Are you sure, Mister Christopher?" Carlotta stood on the other side of the door. She had learned early on not to walk into his bedroom uninvited.

"Just straighten up a bit, then you can go. Maybe set out some fresh towels. That'd be nice. I'll pay you for the day." As an afterthought, "And thanks for the coffee. Smells delicious."

"Yes, sir, Mister Christopher. Thank you. See you tomorrow."

After a few minutes, the front door closed with a click, and he was alone. Once again. He stared at the ceiling. Would life have turned out differently if he and Edward had attended different colleges? Maybe there would never have ever been an issue with Lily-Rose.

Between the fear of returning dreams and the aroma of coffee, there was no way he could go back to sleep, even for a half hour of shuteye. He got out of bed, slipped into his robe, walked toward the smell of coffee. He passed the coffee pot and shuffled toward the library's liquor cabinet. There he poured his ritual morning shot of Macallan 18 Scotch.

Seeing Lily-Rose again had tripped off his longing for her—his need for her company. Like the way the wind whipped her hair over her shoulders. Her fragile presence at both the funeral and lawyer's office almost made him reach out to her. Then both times his ugly memories took over and instead of offering comfort, his words and actions scared her. Maybe even repulsed her.

The day after their meeting with Karn, he went to Lily-Rose's house to see her, tell her he was sorry. But she was gone. Figures, he thought. He now needed to stay around and watch PT until she decided to take care of her responsibilities. Women. They're all alike. The memory still churned in his craw.

Christopher downed the scotch in one gulp then headed back to the kitchen to grab a cup of coffee. He tightened the belt around his thick robe, settled into the chair behind the desk with his coffee mug and reread Edward's local obituary from last spring.

> Edward William Pembrick of Timberdale Township
> died as a result of a tragic accident at his home.

Passing over the boring particulars, he continued to the part that dug deepest into his heart.

> He leaves behind his daughter, Mary and son, Delaney, and the love of his life, Lily-Rose, whom he married in 1951.

"Who knows what our friendship could have grown into. But you swooped in and changed everything. The ever-perfect Edward. Now we'll never know, will we?"

Christopher continued his self-inflicted torture as he finished the article.

> As the only son of William and Sandra Pembrick,
> Edward had inherited Pembrick Transportation
> when his parents died in a tragic car accident in
> 1960. Edward leaves the entire Pembrick fortune to
> his wife and family.

Even though Karn made sure the papers retracted the only son portion of the announcement to include Christopher, the damage had already been done.

It had always been Edward.

Edward had owned her heart. He had been such a fool. Looking back, he could see that Lily-Rose had only seen him as a friend. He became numb to his family's indifference. But hers had cut the most. She had seen his vulnerabilities—his underbelly—and tossed him aside for the noble and righteous Edward. Just like everybody else. No, not just like everybody— she was the worst because she caused more pain than all of them combined.

And she needed to pay.

Christopher finished his coffee and headed back to the kitchen. Maybe he'd make himself an English muffin. Enjoy a second cup of that coffee. Take the edge off the booze.

He ground his teeth as he poured the aromatic brew into a cup. He hated his plan but hated his torment more. Details needed to be pulled together before he got back to the island and ... Margaret, wasn't it? His life of choice waited for him.

He held the cup of coffee close to his lips; the steam embraced his face. His plan. How would he find peace again unless he carried it out? He turned and stared out the kitchen window to where the sun hung halfway over the eastern horizon. He knew the time had come. It time to finally visit his mother and dad. Sharing his plans with them would be appropriate.

He finished his coffee, threw on yesterday's clothes, then grabbed his keys. He popped a few breath mints and headed out the door. He maneuvered the back streets of Lincoln to Wyuka Cemetery and then onto the Pembrick mausoleum. The setting looked astonishingly different than the day of the funeral. The crowds were gone now. So were the padded chairs. No more paparazzi straining for a shot. The winds were still, and the fall sun promised a warm day.

He left his parked car several yards from the mausoleum and walked to the stone building, exchanging the sunny morning sky for stale air in the lobby of the modern-day tomb. His head pounded and he shivered. He should have brought a jacket. The effects of the collective days of drinking began to wear off. He looked to his left, then right, getting his bearings. He was alone now ... with dead people.

Sitting on the bench opposite the interred, he looked at the marble square covering his parents' crypt slots. Christopher cleared his throat, shook his head a bit, blinked hard in hopes of getting rid of the alcohol haze. "It's been too long since we've chatted and, as always, I take all the blame." He raised one hand. "No, no, don't get up. I can see you're comfortable where you are." His hand shook, and he dropped it, then noticed them both lying dormant but quivering in his lap. Were these alcohol tremors? He really needed to stop drinking. Maybe take up golf again.

He leaned back and stretched his legs, crossing them at his ankles. "There's a reason for my visit. I probably should've spoken up sooner. This this side of the marble." He pulled his legs back. Tried to get comfortable on the bench. "The thing is, I'm done dealing with so much rejection. I hope I don't hurt your feelings by being so candid, but you guys really messed me up—both of us, really. Me and Edward." Christopher pulled a flask from his coat pocket. He'd take up golf tomorrow. Right now, he needed trusty fortification. He leaned back against the wall of the marble crypt again, closed his eyes, and took a deep breath. He still remembered the shock—the devastation—when Edward drove a dagger into his heart.

"I always put him first," Christopher muttered. "Yet he couldn't give me what I wanted most."

Christopher took a long swallow from his flask while his mind played scenes from Edward's last year in college.

chapter 24

No space for regret can make amends for one life's opportunity misused.

—Marley's Ghost, *A Christmas Carol*

Memories still haunt Christopher.

He stood in the dormitory hall, talking to his brother on the payphone. "Come on, Chris," Edward's voice said through the line. "Don't do this to me. I really need this. Mother and Dad will be furious if I don't pass. You know how they are. Please, sport. Just this once more. I'm pulling my own in everything but English Writing. I need to make up some work that I dropped before. Dad got them to let me take the course again. I have to get an A this time or he will have a cow."

"I just can't, Ed. I met this girl, ya see—"

Edward's tone changed. "No way. Really? Well, this girl must be spectacular if you'd ditch me for her."

Christopher grinned and leaned against the wall, propping his foot up against it. "I've never met anyone like her, I swear." Confiding in his brother about a girl was nice.

Edward was silent for a moment. "You've never had a girlfriend before?"

"The girls Mother tried to set me up with don't count. Those were to make her friends happy. But this one's different—special."

Christopher dropped his voice to a whisper and cupped the mouthpiece with his hand. "Ed, I think I love her."

"Hold on, pal. Have you told her yet?"

Christopher spoke up again. "No, not yet. But I feel it. I'm sure I am. In love, I mean."

Another pause from his brother. "Why don't you just enjoy her company? Know what I mean? You can get to know someone, when you—you know—enjoy what they have to offer. Right? How long have you been hanging out with her?"

Christopher shifted and leaned on his shoulder. "A couple weeks, but long enough to know how I feel."

Edward's laugh rang from the receiver. "A couple of weeks is way too short to know anything." After a pause, levity left Edward's voice. "Hear my words, Chris. Spend time in her company, but don't count on your feelings lasting. And whatever you do, never tell her you love her. That'll ruin everything for sure. If you do what I say, it'll be a win-win for you and me." His voice perked up. "See. you'll be able to spend time with her—what's her name? Wait, don't tell me. I don't care. Then you can still spend time helping me on my English Writing. Whatcha say?"

Christopher closed his eyes. He wanted to keep Edward happy, but he needed to do this one thing for himself. He gathered his thoughts. "You're my best friend, Eddie. My only friend, really. But this girl—she's the one. I swear." He tapped at a piece of chewing gum wrapper with the toe of his shoe, still holding the receiver to his ear. "I think she sees me only as a friend—but I know I can make her fall in love with me. I just know it."

"Hold it, Chris. Does she call you her friend?"

"Yeah, but—"

Christopher heard his brother groan. "Ugh. Friendship. The kiss of death for a guy. You've got it bad, Chris, I'll say that for ya. Fine. No hard feelings. I'll get with Professor Collins and see what kind of suggestions he can offer. He'll help me out. Probably hook me up with a tutor. Keep me posted on how your friendship goes. Later, dude."

Christopher hung up and headed out for the coffee shop on the edge of campus. He was pretty sure he'd find Lily-Rose studying there. Sure enough, as the bell jingled when he opened the door, he saw her. Sitting in their usual booth. Books opened and sprawled on the table. His heart beat a little faster as he walked up. "Fancy meeting you here. Can I get you the usual?"

She looked up with a smile. "Sure. Thanks."

He put his bookbag on his side of the booth then walked to the counter and ordered two coffees. Carrying them back, he set them on the table.

Lily-Rose smiled again. "What are you studying tonight?"

He pushed his bag against the wall and slid in. "Nothing this time." He drummed his fingers on the table. "I came by to talk with you. I want to ask you something."

She begrudgingly closed her books and piled them to the side. "Shoot." He wrapped his hands around a mug boasting the name of the café.

"What are your plans for Thanksgiving break? It's not that far off. I thought—hoping, anyway—that you plan on staying here. On campus, I mean. If you do, I thought." She watched him take a deep breath. "Would you want to come to my place and meet my family? I think you'd like them. I'm certain they'd like you."

Lily-Rose sat back and sighed as she brought the fresh cup of coffee to her lips. "Tell you the truth, I've been looking forward to having time by myself over the break. Thought I'd get caught up on stuff around the apartment."

Christopher pushed. "No, don't stay by yourself. Come with me. Meet my family. They'd love that."

She stared back—eyes not revealing any emotion. When

she spoke again, her words seemed cautious. "I don't know, Christopher. I think I should use this time to catch up on projects I've let slide. Besides, I'll have the house all to myself. I've been looking forward to having the space. You can understand, right? Besides, we agreed. No last names. No commitments. That doesn't fit with meeting your parents."

Edward continued to push. "If you want to be alone, how about we go to my parents' place for dinner that Thursday and we both come back to your apartment. I can stay the rest of the break with you. We can get to know each other better. Enjoy ourselves. Be alone. It'll be perfect. C'mon, Lily-Rose, whatcha say?"

Her tone changed. "I appreciate it, I really do. Maybe another time, okay?" She looked at her watch. "Oh." She began sliding her pile of books into her bag. "I gotta go. I forgot one of the books I need."

"But I just got here. I thought we could hang out a while."

Lily-Rose seemed a bit off. Nervous. "Sorry. Not this time. I just remembered. I need to talk to—uh—somebody."

"Who?"

The words spilled out as she continued gathering her papers. "You don't know them. Just somebody."

Christopher's voice got loud. "Hey. You said you forgot a book. Now you say you need to talk to somebody. Are you mad at me? Did I do something wrong? It's just a weekend. I love you, Lily-Rose."

Christopher watched Lily-Rose's eyes widen as she scooted out of the booth. He should have seen this coming. Known better. Listened to Edward. He wrapped his palms over the sides of his face. "I'm such an idiot. That's not how I wanted to tell you."

Lily-Rose stood by the booth for a moment, then hoisted her bag over her shoulder. "Sorry, Christopher. I gotta go. See ya around." She shuffled past him and out the door. Once outside, he watched as she broke into a run.

Well, now he'd done it.

Thanksgiving came and went. Christopher looked for her on campus after the break, but she had gone stealth. Yet he never gave up hope. Maybe next semester, he told himself, after the Christmas break. He rehearsed apologies. He'd make this right. Had to. She was different. Figuring out how to make Lily-Rose fall in love with him consumed his days and nights.

Edward seemed different too.

"Why are you acting so goofy?" Christopher asked Edward one evening as the Pembricks ate dinner, enjoying one another's company after their trip to Austria. "What gives?"

"You'd never believe me in a thousand years, but I've met a girl. She's been my tutor. And," he pointed to his brother, "don't give me a hard time on this, but I think she's the girl."

"Give us a break, Eddie," Christopher chuckled. "I could buy enough PT stock to hold a majority if I had a dollar for every time you told us you met a girl and she was the one."

But their mother offered a knowing smile. "That explains why you insisted we get back on time this year. I thought it strange that even the perfect snow couldn't keep your interest. Tell us about her." She picked up her coffee cup and rested her elbows lightly on the edge of the table. "She must be ravishing. You've had your pick of all the girls in the tri-state area."

"Really, Mother," Christopher moaned. "Can you exaggerate any more than that?"

"Christopher," his dad admonished. "That type of sarcasm is not appreciated in this house." He turned back to Edward. "You must bring this young woman to dinner, son."

"Whoa, Dad, slow down. She doesn't know about us," Edward said, shifting in his chair.

Mother put her cup back in its saucer and stirred her coffee.

"What on earth does that mean?"

"Only that I need to break the news to her about our family before I bring her over. She's not from here and doesn't know what being a Pembrick from Pembrick Transportation means." Edward shrugged. "Guess I've been holding back some."

Dad lit his pipe for his after-dinner smoke. "Well, tell her soon, son. If she had you wanting to come home from our vacation, then she must be something. We're all dying to meet her."

"I met a girl too," Christopher said.

"Really?" All conversation stopped as heads turned toward Christopher.

"Yeah. We haven't spoken for a while. She's been busy with the holidays and all."

Dad put his pipe down. "I have to say, Christopher. I'm a bit shocked—pleasingly, of course. I never thought you had it in you to even talk to a girl." He looked at his other son. "Did you know about this, Edward?"

"I heard rumblings." He didn't offer any more of his pre-Thanksgiving conversation with his brother. "But I didn't realize you were so serious." He offered a warm smile to Christopher. "Way to go, sport."

Mother interrupted. "Christopher, hold that thought for a moment, dear, I want to hear more from Edward." Mother gave a sly smile. "So, she's not from here, you say. Where exactly is she from? Who are some of her people? Do we know them?" She caught her breath. "Oh, Edward, dear. I can tell you're serious about this one, aren't you? Tell us everything."

Within a few minutes the plans were settled. Edward would bring this girl to the house the following weekend. They returned to the conversation about Christopher's little friend and promised they'd meet her too. Eventually.

Then, the following Saturday, Christopher's world changed

forever when Edward walked into their family home with his new—and last—love.

अ⁊

Christopher shifted on the bench inside the mausoleum as his thoughts returned to reality. The door to the entrance of the mausoleum opened, and Mark Backus walked in. Seeing Christopher, the pastor startled and laughed.

"Man, you scared me half to death. These places give me the heebie-jeebies anyway. But seeing someone on this side of the marble almost stopped my heart beating." He held out his hand. "You're Christopher Pembrick, right?"

Christopher looked up, ignored the offer to shake, smiled, and gave him a two-finger salute. He didn't stand but continued to lean his head back against the wall of the tomb. "And you're Pastor Backus. I was just having a talk with my parents. Going over old times. Filling them in on what's happened and some of my plans for the future." He smiled. "I thought I'd take advantage of their undivided attention." He leaned toward the pastor as if telling him a secret. "I told them that their favorite son died. I didn't know if they'd heard."

Pastor Backus stared at his mausoleum companion. "I, umm, smell alcohol on your breath, Christopher. Are you alright?"

He patted his pocket. "Right as rain, padre. I've been consoling myself. I've just realized—for the second time in my life—that Edward and Lily-Rose were at the middle of my misery. First time was that night before dinner at my parents." Christopher pulled the flask from his pocket, took off the top and wiped the mouth off with his sleeve. "Wanna swig?"

Pastor Backus grimaced. "No. Thank you though."

Christopher looked at the flask, shrugged, then tightened

its top and put it back in his pocket. "This morning, my thoughts on the subject became clear. Everything with value has been taken by either Edward or Lily-Rose. And now her kids." Christopher squinted his eyes shut, hoping to block out the memories. Changing his focus, he addressed Backus. "How 'bout you? What brings you to the Pembrick palace of the dearly-departed?"

"Me?" The pastor rubbed his light beard stubble. "Well, truth be told, I came by to see your brother. I wanted to apologize. I didn't do a very good job for his funeral. I needed some time to work where I felt I fell short. See what I did wrong. What I shoulda done. Thought I'd come in here, commiserate with God. Then your brother. I thought it'd it easier to make my amends to you and Lily-Rose after that."

Christopher shifted his gaze to the pastor. "Don't worry about me, preacher. We're good. You were cool."

Backus tilted his head. "So, tell me, what do you mean by … what'd you say … everything that matters has been taken?"

Christopher dropped his shoulders and sighed. His voice quivered as vulnerability overtook him. "Nothing makes sense, Pastor Backus. I have nothing of value anymore. I don't have my parents or my brother." He dug his elbows into his knees and rested his head in his hands. After sitting like that for a few moments, he looked up. "I wanted them to love me like I did them. Always did. But that wasn't in the cards. At least Pembrick Transportation was there for me. I poured my heart and soul into that company, so I could carry on what Mother and Dad started. I even dreamed that me and Edward could run PT together. Brothers, you know? Side by side."

Tears formed in Christopher's eyes as he lifted his head and looked at Backus. "But now even that dream's gone. I have nothing. Less than nothing, really. And having nothing hurts. Having no value hurts. So that's where I am now, explaining to my parents that I'm hurting and what I'm going to do to make that pain stop."

The pastor motioned to Christopher to scooch over, sliding in beside him.

"Christopher, I'm sorry you carry so much pain. I'm a father, and I can tell you, parents make lots of mistakes. I didn't know your parents. Maybe they didn't know how to show you what they felt. Could that be it?" When Christopher offered no reply, he continued. "But don't believe for a moment that you have no value, because that's just not true. Sounds to me you've been focusing on the wrong types of scales that measure worth. Can I share what Jesus said about what's really important?"

This was the last thing he needed. "Sure," he said.

Pastor Backus pulled one of the smallest Bibles Christopher had ever seen from his pocket, then opened it and began to speak.

⁊

A cloaked figure huddled in the shadows that hid the payphone outside the bar on Lincoln's O Street. He slipped the coins in the slots, waited for the dial tone, then called a memorized number. A familiar voice answered after two rings.

"Kritter. Hi. It's me. Yeah, long time no talk. Yeah, me too. Hey, want to earn some fast cash? No, no, nothing real bad. I just need you to find someone. A family-of-three someones. Super. I'll meet you at Trixie's Bar tonight around ten o'clock. Regular booth. Don't be late."

He hung up the receiver. This would be perfect. The best chance to make things happen. The less Kritter knew the better. All he needed to do was find Lily-Rose and her disgustingly precious family. But that would be it. Kritter had always been good for a quick job in the past. Always discreet. Never asked too many questions.

Besides, he was always eager to make a quick buck.

He leaned against the glass wall in the phone booth and chuckled. Once his prey was found he'd take over. He wanted to be the one to finish them off. To bring this farce to an end. Pembrick Transportation and the Pembrick money would soon belong to him.

chapter 25

Early Winter 1970

Never shall I forget the days I spent with you.
Continue to be my friend, as you will always find
me yours.

—Ludwig van Beethoven

Lily-Rose never knew friendships could be so sweet.

She stirred the embers, stretched, then looked at the ladies sitting with her, all huddled by the fire's glow. "I can't imagine a time when I didn't know you guys."

Sugar smiled as she poked the embers with her own stick. "It's like we've been friends all our lives. Sisters. I've told you things I've never told anyone else." She leaned in. "Not even Dungar."

"Like the crazy stunts you pulled when you were a kid?" Lily-Rose's eyes twinkled as she crossed her arms and briskly rubbed her shoulders with gloved hands. "We all did goofy things. But here, we can talk about them and laugh. Not feel judged."

Fiona cackled. "Sisters, hmm. We never had any redheads or southern belles in my family. That might take some explaining. Land sakes, Lily-Rose. Can't you get that fire any hotter?"

Sugar added, "I sure do feel like you'uns are my sisters. I talked with Dungar and Granny, and I told them I needed my evenings for the fire. I'd get my work done first, but we all needed to pull together. Be a family. And guess what? They love me bein' happier than not."

Fiona nodded. "Me too. It's like Miss Fergie's shooing me out as well. I no sooner get home from my internship in Cleveland and eat than she makes sure I head on over."

They all laughed.

Lily-Rose faced Fiona. "You like working in Cleveland? That's quite a drive every day."

"Yeah, but I lucked out getting in the accounting firm I wanted." She used her poking stick to rearrange the burning wood. "They only take on a handful of new interns each year. Miss Fergie and a couple professors wrote letters for me." Fiona gave up on fixing the fire and offered her friends a crooked smile. "And, of course, I had my training from the Wendy Ward Finishing School from way back. That helped too." She took a deep breath. "But seriously, I've met some nice people there. I might even bring one to the fire someday."

Sugar piped in. "A firepit field trip. Sounds fun. Can I bring Dungar? Maybe Granny? I imagine they'd like it—as long as they remember they're only visitors."

"Yeah, auxiliary ladies of the fire, right?" A chuckle circled the pit.

Lily-Rose tried her hand at fixing the smoldering wood. "What were you like as a kid, Fiona? Like now, you're driving to Cleveland—Cleveland, for crying out loud."

"Yeah, Weeds, I dun heard about the Cuyahoga River catchin' on fire up there last summer. Even made the cover of Time. That's nuts." Sugar started sniffing. "Y'all smell that? Smells like snow."

Lily-Rose put the stick down once she finished. "Were you so driven then like you are now?"

Fiona's golden hoop earrings danced as she shook her head. "No way. I played outside all the time. Remember—Weeds, tall blades of grass—that's because they could have lost me in 'em if they weren't careful."

Sugar jumped in again. "Yep, smells like we're goin' to get snow."

Fiona reclaimed the conversation. "Maybe I wasn't driven, but I always knew I wanted more." She stared at the fire. "Geez-Louise. It's like talking about myself. I'm not a fan, but I'm getting better. Our time out here at the fire's helped me with that. Gets me out of my shell." She sighed. "But it is something I need to learn how to do more of. Do better." She gave her head a nod. "So that's what I do. Push. Never turn from a challenge. Strive for more." She pulled her jacket collar close. "Like, I wanted more from high school than my friends did. That's why I graduated summa cum laude."

"Wow," Sugar drawled. "I heard of that summie thing. It's somethin' good, right? For me, I managed to walk across the stage and get my diploma and everyone in my family thought that was somthin'."

"I'm not afraid of work." Fiona grabbed the last cookie from the paper plate on the stack of wood and broke off half. "I just didn't know what I wanted. Miss Fergie helped me find that." She offered the other half of the cookie to Lily-Rose, who waved it away. She put the rejected half of the cookie back on the plate. "Now I know I can crunch numbers with a vengeance."

Sugar smiled and piped in. "I told the girls to be real nice if they ever saw you."

"I crunch numbers, not little girls, you southern belle."

More chortling.

Fiona's tone softened. "Sugar, what keeps you going?"

"Guilt."

The jovial spirit—nearly palatable—slipped away. That spirit, a new and welcomed friend, suddenly hid as Sugar straightened the bottom of her bellbottoms.

Sugar continued. "My people said my life was filled with perfection. Bein' the homecoming queen was perfect. Marryin' the homecoming king was perfect too. Then travelin' with him all over the country as he goes to college, then coaches and teaches at more different colleges. That's perfect too." Sugar turned her gaze from the fire and caught the puzzled looks on her friends' faces. "Don't get me wrong, Dungar is terrific."

"Is he perfect?" Lily-Rose watched as her friend squirmed.

"Yeah, matter of fact he is. He's so perfect I have no idea what he wants with me."

"You're loco, girl," Fiona poured more hot cider from the thermos into her cup, then grabbed the other half of the cookie. "What do you want him to do?"

"I used to want him to make me happy. But I learned recently that my bein' happy is my responsibility and not anyone else's." Sugar looked at Lily-Rose and smiled. "A good friend told me that."

Lily-Rose returned the smile. She watched as Fiona and Sugar sat there staring at her, probably waiting for her to share about her past just as they had done.

But she didn't.

Sugar finally broke the silence. "Lily-Rose, you okay?"

Lily-Rose's eyes moved from the fire to her friends. "You guys have no idea how important you are to me. You came into my life when it was pulling apart."

"Losing a husband like you did had to be difficult, girl," Fiona said.

The jovial attitude slipped away again just as a single snowflake, and then another, and another danced around them.

Sugar did her best to right the conversation. "Told you. First snow of the year." She stuck out her tongue and tried to catch the flakes now falling with abandon.

Fiona pulled her hands from her pockets and held them out to catch the falling flakes. "I love the first snowfall. It's the ones in March and April that bring me grief." She looked at Lily-Rose expectantly.

Lily-Rose stared at the flickering flames. When she finally spoke her voice cracked. "It's a bit more complicated than just losing Edward. Oh, but I miss him every day." She stopped and caught her breath, never looking away from the fire. "But I'm so tired of losing. Losing my mother to drugs when I was little. Bouncing from one family to another after that seemed awful at the time." She offered a weak smile and spoke again with more resolve. "I pretty much got over that when I finally landed with Mama Henderson. She was the best. But … I lost her too. Died too young."

Sugar reached out to Lily-Rose and gave her arm a squeeze. "That's okay, honey," Sugar cooed. "You cry if you need. We're here for ya."

Lily-Rose took a deep breath and dusted the few flakes of snow off her lap. "But, there's more." She brought her mittened hands to her face to feel their warmth. Fiona and Sugar looked on quietly until she finally began to speak. She dropped her hands. "I want to be completely honest with both of you. I'm not exactly who you think I am. In fact, I'm in kind of a jam."

Flickering lights danced from the flames as silence grew between them in the waiting, and the snow changed from fleeting to large flakes that coated their jackets.

"It's true that my husband died. Edward was the love of my life. And coming here from Nebraska to get a fresh start was true too. But what I didn't tell you is that I'm from the Nebraskan Pembricks, the people who own the trucking company. Ever heard of them?"

Sugar leaned forward and brushed snow from her shoulder. "You mean those trucks that have Pembrick written on the side and roll up and down the interstate outside town? Those Pembricks?"

"Yep, those are the ones."

Fiona joined in. "Those trucks are everywhere. I never put it together, you'd be some of those people. You never said you were related." She poked at the fire. "So why are you here in Applegate?"

Lily-Rose took a deep breath. This was it.

"Like I said, what I told you about Edward is true. He died in a freak accident. But what I didn't tell you was he owned Pembrick Transportation—we call it PT. Anyway, Edward's brother thought that since he was the only true Pembrick left—his parents died in a car crash years ago—that he should have inherited the company. When he didn't ... when PT was left to me ... well, he kinda threatened me and the kids." That's why we're here-that's why I ran away.

"What?"

Lily-Rose shushed them, looked around as if someone could possibly overhear, and then continued her story of Christopher and their meeting in the parking garage, her decision to throw herself and the kids in the car, running to the bank to get the cash, and then driving all day and nearly all night until they came to Applegate. With a light laugh she told them about finding the ad for the house and making the call. The call that changed everything.

"So," Lily-Rose wrapped up the news. "My meeting with Connie Hastings changed my life. Brought me to Norwood Street." She smiled and raised her eyebrows. "And the fire."

"That's terrifyin'," Sugar said when she was done.

Fiona added, "It's more than terrifying, it's crazy."

"I'm trying to be smart here. We have a home away from Christopher and PT, so that's good. With me gone, maybe Christopher had everything switched over to his name legally and is busy taking care of the business by now. My only hope is that any other distractions he might be surrounding himself with will be enough for him. Maybe give him some time to cool off. He's not a bad dude."

"Really, Lily-Rose. He sounds like a very bad dude." Fiona paced around the fire, leaving footprints in the thin layer of snow.

"That's where the story gets complicated. You see, I met him first—before Edward, I mean. I really liked Christopher—but not like-liked. He wanted more. Then I met Edward and fell in love with him. I didn't know they were brothers until I went to their parents' home for dinner one night."

Fiona stopped pacing. "That still doesn't mean he has the right to threaten to kill you."

"Fiona, he's always been second to Edward. I guess he's tired of never measuring up. But I think he'll calm down. Eventually. Not do something he'd regret."

"Sounds like you love him," Fiona said.

"Like a brother. We had a great time in college before he got territorial and wanted more than I had to offer. And when Edward introduced me to his parents, Christopher flipped."

"He sounds looney," Sugar said.

"Not looney, Sugar. But radically wounded."

Fiona returned to her chair, grabbed her stick, and poked at the fire. She leaned back. "We all have a story. Sugar, sounds like you're afraid of being left behind by your successful husband. My fear is I'll die alone because I always push too hard to succeed. Lily-Rose, we need to figure out how to stop your fears from jumping around in your head. Christopher will never find you here."

"Do you have a gun?" Sugar asked.

Fiona barked, "Sugar—you daft? Lily-Rose has children."

"I know she has chill-dren," Sugar defended herself. "That's why she needs a gun. She needs to protect them. When I was little, we had guns. None of us did anything stupid."

"I'm sure your family knew what they were doing," Lily-Rose interrupted. "But we've never been around them. Bringing a gun in the house now would cause more fear than not. Besides, would I ever be able to use it?" Lily-Rose shook her head. "No, a gun is not the answer. Not for me. Anyway, I think we'll be fine." She smiled. "We have Scout, remember?"

"Well," Sugar said, her drawl showing that she was not convinced, "what's safer than a gun?"

Fiona spoke up. "Growing up I remember my mama spending time on her knees praying when my brothers were out at night. Said there's nothing bigger than the hand of God to keep her boys safe."

Lily-Rose thought of Mama Henderson and her love for the Almighty. Her prayers before meals. The way she talked to Jesus throughout the day as if the good Lord had made himself at home within the tidy walls of her house. She hadn't thought of that for years. "Nothing safer, huh?" Yes, Mama would say the same thing, but not about a gun. Could the safety Mama found in God be meant for her?

For them?

Chapter 26

Walking with a friend in the dark is better than
walking alone in the light.

—Helen Keller

Weeks went by and although they came with challenges,
the winter fires had become Lily-Rose's favorite.

She dusted the snow from another split log and placed it in
the pit. "I'm at the end of my rope," she said to her friends. "I
don't think I can take much more."

The embers burned red and mirrored her level of frustration.
The crisp frigid air almost took her breath away. Not even her
pea coat, earmuffs, and mittens prepared her for the evening.
If it hadn't been for spending time with the ladies, she never
would have stayed at the fire. She was physically miserable
with the front of her body warm and her back cold.

The crunch of the snow beneath her feet as she walked back
to her chair reflected her sense of being—cold, hard, unyielding.
She needed time tonight with her friends to find answers that
would help rid the frustrations that had been building over the
past few weeks. "I've never been beaten by a situation. But I'm
completely stymied right now. Mary's hanging with kids who
have no interest in a solid future. They only want to be cool."
She fidgeted in her seat. "Do you realize the harm in that? And
I think Del's angry, but he doesn't let on. Football helped last
fall, but there's something missing. He stays in his room most
all the time. He goes to school, comes home, then goes to his

room. He comes out to eat, and then back to his room again." She threw her hands up and her brows raised. "Oh. Did I tell you? I spent all day today cleaning. Then I drove to the store for all the ingredients for that new pot roast recipe Sugar gave me. Remember, Sugar?"

Sugar nodded. "Great recipe. Dungar and the kids dance a jig in the kitchen every time I make my pot roast."

Lily-Rose stood and began to pace. "We'd been on one another's nerves, so I thought a nice dinner might help—bond over food, right?"

Fiona agreed. "Makes sense. Doesn't sound like a problem."

"It was going great. I brought everything home and put all the ingredients on the counter. Meat, potatoes, onions, and carrots. We were going to have a grand feast. But I went to my room to change—just for a few seconds—and when I got back, you know what I saw?" She stopped and put her hands on her hips. "I saw Scout grab the roast and drag it to the floor."

Fiona and Sugar perked and looked at each other. "Na-ahh! What'd you do?"

Lily-Rose's speech sped up. "I yelled, Scout. Our dinner. Then Del came in the kitchen and hollered, 'why are ya yelling at my dog?'"

Sugar winced. "Oh-oh. That sounds sassy."

Lily-Rose walked over for more wood. "Then I said, 'This mess happened because you weren't watching your dog.'" She sighed. "My tone was too short." But she gained steam again. "But then he came back with, 'Maybe you shouldn't have left what he likes on the counter like that, huh?'"

Fiona moaned. "That would've cost me a paddlin', I tell you. What'd you do?"

Lily-Rose shrugged and flopped in her chair. "I made vegetable soup for dinner—a dinner we ate in silence, I might add. So now I'm getting attitude from both of them. And Scout's even adding to the drama."

The fire crackled.

Fiona looked at her. "Are you sure it's as bad as you're makin' it? Okay, the dinner, that was messed up. But I've seen those friends of Mary's. They're good kids. Maybe a bit confused. But who isn't these days. People walkin' on the moon. Woodstock. And everyone trying to figure out if Paul McCartney's dead or not. Confusing times for sure. As far as Del, could he just be dealing with the winter blues? They can get nasty sometimes."

"I'm sorry," Sugar said rubbing her mittened hands together. "Thinkin' 'bout losing my babies to the dark side just makes my skin crawl." Her eyes brightened in revelation. "Hey, what about Coach Matheson? Has he helped?"

"Some. And I guess growing up these days would be hard." Lily-Rose kicked the snow off her boots. "I never had the luxury of being confused when I was young." She blew into her cupped hands, stood and turned, warming her back. "I suppose it could be the blues for Del. He has every right to still be mourning his dad's death." She sat back down in her chair. "Even though I feel like we've been here forever, it's only been a year and a half."

Sugar piped up. "You may have two kids dealin' with grief differently. Mary lookin' for distractions and Del hidin' em."

"That stinks," Fiona added. "And being their mama ... telling them what to do and stuff. Probably doesn't make processing their feelings any easier. What are you gonna do, Lily-Rose?"

Lily-Rose shifted in her chair. "To tell you the truth, I'm dealing with stuff of my own." She secured her paper cup of cider in the snow then reached behind her chair for the Tupperware container of cookies. She opened it to the familiar sigh, reached in and took a cookie before passing the container to Fiona. With a cookie in one hand, she picked up her cider with the other. "I'm about as mad as I can get at Edward. He should be here to help raise these kids. They aren't just mine. They're his kids too. How do people parent by themselves?" She finished the last of her cider and tossed the paper cup into the fire and watched the leftover drops dance from the heat. "He's gone, leaving raising these guys all on me. If he wasn't already dead, I'd throttle him."

Sugar and Fiona munched on their cookies, neither saying a word. Not that Lily-Rose blamed them. Were she sitting in their chairs and heard such a declaration, she wouldn't have said anything either.

Lily-Rose exhaled a deep breath, watching a cloud of steam move on. "You two are my best friends here in Applegate. Probably know me better than just about anyone—ever. What do you think I should do?"

Fiona and Sugar looked at each other, then at Lily-Rose. Firelight flickered and reflected on their faces. The smoke of burning wood filled the frozen air. Sitting at the fire was where they had fixed their problems in the past. But this one offered resistance.

Sugar spoke first. "I think this is bigger than us. I think you need to talk to a professional."

"I can't see a therapist," Lily-Rose said, she stood again and paced in the dark. "If word got out that we're the Nebraska Pembrick family, the paparazzi would swarm all over this safest street in town. Then Christopher or his goons might swoop in. We'd all be goners."

Fiona spoke up. "It might help if Mary was part of a church youth group. She'd be with good kids. In a good environment. I remember hearing the kids at college talking 'bout the one at Mercy and Grace. You know, the church downtown? They might even have something for younger kids like Del."

Sugar's eyes widened and she pointed at Fiona. "You know, that's a great idea. I was thinkin' 'bout checking Mercy and Grace out for our family too. It's time me and Dungar got the girls to church. We've been meaning to go, just haven't made it there yet."

Fiona stood and put her backside to the fire. "Me too. I'd get my parents off my back if I'd go. That is, if they'd let me in. Being black and all." She turned her attention to Lily-Rose. "Why don't you ask the pastor?"

Lily-Rose sat up straight. "Why should I ask him?"

"You know him better than me or Sugar, that's why."

Lily-Rose coughed a little. "What makes you think I know him. I don't know—"

"The coach, Lily-Rose," Fiona said. "The coach is the pastor. And you know the coach. Pretty well, I'd say."

Lily-Rose's jaw dropped. "That's right! I forgot Cole's the pastor there. It came up when we were at Al's, but I forgot all about that part of our conversation."

"Conversation?" Fiona piped.

Sugar added, "What were you doing with the coach—or should I say pastor—at Al's? Why didn't we know that?" She looked from Lily-Rose to Fiona who said, "You holding out on us, girl?"

Sugar stared at Lily-Rose then slapped her knees. "Then that's it. Tomorrow's Sunday. How 'bout the three of us go and check the place out? I'll tell Gran she'll need to get up and stay with the girls. Lily-Rose, I imagine your kids will be sleeping in, right? We can do this?" Her face shone in the firelight. "Whatdaya say?"

Fiona pointed to herself. "I still see a problem here."

But Sugar waved her off. "I say let's all go. If they throw one of us out, they throw us all out."

Lily-Rose sighed. She supposed going to church couldn't

hurt. Besides, Mama Henderson would be happy as well as Fiona's parents. "I say it's a date. See you in the morning."

When the fire burned out, Lily-Rose went inside and found Mary and Del watching television.

"I'm surprised to see you two still up. Anything good?"

Del piped up. "Yeah. A movie called *The Birds*." He turned back to the television. "Pretty gross."

"Kids, I don't think—"

Mary never turned from the television screen as she continued chewing her popcorn. Once swallowed, she responded to Lily-Rose. "Mother, you need to stop treating us like we're babies. We know what fiction is."

"All right. Not babies. I'll make a note." Lily-Rose saw her chance. "In fact, since you're not babies, the ladies and I are going out tomorrow morning—"

Mary cut her off. "Cool. Can you tell me later? We're busy, remember?"

"Yeah, Mom, busy."

Lily-Rose walked toward the hall to the bedrooms and spoke over her shoulder. "Okay. There's cereal for breakfast. I'll be back as soon as I can. If you need anything, Sugar's mother will be next door. Okay?"

Both kids grunted. "Uh-huh"

Lily-Rose returned to the living room. "But, if you want me to stay, I will. Make breakfast. We can talk. Plan something fun for the day."

"Mother. The movie?"

Lily-Rose turned and headed back to her bedroom, certain her kids would never need her again. She closed the door, climbed in bed and sobbed into her pillow, positive she was the worst parent in the world.

chapter 27

Still round the corner there may wait, a road or a
secret gate.

—J. R. R. Tolkien

"I'm glad you didn't mind me driving," Fiona said to Sugar
and Lily-Rose the next morning as they climbed in the car.

"Didn't have much of a choice," Sugar countered, putting
on the passenger's seat lap belt. "Coming up my driveway and
honking like that. I could've walked over. I'm just glad Dungar
and the girls didn't hear you."

"Thanks," Lily-Rose said from the backseat. "It's nice to
ride for a change." Her heart continued to stir from the past
few weeks' challenges.

"Well, this way," Fiona said as she headed down the street,
"if they throw me out, I've got my own vehicle to flee the
premises."

Lily-Rose's lips rose in a smile, but inside she frowned. How
awful to have to think this way. Live this way. Especially when
considering going to church.

They reached downtown and pulled into the church's
parking lot. The small, white-framed building held tall stained-
glass windows and red doors that opened invitingly. The bells
ringing in the steeple filled the air with the music of an old
hymn Lily-Rose thought she recognized. A black sign framed
in white by the door read, Mercy and Grace Community
Church, Cole Matheson, Pastor.

"Isn't that something. There. Just like you said." Lily-Rose said to Fiona, "I can't believe I didn't think of this."

"That's why we're here with you." Fiona. Nothing got by her.

They walked in. "Let's sit in the back," Lily-Rose said. "If any of us need to step out, we won't cause a fuss and …" The short memory of her children and the night before swept over her. They preferred a movie about killer birds to spending time with their mother. They'd nearly rushed her out of the room, not wanting her company. Or her concerns about the movie's contents. She'd used up her mothering tickets. Her children had made that clear. Now, if she could keep from crying the way she did last night, with her face pressed into the pillow.

"That's cool," Sugar offered, jarring her back. "We'll sit wherever you want."

The three women claimed a section of the back pew, took off their coats and piled them atop of one another at the end of the row. Lily-Rose glanced around. The sanctuary offered few fineries. In the front, two upholstered chairs flanked the pulpit. Cole sat in one and a dark-haired man in the other. To the right was an organ with a pleasant-looking woman at the keys, playing a soft tune she thought she recognized, but couldn't be sure.

When the music stopped, the dark-haired man left his chair and went to the pulpit. He welcomed those in attendance and instructed everyone to turn to a specific page in the hymnals available in the rack in front of them. When the organist began playing again, Lily-Rose closed her eyes. She smiled as words learned years ago came to mind. She basked over sweet memories as they swept over her. Memories of Sundays with Mama Henderson.

What a friend we have in Jesus,
All our sins and griefs to bear!

What a privilege to carry
Everything to God in prayer!

Lily-Rose kept her mouth closed and her heart open, concentrating on the lyrics sung by those around her. How could carrying things to God be a privilege?

Oh, what peace we often forfeit,
Oh, what needless pain we bear,
All because we do not carry
Everything to God in prayer!

She pulled a pen and a piece of paper from her purse and jotted down the words, then doodled a question mark at the bottom righthand corner. Why? Why had she stayed away from church so long? Mama Henderson had made sure church was a steady part of their diets. But once she started college, she stopped going. Now, with the refrain rising around the room, her parched soul smiled from the comfort she found in the song.

After the singing, the dark-haired man noted those in the congregation who had birthdays that month and that Mrs. Wise—whoever that was—was recovering nicely from surgery. He then turned to the organist and directed her to play the next song. This time, Lily-Rose grabbed a hymnal and tried to follow along.

She stood with the others. Her heart overflowed with sorrow as pictures flashed through her mind—memories of unpleasant times. Fiona and Sugar may have flanked her in the pew, but her loneliness and emptiness placed her on an emotional island. She was ... alone.

The congregation sat after the singing concluded. The man returned to his chair and Cole stood and walked to the pulpit. He began speaking, his eyes searching those sitting before him. He asked those who had brought their copy of the Scriptures to open to a particular chapter and verse. Lily-Rose exchanged glances with Fiona and Sugar. None of them had thought to bring a Bible. Fiona shrugged and Sugar made a face.

"Some of you might as well be buried in the ground," Cole was saying, and Lily-Rose turned back to listen. "… because you feel dead inside. But you can't tell anyone because you have to keep things together. Maybe it's your job or your family. You're barely getting one foot in front of the other. But Jesus is waiting for you. No one can ever love you more completely than he can. He will stick closer to you than a brother. He will never leave you or forsake you. He wants to rescue you from the pain you're in. The only place you'll find peace is in a healing relationship with Jesus."

Lily-Rose's hands offered a slight tremble. How could Cole—a man she had seen only as her son's coach, never realizing the depth of his spirituality—zero in on how she felt? Dead inside. Dead but wanting more. She'd felt alive when Edward had been with them. But she had placed her hope and life in the hands of a man who could not stick around forever. One who hadn't wanted to leave, but who had left just the same. Left her. Her and their children. And, God, how she needed him. How she—

"It's only Jesus." Cole's words found her again. "He will never leave or forsake you."

She wanted—no, she needed—the peace Cole spoke about. This Jesus of her childhood.

Lily-rose blinked back hot tears as Cole continued. "Let's all bow our heads and pray." Rustling filtered through the room as Bibles were closed and every head went down, including hers. "Lord, we come to you today." His tone changed as he directed his words to the congregation. "If any of you will open your heart, He will meet you. But it's up to you to reach out. Take the first step. If you want a relationship with Jesus, tell him. Let him know. He's waiting."

Lily-Rose took a deep breath. Held it. She couldn't go another day with all the weight on her shoulders. Edward's death and Christopher's threats were bad enough. But this pain that Cole's words found—this brokenness—ached greater than all her other pain. And Cole's solution—a relationship with Jesus—offered relief.

She stayed seated as the organist played another song and while people around her stood and began to shuffle out.

Sugar leaned over. "Lily-Rose, you okay? You want us to stay with you?"

"No, but thanks. Do you mind waiting for me? I'm gonna sit here for a moment."

Fiona squeezed her arm. "Take all the time you need. We'll be right outside these doors if you need us." Sugar and Fiona grabbed their coats and stepped away.

Lily-Rose stayed seated in the small sanctuary, her face down as the congregation filed past her. Soon, she was alone.

Alone, but her heart heavy and her mind clear.

Jesus, help me.

※

Cole sat in the upholstered chair and listened as Harriet played "What a Friend We Have in Jesus." He closed his eyes and concentrated on the old hymn and let the words wash over him preparing him to share from God's word.

Cole thanked God every day for Harriet. Every week when he gave her the theme of his upcoming sermon, she always pulled the perfect songs to help prepare the hearts of those who came to hear what God had given him to say. He never told her how much her choices in music ministered to him as well. Redirecting his focus for a moment, he pulled the bulletin from his Bible and jotted in the corner tell Harriet how God is using her and slipped the paper back in place. He needed to make sure she knew he valued her.

After Harriet played the final chords of the last hymn, he stood and walked to the pulpit. He found such comfort standing before his congregation. He had a strong connection with everyone there. The Foster family always sat in the third row on the left. The Cunningham family would be found on the right. Other families had their favorite places as well. He knew by seeing empty spaces around the small auditorium who was ill or on vacation.

It surprised him, then, when he saw three women—one dark, one blonde, and one with wild red hair—sitting in the back where the ushers usually took their seats after the offering had been collected. He then recognized her, the lady with fiery hair, to be Del Pembrick's mother, Lily-Rose. Seeing her lightened his mood and momentarily distracted him from his sermon.

Stay focused. Remember, God has words He wants you to share. Offer the message He's directed. His purpose always comes first—had to come first—and this message needed to be shared with no distractions.

After a glance at his notes, he spoke on loneliness, emptiness, and a loss of purpose in life. Words came from the deepest part of his heart. He shared verses and thoughts he hadn't included for this sermon, but that flowed from deep within. He expressed from his heart how a relationship with Jesus Christ would add more to a person's purpose.

He basked in God's presence in that small sanctuary as he spoke of God's love for them and how God had plans for each one there today. And that he would never leave us.

Cole felt God's hand on his heart—the telltale sign of God's leading—and so he continued offering words of comfort. He tried his best to get across God's desire to heal broken hearts.

Broken lives.

When he had given them all he had to give, Cole asked the congregation to bow their head and close their eyes, then continued, "If any of you will open your heart, he will meet you. But it's up to you to reach out. Take the first step. If you want a relationship with Jesus, tell him. Let him know. He's waiting."

Lord, have my words made a difference for you today?

※

Cole stood near the entrance of the church and shook hands with each person as they left, thanking them for coming. He noted that Lily-Rose hadn't appeared yet. Her friends stood to the side, waiting. But no Lily-Rose. Then she was there, puffy-eyed, yet smiling. He took her hand.

"Everything all right? Your friends are standing tight for you over by the coats."

"I had some thinking to do."

He slowly shook her hand. "I was happy to see you in the back there."

She smiled, holding onto his hand, deflecting his comment. "I hope it was okay … bringing Fiona. We weren't sure."

At first his brow furrowed, then understanding came to him. "Of course. The Lord sees our heart, not the color of our skin."

Her smile grew wider as she changed the subject again. "So, two jobs—coaching and pastoring?"

He grinned back. "Both kinda the same, just different uniforms." He leaned in. "It's really nice to see you today. Really nice."

She smiled. "Thanks. Do I call you pastor or coach?"

He chuckled. "Cole. Please. Call me Cole."

She paused for a moment. "How about I call you pastor here, but when I see you around town I call you Cole?"

She had made her point clear. He smiled and tilted his head. "Pastor it is then. Here, that is. And I look forward to seeing you again, Lily-Rose."

❧

Lily-Rose walked to Fiona and Sugar. Fiona pulled both women close and spoke in a whispered voice. "That's how you do church? There wasn't any clappin' or hankie-wavin'," she said, speaking up and putting on an accent. "When I was little, Grandma Williams said bein' a Christian took shoutin' and singin' to put on God's body armor." She turned to Sugar, "And I didn't hear one amen the entire time." She shook her head, "You white folks need a lesson in worshippin', that's for sure." She focused back on Lily-Rose. "Are you all right? Did something the preacher say bother you?"

Sugar jabbed Fiona in the ribs. "Don't be silly, you heathen. Jesus was talkin' to her. That's what happened, ain't it, Lily-Rose?"

Lily-Rose grinned. "Is that what that was?"

"Yep, it is." Sugar took a deep breath. "Glory be. Sure feels good to be back in church again. I'll bring Dungar and the girls with me next week."

Fiona stared at her. "Far out. Mama'd be happy for you." She looked around. "Do we eat now? Mama's church always had food down in the basement between services. How do we get to the stairs? I'm hungry."

"Well this ain't your mama's church. We need to go home to eat," Sugar reminded her.

"Yes. Let's go home," Lily-Rose said with a smile.

They rode home in silence. Once Fiona dropped her off,

Lily-Rose went to the kitchen and started a fresh pot of coffee. From there, she went to her bedroom and closed the door to change her clothes. The house was still except for the blip-blip from the percolator.

Thoughts of the morning swirled. What did opening my heart to Jesus mean? Would he really meet me if I did?

She knelt by her bed and folded her hands as Mama Henderson had taught her. She fidgeted, not remembering how to talk to God. Lily-Rose cleared her throat. "Heavenly Father, I thank thee for today. That sermon. Cole—I mean, the pastor—told us that you wanted a relationship with us." Lily-Rose continued talking with God, giving up all the hurt she carried. And on her knees, falling tears changed from befouled to cleansing.

chapter 28

Sometimes the person you fall for isn't ready to catch you.

—Unknown

"I saw how he held your hand at the door after church, Lily-Rose. All I'm sayin' is he likes you. There are worse things than that."

Lily-Rose shook the snow off the tarp covering the wood pile and brought three pieces to the fire. "But I can't, Sugar."

"Can't what?" Fiona asked, sending a cloud of warm steam from her breath into the air. "So he likes you—"

After dropping the wood she stood by her chair. "But I'm a married woman."

"Ah, no," Sugar said rubbing her mittens together. "You're a widow. That means your husband ... while you loved him—"

"And still love him," Lily-Rose interjected.

"Okay, fine." Sugar air quoted, "still loves him ... doesn't mean you're not attractive and interesting. I say if he ever asks you out, you go."

Lily-Rose stared at the flames, then gave a sly smile. "I do still love Edward—I do," she paused. "But Cole is really nice. His interest in me seems genuine." She dusted off her hands then shrugged. "And he is good looking, isn't he?"

Fiona laughed. "And you're interested, too, right? You can tell us. We're at the fire. Nothing leaves here."

"I don't know. After seeing him last summer—"

Fiona sat up. "When did you see him last summer? You holding out on us?"

"Yeah, girl. What's up with that?"

Lily-Rose stuttered. "No, I didn't see him—well, yes I guess I did, but only a couple of times. Once at school. I went to talk with him about Del. And I started to cry, and—"

Sugar pointed and laughed at Lily-Rose. "You what? I thought you only cried at the fire. You cheatin' on us, missy?"

"No. Then we only had fries at Al's. I told him I wasn't ready to get to know him in that way. He said he'd be fine to keep it to a professional relationship. You know, me being a parent of two Roughrider students." Lily-Rose sipped her drink and looked over the rim of the cup to her friends. "We've grabbed a coffee or soda a few times. Nothing serious, though. Just coffee or sodas."

Fiona held her cider, warming her hands. "We're teasing you, you know that, don't ya, Lily-Rose?" She took her own sip then set the cup beside her. "This is a good thing. You noticing a man—a good man, and him noticing you back."

Lily-Rose's teary eyes reflected in the firelight. "But what about Edward? I feel like I'm cheating."

Sugar stole a look at Fiona. "Sweetie, me 'n Fiona never met Edward, but sounds like he was a wonderful man." She added a piece of wood to the fire, seemingly using the time to choose her words. "So it rings true that he'd want you happy. Not be alone, pinin' for a man you'll never have again."

"Yeah," Fiona added. "He'd want you to have a full life, right?"

Lily-Rose considered their words, then remembered her dream of Edward after she arrived on Norwood Street. *I know that you'll have a long, full life … you will feel joy, peace … and love again.*

"He'd want me to have more than just an existence." She

nodded slowly as a tear left the corner of her eye. "But this is scary stuff." She shook her hair, knocking the flakes of snow away that had fallen on her. "Besides, Cole reached out for anything other than drinks. Who knows, maybe he won't."

Fiona and Sugar leaned back into their chairs, both raising their cups to their lips. After taking a sip Sugar spoke, "Don't you worry your little head. He'll call. There's no doubt."

As if on cue, Cole called the next morning and asked if she'd meet him at Burgers 'n More. They agreed to meet that evening at seven. Lily-Rose bit back a smile after they hung up, then sobered fully. Before she could do such a thing—simple though it was—she needed to tell the kids about the invitation. She broached the subject during their after-school snacks. "I got a call from Coach Matheson after you left this morning."

Del's face went solemn, and Scout perked up, tilting his head at Lily-Rose. "Am I in trouble? He didn't say anything to me today."

"No, you're not in any trouble. Wait. Is there anything I need to know?"

"No, honestly, Mom. No problems. I swear."

"That's good." Because Lily-Rose could only handle one challenge at a time.

Mary studied her mom. "Why did he call you?"

Lily-Rose laughed. "Don't wrinkle your nose when you say that, Mare. 'Why did he call you?' Am I not supposed to get calls from people?"

"Not men from school you aren't," she countered.

Lily-Rose sipped her coffee. Here went nothing. "He wants to meet me at Burgers 'n More."

"What for?" Her daughter offered no mercy.

"Well," Lily-Rose took another sip of the almost finished coffee, "I guess to take me to dinner." She smiled. "Is that so hard to imagine?"

"Nah, Coach is cool." Del responded.

Mary's expression stayed the same. "No. I suppose it's okay. What time you leaving?"

"We're meeting tonight at seven. I can cancel if you need me here."

Del looked at his sister then shrugged. "Nah, I guess we're good, right, Mare?"

"Right." She continued looking at her mom. "What will you wear?"

Lily-Rose gasped. "I don't know. My bells, of course. Or should I wear a dress? No, too fancy." She moved from answering Mary's question to talking to herself as she began to walk toward her bedroom. She yelled back as Mama Bear kicked in. "That means no friends over tonight. Just studying and television. Have I made myself clear?"

"Yes, ma'am," they returned in unison.

Lily-Rose arrived promptly at seven. Cole waved her over to a booth he held for them near the window. He wore a suede jacket and bellbottom jeans. Casual but nice.

She took a deep breath, thankful she chose to wear her jeans and a sweater instead of a dress. You can do this.

She walked to where Cole stood. He leaned in as to give her a hug, then changed to patting her on the arm. "Hey. Thanks for coming out. Can I take your coat?"

"No, but thanks. I'm good." She shrugged off her wrap and folded it in the booth beside her, placing her purse atop the heap. He took off his coat before he sat and piled it on his side as well, revealing his ivory cable-knit sweater.

Handsome.

"Cold, right?"

Lily-Rose threw up a silent prayer in jest and asked God to kill her now and stop the misery. At least, she thought her request was in jest. "Yeah. Cold."

Cole had taken off his gloves and set them on the table. "Know what you want? Burgers are great here, don't you think?" He grinned.

"Yeah. Great."

"I can order for us if you'd like. You can stay here and hold our spot." He surveyed the room. "College kids'll be swooping in any minute."

Lily-Rose glanced at her watch. What in the world am I doing here? "Sure. I'll take a burger and fries—no, wait, cheeseburger—no, make that a burger. And fries. And lots of ketchup. And a chocolate shake. Please."

Cole stood. "Be right back."

Lily-Rose watched as Cole went to the counter and placed their order. She pressed her lips together at the sight. His back. His broad shoulders. The way his body tapered at the waist. Not your average I've-had-too-many-donuts kind of high school coach. Or the kind who took great care of themselves all the way through college, then let themselves go as soon as they got a job. No. Coach Cole Matheson was—okay, she'd admit it—a fine specimen.

But he was also Pastor Matheson. Or did they call him Pastor Cole? Lily-Rose caught herself staring, then blinked furiously, and looked away as he headed back. Had he felt her eyes on him? Could he even guess what she'd been thinking?

When he returned, he had two shakes, two sandwiches, two orders of fries and several small cups of ketchup. "I like ketchup too." He put the tray on the table and Lily-Rose began divvying the food all the while silently praying that he wouldn't mention her gawking. For heaven's sake, they weren't high school kids anymore.

With everything settled, Cole smiled. "Thanks. Mind if I say grace?"

She smiled back. "That'd be nice."

Cole offered a blessing over the food, then added, "And bless this time with Lily-Rose and me. May you find honor here. Amen."

"Amen," Lily-Rose said, then pulled napkins from the dispenser and handed two to him.

"How are you doing?" Cole placed a napkin on his lap.

"Getting better. Some days are better than others. It's a process, right?"

"That's what they say." Cole took a bite of his burger.

Stillness.

"Sorry, I'm nervous." Lily-Rose confessed after taking a bite of her own burger. "I haven't been out like this with anyone other than Edward for years."

Cole smiled. "You're fine. We've chatted over coffee about the kids, but I thought it'd be nice to get to know one another some. Move on from coach and pastor, mom and parishioner. Is that cool?"

Lily-Rose nibbled on her sandwich, then smiled. "It is. But I apologize now for any hairbrained comments I end up making. Like I said, out of practice."

"Apology accepted."

He is cute and funny.

Cole continued. "I remember the first time we were here, having fries and talking about Del. I seem to remember talking a bit more about us as well. Nice to have that, you know, those things under our belts."

"I remember. You still feel good about your choice, coming to Applegate, I mean?"

"Better every day."

Lily-Rose looked down at her hands searching for something brilliant to say. Cole continued.

"Truth be told, however, I've been feeling restless. Fidgety. I don't know if it's me or God trying to get my attention."

"Really? How's that?"

"I've even toyed with the idea of moving to Ireland. I'm intrigued by their culture. How they love big over there. Maybe start a church somewhere in the country." He shrugged and took another fry. "Someday." He nodded. "Until I get the sense that I'm to move along, I'm perfectly fine where I am."

The conversation stalled. Both worked on their dinner.

Cole finally spoke. "I'm really glad you agreed to come out and meet me tonight." He reached for Lily-Rose's hand on top the table. "I've been trying hard to be professional." He smiled. "How have I been doing?"

Lily-Rose chuckled, "You've been the perfect gentleman. Thanks for giving me the space I need." She shrugged. "I wish I could tell you it's not still going to be a slow-go."

"I can be patient if need be, as long as I have a sense of what's going on around me."

The touch of his hand felt good—and frightening. She slowly pulled her hand away.

"Well, I'm not sure I do." She gazed into his eyes. Thought about how he looked back at her. Listened to her. There was no doubt about it. Cole was an incredible man. "How about this? Let's take this … whatever this is … super slow. Give me time to catch on to life without Edward."

His smile returned. "So not a red light but a yellow one?" The smile grew larger. "Continue with caution?"

"Yes."

He took the final bite of his sandwich in a triumphant gesture. After swallowing, he smiled. "I can do that."

CHAPTER 29

Summer 1971

It's not hard to make decisions when you know
what your values are.

—Roy E. Disney

Bob Biddle missed his conversations with Mr. Bird.

Confidence had begun to build as he put action to his plans.
He could do this. He could right a wrong. He dug through
his desk drawer and found his renewed driver's license—the
license he never thought he'd use again—and took the bus to
the nearest Avis center. "If you don't mind, I'd prefer to take
your insurance and not submit this rental to mine."

The agent took his money and said to Biddle without
looking up, "Cool, no problem. Just check this box ... and
this ... and initial here. I'll get you the keys."

Just that easy. When he drove off the lot, he tried to
remember the last time he had driven. He chuckled to himself
when nothing came to mind. He was glad he kept that piece of
news from the Avis agent. One more secret by omission. But
no more.

He had already contacted his landlord and paid the rent
ahead for a few months. He didn't know how long he'd be
away. Even though his apartment was dark and disheveled,
it had been his safe place—his refuge—and leaving his home
made him sad.

But the hardest part of putting his plans in to action had been finding a new home for Mr. Bird. Fortunately, Biddle recently crossed paths with the talkative young woman in the laundry room who lived above him. When she shared how much she enjoyed listening to Mr. Bird's squawking, it was a clear sign that fate intervened. He asked if she'd be willing to watch his feathered friend while he was away. She graciously accepted.

Everything fell into place. *Sorry to leave you, good buddy. But I have to do this.*

Biddle packed some clothes into a worn suitcase, gathered his cash and slipped the folded letter from Richard Pembrick into his jacket pocket, and walked out the door. Bittersweet. More bitter than sweet. He hoped there would be more sweet somewhere on this venture to confirm his choices were worthwhile.

But before leaving Lincoln, he had one stop to make. His hands trembled as he headed to an address scribbled on the back of an envelope. The residential area was nice. Tall trees. Wide, well-kept streets. Everything he had wanted what seemed a lifetime ago. He drove slowly; following the house numbers until he found the one he sought. The two-story brick colonial sat on a groomed lawn with trimmed bushes. Tranquility. He pulled in the driveway where a young man held a hose and was spraying suds off his car. He looked up and offered a quizzical smile as Biddle pulled in. Upon getting closer, however, he watched as recognition washed over the young man's face, stealing all emotion from it.

Biddle turned off the car, took a deep breath, clenched and released his trembling hands, then got out and walked toward the young man. He held out his hand. "Hi, Johnnie."

The young man bent over and turned off the water. He looked up and raised his chin. "Dad. It's John now." His arms stayed at his side, but he continued to hold the hose.

Biddle pulled back his extended hand. "It's good to see you."

His son offered a cold gaze. "I didn't think you even knew where we lived." He dropped the hose and dusted off his hands. "What brings you here?"

Biddle looked at his feet and kicked at a pebble on the driveway. "I've been following the stories about you in the paper." He looked up and smiled. His son had grown. "Congratulations on your scholarship. Wide receiver for the Cornhuskers, right? Can't get much better than that in this part of the country."

John crossed his arms and asked again. "What brings you here, Dad?"

"I … I wanted to see you. Tell you—"

"Yeah, well, I wanted to see you too. For years. But that stopped a long time ago."

Biddle stared at the confident young man in front of him and remembered the boy, hungry for his father's attention. What a fool he had been to choose success and fame over that admiration. "I'm sorry, Johnnie—John. I should have never done you and your mother the way I did." He looked at his hands. "I was a fool." With his head still down, he turned to walk back to his car. He stopped and faced his son again. "Do you remember when we cut grass together?"

John stared at his dad for a few moments, then offered a reflective grin. "Yeah, I remember. You'd let me hold on to the brace midway up the handle." He snickered. "That was fun. Not safe, but fun."

Biddle gave a soft chuckle. "Yeah, not safe at all. But it was fun, right?" He reached for the car door handle.

"Dad … wait."

John trotted over to the rented car. "Thanks for stopping

by." He held out his hand.

Warm tears filled Biddle's eyes as he took the warm, slightly damp, hand in his own. "Good to see you again, son. Thank you." He got in his car as his breath caught in his throat and John went back and picked up the hose. Neither one had offered to see the other again. Just as well. After Biddle backed out of the drive and pulled onto the street, he waved. And his son waved back.

One amends made, one more to go.

Muscles in his jaw twitched as he drove across Route 30, vacillating between manhandling his map and finding a radio station to help pass the time. As he drove through Iowa, the day's brilliance enhanced the colors of the summer's fields, readying for a fall harvest. The corn reached for the sun, pushing its tassels upward. Rows of soybean plants danced in unison as wind blew through the rows. Miles of hypnotizing simplicity and comfort.

Biddle finally gave up trying to find a radio station and twisted the knob to off. Reflection. That's what he needed. He looked at himself in the rearview mirror and offered a wry smile. "There's no victim here. You made your choice—long ago." He looked back at the road. "This is the right thing to do." After a few moments he looked again at his eyes in the mirror. Resolute. Determined.

How ironic that honesty came so easy for a dying man.

He had hoped the private investigator would make finding Lily-Rose easier. However that had taken more time than he anticipated. The months of searching came at a cost—most of his money was gone. But what good was money to him, anyway? Signs of Lily-Rose finally surfaced in a small town in Ohio where she had registered her children for school. Now his focus was reaching Applegate. He'd figure out what to do afterward—if there was an afterward for him.

Biddle looked again in the rearview mirror and studied his red-rimmed eyes pooled with tears. Would Mr. Bird miss him? He hoped not. Soon enough he'd need a new owner anyway.

He glanced out at the fields as he drove. Then coughed. He covered his mouth with a napkin as he coughed again, fresh blood staining the rag.

At his last visit the doctor said it wouldn't be long now.

What a waste of a life.

"No. I can do this," he said aloud. He had to find Lily-Rose and tell her of the secret he never should have kept. He was ready to make amends to the remaining Pembrick family members and get the weight of ruined lives off his chest. If finding peace meant leaving everything he owned behind, he had to do this. Fixing everything with Lily-Rose might be the last right thing he would ever have the chance to do. He had to trust that she'd take over from there. Make the past Pembrick choices right.

Reaching into his pocket, his fingers found the smooth plastic of his bottle of pills. He let out a breath. Knowing he had them close brought comfort. Lately, they'd helped when the pain became too intense. When it was time to stop for the night, he'd take the prescribed amount. That and a good dinner would help him get some sleep.

Fatigue had already tried to own him today. He had pushed hard—maybe too hard. But he needed to find a place for the night soon.

Blasted fatigue. The exhaustion and lethargy had started soon after the doctor told him about the tumor in his lungs. Said his physical condition would get progressively worse. What exactly had the doctors said? Ah, yes, diminished quality of life. A gentle way of saying death wasn't far off.

Hopefully, he'd find a motel soon with a nice bed and a diner close by. Maybe a room with a window he could open for fresh air. That seemed to help. Possibly even stay a day or two if he needed. He didn't like the thought of spending the money or the time, but he just might have to do that to get his strength back. He'd waited for years to do this; he hoped he could wait a couple more days. He needed a sharp mind for what he had to do. He had to get to Applegate.

Before it was too late.

But now he needed to focus on dinner and some sleep. He would worry about dying later.

Mr. Bird, you o' squawker, I sure do miss you.

⁂

Lily-Rose woke early Sunday morning after another restless night. She rolled over and stared at the ceiling.

Single parenting was for the birds.

The off-and-on disconnect between her and the kids had worn her down. She tried to break through—talking, special dinners, one-on-one time with each of them—but nothing seemed to make a difference. She hadn't felt this level of frustration and helplessness since before moving in with Mama Henderson. Oddly enough, she had tasted peace that first Sunday attending Mercy and Grace and wanted more. Not just on Sundays, but every day. The newly found peace was real—no doubt making her a different person. But she was still a mother who longed for a better relationship with her kids.

Lily-Rose stretched, pushed herself out of bed, and shuffled to her closet. She picked through her summer clothes and settled on a maxi-skirt, paired with a blouse and matching sweater to go with her sandals, then sauntered to the door and cracked it wide enough to stick her head out.

"Kids," she yelled into the hallway, "choose something nice for this morning. Remember, we're going to church, not a baseball game."

After dressing, she went into the kitchen to make breakfast. Lily-Rose drank her coffee as she stood at the stove frying bacon and eggs. Del walked in and flopped his arms around her shoulders, then leaned into her.

"Hey, sweetie," she mused. "When did you get so big? You're almost as tall as I am." She turned her head and gave him a quick smooch on his freshly washed hair.

"I am fourteen, you know," he answered, voice cracking.

Lily-Rose leaned her head against Del's. "I'm keenly aware that you're all grown up. I just don't know how it happened." She straightened and turned her attention back to the stove. "But right now I want you to have a good breakfast before church. Ready?"

Del nodded. Lily-Rose put two eggs on his plate, and he pulled four pieces of bacon from the paper towel where they were draining. Del took his breakfast and sat at the table. Lily-Rose stood at the counter and began pulling apart an English muffin before slipping it in the toaster. She then went to the cupboard and pulled out the honey and placed the jar by Mary's spot. She poured a glass of grapefruit juice and called, "Mary, your skinny-person food is ready."

"Oh, Mom, really?" Mary entered the kitchen. Her smile told Lily-Rose she took the well-meant jab in fun.

When the breakfast dishes were done, they climbed in the car and headed to church. The air was cool, but the sunshine warmed them through the car windows on their short drive.

"Mom?" Mary asked as they walked to the doors of Mercy and Grace Community Church, "God's real to you, isn't he?"

"More real than I ever imagined. Why do you ask?"

"No reason. Just asking."

They walked in together as they heard Harriet play the first notes of a hymn. Lily-Rose caught the eye of several of the new friends she had made over the past several months, waved, and headed to her typical spot, her children behind her. Mary spoke. "Mom, can we sit with you?"

"What? Neither of you sitting with your friends today?"

Del looked at Mary then back at Lily-Rose. "Not this time. Can we stay with you?"

"Of course you can." She reached out and gave them both a quick hug. She looked up and waved at Sugar as she led the girls in, followed by Dungar, and watched them go to their usual pew as well.

Harriet's choice of music was especially sweet today. And Cole's message sent Lily-Rose's children squirming. She knew her children, and she recognized that they had more on their minds than usual. She leaned in and whispered, "You guys want to go home right after church? No dilly-dallying?"

"Yeah," Mary answered, and Dell nodded.

They left church without a word to anyone. After pulling up the drive, they all went into the house. Del let Scout out the back door as Lily-Rose made turkey sandwiches and set out some chips along with glasses of milk. Mary sat at her place and pulled a potato chip from the bag.

"Mom. How'd you get to know God?"

Del and Scout walked into the kitchen in time to hear Mary's question. "Yeah, Mom. How'd you do it?" He went to the sink and washed his hands.

"You both want to hear?"

"We talk, Mom," Mary offered softly. "We've watched you. You're cool since we started going to Mercy and Grace. Cooler than any time since Dad died. I think—I think we just want what you have."

"Yeah," Del piped in.

Lily-Rose stood from the table and gave each of her kids a long, substantial hug. Okay, maybe life wasn't so hard after all.

"It'd be my pleasure."

Over lunch, Lily-Rose told them about the days she and Fiona and Sugar had gone to church and about how, after she returned home, she'd knelt and talked to God in her bedroom.

Del asked, "Can we do that too?"

Lily-Rose smile. "Yes, sweetheart. You can do that too."

Del and Mary looked at each other, then Mary spoke. "I'm going to my room now for a while."

Del answered, "Me too. Mom. Can you keep Scout with you for a while? I'm gonna be busy. Talking to God."

She reached down and scratched behind Scout's ear. "I'd be happy to."

CHAPTER 30

Life is not easy for any of us. But what of that? We must have perseverance and above all have confidence in ourselves.

—Marie Currie

"This Lily-Rose situation should have been handled by now, Karn. It's been too long."

Karn's jaw tightened as he eyed the man on the other side of the booth. He didn't like his tone but had to tread lightly. "These things take time, sir. We don't want anything pointing back at us—"

"Don't take me for a fool. You don't want anything coming back on you." The muscles in his jawline pulsed. "Thoughts of her and that ragamuffin family are like a burr digging into my skin." He took a drink of his coffee. "There needs to be a break soon."

Karn looked around the diner. Whoever said this was easy money must have been one bulb shy of a full box. He spoke in a hushed tone. "Your guy's looking. He'll find something soon. He's got to. Right?"

The man put his cup on its saucer, nodded and smiled. "Gotta hand it to that girl. She has instincts. All that hard living paid off for her." He took a bite from his piece of pie. "I've had my people watch for any traceable movements from her. Nothing. They did find her car at a dealers' lot outside of town where she picked up a new one. But that was the day after the funeral." He took another sip of coffee. "Then nothing." He sat back into the booth as he placed his fork on the plate then pushed it away. "If this wasn't so frustrating, she'd make finding her an exciting hunt."

"We'll get news soon." Karn signaled to the waitress to bring more coffee. "I can't sleep at night knowing she's out there, ready to expose us. She could send us to prison if she knew our plans."

"Shut up, will ya? You're just paranoid." He picked up his cup for another drink, then realizing it was empty, put it down. "Look. You're not going to prison. She's on the run, but not from us." He chuckled. "That's why this is so perfect. In fact, better than perfect. We do 'em in while they're living far from Lincoln—there won't be so much as a blip on the news. By the time Lincoln cops figure out who didn't do it, we'll be long gone.

Karn nodded at the man as the waitress brought over more coffee. He dropped three spoonfuls of sugar into his cup; the spoon clinked as he stirred his drink. He tried to think of a way to move this "situation" along. "I don't think you know what's at stake for me, sir. I could be disbarred. I could lose my livelihood and never practice law again."

The man chuckled. "Disbarred? Dude. Where's your head?" He stretched his arms over both sides of the booth. After a moment he leaned forward and whispered. "First, we're not going to get caught. And second, you and I both know you hate practicing law. After we're done, you'll have so much money you'll never have to practice again." He arched his brows. "And you can stop watching your assistant from afar. Janice, right?" He looked at Karn and sneered. "Yeah, once this is over you can finally wow her. In style." He leaned back again. He looked down and slightly tugged a loose thread from his cuff. "So, stop trying to snow me." His eyes met Karn's. "You want this as much as I do." He finished his coffee, stood, and tossed a twenty on the table. "Look, Karn, we control this. You leaked the story about Christopher's blow-up all over town just like I told you. Everyone thinks he's a hotheaded kook. If something happens to Lily-Rose, he'll be the first person they question. We've done everything right so far. Stop worrying."

How Karn hated arrogance—except for his own. "Okay, I get it." He stood too.

"I hope you do." He grabbed Karn by the arm like a vise and whispered in his ear. "I know what I'm doing. Got it?"

Karn winced. "Things can go wrong, man. That's all I'm saying."

"I said, 'got it?'"

Karn winced again and tried to free his arm. "I got it, I got it, okay? No need to get physical."

The man's steely eyes stared into Karn's. "I hope there isn't. Remember, dead men tell no tales."

"Message received. Loud and clear."

۾

As the sun found the horizon, Lily-Rose carried a tray holding a pitcher of lemonade and Tupperware tumblers to the firepit. She set the refreshments on the ground and straightened as she draped the towel she had on her arm over the back of her chair. She studied the seating, then pulled them back a few steps. Summer fires were often too hot. Drinks would help, but a bit of distance wouldn't hurt. Fiona had said that Miss Fergie offered their air-conditioned place for those hot evening get-togethers, but nothing matched their time at the firepit.

She smiled remembering how air conditioning had been a part of her Lincoln life. But that was in the past. Now she had an attic fan to cool her house at night and a new life, lived by a new person. She found comfort—and wisdom—with her friends. They brought a fullness to her life she had never experienced. At the fire, she learned how to keep a balanced life, hold her children as top priority, all the while finding a way to meet her own needs.

Sugar taught her—even when she periodically suffered dark times due to loneliness—how to never shy away from responsibilities. Even when she was wrapped in depression, she was completely devoted to Dungar and the girls. And while Fiona had recently spent more time in Cleveland than Sugar and she had liked, Fiona had made most of the fires she attended and brought her own pizzazz to the mix. Unfortunately, her time away had raised Sugar's annoyance. Lily-Rose worked extra hard to keep Sugar calm of late. The recent fires had all become the same—bumpy start for Sugar and Fiona but smooth landings for all.

"For real, Fiona, what could be so important that you can't get home at a normal hour?"

"Stop mothering me. And there's nothing wrong with my schedule, you backwoods hillbilly."

"Hillbilly, huh? Well, at least my nickname—"

"Don't start picking a fight with me, you crazy fool. I'm here now, aren't I?"

"Ladies." Lily-Rose had tired of the spats. If she hadn't loved these two as she did, she would have stopped refereeing and halted the fires long ago.

Sugar would look her way and always try to have the last word. "No worries, Lily-Rose. Me and this pinko-feminist love one another. Right, Fiona?"

And Fiona never allowed her that treat and fired back with a smile and comment like. "Right on, you possum-eater."

Yep. These fires were exhausting at times, but always worth it by the end of the night.

Lily-Rose started a low-burning fire and sipped on her lemonade. Sugar soon arrived, carrying a plate of Rice Krispy treats. Seeming preoccupied, she craned her neck in the direction of Fiona's house. "Is she coming? Her car's in the driveway, but I haven't seen hide nor hair of her yet."

Just then Fiona rounded Lily-Rose's house with paper bag in hand. "Surprise. I thought I'd come home early for a change. I grabbed a bite to eat and am ready for a fire." She held out the bag. "Miss Fergie told me to bring these over. Gotta eat them quick, though." She pulled out three Fudgesicles, passed them around, then pushed the empty bag into the embers with a stick.

"Oh, these will hit the spot. Thanks." Lily-Rose used one hand to hold her treat and the other to grab more wood. Fiona's—as well as Miss Fergie's—attention to their needs was one of the many points she loved about the women.

Soon flames grew and licked into the still air. "Miss Fergie takes good care of us." Lily-Rose shifted in her chair and looked at Fiona. "Did you remember to bring your hair clippers? You said the next time you were out here you'd trim my hair, remember? It's not too late, is it?"

"Of course I remembered," she replied pulling a comb and pair of scissors from her pocket. "I've practiced cutting Miss Fergie's hair over the years. White people's hair sure feels different than I'm used to. But she was patient, and I got used to it. Happy to be of service."

"Cutting hair by firelight. This will be a first." Lily-Rose finished her ice cream and tossed her stick into the fire. Finally. She'd been bringing the towel out for several fires that Fiona missed. Now. Down to business.

"I been waiting all day for this fire," Sugar absentmindedly stared at the flames.

Fiona tossed her cleaned ice cream stick into the fire as

well. "It's a beautiful one, all right. I just wish the night were a bit cooler. A breeze would help. But it's fine." She looked at Lily-Rose. "Good job, Lily-Rose. As always."

Lily-Rose wrapped the towel around her shoulders, pinning the ends together. She took a deep breath and sat straight as Fiona nonchalantly poured them both some lemonade, setting a cup on a stump and placing the other into Lily-Rose's waiting hand.

Fiona clicked her scissors. "Just a trim, right? Nothing fancy. I don't know if I can do fancy."

Lily-Rose snickered. She appreciated the clarification before Fiona started. Nothing like cutting too much off. "No, nothing crazy. Just trim the ends. Maybe an inch, you think?" Her hair always had a mind of its own, but Lily-Rose hoped the locks would respond to the attention.

Sugar cleared her throat and muttered softly, "You'uns, I have something ta say."

"You always have something to say, girl. No sense making an announcement of the inevitable," Fiona said as she ran the comb through Lily-Rose's hair.

Lily-Rose reached up and placed a hand over Fiona's. Sugar's tone ... the look on her face ... was different this time. It reminded her of how she looked when she found her at her worst. "Hang on, Fiona."

Sugar pulled the ice cream stick from her mouth. "There's no easy way to say this, so I'm just gonna say it." She took a deep breath. "Dungar's takin' a job with the Baltimore Colts. Assistant offensive coach. A chance of a lifetime for him. He has to take it." She took a breath. "That means we gotta move."

"Oh, no," Lily-Rose cried. More loss? This was as sudden as losing Edward. The unexpected knife plunged deep into her heart and took her breath away.

Fiona dropped the comb and shears. "Are you sure?" She

bent over and picked them up out of the grass and returned to her chair. "When's this happening?"

"In a few weeks."

Lily-Rose stared. "That's too soon." This can't be happening. Not Sugar.

Sugar's words softened. "Oh, it's just him for now. He's goin' down to get set up with the team and other coaches. The team's puttin' him up in an apartment for a few weeks. Once he learns the area, he'll get a house for us. After that he'll come back for a U-haul and take us and our stuff"—Sugar took a breath—"to our new home."

The fire's crackle drowned out the silence between the ladies.

Sugar continued. "I'll stay behind and close up our Applegate lives. Shouldn't be too tough. The girls aren't in school yet, so that helps. And I'll have Connie put our house on the market." She took a breath. "I imagine me, Gran, and the kids will be gone in a few months, not much more."

Fiona sat stoic. She just stared at the fire as Sugar spoke faster. "I couldn't say anything till we was sure." The light of the fire reflected the tears in her eyes. "Believe me when I say I need you'uns now more than ever." She stifled a sob and her words became deliberate. "You've become my family—closer than family. You. Are. My. Heart." Tears began to fall as Sugar wrung her hands. "What am I gonna do?"

Both Lily-Rose and Fiona stared on. Lily-Rose needed to say something—anything—to offer comfort to Sugar. But her own pain was too great. Not more loss.

Sugar pulled herself together and stepped to the woodpile. She picked up two pieces and laid them by the fire. She stood before the ladies and dusted off her hands. "I know I'm simple. Backwards sometimes. Not as strong as you'uns." Her tears began falling again. "I'm not ashamed to say I'm scared." She sat in her chair. "How am I gonna do this without you'uns?"

She looked at Lily-Rose. "If it hadn't been for you comin' over and talking sweetness into my life again I don't know where I'd be." She pointed at her. "No, that's not true. I do know where I'd be. I'd be either in a padded room somewheres or even worse. That slow train to Depressionville was not gonna stop until stoppin' at death's door."

Sugar turned to Fiona. "And we fuss all the time." Tears now streamed on her cheeks. "But, Jiminy Crickets, you've shown me I got spunk—spunk just like you." She wiped the tears from her face. "I promise. Don't know how, but one of these days you'll both be proud of me."

Lily-Rose pulled the towel from her shoulders, went to Sugar, and gave her a long hug. "Proud of you? Sugar. You're a part of us. How can we not be proud of you?" Her words didn't fit somehow. But they had to do.

Fiona finally looked up from the fire. "Don't hold me up like I'm a superwoman, hear-me-roar-woman, thinking I have it all together, Sug. Remember, you're the one with a husband and kids. Time's not stopping for me. Truth be told I'd give anything to have those." She picked up a stick and poked at the fire. "I guess I fuss at you because it's safer than saying nice things." She sniffled and spoke in a soft tone. "Truth be told, you're far wiser than me. I wish I had what you have. You're my hero," Fiona took a breath. "And I'm going to say it. I'll be lost without you."

The moon continued to rise in the clear sky as smoke whiffed through the still air. The only sounds in Lily-Rose's backyard were the occasional sniffle and hypnotic crackling of the burning wood.

chapter 31

Out of difficulties grow miracles.

—Jean de la Bruyere, French Philosopher

Summer was almost over.

Sugar fumed as she walked to the fire pit and put a plate of cookies on a side table fashioned from one of the larger logs standing on its end. "If Gran weren't here, I don't think I could do this—this—single parent thing. Dungar's only been gone a few weeks, and I'm about ready to pull my hair. Being both Mommy and Daddy's hard work." She flopped in the chair and bounced her foot. She looked over at Lily-Rose, then gasped. "Oh, I'm so sorry. What's wrong with me? You've been both Mommy and Daddy ever since you pulled into Applegate. Argh. I'm so frazzled; I'm sayin' the meanest things without thinkin'." Leaning in and propping her elbows, she held her hands in a prayerful grasp. "I've never had a friend like you before, and all I do is say terrible things. Can you forgive me?"

Lily-Rose smiled. "No problem, sweetie. Those words are true enough. It is hard work." She poured some iced tea for Sugar. "Do you hear much from Dungar?"

After taking a drink and setting the tumbler on the ground, Sugar started, "We don't talk nearly enough." She broke a cookie in two, then took the larger piece. "We've never been apart like this since we've known each other. Says he's missin' me like crazy." She chewed a bite of cookie for a moment. "It's so hard." She left her chair and nudged the bottom log in the fire with her stick, causing the others to shift, loosening embers. "Long-distance calls get expensive. And because his schedule is so whacky, we can only talk before or after practices and meetin's. Because the girls are sleepin' mostly at the end of his day, I sometimes try and keep 'em awake so they can talk with him later. But those are the times he doesn't call in the evenings when the calls would be free, but then he calls the next morning, hopin' to talk with 'em before breakfast." Sugars scrunched her nose. "They miss him a bunch, but what else can we do, but keep tryin'."

She took the smaller broken piece of cookie from the plate. It was cool talking with Lily-Rose, never needing to explain her feelings or thoughts. Lily-Rose just listened ... and was her friend.

Sugar finished the cookie and leaned back into the chair. "Lily-Rose, no offense n' all, but how do you do this? If Dungar died, I don't know what I'd do."

Lily-Rose stared at the fire then shrugged. "Just take one day at a time, that's all. Some days turn out just fine. Then there's others that really stink." She took a breath, offered a sad smile, and closed her eyes. "I still miss Edward all the time."

Sugar ached for her friend as Lily-Rose seemed to visit a memory—a time and place she'd never see again. "But the pain lessens." A smile wrapped in wisdom showed on her face as she got up and stoked the fire, then tossed a smaller log on top of the burning wood, sending embers up with the smoke. "I sometimes pretend he's not dead. Just on a business trip." Her smile faded. "It's like if I don't talk about it—him being dead—maybe I'll see Edward walk around the corner." She leaned over and slid a cookie from the plate. "I know he's gone but pretending helps get me through some of the loneliness."

The look on Lily-Rose's face broke her heart. At this moment she wasn't a tower of strength or source for wisdom.

Not tonight. Instead, here sat a broken widow missing her husband something fierce. Sugar nodded.

Change the subject. Maybe that will help. "What's new with Cole? I see how he looks at you when we're in church." She'd been proud of herself for not prying, but now was time to get to the bottom of things—whether Fiona was there or not.

Lily-Rose's mood seemed to lighten, and her eyes twinkled. "Funny you should ask. Last Sunday, he asked me to go to the local music festival with him." She smiled. "It might be fun. We've grabbed burgers a few times, but nothing to write home about." She leaned on one hand under her chin, rested her elbow on the arm of the chair, and took a deep breath. "He is a really nice guy. I think he wants to get closer. But I still need space, so he's giving it to me. Never pushes." Lily-Rose tilted her head and grinned, sending red ringlets of hair cascading over her shoulders. "He's not one of the ladies of the fire, but he's a good friend."

Sugar leaned toward Lily-Rose, honored to hear her deepest thoughts. "Girl, it's written all over his face. He wants to get to know you better." She stirred the fire. "He's a good man, Lily-Rose. But you do what you need to do to take care of yourself."

Lily-Rose had made an impact on her from the moment she saw her sitting alone at the fire that first night. She made sense. Lily-Rose understood brokenness and had learned that there's life after tragedy. A lesson Sugar would take with her to Baltimore.

Sugar came back to reality and focused again on Lily-Rose's voice. "Knowing you're leaving soon has reminded me of the pain that surrounds loss. Like when I lost Edward." She reached for Sugar's hand, "But now I have friends—and a renewed faith—to lean on." Her mood lightened. "And Fiona's here. That makes all the difference in the world. I don't know where I'd be without all that. And you." She swung Sugar's hand back and forth. "You'll take our friendship with you. And your faith, as well, right?"

Sugar stopped their swinging hands and grasped Lily-Rose's with both of hers. "Of course we'll still be friends. But how am I gonna find someone that understands me and my big mouth?" She let go of Lily-Rose's hand then leaned back into her chair. "I think the girls will be fine. They'll be able to make friends fast at church there. Dungar says there's a rash of 'em to choose from." Her knee started to bounce. "We'll land okay, but I'm still gonna miss y'uns and our time at the fire."

Fiona approached. "Am I walking in on a private conversation? I can come back later if you like."

Sugar's mood perked up. "No, no, no. Please join us. We have no secrets. Besides, you'll save me from putting my foot in my mouth again. We're talking about missing our husbands. Something you wouldn't know anything about—" Sugar stopped and stared at Fiona. "Oh, Lordie, I done did it again. Weeds, I'm such an idiot. Sorry." She shook her head. "There I go, saying something hurtful. I should just go back home and curl up in a ball somewheres."

Fiona and Lily-Rose burst out laughing.

"You're okay, Sugar." Fiona grabbed a poking stick.

"Lady," Lily-Rose looked at Fiona and added, "there's nobody like you. We learned long ago to use the Sugar filter when you start getting excited or upset."

Fiona stirred the fire. "Besides, you can't hurt my feelings tonight. I'm on top of the world right now." She offered a coy smile and playfully tried to change the subject. "Hot tonight, right?"

Lily-Rose and Sugar stared at Fiona, their mouths gaped.

"What?" Fiona smiled as she sat in her chair. "Haven't you ever seen someone happy before?"

Sugar deadpanned. "Someone happy, yes. But you, no. Are you all right? Did you hit your head on something?" Putting her hand to Fiona's brow, "Should we get Miss Fergie for you?"

Fiona playfully pushed Sugar's hand away. "No, it's just that I'm in love, you crazy woman."

"What?" Lily-Rose and Sugar squealed as they grabbed her and began jumping up and down like giddy schoolgirls.

Fiona laughed. "Careful ladies, all this jumping and you'll end up throwing me in the fire. Sit. Sit. I'll tell you all about it."

After the dancing finished, Lily-Rose grabbed some loose twigs, broke and tossed them into the fire, then returned to her chair. Sugar waited, perched, leaning in as if not wanting to miss a syllable. This had to be good.

"Well," Fiona started as she plucked a cookie from the plate then settled in the nearest chair. "It's been a whirlwind romance, for sure. His name is Derrick Boyer. I met him at the accounting firm in Cleveland. He's one of the senior executives there. I told you about him, right?"

"No, not a peep," Sugar said. Cookie crumbs fell from the corner of her mouth. "But we'll get back to that later. Keep goin', keep goin'." Just like talking to her daughters, trying to figure out who spilled the juice. No, we'd get back to this. You can gar-un-tee that.

Fiona chortled. "Wipe your mouth, mountain woman." She poured herself a drink and took a deep breath. "Now, where was I? Oh, yes. I met Derrick while I was Xeroxing. I thought he was cute 'n all, but didn't think he'd pay any attention to an intern like me. But he did. And we started talking. Then one thing led to another."

Lily-Rose straightened, and her eyes widened. "Tell us 'bout the one-thing-led-to-another thing."

Good girl, Lily-Rose. Spoken as a hound dog of a momma.

We'll get the story from her, for sure. Sugar listened and marveled as Fiona talked. She should have seen the difference in Fiona. Completely gaga over this man.

"At first he'd follow me back to my desk, and we'd talk more." She stood and looked to her right and spoke in a deep voice. "Looks like it's going to be a fine day today, Fiona. What do you think?" She then turned to her left and answered the question in a regular voice. "Why yes, I think it will be a beautiful day ...Derrick." She smiled. "Then I said something like 'Did you see the new Standard Oil sign by the pumps?' And he said, 'Yes. The price starts with a zero and decimal point before the thirty-three cents a gallon number. Can you imagine, needing a sign that shows a price over a dollar? That's crazy!'" She put her hands on her hips and smiled. "That's how we started."

Sugar leaned in closer, wiping cookie crumbs from her mouth with the back of her hand. "Ooh. Did he ask you your sign, Weeds? That's what they do on television. Did he ask your sign?"

"No, we didn't get to that. And be careful. You'll fall in the fire if you get any closer." Fiona's eyes sparkled as she looked from Lily-Rose to Sugar. "So once we covered the weather and the cost of gas, he asked me if I wanted to grab lunch sometime."

"Ooh-ooh-ooh. Lunch." Sugar sing-songed as she leaned back. Where had this side of Fiona come from? Light. Almost giddy.

Fiona pretended a scowl. "For pity's sake girl, you want me to finish my story or not?"

Lily-Rose poked fun. "You can't stop now, Fiona. Tell us more."

Fiona sat back in the chair to continue. Eyes widened. "Not only did he take me to lunch"—she raised her brows—"but we went to Otto Moser's."

Sugar squinted. "That's a someplace, right? I think I heard of it on television." Sugar reached for another cookie. "My word, I'm gonna need more cookies. Good news makes me hungry."

"Yes, Sug," Fiona smiled. "It's a someplace all right. That's where Hollywood types meet when they come in from California. Or New York. Maybe after they perform at the Hannah Theater." Fiona folded her arms. "We even saw Katherine Hepburn having a sandwich."

Sugar gasped. "Ohh, have mercy. Did she look more like Christina Drayton, from *Guess Who's Coming to Dinner,* or Eleanor of Aquitaine from *The Lion in Winter?* Wait. Those kinds of clothes would cause a ruckus. She probably looked like Christina, right? Wow. Celebrities, eatin' sandwiches just like us." A quick breath. "What kind?"

"What kind of what?"

"Sandwich. What kind of sandwich did she have?" Sugar needed to round out this information.

Fiona laughed. "Girl, I have no idea. I was too focused on the sweet slice of chocolate cake I was sitting with."

"That's nice about Katherine Hepburn," Lily-Rose smiled. "But tell us more about your date."

"What's he look like?" Sugar asked, nibbling.

Fiona fingered her hair. "He's tall, dark, and handsome, that's for sure." She covered her grin. "I started watching him—like when he didn't know I was looking. How he treated other people. If he acted one way around me and another way when he thought I wasn't there." She sighed and smiled "Not only is he super fine, he's super nice to everyone at the office." Her eyes rounded. "Seriously you guys, he's a good dude."

Fiona's gaze went from one friend to the other.

"I know this seems fast. It was for me too. But once we

started having dinners together—"

"—it was 'cause of a man?" Sugar squealed, reaching for the cookie plate again. "You were coming to fires later and later because you were in love? I thought you was just workin' too many hours. I never thought in a million years it'd be because of some man."

Fiona turned to Lily-Rose. "He really is a good guy. He likes me for who I am. No, that's not right." She took a breath and began again. "He respects me for who I am. I've been watching for flags—warnings—reasons to run from this relationship." She got up and poked the fire. "I haven't seen a one." Startled, she looked back to Sugar. "Hey. What do you mean 'never thought'? C'mon, now. Really you guys? Can't you have a bit of faith in my womanly prowess?" Once the laughter stopped, she continued. "Anyway, we plan on flying to Belize for a private beach wedding, then onto our honeymoon. We're looking at an early fall wedding."

Lily-Rose fought to keep her smile. "Oh, Fiona. This seems a bit soon to me. Are you sure?" She shifted in her chair. "Don't you want to date a bit more?"

Sugar crinkled her face. "What's a Belize?"

Fiona smiled. "It's a country in Central America. And no, Lily-Rose, I'm sure about this. We love each other."

"Why would you go so far away? You got people there?" Sugar shook her head. "I don't understand."

Fiona's voice softened. "Be happy for me, you guys. Please?"

Lily-Rose was the first to speak. "How romantic. You've got to bring him to the fire." She shot a look to Sugar. "We can't wait to meet him. Hopefully, you can get him down here before Sugar leaves."

Fiona's face changed. Her gaze dropped. "That's what I wanted to talk to you guys about." She poured herself a glass of tea. "As soon as we get married, we're finding our own place.

Closer to Cleveland, but still close enough to Applegate to get back if either Miss Fergie or my parents need me." Her gaze moved between her two friends but landed on Lily-Rose. "Sorry, sweetie. Looks like I'm leaving the fire about the same time Sugar is."

All sense of gaiety stopped. The somber reality blanketed their time at the fire, just as listening to a Rod McKuen album could quiet a person's heart. Still, the fire continued to crackle. Sugar put down her cookie and looked at Lily-Rose and spoke in a whisper. "You gonna be okay? The fire? Lily-Rose? Whatcha gonna do?"

Lily-Rose looked at her friends and smiled. "I get it. Life moves on." She then frowned. "But it's an omen. A premonition. Something bad's coming. I can feel it. It's in my Knower. And my Knower's never wrong."

Sugar stared. Guilt had wracked her, being the one who started the trend to leave the fire. Now it was Fiona's turn. And Lily-Rose was getting premonitions that something bad was going to happen. Poor Lily-Rose. What was she going to do?

CHAPTER 32

The sad truth is that most evil is done by people
who never make up their minds to be good or evil.

—Hannah Arendt, German-American philosopher

Waiting for no reason was the worst.

Kritter looked at his watch. Only three minutes had passed since he last checked the time. Sweat trickled down his temple. He chewed the cuticle on his thumb and spit a sliver of nail out of his black Mercury Comet window. Terrible habit. Maybe he'd try to stop once he got home. His stomach growled, and he pressed his fist under his ribs, hating that he left his room without the bologna sandwich he'd bought earlier.

No doubt about it. She was going to be a goner. Too bad, really. Cute family. And from what he had gathered, not very demanding. Just up and vanished. Like all she wanted was to be left alone.

But word was the boss wanted her and the kids gone—permanently. So, he hired him to find them. He got his job over a year ago. His reputation was what brought them together. Years of finding people who didn't want to be found made him a legend in the Lincoln underground.

He looked at his reflection in the rearview mirror. Yeah, he was good at his job.

He figured she'd probably leave the Lincoln area, but he needed to start somewhere. Nothing close. Then, he went west toward Scottsbluff. Nothing there either. He widened his radius to cities outside of Nebraska. Kansas City. Sioux City. Denver. Even Minneapolis then Dallas. Still nothing. None of the airports had her leaving the country. She had to be somewhere. He looked east. Chicago. Then Cleveland. Not a sign anywhere until last month when he put out the word that anyone who gave him a solid lead would get a G in twenties. Brilliant idea. Should have come to him months ago. All the cockroaches had crawled out from under their rocks to find her. That's when a cockroach in northeast Ohio said two kids with the last name Pembrick were registered in a school south of Cleveland.

Bingo. Yessiree, Lady Luck had taken her time, but had finally smiled. Had it been Lily-Rose's cunning or just dumb luck that kept her safe? He didn't know, nor did he care. He wanted this job over—the sooner the better.

He looked at his watch again. Ten more minutes passed. Fishing. That's what he'd do once he got home. Go fishing.

He watched as Lily-Rose and the blonde chick huddled at the fire. They had to be hot, that close to the flames. At least the fire wasn't roaring tonight, not like some of the others he had seen. Without looking he reached for his drink and knocked it over, spilling warm cola over the passenger's seat.

Kritter muffled a growl and set the cup upright on the dash. He grabbed a dirty shirt from the floor and wiped off the faux leather. His expense log had taken the spill full on. He held the book upside down by its binder and gave it a shake. What a mess. He just wanted all of this over. So he could go home.

He had tried to talk the boss out of making him stay later than necessary. He'd sent the film back days ago, confirming that he had found her. But the boss wouldn't hear of it. Only a few more days he said. Until the film arrived and he got a good look at the pictures. Had to be sure he said. Keep an eye on her so she doesn't slip away.

He'd gone from hero to lackey. A babysitter.

Kritter looked again in the rearview mirror and sneered. Offer a suggestion more than once and you're labeled a wise guy. He had worked for this fella before. He was legit—the real deal. And a little crazy—which usually confirmed legitimacy. But it'd always been petty jobs. Nothing like this.

He wiped the sweat away on his temple. No way around it. He'd have to stay here—and sweat—to make sure he got his money.

"Perfect," he muttered sarcastically.

He looked back to the fire as Lily-Rose stood up and hugged the blonde. Somber faces.

What a pity.

Talking, talking, talking ... then Lily-Rose and the blonde held hands and set them swinging.

She had no idea what was coming.

That's when the third friend—the exotic one—showed up. Kritter picked up and wiped off his Canonflex with the end of his t-shirt, thankful he hadn't attached the lens yet. He carefully placed the camera in his lap then reached for his night zoom lens. After twisting the lens onto the camera and hearing the attaching click, he brought it to his eye.

Surveilling Lily-Rose and her friends hadn't been all that bad once he had arrived in Applegate. There were perks. These were some beautiful women.

He'd found a street adjacent to hers—behind Norwood Street—where he could sit in his car and have a straight shot into her house and backyard. Being a creature of habit had made his job easy. She and her friends had a fire almost every night since he'd arrived. And the light from them made taking pictures a cinch.

Kritter pulled the camera down and moved his head to the right then left, waiting for the relieving crack in his neck.

Too bad this wouldn't turn out good for Lily-Rose or her kids. He'd learned long ago to never ask questions about his jobs. Just do what he was told. But he saw the tells. This boss was like a dog after a bone. He wouldn't let this young mother slip away.

He was glad his only assignment was taking pictures and gathering information. He'd lost his stomach for hurting pretty women and their kids long ago. No, this was not going to turn out well for Lily-Rose.

Kritter rattled his cup to see if anything was left, then tipped it to his mouth, patting the bottom to bring the last few drops down. Maybe he'd try fly-fishing. Heard that was fun. Take a trip to Elm Creek. Try his hand at catching some rainbow trout there.

Suddenly the gals whooped it up and hugged the exotic one, jumping up and down. He snapped a few more pictures. Yes, Lily-Rose was a beauty, for sure. He'd take a few more shots of the three of them for good measure. Maybe keep some for himself. Hopefully tomorrow he'd hear that he could leave.

Abruptly faces went from jubilant to sorrowful. What happened? He looked above the lens, then back through the lens again. They all seemed to be consoling Lily-Rose. Somber faces.

Yes, pity.

Kritter leaned back and stretched. He looked at his watch again. As much as he sometimes wanted the entire story, asking too many questions was the kiss of death in his business. This much time and energy were never spent on anything—or anyone—trivial.

All he wanted was to say goodbye to this Podunk, no-nothing town. Return to Lincoln and leave all this behind. Definitely look into fishing. He wiped his forehead with his sleeve. He had to wait until the ladies called it a night, then he'd go back to his room and wait for the phone call telling him he could come home.

๛

He needed to eat better. But not this morning. Today he was celebrating.

Karn sat perched on a barstool at Nathan's Bar and Grill and gnawed on his third piece of greasy warmed-up pepperoni pizza.

Bartender Sam looked on and shook his head. "You want some more napkins, pal? You're making a mess on my bar."

"Nah. I got it." He shoved the remaining pizza in his mouth and wiped his hands on his shirt over an ever-growing beer belly. "No big deal. Glad you had this around from yesterday." Swallowing the last of his food, he looked down then smiled, still rubbing his middle. "I'm gonna get new clothes soon—a whole new wardrobe. Besides," he added, "this shirt doesn't fit anymore. Musta shrank it." He shot back the last of his beer and promptly belched.

He felt Sam's eye on him. That barkeep better watch himself— he didn't know who he was dealing with. Karn straightened his back. He'd dealt with the high society in Lincoln. This Sam character? Nothing more than an insignificant bartender in an insignificant bar. No better than him. After this, he won't bother with visiting stinking hole-in-the-wall places like this one.

Sam's voice brought Karn back to focus. "When she s'pose to call?" Sam methodically pumped one glass after another over the soapy, twirling brushes in the sink behind the bar. When finished, he stopped and wiped his hands as he turned to Karn.

"Who said I was waiting for a woman's call?" Did this loser

think he was clairvoyant? Karn slid his empty mug toward Sam. "And I'll take another, when you're done with your ladies' work."

Sam huffed. "Just that most guys who come in at this hour to get calls are getting them from women they're not supposed to be talking to, that's all." He raised his brow. "Especially when I get hush money for covering the call."

Just then the ringing of the phone from under the counter made Karn jerk. Sam looked at him, then pulled the receiver and answered. Karn looked at his watch as Sam spoke. Eleven thirty.

"Yeah, he's here." A pause. "About thirty minutes." Sam snickered. "Four beers and just asked for his fifth." Sam nodded. "No problem."

Karn could tell the call was for him. He didn't like the way Sam talked. He didn't like only being privy to half of the conversation. Sam held the receiver in one hand and grabbed the phone base with the other and set it on the bar in front of Karn. "For you."

Karn cleared his throat as Sam wandered to the other end of the bar. "Ha-hello?"

"Man, you're drunk already, aren't you? No. Never mind. We can talk about that later."

"Nah, I'm fine. Really." That Sam was a squealer. He'd deal with him later.

"Sam says different. Is there anyone else in the bar but you two?"

Karn took the receiver from his ear and stretched his neck as he looked around. "A few, but not close enough to hear anything."

"Be on the safe side and don't say my name—don't say any names. Understand?"

"O-okay. Do you have any news?"

"Yes. I have pictures in hand. Seems our Pembrick heiress went all the way to Ohio for a new life. Applegate. I also have an address and a brief rundown on her daily habits. She's pretty much a homebody." Karn imagined the man on the other end of the phone sitting, holding photos and sneering. "This will be a piece of cake."

Karn hacked. Too many cigarettes. "Can't we just get the money and run? I don't know if I wanna be a part of—"

"Karn, you're too far in to back out now. Besides, it's almost over. You keep going to work like everything's fine. I'll run out to Ohio and take care of business. I need you here to handle things from this end. Just like we talked about." The voice on the other end of the phone paused. "Can you do that?"

Karn downed his drink and belched before speaking into the receiver. "You can ca-count on me, sir."

"Let's make sure, Mr. Karn. Let's make sure." Another pause and then he cursed. "Every time you get drunk, you get stupid. Don't get stupid on this. It could cost you. More, I think, than you want to pay."

chapter 33

Evil counsel travels fast.

—Sophocles

He hated driving on unfamiliar roads at night during a storm. Maybe starting out after the weather had calmed down would have been smarter. But he was too keyed up. He had to get to Applegate and get this part of his plan over.

Crack.

Yellow streaks of lightning flashed across the sky as rain pelted his windshield. The wipers slapped back and forth offering an annoying tune as they tried to clear his view. He had dealt with this storm from the beginning of his trip and had squinted for most of the drive. His head hurt, shoulders ached, and he was ready for sleep. But no stopping. Not until Applegate.

He had received Kritter's package in the morning mail and headed out within the hour to his friend's photography store to develop the photos. Even though they were pals, the work had cost him plenty for immediate results … and to keep his buddy's mouth shut. He called Karn to make sure he was still in the game, and by noon he was on his way out of Lincoln, heading east.

He cupped the crumpled paper over the steering wheel. The sweat from his hand smudged the directions to the Applegate Motel and Lily-Rose's home. While Kritter had cost more than he had wanted to pay, he had earned every cent of his money.

Huh. Applegate, Ohio.

What a nondescript kind of town. No wonder Kritter had a hard time finding her. He smiled. Maybe the town had a deputy that only carried one bullet. He could only hope.

Crack-boom.

He flinched and swore aloud. He hated summer storms. They could be unpredictable.

He reached for the wiper controls and tried to increase their speed, only to find they were already set on high. He swore again, then rubbed his eyes. He should have replaced the wiper blades months ago. Thankfully, not many cars out on the road. Most people had sense enough not to be out tonight.

He turned on the overhead light and quickly looked at his map. Only a few more miles to go. He'd been on the road for over thirteen hours and was ready to get there.

He pushed the map to the side without refolding it, then reached for the last of his coffee he had purchased hours ago. He braced himself before drinking it—he knew the taste would pucker his lips, and he was not disappointed. He grimaced as he swallowed the last of its dregs, then rolled down the window to get rid of the cup. Water drenched his left arm.

He hated his life. But he would have a new one soon enough.

After tossing the cup, he squared his tense shoulders. He had a job to do, and he'd get it done. No turning back now. He was too close to what he'd always wanted—deserved.

His nerves were almost shot when he came to his turnoff. He was exhausted, ready for sleep. He followed the signs to Applegate Motel. Kritter had promised this place was the least dismal lodging establishment in town.

A large arrow—barely visible—pointed from the road into a grove of pines. Following the gravel drive, he came upon a run-down motel. His eyes strained to see his way through the swishing wipers toward a vacant parking spot. His tires splashed through puddle after puddle until he parked. He exhaled, "What a dump." But he was here. And he'd be gone soon enough. He put his felt fedora on his head and flipped up the collar of his jacket. Inhaling quickly, he opened his car door and bolted to the door labeled Office.

The bell tacked to the top of the door clanged when he entered. He paused for only a fraction of a second, taking in the view of the room before he walked to the counter. He saw a white-haired elderly man sat on a worn BarcaLounger behind the counter listening to a police scanner. He stood at the counter a few moments and waited for the gentleman to acknowledge his presence. Yet he offered no response.

"Didn't you hear the bell, Gramps?"

Not turning, the elderly man answered, "Watch yourself, boy, or I may need to make soup."

He tilted his head. "I didn't say anything about having soup. What's that got to do with me coming in here to rent a room?"

Still not moving, Gramps continued, "It ain't got nothin' to do with rentin' you a room. But if I don't want to rent to ya, one excuse is just as good as another. The music festival's bringin' in all sorts of folks. Their money's just as good as yours. And that hippie kind will definitely be nicer to me than you just was."

His stare moved from the side of the old man's face to the scanner, then back to the old man. He laughed. "You're all right, Gramps. I dig ya." He cleared his throat and pretended to straighten an invisible tie. He started again. "Excuse me, sir. Do you have a moment? I'd like to inquire about some lodging for a day or two."

The old geezer slowly rose from his chair and sauntered to the counter. "Don't want no trouble."

"You won't get any from me. I guarantee it."

The elderly man put a blank motel registration form and pen on the counter. "Well, I s'pose you'd say that one way or ta-nother. How long will you be stayin'?" Gramps eyed his guest. "You don't look like a music lover to me."

"I'm not. And only a couple of days." He finished registering. "A music festival, huh?"

"Yeah. Ever since that hippie-fest Woodstock a couple years past, the farmers here have been tryin' to cash in." He squinted. "You here on legal stuff?"

"Whatcha mean?" Did the old man know something?

He shrugged. "Don't want no trouble, that's all."

He blinked. Relax. Must be the old man's shtick. The fella didn't have a clue why he's in Applegate. "No, here on some business. I won't be here long."

The old man placed a room key on the counter. "Checkout's noon sharp. Not a minute later or I'll have to charge you for an extra day."

"That's cool." Thunder clapped overhead, and he flinched. "Any idea how long this storm supposed to last?"

This question seemed to spark an interest in Gramps.

"The festival folks stayin' here are besides themselves with worry. Been comin' in here most every hour checkin' to see if I had any news from the po-lice." He shuffled back to his recliner. "From what they're sayin' on the radio, storms 'bout over."

Staying in a town where people were coming and going didn't sit right with him, but he had few options. Maybe he could somehow use it to his advantage.

The night manager settled in front of the scanner again but pointed over his shoulder to a pile of papers on the counter. "You can take one of the flyers there on the counter 'bout the Applegate Festival. They're free."

He picked up the flyer. "Probably lots of strangers in town to catch the party, right? And lot of the locals will come by and hang out … meet up with friends?" He looked out the window. The storm, indeed, seemed to be lessening. He refocused his attention to the motel keeper. "Where are all of the visitors staying anyway? Doesn't look like you have enough room for all the festival goers."

The old man looked at him and smiled. "Stayin' in tents on the McKinney's farm. Bet if any of 'em are city slickers they're rollin' in the mud by now." He grunted. "Kids these days. Some don't know enough to come in out of the rain."

Getting information from the old coot was like taking candy from a baby.

He leaned in. "Tell me, is there a place—a nice sorta place—to grab a bite to eat while the music people are here?"

"Matter of fact there is." Gramps sat straight in his chair. He'd become more approachable than before. "The Legion's Auxiliary ladies are puttin' on a feast for the next few days that's better 'n any food in all of Ohio. At least these parts, anyways. Chicken and biscuits. Salisbury steak. Mashed taters covered with milk gravy." He shook his head. "None of that canned stuff."

"Well, yes, that does sound wonder—"

"And pies and cakes." Gramps continued talking about the fair food as if his off switch had failed. "Bernetta makes the best apple pies—and don't forget to try some of her dumplings."

"Well, well, well," he said as he picked his key off the counter and headed out the door. "This trip is turning out to be more entertaining than I anticipated."

꘎

The rain began letting up as Christopher drove through

the trees and over the gravel toward the Applegate Motel. He took a deep breath as he allowed his shoulders to relax. It had been a long day. The weather had been treacherous, so he had stopped here and there before finally arriving in town. His beard stubble itched, his eyes burned, and his mouth was like cotton. He was ready to climb into a bed and get some sleep. He couldn't wait until he got with Lily-Rose and begged for her forgiveness. He had been such a fool, blaming her for everything bad in his life.

God, with your help this nightmare will soon be over.

Approaching the parking area, his headlights illuminated rows of cars. Passing one after the other, his eyes caught a black on silver license plate with Cornhusker State running across the top of it. A Nebraska tag? He squinted to read the back-bumper sticker, Lincoln's Finest Chevrolets.

Coincidence?

Gravel crunched under his tires as he pulled behind the car for a closer look. He got out and walked to the other car's passenger side and shone his flashlight onto the seat. Laying there was an unfolded map and crinkled receipts—and a picture of Lily-Rose. He slid his hand over the hood of the car. Still warm.

He frowned. Why would someone have a picture of Lily-Rose?

He quickly got back into his car and closed the door with a soft click.

This couldn't be good. He had to think.

He drove around the motel, looking for any other explanations or clues to why someone would be there from the Lincoln area. Tried to convince himself. Maybe this was a coincidence—someone traveling through going home to Nebraska. Yet his Knower knew better. He wasn't sure why, but that car meant trouble.

Lily-Rose.

He circled back to the front area of the motel and parked his car where he could see the office door. If the person from back home had just arrived, maybe—just maybe—he was still inside renting a room.

No sooner had Christopher gotten comfortable, when the office door opened and a man walked out, his collar up and his fedora pulled down, shielding his face. The man walked to the Nebraska car, gathered his papers from the passenger side, and went to the door labeled Room N. In a moment, he was out of sight.

What was going on?

He left his parked car and dodged puddles as he ran to the office. Opening the door, a friendly clang of the bell rang over him. An elderly man sat in the back.

"Excuse me, sir. Do you happen to have any rooms available?"

The old man looked his way. "Just one left. You here for the music festival?"

Christopher smiled. "No, but a music festival sounds nice. I'm here on personal business."

The man gave Christopher a registration form. "Lots of people comin' and goin'. That's for sure. Just had a guy come in a few minutes ago for a room. A bit snarky, that fella. I can tell 'bout people. He said he was here for business, though." The elderly man rubbed his stubble. "Funny, all I got are music people around me and in walks a business fella." He chuckled. "Not much business goin' on but music." He looked at Christopher's information. "Hey, you're from Nebraska, just like that other fella." His brow furrowed. "Everything legal? Don't want no trouble."

Christopher smiled, trying to put the old man at ease. "I'm very legal. In fact, I'm here to right a terrible wrong I did years ago." He leaned against the counter. "Nebraska's a big state, but maybe I know the guy. What's his name?"

The old man studied him. "I believe you're a good guy. Like I said." He reached for the last key on the pegboard. "I can tell 'bout people." He slid the key toward Christopher. "But I can't tell ya who's stayin' here. Against the rules." He headed back to his chair. "Have a good time in Applegate, young man. Maybe even stop by and hear some music. Or grab a bite to eat. Best grub in these parts." He nodded toward the side of the counter. "Flyer's there, free for the takin'."

"Yes, sir." Christopher picked up the key, grabbed a music festival flyer, and left the office. Instead of going to his room, however, he returned to his car and hunkered down in his seat, settling in for a rest. He'd wait here until the owner of the Nebraska car came out. He'd follow him to see what was going on.

Too many questions bounced around in his head. He came to make amends and possibly heal his relationship with Lily-Rose. But would he need to protect her instead?

Lily-Rose.

CHAPTER 34

As long as you do not accept reality,
you are powerless to define the role you will play.

—Iyanla Vanzant

The man in the motel cursed. Those Pembricks. Never were reliable. She just needed to be home with the kids and this would all be over.

But there was no answer when he called the house. He looked at his watch. After eleven o'clock in the morning. Good thing he called. He'd been prepared to hang up when Lily-Rose picked up. But with nobody answering, his plans needed to change.

What to do now?

He went into the bathroom and rinsed his face. Dried off with his stiff, musky-smelling towel and stared at his reflection.

Think.

He didn't dare go to her house to wait for her return. Couldn't risk someone seeing him hanging around during the day. He cursed again. Should've kept Kritter here to make sure all the moving parts lined up.

No, the fewer who knew for sure what was going down, the better.

"Won't be long now, Christopher." He spoke again to the reflection. "You've been looking down your nose at me like I was some lackey." His smile turned sinister. "Who's the lackey now?"

He headed for the motel office to check out. Maybe have a chat with gramps. Who knows, the old guy may even have some idea where he could find Lily-Rose. When he opened the office door, he winced, hearing the annoying clang from the bell. He walked to the counter and slid his key over.

The old manager looked at the wall clock and stayed in his chair. "Checking out? It's just before noon, so good timing if you are." He groaned as he hoisted himself from the recliner and shuffled to his side of the counter.

"Yeah. I have some errands to run. Things to take care of. Once I do, I'll head on out."

He decided that speaking softly would carry a bigger weight. "Say … I tried to reach a friend of mine, and they didn't answer. You say everyone's at this festival. Or maybe at the auxiliary getting ready for lunch. Can you point me in the right direction? Maybe I can catch up with them at one of those places."

"Good luck. Auxiliary will be swamped. Lunch time. And I hear there are so many people millin' around the festival a person can't hear themselves think."

"Confusion, huh?"

Gramps handed him his receipt. "Too much happenin'. I wouldn't be caught dead there."

He snickered. "Caught dead. Good one, Gramps."

※

Christopher stirred from a deep sleep as he heard the door close from Room N. Gathering his senses, his eyes focused on the back of the man walking to the motel office.

But he couldn't see his face.

The sun was high now. Christopher rolled down his window to get a fresh breeze through the car. He rubbed his eyes and shifted in the car seat. His thick, dry tongue reminded him of the coffee he relied on to get him to Applegate.

He leaned over, opened the glove box, and rifled through the napkins and straws looking for something to eat. Finding a wrapped but worn candy bar, he peeled away the covering and quickly ate his stale breakfast. He needed more coffee, but there were only dregs from last night's swill. Coffee, a better breakfast, and time to clean up would have to wait. He was too close to finding out who held such an interest in Lily-Rose.

The office door opened. Christopher scooched down and looked through the steering wheel as a man exited from inside.

"What?" he spoke into the thick air. "That can't be."

He watched, his eyes narrowed, as the man walked to the driver's side of the Nebraska car and tossed a bag onto the back seat. He pulled his sunglasses out of his jacket pocket and put them on. He then folded it neatly and laid it on the back seat as well.

Christopher shook his head in disbelief. Thoughts dropped like dominos in his mind—one after the other.

He should have known. He should have seen the signs. Looking back, everything made sense.

And the new knowledge made him afraid for Lily-Rose.

He slid lower in his seat as the car pulled out of the motel parking lot. And then—quickly as he could—he followed.

But not too close. He knew who it was now. The last thing he needed was to do something stupid.

Lord, help me.

He tried to conjure a plan, but his mind froze. All he could do was watch the car ahead of him.

He'd been so stupid. How did this happen? Why hadn't he seen it before? He slammed his fist against the steering wheel.

Stop thinking like that. He took a breath. Don't let this fool steal all the peace you've found.

Christopher followed the car through town. Past the bakery and the realtor's office. People milling through the streets as if nothing were wrong.

Why can't you see something bad is about to happen?

Lily-Rose.

ॐ

God, my life is yours. But now what?

Cole left Mercy and Grace Community Church after the weekly Saturday meeting in preparation for the next day's message and walked to the front of the parsonage. He stared at the door before going in, noting every line in the wood. Blessed. He had been blessed since arriving in Applegate. Life could have—would have—turned out differently if he had listened to his father's voice instead of God's.

He unlocked the door and walked in, putting the morning behind him. He'd been a bit distracted and hoped the worship team hadn't noticed. He set his keys and Bible on the hallway table, grabbed the unopened envelope, and carried it to the kitchen. He tossed it onto the table before walking to the fridge.

He finally received word back to his inquiry.

He looked in the fridge. Not much available. He'd arrived too late at the grocery store the night before to buy anything, so no feast today. He sighed, pulled out the bologna, then mustard and pickles. He scooped up the bread and chips and headed for the table. A sandwich would have to do.

He stared at the letter. He shouldn't put off reading the news any longer. These could be time-sensitive materials. He shrugged. Today was Saturday. Reading the letter could wait a bit longer.

He offered thanks for his lunch and ate without tasting it.

After he finished, he picked up the envelope again. Tapped it against the table.

Cole held onto the letter as he walked to the window and stared out at nothing in particular. He sharply exhaled, then spoke to an empty room. "I've been patient, Father. Haven't pushed at all. But you know about what I have here. The possible offer. May be what I want. Asked for, really."

But she's perfect … and so beautiful.

Cole had seen gorgeous women all his life. Either through his father's church or at college. But Lily-Rose's radiance overshadowed them all. Her love for her family and friends surpassed the flawlessness of her exquisite features. Porcelain skin. Wild, flaming hair. He sometimes lost his breath at the sight of her.

He told her he'd give her space, and he had been a man of his word.

But she consumed his thoughts. During the day, he prayed for her and her kids. Wondered how she was doing. At times even pondered a future with them. Did he dare hope that he could have a life serving God with Lily-Rose and her kids?

He paced in the living room, praying aloud. "Father, I want what you want. That's first and foremost. But dare I ask? Before I open the letter, will this be an answer to my prayer? Are you closing one door and opening another?" He stopped and closed his eyes, silently hoping God would offer an audible answer.

Nothing.

He looked at the envelope. He half hoped it had been lost in the mail. Not only had they received his inquiry—they replied. His eyes traveled to the return address: Christian Missions in Ireland.

He sat hard on the chair, leaned back, and let go of a breath. He was confident that Lily-Rose had everything he was looking for in a wife—a partner. Intelligence and beauty. He knew all that the night they had grabbed fries and drinks to talk about Del. But then he watched her love for God grow, and that sealed the deal in his mind. And his heart. But she had made her needs clear from the start. She was still in love with her husband—her dead husband. He knew winning a battle against the memories of a ghost would be impossible. Ghosts always win.

He had done everything he could to walk the line but still be close to her. Always talked with her after church. Even grabbed a private moment or two. But never broke his word and never pressed. Dinner at Burger's 'n More had given him hope. But still, if there would ever be a relationship between them, she had to be in control of her choices and the timing.

Last Sunday he floated out the idea—the possibility—of attending the local music festival together on its last night. That would be tonight. He was thrilled when she said she'd think about it. Two days ago, however, the letter from the mission board arrived. Until he opened the envelope, he was able to straddle both worlds—one of following his calling and the other following his heart. Once he opened and read the letter's contents, his fate would be sealed.

Thy will be done.

Cole turned the envelope over in his hands. He exhaled sharply, then ripped the end of the envelope and blew in it, showing its contents. He held his breath as he pulled the letter out, unfolded it, and began to read.

> Greetings, Pastor Matheson, in the name of our Lord!
>
> We are eager to let you know that our team of missionaries have been praying for you and your request to join us in Ireland. This letter confirms for you that …

❧

"But Mom. It's a school lock-in. What could go wrong?"

"First of all, young lady, stop yelling. I'm right here." Lily-Rose took a calming breath then looked over the edge of the Saturday morning newspaper. They had been gone since eight doing errands and this was her first moment of quiet since they returned. "I don't know, sweetie." She had hoped to grab a moment of rest while reviewing the latest current events. No such luck.

She tried to keep in mind that Mary's tenacity was a positive trait, but, bother, her spunk was fierce. Lily-Rose watched as Mary threw her hands to her hips. "But all the kids will be there. And Del can come too."

"I know, but—"

"I'm not a child anymore. When are you going to start letting me make some of my decisions?"

Even though they had all been getting along much better these days, her daughter still knew her buttons, that's for sure. "Mary, I never said—"

Del and Scout entered the living room. "You guys talking about the lock-in tonight?" He looked at Mary. "We going?"

"Wait. Del. You knew, and this is the first I'm hearing about it?"

Mary looked at her brother, ignoring her mom. "She's not sure. Doesn't think we'll"—she stressed with air quotes— "make good decisions."

"Now wait one moment, Mare." Lily-Rose's ire flared. "You have no idea what I'm thinking." She dropped the paper fully, looked at her daughter, and started ticking off her points. "One: I don't know where they're holding it. Two: I don't know who's all going to be there." A sudden flashback of her battles with Mama Henderson washed over her, but she was on a roll.

"And three: I don't know who the chaperones are? And those questions are just for starters."

"But, Mom—"

"Honey, you haven't even told me when I need to get you there or if you need to take anything with you. Is there a fee for this?"

Yes, they were all getting along so well. What was the harm in letting them go to a school-sponsored function? She had to admit, at least to herself, that she was overreacting.

Honesty. They needed honesty.

She closed her eyes for a moment and exhaled. "Okay, yes. I admit I still get spooked when it comes to you guys being out of my sight—"

Del piped up. "But Unc-a-bunk's never shown up. I bet he hasn't even looked for us. That he's forgotten all about us. Can we go, Mom, can we?"

Scout walked to Lily-Rose and nuzzled her hand. She scratched the dog's ear. "And what about your dog?"

Del looked at Mary, then back, smiling. "Can I take him with us—to the lock-in, I mean?"

Mary squealed. "Yeah, Mom. That'd be great."

Edward had called it years ago. "Once they start working together against us, we're goners."

They were working together now and seemed to outnumber her. She started folding the paper. "Tell you what, Mary. You find the answers to all my questions, come back, and we'll revisit this. And if I'm satisfied with who is chaperoning … and if they agree to Scout tagging along … then you can both go. Is that a deal?"

Lily-Rose stopped folding the paper and tried to find where she had left off, but her thoughts stayed on the kids. Strange that Del's first input was about Christopher. Was her son still looking over his shoulder too? He was probably right. There hadn't been any inkling that Christopher was looking for her. Or them. She'd make a point from now on to lighten up—let her kids have normal childhoods.

Mary's phone conversation wafted from the kitchen. After several minutes, she hung up and started talking to Lily-Rose even before she walked into the living room. "The junior class is putting it on at the school. We can get there up to six o'clock tonight. That's when they lock the doors. They won't let us out until six in the morning. There's a cover charge—but I got it." She came closer to the couch. "Guess I did spring this on you a little late. Sorry."

"But what about—"

"Oh, and the O'Donnell's are chaperoning along with Principal Miller and his wife."

"Did you ask about Scout?"

Mary curled up on the couch beside Lily-Rose. "Uh-huh. We have to bring a couple of bowls plus his food. And a scooper. Mrs. Miller said if I was responsible, she'd let me take Scout outside—but I wasn't to tell Mr. Miller." She smiled and scooched closer. "She'd unlock the lock-in for Scout." She cuddled playfully. "So, can we go?"

Lily-Rose smiled and pulled her tight. How she loved cuddling with her kids. She then looked at her watch. Just past one o'clock. "Looks like you got it."

The phone rang. Del and Mary raced to pick it up.

Del got there first. "Hello? Oh, hi, Coach. I'm fine. Yeah, she's here." Mary headed to her room after hearing the call wasn't for her. Del pulled the receiver from his ear and covered the mouthpiece. "It's the coach. He wants to talk to you."

"Oh. Okay. Tell him I'll be right there. And remind Mary of the time. You two need to pack what you need and take showers."

He talked into the receiver. "She'll be right here. You too."

He laid the phone receiver on the table. "I'm going to my room, Mom. Let me know when it's time to go."

She walked toward the table and picked up the phone. "Hello?"

"Hi, Lily-Rose. It's Cole."

She smiled.

"So, uh, Lily-Rose. How you doing?"

She tilted her head and twirled her hair. "Good," she answered. "I'm good." This preacher, much as she didn't want to admit it, made her heart skip whenever she heard his voice.

"Great … great." She heard him take in a deep breath. "So, Lily-Rose. About the festival. Have you thought anymore about it? If you want to go, I could pick you up around three, that is, if that time works for you. I figured we could get something to eat first. I hear Bernetta's cooking for the auxiliary at the Grange Hall. Guess she's making her blueberry pies for the occasion."

Lily-Rose smiled. "Not apple? That's scandalous."

Cole chuckled. "Should be a treat, right?" He paused. "And there's something I want to talk to you about."

Her brow furrowed. "Everything okay?"

Cole's words tumbled. "No, no. Everything's fine. Better than fine, really. That's what I want to talk to you about. So can I pick you up, say, 'bout three?"

Lily-Rose raised her brows. The timing was perfect. The kids would be done with their showers and give her time to get ready without a rush. Mary would drive to the school and even Scout would be taken care of for the evening.

"Sounds like a date. I'll see you around three."

She hung up then went outside and sat by the firepit. The circle looked dark and dirty without the flames jumping from the wood held in its circle.

"Kinda early for a fire, isn't it?" Sugar called through the hedge.

She smiled. "No fire yet. I'm just out here thinking."

Sugar rounded the bushes, wiping her hands on a kitchen towel. "'Bout what? Or is it a secret? Remember, we don't hide things from one another, right?"

Lily-Rose grinned. "I have a date tonight. With Cole."

Sugar howled. "Girl, it's 'bout time he asks ya. Where you goin'?"

"First to grab a bite at the hall ... Bernetta's desserts, for sure ... then onto the music festival."

"I swear, all you have to do, Lily-Rose, is say the word. That man's been pining after you for months. I see how he looks at you after church."

Suddenly a crash came from Sugar's house. Sugar looked over her shoulder and wrinkled her nose. "Lordy. I gotta get back to Gran and the girls. We got a call from Dungar early today. He'll be home tomorrow to start packing. Said we should get a head start." She headed toward her house and yelled back. "Mark my words. Tonight's gonna change your life. I can feel it. I hope there's time to have a fire after. You can fill us all in then." She turned and stared, her eyes sad. Pensive. "Lily-Rose. We're leaving Monday morning. We're running out of time for our fires."

Lily-Rose offered a weary smile. "We'll have a fire before you go, I promise. If not tonight, then Sunday for sure. I'll fill you both in then." She stiffened her lip and sighed. "I can't believe it, talking about our last fire. Of course, there'll be a fire. Nothing could stop it."

chapter 35

Love is begun by time,
And time qualifies the spark and fire of it.

—Shakespeare's *Hamlet*

She hoped she had made the right decision.

Cole was a great guy. There was no doubt. But he was her friend. And Del's coach. And their pastor, for crying out loud.

She smiled and poured herself a glass of iced tea, then looked at the clock. After the kids left she had an hour to get her act together. She leaned against the counter and took a sip.

A date—not just a date, but a for real planned date. The first time they met was e about Del, but she knew from the start it had been more. It had been … sweet. Non-committal. Mostly just getting to know one another and for her to establish some boundaries. Nothing special really. Then after that they met over a burger and fries, checking in to see if there was still interest.

And there was, on both of their parts.

She was always glad to meet for an impromptu cup of coffee or soft drink. and had been thankful he had heard her heart when she said she needed to take everything slow.

Edward.

The kids were finishing getting ready for the lock-in. Their overnight bags were already packed and by the door. She could hear them in Del's room making plans on his phone with their friends. They were fine. Even Scout seemed excited.

She took another sip then called to the kids. "Are you done in the bathroom for a while? I'd like to take a long hot bath."

A duet of "we're good" greeted her.

She felt herself still smiling. She was going on a date—a for-real date this time.

The timing felt right.

She slipped her robe from the hook on the closet door in her room, grabbed the transistor radio from her nightstand, and went into the bathroom and began filling the tub with hot water. After the radio station had been set, she inflated and secured her seashell pillow to the back of the tub. It had been a long time since she'd pampered herself with a luxurious bath, but today called for it. She sprinkled Calgon in the water and watched as the crystals dissolved and created a cloudy mix. She laid out her arsenal—Camay bar soap, loofah sponge, a razor, and a new can of Lady Gillette. She looked at her nails. Better set the hand brush and cuticle remover on the side of the tub as well.

She wrapped her hair in a towel then leaned back and soaked in the steaminess, listening to music. Warm water soothed the tense muscles in her body as her mind relaxed.

Edward.

Memories of the dream she had after arriving on Norwood Street came to mind.

I know that you'll have a long, full life ... you will feel joy, peace ... and love again.

She closed her eyes as tears glided down her cheeks. From the radio, the Bee Gees sang in their falsetto voices of how to mend a broken heart. She pulled the cloth from the steamy water and laid it over her face and hummed along when they sang about living again. How appropriate.

The water began to cool. Lily-Rose uncovered her face and stared at the ceiling. Was she ready? Well, she sure didn't feel it.

Should she consider Cole as more than a friend? He had made his intensions clear that he wanted something more. What about the kids? She exhaled, then sat up and skimmed her hands back and forth through the water for a few moments. So much to think about. Things to consider.

She climbed out of the tub and wrapped the robe around her flushed body, then padded to her room. She stared at her clothes hanging in the closet. "What does one wear to a music festival?"

She pulled out a peasant skirt, white cotton top, and a fringed suede vest and draped them over her bed. Top this off with a floppy hat and sandals, she told herself, and she'd fit right in.

Mary called her from the kitchen. "Mom. We're going now."

Lily-Rose went to the kitchen in her robe and looked at the wall clock. "It's early, isn't it?" She turned to her daughter. "You both sure you want to go? We can always stay in and have popcorn." If they wanted to be with her, she'd call Cole and reschedule. Her kids came first.

Mary answered. "Going early isn't a problem. The Millers are there already." She raised her brow. "Hey. What's with taking a soaking bath in the middle of the day?"

Lily-Rose stammered. "I-I forgot to tell you. Cole's coming by to pick me up a little after you leave. We're headed out for a bite, then on to the festival."

Mary walked to her mom and gave her a hug. "Getting gussied up, are we?"

"You know ... I could stay—"

Del offered a crooked smile. "She's teasing, can't you tell?" He gave a hug as well. "Have a good time, Mom. Really."

"You guys sure?"

Mary grabbed her bag. "Yes, we're sure. Del, get your bag.

I'll bring Scout's things, and you get him." Before Lily-Rose could protest, they were out the door. Mary called back. "Love you. See you in the morning sometime after six."

"Love you too." She heard the car doors close, then the music from the radio at full blast. Yep. Mary was in charge. The song faded as they pulled out of the driveway.

They were gone.

Lily-Rose returned to her bedroom. After dressing and brushing out her hair, she stole a glance in the mirror and smiled again. She was getting ready. For a date! Nothing could dampen her mood. Her kids were happy, and she felt Edward's blessing on her life. And she had two of the best friends any woman could want.

Life was perfect.

The doorbell rang as she finished putting on the last bit of blush. With a final check in the mirror—yes, she looked fine—she hurried to the door

There Cole stood—bellbottoms, linen shirt, and sandals.

He smiled and stepped in the door. "Wow, Lily-Rose. You look like a hippie. You'll fit us right in."

"You look good yourself. Ready to go?"

Cole held the door. "I'm looking forward to Bernetta's blueberry pie. How about you?"

"Can the blueberry be as good as her apple?"

They walked to the car where Cole opened the door for Lily-Rose, then sprinted around the front of the car and got in. Within seconds, they were headed to the Grange Hall outside Applegate where the Ladies Auxiliary served their goodies.

Cole held the door again for Lily-Rose, and they entered the hall. Laughter and the shuffling and clinking of plates filled the air. They were led to a table and settled in.

Cole looked at Lily-Rose. "I'm really glad you agreed to come out with me today. More for than just a cup of coffee."

Robin Luftig

She smiled as she picked up her menu. When had life become sweet again after Edward died? Talking to Cole seemed so … easy. Like she had known him her entire life. "Thanks for asking. The festival should be fun." Turning her attention to her choices for an early dinner. "What are you going to order? Everything looks delicious."

Cole shrugged. "The special, whatever that is. I'm sure it'll be good. And ordering before hearing what our choices are adds a bit of excitement, right?"

The waitress came to their table with glasses of water. They ordered the special in unison before she had the chance to read their choices from her notepad.

This was living life on the edge. The type of edge that she preferred.

He began rolling the corner of his paper placemat under his fingertips. "Okay," he said finally. "I also wanted to see if I was any closer to a green light with you. If you remember, what seems to be about a million years ago, we left it that I only had a yellow one." He held up his hands, surrendering. "But, no pressure, Lily-Rose. Just wanted to have dinner. And hopefully check the flow of traffic." He smiled. "Know what I mean?"

This was turning out to be a wonderful date. She knew what he meant. And yes, she was ready At least she thought she was. It was now or never. "No problem. And I did say yellow, not red." She smiled. "Yes. Traffic's ready to move on down the road."

Cole's eyes widened, and a smile filled his face as though he'd not expected to hear her answer. "Excellent. I'm happy to hear that. There's so much I want to talk with you about, but I also wanted to honor that space thing."

"Honoring my space is huge." She stirred the ice in her water with her straw. "I met Christopher … Edward's brother

… before I met Edward. I thought we were friends, but he wanted more." She took a sip. "His obsession scared me to death. I learned a big lesson then."

"Really? What's that?"

"How situations look doesn't always match what they are."

Their waitress returned with two plates filled with fried liver and onions and a scoop of mashed potatoes with gravy. They looked at one another. Lily-Rose pressed her lips together while Cole's cheeks puffed out. "Anything else I can get you?" the waitress asked.

Cole looked up with a shake of his head, but once she walked away, he shrugged. "We could get something else if you'd like."

They both laughed.

Lily-Rose unrolled the napkin off her flatware and placed it in her lap.

"This is perfect. I haven't done this in years."

"Me too. And I bet everything is great. Can I say grace for us?"

"Please."

They both bowed their heads, and Cole offered a short thanks, then came back to where their conversation left off. "Believe it or not, liver and onions used to be my favorite, but Mom thought internal organs weren't dignified enough." He arched his brows. "I think that's why I liked it so much." He cut a piece of liver and speared some onions with his fork, then looked at Lily-Rose and smiled. "Funny how life changes."

She took a bite as well. "Sure is." She chewed, then her eyes widened. "This is delicious. Great suggestion. I can't wait to tell the girls."

"Your two friends?"

She smiled. "Friends. Somehow that doesn't say what we are exactly. But yes, Fiona and Sugar."

"You tell them a lot?"

She smiled. "I tell them everything. And they do me as well. I have a backyard firepit. That's where we meet."

"Like ladies of the fire, huh?"

"Exactly. That's why the word friends just doesn't measure up." She took a bite of potatoes. "These are delicious too. I need to bring the kids here. Steer away from always going to Burgers 'n More."

For a while, they ate in silence, Lily-Rose sensing that he wanted to talk about more than fires and mashed potatoes. Maybe this was her turn to give him space. To see what happens.

"So, Lily-Rose." He wiped his mouth with his napkin, then took a drink of water. "I told you there was something I wanted to talk to you about."

"I remember. You said everything was okay, so I tried not to worry."

He nodded. "Nothing to worry about, but it is big." He took another sip of water, paused, then let the words flow. "I've been accepted by the Christian Missions of Ireland. They want me to go there and start a church … in Northern Ireland. They're sending me the specifics if I tell them I'm coming."

She had forgotten all about the Ireland part and hadn't seen this coming. "I remember you mentioned that over burgers. You said you'd been a bit restless, not knowing if God was nudging you or not. You must have gotten your answer."

She paused. "Wait. Isn't there a war going on there?"

"Yes, but I don't imagine it lasting too long."

Lily-Rose's heart sank. She felt silly that she sang along with the Bee Gees on the radio. It'd been too long since she dated. She thought Cole wanted more—wanted a relationship with her. Obviously, he didn't. But Cole reached for what he wanted. Very impressive. She'd be happy for him.

"We'll miss you. Applegate won't be the same. And Del

… well, we'll work it out." She took a deep breath. Exhaled. "Congratulations, Cole. This sounds exciting."

Cole reached across the table for Lily-Rose's hand. She let go of her fork and reached for his as well. His hand was warm. Soft. His touch reminded her of their last time together and how he had reached for her hand then too. His touch felt wonderful. And it'd been a long time since a man looked into her eyes the way Cole did. "That's what I want to talk to you about, Lily-Rose. I want you to come with me."

"What?"

She jerked her hand, and he leaned back in his chair. "Probably should have snuck up on that a bit. Sorry." He smiled, nervously wiping his mouth with his napkin. "I imagine this is a surprise for you." He leaned forward again. "But I've been praying about this—about me and you—for a long time now."

What was he saying? Each word he spoke was understandable, but the sentences made no sense.

He smiled. "You're shocked. I see it on your face."

"Shocked doesn't come close to explaining what I feel." Was this Christopher all over again?

As if reading her mind, his gaze softened. "You can say no, Lily-Rose. And if you do, I'm not going to wig out on you." His eyes searched hers. "I've held back, like you asked. But I can't deny that I'm falling for you. Hard."

She exhaled. Hard. "You don't know me, Cole. And I have kids to think about—"

"I get that. I know you do."

"And you're asking me to take my kids and go with you to a country in conflict." She stared. "I'm … I'm speechless." How could this be? She began again, "What's … how's …" She shook her head. "The words aren't coming."

"I should have come at this from a different direction." He reached for her hand again. Funny, his touch felt confining this time. She pulled her hand away.

"You're a good guy, Cole. And I really like you. I just never thought—"

"Think about it, will ya?"

"Okay. But I have to say." She took a breath. "This is like Christopher all over again."

He looked at her puzzled. "Christopher?"

She looked down at her plate. "Someone I really cared for but who ended up hating me because I didn't turn out to be who he wanted."

Cole's eyes widened. "No, Lily-Rose. That's not it at all. I'd be lying if I said I didn't want you and the kids to come with me." He leaned forward and reached again for her hand. "But you can say no. Right now, all I want you to do is say you'll think about my offer. Okay?"

What else could she think about? His passion for ministry was real. She didn't doubt that. But would his passion be enough for her to consider taking his offer and moving her family to a war-torn town in a different country? Mary would be in college soon. Would moving to another country dampen her chances? Del really liked Cole, but would following him to Ireland be good for her son?

She looked into Cole's eyes. "I will think about it."

chapter 36

Make us worthy, Lord, to serve those people
throughout the world ... and by our understanding
love, give them peace and joy.

—Mother Teresa

Bob Biddle's body ached from exhaustion. A wracking
cough had stolen most of his strength. He had no time to
waste.

Pushing past the pain was his only option. He shouldn't be
on the road. Driving had stopped being safe hours earlier. But
he had to risk it. He had to get to Applegate. Had to see Lily-
Rose before it was too late.

He had initially planned to find a room and get some rest
when he hit town. Had wanted to be on his best game when
he met with Lily-Rose and told her his news. But because this
exhaustion was almost crippling, he feared he'd never get out
of bed if he took a break. He had to keep going. Didn't have
time to rest. She'd have to take him as he was. His words would
need to convince her. Nothing was more important than what
he had to say.

Not even his life.

Change in plans. He headed for the address written on the
index card his private investigator gave him. Norwood Street.
He needed to find Lily-Rose first. Motel room later. He'd rest
then. After that, well, not much mattered after that. He'd face
the Pembrick music. He was sure they'd have a word for him.

Biddle looked at his eyes in the rearview mirror. He deserved all the venom they could possibly spew his way.

That didn't matter now. He needed to make amends—before he died.

The sun's rays cast shadows under the trees in her front yard as Biddle pulled into Lily-Rose's driveway.

Nice place. Cute. She had done okay for herself.

Biddle gritted his teeth as he struggled to get out of the car. He played the rehearsed speech over in his mind as he walked to the front door. Pressed the doorbell and waited for the chime to echo through the house. No answer. He never considered a scenario where Lily-Rose wasn't home. So, he knocked. Proverbial cotton balls filled his mouth and words lost their form.

He could do this. Stay focused. Figure out what to do now.

Biddle slowly left the front porch and walked around the side of the house. He passed the firepit and headed for the back door.

"Can I help you?" a sweet southern voice came from beyond the shrubs.

"Hello?" He coughed. "Ah, hum, yes, um, I'm looking for Missus, I-mean, I'm looking for Lily-Rose Pembrick."

A kind-looking blonde came into Biddle's view around the end of the shrub. "That's her house, but she's not home now." She stuck out her hand in greeting. "My name's Sugar, Lily-Rose's neighbor. Can I help you?" She took a breath. "I didn't catch your name. Say, mister, you don't look so good."

He didn't take her hand. "Thank you for your concern, but I'm fine." He coughed again, then swayed. Regaining his balance, he exhaled. "I need to see Lily-Rose. It's imperative. Do you know where I can find her?"

This woman must have kids, the way she pushed past his reserve. She held his arm and steadied him. "She should be home later ta'night." Her eyes sought contact with his. "Are you sure I can't offer you some help? Maybe a glass of cool, sweet tea? Could bring a bit of color to your cheeks."

Biddle offered a faint smile. "Thank you, dear. Maybe a cool drink and a moment to sit and rest would be best. Do you think she'd mind if I sat here, at the firepit, for just a moment?"

Sugar guided Biddle to a chair then went back to her house for some tea. He waited between the beats of silence and crickets and a few croaks from some yard toads until she returned with a tall glass of liquid sweetness over ice. Her other hand held a paper plate with a bologna sandwich and chips.

"Here's a little somethin' more to go with your tea. Are you sure you're okay?"

Biddle pulled his handkerchief to his mouth as he coughed. His breathing thickened as a red spot widened on the rag.

Sugar stood over him. "Bless your heart, mister, you're real sick."

He closed his eyes and leaned back into the chair. "I'll be fine, dear. Forgive my bad manners. My name is Biddle. Bob Biddle."

Sugar cocked her head. "I don't remember ever hearin' Lily-Rose mention you."

Biddle grinned. "Oh, I'm confident that she hasn't. We've never met. But it's essential I speak to her." He coughed. "About a Lincoln, Nebraska matter."

Sugar pulled a baggie filled with chips from her pocket. "Lily-Rose told us she was from Lincoln. Said she left some … um … family ugliness behind."

Biddle sipped his tea. "Yes. I'm afraid she did. Quite ugly. And it's all my fault." He offered a hesitant blink. "Oh, not about Edward dying, but about the nefarious treatment that Christopher endured. Poor fella."

"Nefarious." Sugar pinched her lips together. "I don't know

that word. But if it means he's a bad guy gettin' ready to hurt Lily-Rose, then you better know she's onto him."

He held the sweating glass to the side of his face. Its coolness—as well as speaking to this delightful woman—refreshed his spirit. "No, not at all, my dear." He cleared his throat. "Christopher may not have died, but his life was ruined—years ago. Bad choices his parents had tried to fix. That's why I'm here. He was one of the casualties that wasn't meant to be." He coughed, then gasped for air. "That's why I have to speak with Lily-Rose."

Between bites and sips, Biddle shared an abbreviated story of greed and selfishness that led him to his involvement with William and Sandra Pembrick and Pembrick Transportation, and that they commissioned him to write a later—and last—will.

Sugar sat and stared. "Oh, Mr. Biddle, sir, I'm so sorry. You lost your wife, son, and career while chasing after what you couldn't have." She put her hand on his arm. "Funny, ain't it. We sometimes don't realize what we got 'til it's gone."

"No wiser words have ever been spoken, dear." He wiped his mouth on his handkerchief. "That's why I need to see Lily-Rose before—well, soon. As soon as possible."

"Like I said, I'm sure she'll be home later. She's on a date with the preacher. They was grabbin' a bite before goin' on to the music festival."

Biddle looked deep into her eyes. "Sugar, you've been kinder to me than I deserve." He leaned forward and started coughing again. After catching his breath, he closed his eyes and whispered. "You see, I don't think I can wait." With his eye still closed, he leaned back and grinned. "Odd, hearing those words come from my mouth." He opened his eyes, sat back up, and looked again at Sugar. "Would it be possible for you to take me to the festival?" He reached for her hand. "Please.

Help me find her."

Biddle began coughing again. Sugar squeezed his arm. "You sure now? Wouldn't you rather rest for a bit?"

His vision began to blur. "Kind lady, I don't know if I have the time to rest. Maybe if I lay back in the car while you drive, I could get some strength back."

She searched his face a moment, then took a deep breath. "Give me a minute. I need to tell Gran I'm leavin'. She'll need to stick around with the girls 'til I get back. We'll take your car, okay?" Sugar stood. "Finish your sandwich. I'll be right back."

He closed his eyes for what seemed a breath of a moment until Sugar was back, purse in hand. "Okay, I'm ready," her voice reached to him through his fog. "Mr. Biddle? You awake? You sure you're up to this?"

He opened his eyes. "Thank you, yes." Biddle continued to mutter as she helped him stand. "If you don't mind, I'll close my eyes while you're driving." After she got him in the passenger's seat, he exhaled. "Do you think we should head to where they were eating, or just go straight to the festival?"

But before he heard her answer, he had passed out.

⁂

She hoped Lily-Rose wouldn't be mad about this.

She had taken quite a few liberties regarding this Biddle fella. Left her babies at home with Gran so she could track Lily-Rose and Cole down at the music festival for a stranger who looked like death warmed over.

Was she out of her mind?

She thought back to the fire—telling her friends she'd make them proud of her. Was this a way she could make a difference? Could her decision to take a risk help this Biddle fella find peace? She needed a plan.

She chose to steer Mr. Biddle away from Lily-Rose's dinner with Cole. At least the couple could have a bit of privacy at the Grange. The place would undoubtedly be crowded, but nothing like the festival. Sugar looked over at the sleeping gentleman. Interesting fella. Seemingly helpless yet driven with purpose.

She sat straight. If Mr. Biddle could travel across country to make a difference in Lily-Rose's life, she could make an impact in Applegate before she left. She wanted to make sure her time there meant something … made a difference to somebody.

Sugar headed for the McKinney farm, then followed the signs for parking. She drove over ruts and through mud until she reached a flagman. She smiled when she recognized Earl Hastings directing the parking area traffic. She rolled down her window. "Hey, Earl."

Earl smiled, pushed back the bill of his ball cap, and leaned down to the opened window. "Hey, Sugar. Get a new car?" He looked in and saw Biddle asleep. "Takin' a sleepin' guy to hear live music. That's a new one." He rested his arm on the window frame and whispered. "He won't miss much. Not all that good if you ask me." He shook his head. "But my opinion doesn't count. I'm just directin' traffic."

Sugar smiled. "This here's my friend's car." Changing the conversation. "Say, Earl. Is there any handicapped parking in there? My friend here. He ain't able to walk none too good."

Earl straightened. "I don't know, Sugar. We're s'pose to reserve those spots for folks with those blue stickers in their cars."

"I know, I know. But c'mon, Earl, don't you think you could let me get by just this once?" It was Sugar's turn to whisper. "Connie's gonna make a nice commission from sellin' our house soon. Don't you think you could do me this one little favor?"

Earl looked at Sugar, then at the sleeping man. "All right." He straightened and adjusted his cap. He looked forward and pointed. "I guess if anyone needs to be close, it's him. See that fence down yonder? Go all the way there, then turn right. You'll see signs sayin' Infirmary. Follow them 'til you get next to the front stage. The infirmary's right there. That cinderblock building that held farm tools just last week? Nothing fancy. Park beside it." He wiped his mouth. "And if anyone tries to stop you, act like you belong there. Just don't tell 'em I was the one who sent you. Capisce?"

Sugar flashed a smile. "Hey, Earl, guess what. I know what that means. I saw it in a movie. Capisce right back. And tell Connie I said hey." She started to drive off, then slammed on her brakes. She looked over at Biddle. He looked back, but quickly closed his eyes again. She spoke softer. "I almost forgot. Have you seen Lily-Rose yet?"

"Not yet. When I do, I'll tell her where you're parked. Now move along. You're holding up traffic."

Sugar stuck her arm out and waved as she drove off. "Okay. Ciao. That means goodbye."

She did what Earl instructed—drove in like she owned the place. The car jutted and jerked as she maneuvered over the bumpy terrain. Nobody stopped or even noticed them.

She pulled into a parking spot and got out of the car, then stepped up on the car's running board and shielded her eyes as she looked around. The view from their spot was perfect. She could see everything. Both stages—and if she squinted—the park entrance.

Biddle began to stir.

"We're here, Mr. Biddle. But Lily-Rose ain't here yet. We'll need to wait. But I've got us close to the infirmary in case you need somethin'."

"Thank you, dear. I'm ready for this to finally be over."

chapter 37

The past cannot be changed, forgotten, edited or erased; it can only be accepted.

—Unknown

Christopher's mind raced as he followed the Nebraska car into the music festival parking area. He stopped his Pontiac a few spots away from where the man he was following parked. He'd confront him, but not just yet. He trusted the right time would present itself.

As he stepped out, music poured from speakers perched on towers throughout the fields. The sunlight still warmed his skin, but the rays were coming more from the west than straight above. Soon, they would be getting ready to finish the day. The sky was clear, offering the promise of a perfect evening under the stars for the last night of the festival. Too bad he had to chase down trouble. He walked, the beat from the percussions pounding in his chest. Distracting. He could barely think.

"Hey, dude. Isn't this rad?"

Christopher looked down to a young girl, not much older than Mary, who crawled in the mud. He reached for her. "Is something wrong? You'll get trampled for sure if you stay down there."

She grinned; eyelids drooped. "I'm cool. I dropped a 'shroom—you're not the fuzz, are you?"

He gave a light hoot and shook his head. "Little lady, now

there's a first. Nobody's ever mistaken me for a cop." He pulled her to her feet. "Enjoy the music, but lay off the other stuff, okay?"

She squinted as she found her balance. "Whatever you say, pops." She staggered off into the crowd, whooping and waving her arms along with the beat.

Pops? He returned his gaze over the crowd, hoping to find the man from the motel.

Gone.

Christopher growled, then took a deep breath. Glad God's got this. He pushed his way through the crowd in the direction he last saw the man, hoping to spot him again. He'd make him explain why he was hunting Lily-Rose. Then he could do what he had initially set out to do. Talk to her. If he could prove that not only did he want to make amends but was also looking out for her best interests here in Applegate, maybe she'd hear him out. Believe him when he'd tell her he had become a new man.

He continued to scan the crowd. Nothing. Maybe from the clearing he could see better. He walked to the edge with little problem. Most festival goers pushed toward the stages, not away. Only a few hipsters danced the perimeter of the festival's activity. Once on the edge of the crowd, he strained his neck to look above the heads of celebrating music lovers.

"Fancy meeting you here. I didn't know you liked this kind of music."

As Christopher turned, something hard hit him on the side of his head, sending stars exploding behind his eyes. Then all went black.

chapter 38

Some journeys take us far from home.
Some adventures lead us to our destiny.

—C. S. Lewis

Cole held Lily-Rose's hand as they worked their way through the crowd toward the infirmary. It felt good, her hand in his. Maybe a forever-type of feeling good? She looked up at his face and he smiled.

"We fit together." He must have felt it too. They stopped walking. He looked into her eyes—then inhaled sharply as if focusing his thoughts, then looked up to scan the crowd. "Hope we can find the car Earl told us about."

"An out of town Pontiac by the infirmary tent. Shouldn't be too difficult to spot."

"Earl didn't make any sense, that talk about a sleeping old man. We'll get there soon and hear from Sugar. And see what she's doing with some strange guy."

Cole led the way toward the infirmary. As they got closer, she caught a glimpse of Sugar peeking through the block building window about the same time Sugar spotted her and began waving her arms.

"Lily-Rose. Over here."

Walking through a lifted flap of a door, Lily-Rose saw crates and boxes marked Medical Supplies stacked in a far corner. A single table stood alone among a smattering of cots, all but one empty and that one cot held an older man—not the music festival type. Sugar was kneeling beside him. She rose again as they came closer, her face pinched. "I've been bouncin' back and forth between bein' by Mr. Biddle and looking out the winda for ya. Glad you're finally here." She reached out and gave Lily-Rose a brief hug then led her and Cole to the cot. "This man here? He's Mr. Biddle. Came to your place looking to talk. He didn't look so good and seemed a bit anxious, so I thought I'd bring him to the festival to find you'uns. I worked it with Earl and parked his car close and decided to wait with him." She turned to Lily-Rose. "You ain't mad, are ya?"

Cole remained close as Lily-Rose let go of his hand and focused on her friend. "Of course I'm not angry. You're a good person, Sugar."

Sugar nodded toward the door. "The nurse—a no-nonsense kind of a gal—just left. Either her hairpins were pokin' her or I made her nervous. When me and Mr. Biddle walked in, she 'bout had a fit. Didn't even want him here. Said he was too sick. I told her he wasn't a leper. Just needed a place to lay down."

Cole cocked his head and raised a brow. "Did she call for an ambulance?"

"Not that I know of," Sugar answered, craning her head to look beyond them. "Said she'd have to root through her supplies to see if she had anything to make him comfortable. She doubted it. Said it took days to get these supplies ready, you know. Things like oxygen tanks, gauze, and bandages. Rubbing alcohol and mercurochrome antiseptic, splints and stretchers. Stuff that ya might need at a music festival, I guess."

Lily-Rose pulled her friend from the rabbit hole. "That's good, Sug. Anything else about this Mr. Biddle?"

"Oh ... yes. Sorry." Sugar fidgeted. "Nurse said one look at him, and she knew he needed attention. I promised her we'd get him to the county hospital after we caught up with you'uns. But right now he just needed a place to chill."

Cole looked around the room. "Pretty primitive setup. From the looks of things, all this place is good for is cuts, sprains, and maybe some heat exhaustion." He turned back to Sugar. "You didn't say. Why'd she leave?"

Sugar's eyes danced. "She was making me nervous, so I suggested she check out the show. You could tell she wanted to. She said she already looked over when we walked in and knew she couldn't do anything for him. Just keep him comfy and all. So I told her to stay close to the stage here but check out some of the bands. I said I'd know where to send someone if I needed her." She continued to fidget. "Besides. She's excited that Barry McGuire or Norman Greenbaum, whoever they are, that'r suppose to be coming up real soon."

They walked to the occupied cot. Lily-Rose knelt beside the makeshift bed and began whispering to the man in a smooth, soothing voice. "Mr. Biddle. It's me, Lily-Rose Pembrick."

"Excuse me, Lily-Rose," Sugar added. "All that lemonade I drunk gave me a potty dance. If you'uns don't mind, I gotta find the latrine. I'll be back before you know it. Okay?"

As soon as Sugar left the building, Cole's look went from Lily-Rose to the man on the cot. He walked over and took a coach's stance. "What can I do?"

Mr. Biddle open his eyes at the sound of Cole's voice. He struggled to sit upright. "Shh, now," Lily-Rose said, patting him. "Stay down. Relax."

He stopped struggling for a moment and looked at her face. Into her eyes. Then beyond Lily-Rose and directly at Cole. He took a deep breath and began pushing to sit up. Cole leaned down and reached for the man's arm to steady him. "You can stay down, Mr. Biddle. If that's okay."

But despite their efforts, Biddle pushed beyond his comfort and sat up. His face was paler than before. She could tell it took all his effort to focus on her.

"Please allow me this, Mrs. Pembrick." He placed his feet on the floor and struggled again to stand. Cole hovered close as Biddle gained his balance. The feeble man took a deep breath and exhaled. "I've waited a long time to talk to you." He looked into her eyes, then to the floor and offered a soft laugh. "Now I don't know where to—"

A noise at the opened door caused them to turn their heads as a man lumbered in. He held his head; blood oozed through his fingers.

Christopher!

Lily-Rose looked for an escape. The windows wouldn't work. Too small. And he stood in front of the door. She was trapped. She tugged at Mr. Biddle, dragging him behind Cole. "That's Christopher," she whispered over his shoulder.

"The Christopher, the one you ran from in Lincoln?"

"Mmm-hmm," she said as Christopher fully entered the room.

"Lily-Rose," he managed as he dropped his hand to survey the blood pooling there. "I'm—glad to see you—uh—a lot to catch up on." He cut his eyes upward. "I—uh—are there bandages in here?" His voice sounded weak to Lily-Rose. Not at all the way it had sounded the last time they'd spoken.

"Some disinfectant maybe?"

Cole leaned back to Lily-Rose. "He's hurt pretty bad," he said, then added, "I can take him. I know I can. Want me to put him down?"

Lily-Rose wasn't sure she knew the answer to that. Something about seeing Christopher with blood trailing down his face gripped her heart. Then there was the old man saying he needed to see her. And who, for pity's sake, had hit Christopher over the head?

"Wait a minute, mister," Christopher said, raising the other hand. "No need for trouble, although I think I've already walked into it." He squinted as if focusing his eyes. "Look, Lily-Rose," he breathed deeply. "I don't mean any trouble, but someone is hunting you."

"Wha—" Lily-Rose started, then stopped as Biddle coughed.

"Christopher Pembrick," he said, then, coming around Cole. He held out a shaky hand. "I never dreamed I'd be lucky enough to see you too." He looked back at Lily-Rose. "Now you're both here."

Christopher winced, as he pulled his hand down, obviously in pain. "If you don't mind," he looked at Biddle, "can I ask who you are?"

Biddle took a breath, his face nearly devoid of color. "My name is Bob Biddle." He wheezed. "Your parents hired me to do some legal work for them."

Beyond the confines of the building, the emcee announced another band to the stage and the crowd went wild. Lily-Rose looked from the open door then back to Christopher who was studying the feeble man. She struggled to concentrate on Biddle's words and his purpose being there. But it was next to impossible.

Christopher's hand went back to his head, and he exhaled. "That's impossible, Mr. Biddle. My parents died years ago." Lily-Rose couldn't take another moment of seeing the wound on his head ooze blood. She stepped from behind Cole and over to a table where bandages and peroxide were laid out.

"Lily-Rose," Cole warned.

But she raised her hand, letting him know she was okay. She wasn't sure how she knew it, but she knew.

Christopher, on the other hand, showed no emotion to what Biddle had said. "Not you," he told the old man. "They had lawyers—Counselor, then Kid Karn." Lily-Rose kept her distance as she handed Christopher several squares of gauze along with a bottle of peroxide. "Why would—thank you—" he said briefly, "Why would they need your help?"

Lily-Rose stepped back toward Cole, who now made his way over to Christopher, then helped him by opening the bottle of peroxide and pouring some onto the gauze.

Biddle reached into his left breast pocket. "I have proof. Here's the letter of offer they gave me when they asked me to join Pembrick Transportation." He carefully smoothed the tri-folded single sheet of paper against his chest. "See. It's all here. On letterhead. The date. Your father's signature too." He held letter out for Christopher to take. "They gave the offer to me at dinner the night of the accident. Told me to read everything over and bring it back in the morning." Biddle reached for a rag from his coat pocket with his other hand and wiped his mouth. He looked down. "But then the accident ... I couldn't get Karn involved. He wouldn't have believed me."

Christopher looked at the old man's hand and the letter it held but didn't take it. Instead, he turned his wounded head toward Cole who said, "I don't know what's going on, Mr. Pembrick, but I can get the sheriff here in two minutes if you do something foolish." He pressed the gauze against Christopher's head.

Christopher looked at Cole with a wince, then pulled away. "Foolish? Who are you anyway?"

Lily-Rose interrupted. "He's my friend. Cole Matheson."

Cole locked eyes with Christopher. "Maybe you think it's time to make your threat good. Is that it?" Cole leaned into Christopher's space. "Know this, Mr. Pembrick, I'm a fairly nice man, but I'm not an inconsolable widow that you can threaten."

"I didn't come here to threaten anyone," Christopher said, pulling the gauze away from his head—red against the white.

He stood, squaring his shoulders for a fight. "But if you want, we can change that right now." Christopher stared back at Cole.

"You guys, stop." Lily-Rose wedged herself between them. "Cole, thank you, but calm yourself." She looked at her brother-in-law. Her old friend. And nemesis. "Christopher, what are you doing here?"

Christopher tossed the bloody gauze in a nearby trashcan, then nodded toward Biddle. "Who's this guy and why is he stirring a pot that's been left alone for over ten years?" He took a breath and closed his eyes. "Look … man, my head hurts … I've finally come to terms with my life, Mr. Biddle," his hooded eyes resting on the old man. "I'm in a good place now. That's why I came here. To make amends." He looked now at her. "To Lily-Rose." He pointed to the letter in Biddle's hand. "Please. Whatever that is, let it go. I can't take more disappointments regarding my parents." He paused. "Besides, why now? And how do we know you're not lying?"

Through labored breaths, Biddle told Christopher, Lily-Rose, and Cole that William and Sandra Pembrick had hired him to write a new will—newer than the one Karn had read after their funeral. He went on to explain that Christopher had been left the majority of the family fortune and Edward a smaller amount.

Biddle coughed again. "Mr. Pembrick, why would I lie to you? I have nothing to gain by this." He wiped his mouth and looked at Christopher through clouded eyes. "Look at me. Mr. Pembrick. Christopher. You've got a nasty gash there, true. But I'm dying. There's nothing in this for me one way or another. My family's gone. I've spent most of my money tracking down Lily-Rose to make this right. I needed to do one good thing." He started coughing again then swayed like a fighter in a ring listening for the final bell.

"Please, stop," Christopher begged, his voice breaking. "All I ever saw was how they loved Edward. 'Edward, the favorite.' 'Edward, the business mogul.'" He looked at Lily-Rose. "'Edward, the perfect husband.' I was always second." He looked away and raked his hair with his fingers, then winced when his fingers hit the wounded spot. Taking a deep breath, he turned back. Lily-Rose's own breath caught in her throat as she watched and listened to Christopher's lament. "But I've worked hard to come to peace with that. Like I said. I'm good now. My life has a deeper purpose—" He looked at Lily-Rose. "It's more than chasing after empty pleasures."

Biddle pulled back a bit and coughed. "You don't understand." He offered the letter again to Christopher. "Go ahead. Look at it."

Christopher's patience seemed to have worn thin. He ripped the letter from Biddle's hand. "All right, I'll call your bluff. I'll prove to you that you and this letter are fake. Few people ever noticed how Dad signed his legal papers. Mother said he was paranoid, and Counselor was sworn to secrecy. But he always included an extra hump on the 'm' in Pembrick. Let's see what this letter shows."

Christopher looked at the letter, then back up at Mr. Biddle.

Lily-Rose took a single step forward and touched his arm. Something had changed—or nearly changed—in this man. "What do you see, Christopher?"

Christopher whispered. "This has to be a trick." He stared at Biddle, his tone sharpened. "This has to be a trick. If this document is real, that means …"

He took in a deep breath and slowly blew it out of his nose as he looked back again at the letter. "All these years. Lost."

He turned away, put the hand that held the letter on his hip and the other, fingers curled, under his jaw. His tone softened. "Does this mean they loved me? Like the times I was a rebellious teenager?" He looked at Lily-Rose. "I only did that to get a reaction, you know." He looked back at Biddle. "I was such an angry man when I was younger. I dared anyone to get close enough to love me." He looked at Lily-Rose and Cole, then back to Biddle. "Are you telling me all that pain was for nothing?"

Biddle's voice was soft. The single light hanging from the top of the room illuminated the space. "They told me they had planned to offer you what you desired. A place at the Pembrick's business table. But the gesture had been snuffed out in the car accident. Until now."

Lily-Rose glanced toward the opened door. Where was Sugar? Had she gotten lost in the crowd? The sun had set, and darkness had settled over the festival. Outside the crowd cheered as the emcee introduced the next group. "Give it up for Minnesota's newest group, The Dairymen."

"I came here to make amends."

"Wait a minute. You said 'amends.' I thought you wanted me dead?"

Christopher shifted his gaze from the paper, then back to Lily-Rose and exhaled. "I was a miserable person who said some terrible things before. And I'm truly sorry for all the pain I put you through. That's why I'm here. In Applegate. I came to ask your forgiveness."

He reached again for the back of his head. "But there's more." He glanced over at Cole. "When I arrived, I found a man also looking for you." He stopped. "You're in danger, Lily-Rose. I came to warn you, but then—" He touched the cut on his head.

Lily-Rose crossed her arms, then took a step toward Christopher. "So, if I'm not running from you, then who am I running from?"

"Well, well, well," came a voice from the infirmary's entrance. "What a beautiful family reunion we have here."

chapter 39

Life's tragedy is that we get old too soon and wise
too late.

—Benjamin Franklin

Christopher turned as Gaylord Johnson walked in.

Lily-Rose felt her brow furrow. "Mr. Johnson?" Why would
her banker—

Her eyes shifted as the flashing lights from the psychedelic
pulses on stage came through the window and glistened
against the revolver's barrel. Had he followed Christopher out
of Lincoln? To Applegate? To protect her?

"Lily-Rose," Christopher said, one arm extended toward
her. "I think—"

Cole turned to Lily-Rose. "Who is this—"

"Mr. Johnson. He's been our banker and one of Edward's
closest friends for years." She looked at the man blocking the
doorway. "It's okay," she said, nodding. "Really, you can put
the gun down."

Johnson stared with steeled eyes and sneered. "Yeah. I
don't think so. It's funny, I've been watching, biding my time
all these years. Hating the fact that you Pembrick boys had
everything given to you. I knew one day I'd find a way to make
my move. Grab all the chips." He smirked. "Christopher, my
boy. You made this too easy.

"I almost ran into you and Lily-Rose that day after
Edward's funeral ... on my way to Karn's office. You know, in

the garage? Where you threatened Lily-Rose?" He arched his brow. "Lucky for me, right?" He gave a laugh. "Chris, ol' man, you were fired up!"

Lily-Rose frowned and cocked her head as she took a step back, closer to Cole.

What was he saying? Had it been him, all along?

She recalled their last meeting. At the bank. Had she said too much? Thoughts swirled in her head. Her focus returned to Johnson and his gun.

"When I heard you threaten Lily-Rose like you did, well, all the pieces fell together for me," he said, bringing her back to the muddled present. "I rushed back to the bank to start pulling a plan together. Got there in the nick of time too. Just before you popped in for your money."

He paced slowly. "It was easy to remind folks around town of your crazy outbursts over the years. Kind of legendary stuff there, you know. So, you became the perfect patsy. We take care of Lily-Rose and her kids—me and Karn—and leave breadcrumbs of clues back to you. Everyone would put two and two together. Then I'd tell the cops what I heard … you threatening Lily-Rose and her kids." Johnson chuckled. "Yesiree. Then they'd blame you. Because everybody knew you're a hothead-no-good loser. Easy."

Cole had wrapped his fingers around Lily-Rose's arm and pulled her back, slowly, she knew, so as not to startle Mr. Johnson. "I'm confused," she said.

Christopher kept his eyes on Johnson. "That's what I was trying to tell you." His fingertips graced his forehead. "My bet is that Johnson here is the guy who knocked me over the head."

Johnson looked at Lily-Rose. "Your instinct was good to run." He smiled, although the smile seemed anything but friendly. "I did my best to have you tell me where you were going. And even made it possible to track your whereabouts when I gave you those letters of authenticity. All you had to do was give one of those to a bank. They'd call for verification, then bingo. I'd have you." He shrugged. "But you never took me up on my offer. Guess between the cash you already had and what you took from the bank really was good enough. Pity. Looks like Edward really did take good care of you."

"You can't do this." Biddle began coughing again, this time doubling over.

Johnson chuckled. "Look. That boy doesn't need anything." He jerked the gun toward Christopher. "He's lived high all these years. Me and Karn have been holding down the fort all along. Ever since Karn took over Pop's place at PT, he's been redirecting phony payments to a bogus account for me. In turn, I took care of him by setting aside a few bucks here and there. That was, until you left town." His leer came back to Lily-Rose. "All of a sudden, he grew a conscience and tried to stop giving me info. It took some time, but I got him back on course." He took in a deep breath. "Tracking you down has been a challenge, Lily-Rose, but worth it."

Johnson walked farther into the infirmary, gun still pointed toward them.

Christopher glared at Johnson while still holding the letter. "Did you know about this?"

"What is this?"

"A document that proves my parents actually loved me."

Johnson snapped. "Of course they did, you fool. So they tried to live vicariously through son number two. What's wrong with that?" He looked directly at Christopher. "Guess they realized they did you wrong, huh. Too bad you found out so late." His voice grew stern as he motioned with the gun and chuckled. "You have more pressing things to think about. Mainly meeting your Maker. Now. All of you." He waved the gun. "Back corner."

Lily-Rose turned her attention to the music that continued to blare outside the infirmary. If he killed them—when he killed them—no one would hear the shots. Lily-Rose glanced around. Her children … what would happen to her children? And where was that nurse? And Sugar. *Oh, Sugar. Wherever you are, stay there. Please.* She glanced up at Cole, who seemed intent on following whatever he was told to do. Was he buying time? Or was he as afraid as she?

Biddle pressed past the coughing and continued his focus on Christopher. As if not paying any attention to Johnson or his gun, he pushed as if he knew his time was short—one way or the other—and he had to say what drove him all those miles, past his pain. "They loved you, Mr. Pembrick. Christopher." He sighed as they all moved slowly away from the door. "Their last night … that night at The Cedars … all they talked about was how they could show you in a way you would understand. They wanted you to know that they loved you just as much as Edward. They knew you found pleasure in things. Possessions and titles. That's why they wanted to change the will. They wanted to show you, not just tell you."

No.

She wasn't going to simply walk to the back of the infirmary and let this man shoot her. Shoot Cole. Mr. Biddle.

Lily-Rose felt her face heat as she faced Johnson. She jerked her arm from Cole's grip.

"How could you be so evil?" Her eyes met his. What did she have to lose, after all? "You were like a part of our family. Edward looked up to you. Trusted you. Relied on you after William died." She growled between clenched teeth, her mother bear instincts rising. "And if you do anything to my kids, I swear, I'll see that you pay for it."

She felt Cole reach out and grab her arm again. This time

maneuvering her behind him a bit more. "Lily-Rose. Try not to upset him. He's got the gun."

Johnson chuckled. "Very touching ... whoever you are. Those are some wise words. Yes, I'm the dude with the gun." He cleared his throat. "No worries. After I'm done here, I'll find those kids of yours. I'm sure they're hanging around somewhere in town—"

Lily-Rose started after him, but Cole's grip stopped her. "You leave my children—"

"Alone? Can't. They're next in line to inherit PT. Besides, they probably know too much."

"They know nothing."

Johnson's brow raised. "Don't worry, Lily-Rose. You'll see them soon. That's what you do-good people believe, right? Streets of gold and all that?"

She started for him again, but Cole's grip stopped her.

"My plan," Johnson continued, "was to have Christopher sit in jail the rest of his life. But I guess he's going to have to die in the scuffle. Then I'll carry on as the dutiful executor of the estate." He laughed, enjoying himself. "Hey. I'll be the good guy in all this. Other than knocking you guys and the kids off, of course." Johnson pointed the gun their way. "So long, Lily-Rose. It's been swell knowing you."

Cole shielded Lily-Rose with his body and tried to protect his head with his arm. "What kind of a man—"

A flash of blonde came rushing in the room for Johnson. "Not today, you pot-licker." Sugar barreled into Johnson and jerked his arm upward as the gun went off.

"Sugar!"

In a sprint, Christopher and Cole leaped at Johnson as he tried to regain his balance. Together, they tussled until they knocked his gun to the side. "I think she broke my ribs," Mr. Johnson moaned.

Christopher spoke as he and Cole secured him to the floor. "That'll be the least of your worries, pal. Lily-Rose, look through the supplies over there and see if you can find any tape or zip ties. Anything to take care of this roach. We'll hold him down until we get him secured." He looked at Sugar. "Crazy woman. See if you can't get the gun without shooting somebody."

"Who do you think you're talking to? One thing I know is how to handle a gun," Sugar said in defiance.

Lily-Rose rifled through the boxes and found a spool of medical tape. "Will this work?"

"Perfect."

She handed the tape to Christopher, then joined Sugar, giving her a long hug. She finally pulled back. "You knocked him down flat, Sugar. Whatever made you do that?"

"Thought I'd give you some time with Mr. Biddle." She shook her head. "Those bathroom lines were crazy-long. Then walkin' up, I heard that fella there on the ground talkin' all sorts of trash. Terrible things." She put her hands on her hips. "I watched Dungar take down blockers when we was in school. Hit 'em high, and they go down hard. Looks like that works real good with bad guys too."

Lily-Rose pushed the hair away from her eyes. "Good thing you did. You saved our lives. All of us. Including … Mr. Biddle?" She turned. Mr. Biddle lay crumbled on the ground, a pool of blood forming around him. "Mr. Biddle!" She rushed to him, Cole behind her.

"What happened?" Lily-Rose gasped as her head whipped toward the door. A stout woman wearing a nurse's uniform stood with her hands spread wide. "I was gone for just a few minutes."

Sugar snapped back. "Longer than a few minutes."

The nurse rushed over, then knelt. "Sir, can you hear me?" When Biddle remained silent, she ripped open his blood-soaked shirt. Lily-Rose looked on to see a bullet hole in Biddle's chest.

The nurse placed her fingers against his neck. "He's still with us." She looked up at Cole. "Pull some towels and gauze from the crates. I need more towels."

Lily-Rose focused on the wounded man. "Hang on, Mr. Biddle. We got you."

Cole rushed to one of the bins, then returned with a stack of old but clean towels. The nurse grabbed two, held them against the wound, and took Lily-Rose's hands and told her to apply pressure. She jumped up then and rushed over for additional supplies.

Two men who had clearly been enjoying the festival, staggered into the infirmary. They looked at Biddle then to Cole and Christopher securing Johnson. "Dude. I told you I heard something."

Christopher yelled to them. "Go get help. A man's been shot."

They stood wide-eyed. "Bummer."

Cole fired back. "Go get Earl. He'll know how to get the sheriff."

Sugar handed Cole the gun, then grabbed one of the men by the arm. "You look like you might need some help. C'mon. I'll lead the way." She called back over her shoulder. "Be back when we know something."

Lily-Rose, kneeling beside Biddle, whimpered through sobs. "Mr. Biddle, can you hear me?"

His eyes fluttered. Blood began trailing along his jawline from his mouth. By now, the nurse had returned. She took Lily-Rose's place at applying pressure. With a free hand she wiped away the blood from his mouth, then looked at Lily-Rose with a shake of her head. The man was dying, her eyes said. And it wouldn't be long.

But Lily-Rose continued. "You're going to be fine, Mr. Biddle. Just stay still. The ambulance is on its way." She took off her suede vest and slipped it under Biddle's head. His eyes opened. She smiled at him. "Is that better? Stay with me, you hear? We've sent for help. They'll be here soon."

"There you go, Johnson. Try to get the upper hand now," Christopher said, and Lily-Rose looked to see that he'd taped their almost-killer to a table leg. He hurried over to where Lily-Rose knelt.

"I'll keep a watch," Cole said, turning the gun toward Johnson.

"Mr. Biddle," Christopher stayed close. "Hang in there. Help's coming."

Biddle began whispering too softly for Lily-Rose to hear. She covered one of her ears to block out the music and leaned closer to catch his raspy voice in the other. "What? What can I do for you?"

"Papers. In pocket."

"Shh. Don't worry about anything." She stroked his forehead. His color faded. Gray settled in.

Biddle persisted. "Papers. Right pocket," he repeated. He squinted his eyes. "Proof you'll need."

She used her bloody hand and reached into his coat pocket. There she found several pages of paper and slipped them into her lap.

Biddle tried to speak. "Tell Johnnie ... I ... good man ... made my wrongs right."

Lily-Rose's tears fell. Her hands returned to offer help applying pressure to his wound. She'd figure out who Johnny was later. "I'll tell him. Promise."

The nurse cursed under her breath, placing her hands atop Lily-Rose's. "I hope that ambulance gets here soon," she whispered.

Lily-Rose pulled her hands free then handed the folded papers to Christopher.

Biddle offered a weak smile to her brother-in-law. "I got … got here in time … didn't I?"

Christopher's words were soft. "Shh, Mr. Biddle. Yes, you got here in time. Now lay still."

His breathing became strenuous, his eyes widened as he gagged. A gurgle rose from the back of his throat and, in a moment, his body went limp as a labored breath escaped from his falling chest.

His eyes fixed, stared ahead.

The nurse searched again for a pulse, then shook her head. "He's gone," she said, then looked at her watch. "9:23."

⁂

The sheriff and crew shut down the festival once they arrived. Yet deep into the night, activity swirled around the infirmary. Christopher, Cole, Sugar, Lily-Rose, and a smattering of other people stayed to answer questions long after the medical examiner sent Mr. Biddle's body to the morgue. Dungar was called to take Sugar home. Cole stayed at a safe distance while Lily-Rose and Christopher sat on a cot at the far end of the cinder block building.

She looked at him as she absent-mindedly worked the sticky blood from her nailbeds. She took a deep breath. "It won't be long now. You know how this will go. Soon the news of what happened tonight will reach beyond the borders of Ohio."

He nodded. "Then camera crews and news reporters from all over the country will swoop in. Teams from radio and television stations will invade the quiet town by tomorrow."

She smiled as a chuckle escaped her. "Did you know I live on the safest street in the country?"

He grinned back. "Safest in the country? You don't say."

She dropped her head. "That is, until all this gets out." She sat up and waved her hand across the air in front of her. "I can read the headlines now—Lily-Rose Pembrick, runaway heiress to the Pembrick fortune, has been hiding with her kids in a small town in Ohio, only to have her banker attempt to kill her." She paused, then waved her hand in the opposite direction. "Oh, and how about this—estranged brother-in-law to take over transportation dynasty."

Christopher reached for her hands and pulled them down. "I really am sorry. For everything."

"I can see that." She leaned against him and rested her head on his shoulder and closed her eyes.

Maybe, just maybe, if she kept them closed long enough, she'd fall asleep long enough for the nightmare to be over.

chapter 40

Darkness cannot drive out darkness: only light can
do that. Hate cannot drive out hate: only love can
do that.

—Martin Luther King Jr.

As Lily-Rose predicted, swarms of local news reporters
invaded the McKinney farm by midnight. Local police did
their best to shield Lily-Rose and Christopher after their on-
site testimonies were given. It wasn't until one of Applegate's
own spoke up that calm wrapped the crowd in a trusty blanket.
And, of course, Cole was the one who walked between Lily-
Rose and Christopher and the reporters shielding them as they
left. "Okay folks, show's over. It's late. You have your stories.
Time to let these folks go on home. Hope to see some of you
in church later." His voice rose on the last sentence.

But a man from the *Cleveland Press* pushed on. "Why are
you protecting them, Cole? They're looking pretty cozy right
now. Think they're conniving on how to spend their money?"

"Look," he said, his voice weary. "You got your story.
Johnson's the one who came here to cause trouble. Go check
him out."

"He's gone," someone from the crowd shot back. "Sheriff
took him away in cuffs."

Cole encouraged the reporters the best he could as they
packed their equipment to leave. "Go on home. Get a fresh
start in the morning."

Christopher left Lily-Rose and walked closer to Cole and reached out his hand to shake. "You have a way with crowds."

Cole took the offered hand. "Yeah, well, talking to people's my thing. I do it for a living."

Christopher stared. "Is crowd busting a thing?"

Cole chuckled. "No. I'm the pastor at Mercy and Grace Community Church in town. Love to have you come by. See how I work the crowds for the Lord."

Lily-Rose sighed as Christopher and Cole continued their conversation. These two men in her life—two men who were different as day from night. Christopher, who always stood outside the loving arms of his family, and Cole, whose family involvement almost smothered him. Both took control of their lives in their own way—one through serving God and the other through serving himself.

Two men remarkably different from one another. And she she loved them both.

Her voice was soft as she spoke to them. "Funny what drives a person. Mr. Biddle spent everything he had to find me, just to tell me he was sorry." Her gaze went from one to the other. "He got shot in the process. Died. Yet the last thing he said was he made his wrongs right." She looked at her hands and tried to wipe away the dried blood. "Funny."

Cole bent down to look into her eyes, remaining until she finally looked up. "Evil came to your door, Lily-Rose. But God used Biddle to protect you." He attempted a laugh. "That is, with the help of Sugar Bowersox." After a deep breath. "It looks like you don't have to look over your shoulder anymore." He gently brushed the hair from her eyes.

Christopher cleared his throat. "Well," he said with a sigh. "Time for me to get some sleep. Then head back to Lincoln." He pulled Biddle's papers from his pocket, paused. "Of course, I'll stay here for you and the kids. If you need me." His gaze shifted to Cole then back. "No. You're safe now, Lily-Rose. Anyway, I need to spend some time looking over these papers. Get Lincoln ready for the Pembrick shuffle. I'll start asking around for names of legal firms that might want to represent us. Maybe hire an advertising agency to help clean this mess up." He smiled. "I'll get Lincoln ready for you—that is, if you want to come back."

Cole lightly patted Christopher's shoulder as he steered him in the direction of the others leaving the infirmary area. "Good idea. Sleep. Your day was a full one." They stopped walking but Cole kept his hand on Christopher. "And you're right. This might be a real legal mess. I'm confident you can work everything out."

Lily-Rose sat silent as Christopher walked away from the infirmary. As he and the reporters continued to leave, he turned back to Lily-Rose. "Call if you need anything. No. Call me no matter what."

"Okay," she said with a nod. "See you. And thanks."

Cole returned his attention to Lily-Rose. "Well, now. That's taken care of. Christopher's off to Lincoln. He'll get the ball rolling, for sure." He took on his coach's stance, looking confident. "It's amazing how everything worked out. You're a free woman now, Lily-Rose. You can do what you want."

Lily-Rose's mouth gaped. "Is that what you think?" She wondered if the heat showed on her face as a lifetime of pent up anger, fear, and resentment welled up inside her. "I've dealt with loss my entire life. Loss of my parents. Then friends because I moved so much. I spent years struggling financially while living with Mama and Papa Henderson and then college. I met Edward and fell hopelessly in love, only to lose him too. Then I'm convinced Christopher's crazy enough to kill me and my kids, so I run to a small town in Ohio." She took a breath. "And the first thing you say is, 'I'm a free woman now'? You have got to be kidding me."

Cole stared back; his brow furrowed. "What? It's true, isn't it? You can get the Lincoln finances back now. That makes you free."

"Cole," she said, her voice trembling even as she tried to keep it calm. "Don't you understand? None of what I've done over the past few years has ever been about the money."

"I don't get it. What'd I say? We can make sure everyone has enough and loads left over for the kids. It'll all be fine."

"We?" Her eyes widened. Who was this Cole? He sounded like a completely different person. Her hands began to shake. She clinched them, trying to gain control. "Stop talking. Just stop talking." She took a deep breath. Tears pooled around her eyes.

Two years earlier her world had turn upside down. She had gone from being a Lincoln socialite to a mother on the run with her kids. She had lost the most important person in her life, only to find an untapped internal strength of her own. Money had been—and still was—the last thing on her mind.

Edward.

She walked back into the infirmary and sat on a cot. Cole followed.

He exhaled hard as he stood in front of her. "I'm sorry. I'm sorry that Biddle died and Johnson wanted you dead for your money. I'm sorry that you had to lose Edward the way you did. And I'm sorry you've had one letdown after another in your life." He sat beside Lily-Rose and reached for her hand, weaving his fingers with hers. "But I have a proposition—a proposal."

Lily-Rose pulled back and looked into his eyes. "What?"

"Lily-Rose, I'm trying to say something important."

"This entire night has been important. When did all this shift and become about you?"

Cole cleared his throat and squared his shoulders. "Let's get married, Lily-Rose. Come to Ireland. We can make a difference together. You. Me. The kids. What do you say?"

She said nothing. Not because she didn't have an answer, but because—suddenly—every emotion she'd ever felt was swirling within her, like a cotton candy machine creating its fluffy treat. Only this wasn't sweet. It wasn't pink or blue and wouldn't leave a stain on her lips and tongue. But these feelings may scar her spirit, if she allowed it.

"Lily-Rose?"

How much strength did she need before this nightmare came to its grand conclusion?

"Cole." Her voice remained controlled, a fact that shocked her. "This has been quite a day. Right now, I need to go home and hug my kids. I hope you understand. By morning's light, news crews from Lincoln will be here. I need time to prepare for the invasion. Besides, you have a service in the morning." She looked at her watch. Tapped its face with her fingernail. "Today's Sunday, remember?" She took a deep breath. "You really need to give me—give us—some time. I'll get back to you on your proposal. All right?"

"Oh, sure. Sure," Cole stammered and stood again. "I'll take you home."

Lily-Rose stood as well. "No need. I'll have one of the deputies take me to the school. Mary has the car there. I want to tell them about everything that happened before someone else does. Hopefully, we can share some peace and quiet before all our lives change again. After tomorrow, nothing will be the same for them … for the rest of their lives. Again. I hope you understand. We're safer now than we've been in years. And they are my first concern. I need to give them hugs."

chapter 41

You can't calm the storm ... so stop trying. What
you can do is calm yourself. The storm will pass.

—Unknown

An Applegate deputy called ahead to Principal Miller to
make sure Mary, Del, and Scout would be allowed to leave the
school. A sob caught in Lily-Rose's throat when the squad car
rounded the corner and the school came into view.

Safe.

Her kids had been safe there. She didn't just want to hug
her two babies, she needed to hold each one until that need
passed.

The deputy parked under mercury-vapor light and waited.
Mr. Miller stuck his head out and waved, then sent Del and
Mary out the door. Scout bounded alongside. Lily-Rose got
out of the squad car and walked toward them, then stopped,
watching as they lumbered toward her.

What a beautiful sight. She smiled.

Mary's complaining greeted her before she was within arm's
length. "Mother, this better be important. Sarah and I—" She
froze. "Wait—a cop car?" She began walking again. Once
closer, her eyes widened. "Mom, what's that on your hands?"
Del and Scout followed.

"It's blood, but—"

"Blood?"

"Yes, but I'm okay." Lily-Rose wrapped her arms around

her two kids. After a moment she broke the silence. "Let's get the car and go home. It's been a long day."

"But Mom—" Del inserted.

"Please, honey. I promise I'll tell you everything. But let me at least drive us home first. We'll talk when we get there."

They drove in silence. Once home, Lily-Rose broke the ice. "You two go climb on my bed. We can chat there. I just need to wash up first."

She left the bathroom drying her hands on a towel she decided to throw away later, then headed to her bedroom. There, she found her children—Scout between them— propped up on the pillows. She smiled as she put Scout on the foot of the bed, then scooched between them as Del's pup tucked his snout under his back paws in a canine curl.

"I met a man today—well, last night, really—by the name of Mr. Biddle. He drove here from Lincoln to see me."

Mary straightened and looked at her. "Mom. The blood?"

"I'll get there, Mary." She yawned. She really needed sleep. But her children needed to hear the story from her first. "He came here to tell me that there had been a mistake years ago. Seems Unc-a-bunk was supposed to control PT, not your dad."

Del pushed for more. "But what's that got to do with your bloody hands?"

"Shh," Mary ordered. "Mom, go on"

"Mr. Biddle came to tell me the news, and Unc-a-bunk arrived about the same time."

"It's Unc-a-bunk's blood?"

"Mary, stop." Lily-Rose patted her daughter's hand. "Stop and listen. We were in the music festival's infirmary—Cole, Sugar, Mr. Biddle, and Unc-a-bunk—when Mr. Johnson came in. You remember him, right? From our Lincoln bank?"

She paused to let her kids wrap their minds around what she had just told them. But she had to tell them more. What was the age-appropriate information when telling a child that someone tried to kill their mother?

Mary tilted her head. "The bank's Mr. Johnson?"

Lily-Rose gently pulled Mary into her arms. "Mr. Johnson shot Mr. Biddle when Biddle stepped in front of me. Mr. Johnson meant to shoot me but got Biddle instead."

"Meant to shoot you ... Why?"

Del whispered, "Is he okay?"

Lily-Rose pulled him close as well. "He died, sweetie."

Her son began to cry. "Why did he try to kill you? Did Unc-a-bunk try to kill you too?"

Lily-Rose smiled and handed him a tissue from her nightstand. "No. In fact, he had come to warn me that we were in danger." She drew her two children even closer as she finished telling them of all that transpired at the music festival. About Mr. Biddle. And finally filling them in on what she knew about Mr. Johnson. Capping it off with "And Sugar saved us all."

Del stammered. "Gosh, Mom, are you okay?"

Lily-Rose nuzzled her kids as she began to weep. Tears of relief that she hadn't been able to shed for over two years had finally broken free. Their ordeal was over. They would be able to get their lives back again.

"We're finally safe, kids."

Mary shook her head. "That's incredible, Mom. But are you sure? Safe, I mean?"

"Very sure. Unc-a-Bunk is heading back to Lincoln to get things sorted out there." She paused. "But there's more, you guys."

Scout whined, deciding that he'd had enough of being at the foot of the bed.

"Scout." Del pulled the dog close. "Go on, Mom."

Lily-Rose smiled, tears still falling. "An opportunity has

come up."

"What opportunity?" Mary asked.

Lily-Rose shifted as Scout rooted under the covers for a place to make his own.

"There are lots of opportunities ahead of us now. We can go back to Lincoln. It'll take some time to work out the details, but with everything that's transpired and with Unc-a-bunk leading the way, I'm confident we can pass Pembrick Transportation over to him."

Mary frowned. "Are you sure we're not afraid of him anymore? I thought we left Lincoln because he was up to no good."

Lily-Rose touched her cheek. "He was up to no good, but after we left, he had a change of heart. That's what brought him to Applegate. He came here to make it right."

"Mom, are you sure?"

She offered a motherly nod. "Yes, honey. I'm sure."

After moments of silence, Del finally spoke. "Do you think he'll want to be our uncle again? That is, if he's safe and all." He looked at her with those blue eyes—Edward's blue eyes. "As long as you're okay with that, I mean."

She tussled his hair. "I think that's a fantastic idea, sweetie."

"Wait," Mary said, pushing back from her mother. "If we can go back to Lincoln, that means we don't have to stay in Applegate anymore."

Lily-Rose and Del shifted as well. "That's true. We came here for a reason. Now the reason's gone."

"Gee, Mom," Del said. "I never thought we'd leave here. I know we don't have all the stuff we had in Lincoln, but—"

"But what, baby?"

"I kinda like living here."

"I know, sweetie." Lily-Rose paused as she rubbed the lumpy imprint of Scout with her foot. "But there's another opportunity I need to tell you about." She took a breath. "Coach Cole's asked me to marry him. He's moving to Ireland and wants us to go with him."

Silence.

Mary frowned. "What? Ireland, like Ireland-Ireland? Like the IRA Ireland? There's a war going on over there, Mom."

Del shrugged, passing off the geography lesson. "He is a nice guy, I s'pose." He hedged. "Is that what you want, Mom?"

Lily-Rose chimed in. "You're right. He is a very nice man. But I just don't know. He only asked me this afternoon."

Mary's eyes narrowed. "Was that before or after the gun shots? Does he love you, Mom, or is it the Pembrick money he learned about?"

Lily-Rose leaned down and kissed Mary on the cheek. "Pull in your fangs, lovely daughter. He brought the subject up before the shooting, but he asked after. He said he'd been praying about how to settle his heart, and this is what he came up with."

"Mom?" Del began, "Did you get that in any of your prayers?"

Once again, her son's wisdom went beyond his years. "No. Not a peep. My focus has been on you guys. And on who I need to be." She made a silly face. "Getting married again wasn't even on my radar— let alone moving halfway across the world."

"What did you tell him?"

Mary, always wanting the details.

"I told him I'd have to think about it. That I didn't have an answer. I told him he was a nice guy and I liked him a lot." She rubbed Scout's imprint again with her foot. "But my plate's a bit full right now."

"Mom," Del snuggled in his spot. "I'm tired of changes. Can't we just stay here? Like we are?" He muttered. "Besides, we have friends in Applegate. Real friends."

Mary followed his lead. "Yeah. Like Del said. Real friends. Honestly, it's been nice living on Norwood. Sarah likes me because she thinks I'm nice. Not because I'm a Pembrick."

"It's a great place here. And my room—" Del paused, his voice cracked.

"Go on," Lily-Rose said, stroking his arm.

"I picked out what I wanted in my room. The colors. Posters. Everything. And it's the best room I ever had. In Lincoln, the guys I hung out with always bragged how they had great stuff. Pretty boring. 'specially since it was the only time they really ever talked to me. Braggin'. Hoping they were better off than me." He wiped his eyes, rimmed in red from lack of sleep, then swallowed a yawn. "It's nice to be around fellas who don't know we have money."

"Wow," Lily-Rose sighed, then yawned herself. "When'd you guys get so wise?"

"It's you, Mom," Mary looked at her. "You were kinda cool before, but now you really listen to us. You include us in what you do. It's like you like us."

"I do like you—I love you."

"But it's different here—you're different."

"Yeah, Mom. Different," Del said.

Lily-Rose couldn't speak.

"Look, Mom," Mary reached for Lily-Rose's hand. "Del and I talk. We knew you cried all the time after Daddy died. We saw you kinda shrivel up. That made us sad. And mad. But then you threw us in the car—"

"I didn't throw you in the car."

"Mom." Mary looked at Del. "Would you feel bad if we said we wanted to go back to the lock-in? You told us about your options. But if we either go back to Lincoln or to Ireland, we'll need to say good-bye to our friends." Mary continued to hold her mother's hand. "Can we spend more time with them tonight? I mean, everyone's safe, right? Please?"

Lily-Rose pulled both of her kids close. "Oh, you guys. Not tonight. Our lives have just been rocked significantly. I think I need you here. With me. And you might not get it, but I think you need to be with me too."

"Mother, but if we have to go—to leave again—I don't want it to be like last time. I at least want the chance to say good-bye to my friends."

"Yeah, Mom," Del added. "Besides, you'll be talking to your friends at the fire anyways."

"No fire tonight, my lovelies. I'm exhausted."

She held her kids close. She had almost lost them. Almost lost them.

"I promise. You can see all your friends tomorrow. In fact, it'll probably be best for you if you're not around. It's gonna be a bit hectic here once the word gets out about what happened." She shifted her position to see them both at the same time. "What if Mary takes you both out of here and hangs with Donna Masters and her family."

"What about church?" Mary, always looking for more answers.

"I think we'll have our own church, before you head out." She snuggled with them. "Lord knows we have a lot to be thankful for."

"Yeah, we do." Del yawned and snuggled back.

Lily-Rose felt Mary's and Del's bodies slowly relax into her as they fell asleep. Scout's breathing settled into a rhythmic snore. She scratched at the blanket with her foot. "Lucky day for you ... sleeping in Mommy's bed." Scout's head stayed burrowed, but his tail wagged.

She felt herself giving in to sleep as well. Her mind slowing down. Her own breathing shallowing. In her mind, she saw and reached for him.

"Edward?"

She felt his hand cup her face. "I told you, this house was my gift to you. You're safe now."

She needed to speak with him. Was this a dream? Did she speak aloud or just in her mind?

"Edward. Mr. Johnson. He—"

"Shh, I know. But it's all over. Your fear. Your hiding. It's all over. You're safe. You're safe here."

"But what do I do now? I miss you, my love. I need you desperately."

"You're fine now. But know I'm always with you." He leaned down and kissed her lightly on the lips. He then pulled his hand back, and he was gone.

chapter 42

Their last fire

Summer friends will melt away like summer snows,
but winter friends are friends forever.

—George R. R. Martin

Lily-Rose poured the last of the wine in their cups. "That's it, ladies."

The once-roaring late Sunday to early Monday morning fire had turned to glowing embers of yellow and white. The deep blue-black morning sky began to lighten. No birds in the trees or cars driving down the street had dared intrude on the moments. Only the crackling from the firepit.

"I'm leaving in a few hours," Sugar reminded them with a glance to her watch. "Dungar has to be back for practice, and we need to get the kids settled. I'm glad he's good with drivin' the whole way. I'll sleep in the moving truck, and Granny will have the girls in the car."

"I'll be leaving too," Fiona said. "All packed and ready to go. Derrick's going to be by later this morning. Wants to show me a house up by the lake. I'll be staying with his family until the wedding. There is so much planning to do. So … I guess this is it for me too."

Tears welled as Lily-Rose looked from one to the other. "I couldn't have gotten through the past two years without your help."

"Lily-Rose, you're one of the strongest women I know." Sugar laughed. "I'm guessin' you're from mountain people stock. Somewhere back in your history there's mountain people. I know it."

"Sure, she's strong." Fiona stared at the embers. "She's also kind. And wise." She looked at her friends. "I would never have gone to Cleveland if you hadn't showed me I was worth the effort. You two and Miss Fergie. The kindest white people I'll ever know."

Lily-Rose knew it was time for goodbyes but couldn't pull herself to be the first to say the words. Nearly two years of conversations were coming to an end. Tears. Laughter. But most of all discoveries. Lots of discoveries. For all three of them.

But still, another goodbye.

"I saw the fire. Thought I'd stop." The voice caused the three friends to turn as Cole rounded the corner of the house.

Lily-Rose swallowed a gasp. "Cole, what are you doing here?"

"Checking in on you. I missed you in church this morning." He looked at Fiona then Sugar. "Ladies. Good seeing you as well."

Lily-Rose squirmed. "I've been a bit preoccupied with the sheriff and reporters. I didn't get a chance to breathe until late this afternoon."

Sugar leaned in. "Yeah, me too, pastor. Kinda busy for us as well."

Fiona studied the pastor. "You show up at everyone's place well after midnight when they miss a Sunday?"

He laughed. "No, not hardly." He looked around for another chair, finding none. "Am I interrupting?"

Lily-Rose exhaled sharply. "It is our last fire together."

Fiona zeroed in on Cole. "And it's kinda early for casual

visits, Padre. Don't you think? What'd you expect to find?" She crossed her arms. "Preacher or no, what brings you to a woman's house at …" She looked at her watch. "Four o'clock in the morning?"

Cole stammered. "Tru—truly, I meant no harm. I couldn't sleep so I thought I'd drive. Clear my head. Lily-Rose told me about your fires, and I was curious, so here I am." He looked from one woman to the next. "Saw the fire and thought I'd stop to see if she—"

"Ta see what, pastor?" Sugar munched on a forgotten cookie she just pulled from the plate.

"Well, to see if she had an answer for me."

Lily-Rose shot a not-now look at him. "We can talk later, Cole."

But Fiona engaged as well. "What are you holding out on us, girl?

A lonely sizzle escaped the fire. Finally, Cole focused on Lily-Rose. "I came to see if you had an answer for my proposal."

"Proposal?" Fiona and Sugar chimed. Both leaned in, not wanting to miss a thing.

Lily-Rose cleared her throat. "Uh, yes. Cole asked me to marry him while we were still at the festival. Didn't I mention that?"

Sugar mimicked Lily-Rose. "No, you didn't mention it." Then added, "Do ya have an answer?" She turned to Fiona "We got wine left in our cups. The sun hasn't come up yet."

Cole knelt by Lily-Rose's chair. His eyes sparkled against the firelight. Was that hope she saw there? He was incredibly handsome. A terrific person. Guys like this don't come around often. She'd already loved one. Would this be her last chance? "Yes, Lily-Rose, what's your answer?"

Lily-Rose spoke in a soft, yet clear voice. "My answer is thank you … but no."

"Sugar." Fiona looked from Lily-Rose to Cole. "I think it's time for us to go. C'mon over to Miss Fergie's with your cup. And don't forget the rest of the cookies."

"Man, never a dull moment here. Gonna miss this in Baltimore. Goodnight all—I mean good morning."

Sugar and Fiona each hugged Lily-Rose. It was an anticlimactic ending of the short life they shared together. Just as each had stumbled into her life, now they moved on. Would they stay in touch?

Without a doubt. She knew this in the depts of her Knower. Lily-Rose bit the inside of her mouth to keep from crying.

Fiona and Sugar were gone.

Cole reached for Lily-Rose's hand. "Now it's just the two of us. Maybe you can tell me why you won't marry me. Have I been fooling myself? I thought for sure you felt the same way I do. Loved me like I love you."

Lily-Rose studied his eyes for what seemed an eternity, then slowly pulled her hand back. "Maybe I do, Cole, but we never spoke about it—about love." She looked down. "I don't know what that means anymore." She settled into her chair and leaned over and picked up a stirring stick to poke the embers. "I loved my momma, but she left me. Then I went from one home to another, all telling me they loved me but treated me less than lovable. Then I met Christopher, and he loved me to the point of obsession. After that, I met Edward and fell madly in love with him, only to lose him in the end." She looked up from the embers. His eyes rimmed with tears as they glistened by the glow of the firepit.

She put the stick down and turned as Cole hung his head. "I'm not saying you're like any of them, Cole. You've always been kind. You even picked up where Mama Henderson left off, showing me Jesus. And I will always be thankful for that. But I need to take stock of what's going on in my life."

She stood, and in turn, Cole stood as well. "I have kids who are dealing with more pain than they even know. That's not going to be easy. And now we can go back to Lincoln and live in the open if we choose, carrying on the Pembrick name."

Cole finally spoke. "Is it Christopher? Did seeing him spark old flames?"

"I love Christopher, but it's not like that. It's never been like that for me. I love him more like a brother." She looked away, then back. "And, I'll be honest—it feels good, Cole, to love him like that." How could she make him understand? "And now we also have this sweet home in Applegate. Do we stay here, even if we don't need to hide?" She slipped her hands in her jeans pockets. "We learned to live without the Pembrick entitlements while in Applegate. That was a great lesson. But now we have them again ... if we want." She shrugged. "I need to know what to do with all my choices. Besides, Edward made this easy for us. He helped get us set, and now I'm confident I can work something out with Christopher and the new attorneys." She paused for effect. "I just began to figure out how to take care of the kids and me. I don't think I have any business getting married right now."

Lily-Rose stepped up to Cole and reached for his hands as he looked deep into her eyes.

"But we could do so much for God in Ireland," he said, his voice a whisper. "And your roots are there, right? You could investigate your history. Show the kids their ancestry."

Lily-Rose shook her head slowly. "God brought me here for a reason. I think Fiona and Sugar were part of that—and you were a part too." She offered a wry smile. "But my heart hasn't gotten the release to go off to Ireland with you. God still has work for me here—plans. And he has them for Mary and Del as well. And I think those plans include us staying in Applegate. For now, anyway."

Lily-Rose searched Cole's eyes to see if he understood. "You told me over dinner that you have a love for Ireland and the people there. It's important to take care of that."

Cole's voice cracked. "I thought for sure you had feelings for me."

"There's a part of me that is in love with you too. I see that pretty clearly." She took a deep breath. "But you need to go." She added with finality, "and I need to stay."

"Lily-Rose," he grappled. "Don't you see you're breaking my heart? If you think this is what you want, then go for it. But know you're making your decision without my endorsement. We could have a perfect life and ministry together. But your decisions are all on you—"

Cole's eyes widened as he stood silently. He then turned away, shaking his head. "I sounded just like my father when I told him I wasn't going to stay in the family ministry." He sat in the closest chair and hung his face in his hands. "What have I done? I'm sorry, Lily-Rose. Forgive me. I have no right to question what God's plans are for you."

This time, Lily-Rose knelt beside the chair. "It isn't that I don't appreciate what you've done for me and my family. I do. But I've just started to understand there's more for me to learn—about being the mom and person I'm designed to be." She sought his eyes. "We're cool, Cole. Yes, I love you—but the love I have for my family comes first. And we need to figure out our lives. Here in the States. Can you understand that?"

Cole stood and gently pulled her into his arms. His heartbeat met hers as his tears fell on her hair. "I understand more than you know. Would it be all right if I write you? Tell you what's going on in Ireland?"

Lily-Rose's words muffled against his chest. "I'd like that. A lot. And I can tell you what's going on in our lives as well."

"Can I hang on to hope that our story isn't over?"

She took in his scent, memorizing it. "I hope you will. Because I'm hoping the same thing. But right now, I need to take care of me and my kids."

His voice trembled. "Goodbye for now, Lily-Rose. Continue listening to God's voice. He brought us together once, maybe he'll choose to again."

Tears blurred her vision. Part of her heart wanted to go with Cole, but she knew he'd never be enough. She stepped back from his embrace. Cole bent down and gently kissed her forehead. Without a word, he turned and walked away from the fire. The closing car door and crunching gravel let her know he had left, then driven down Norwood Street, the safest street in town.

Lily-Rose sat in her chair and stared up into the midnight blue-filled sky. She thought of all the loss, then all her gain. Edward's voice in her dream from last night as well as all those months ago came back to her.

You'll have a long, full life. You will feel joy, peace … and love again. Much of it will come from your decision to buy this house. My gift to you. I'm always with you.

After what seemed only moments, the sky began to lighten. Sunlight peaked through the painted oak and maple leaves and sparkled against the dew on the grass. A new day had begun.

Lily-Rose stared at the smoldering ashes—pondering choices offered and choices made. More crunching gravel sounds, then the back door creaked. She turned to see Mary and Del, both looking a bit disheveled as they walked toward her, Scout loping behind.

"Neither of us could sleep too good," Del rubbed his eyes. "So I got Mare. She was awake too. We left a note for Donna Masters' parents and came back. Thought we'd find you out here."

"Yeah, Mom, you love your fires. It was easy to figure out."

"Perfect timing, kids," she called opening her arms to them. "Come join me."

They gave her a hug. Mary's hand lingered a bit and rubbed her back. "You okay, Mom?"

"I will be," Lily-Rose smiled. "A fire can fix any problem you have if you sit long enough. Open yourself to its beauty."

Lily-Rose took a breath. "I told him we weren't going to Ireland."

"Coach must be pretty sad." Del patted Scout as he nuzzled his hand. "Do you think we'll ever see him again?"

"My heart's open to that, honey." She picked up the stirring stick and poked at the warm ashes.

He continued. "The ladies are gone too, huh. Do you think you'll ever see them again?"

Lily-Rose took a deep breath. "You can count on it, sweetie. You can count on it." She tilted her head and smiled. "Say, I know we all need some sleep, but let's have a morning fire, just the three of us. A good fire chases a damp chill away and always brings answers. Even in the toughest times."

Mary smiled. "Sure, Mom. What'd you teach us … Pembricks always rise to the occasion?"

"That's right, honey. No matter what."

Lily-Rose and her children settled into their chairs—chairs once meant for Fiona and Sugar, but now meant for them. And somewhere, not too far away, the sun continued to rise.

> O most merciful redeemer, friend and brother, may
> I know thee more clearly,
>
> love thee more dearly, and follow thee more nearly,
> day by day. Amen.
>
> —Saint Richard of Chichester

The End

About the Author

Ladies of the Fire is Robin Gilbert Luftig's debut novel. She has written, *God's Best During Your Worst* (Bold Vision Books) and *Learning to Bloom Again*. Luftig is a sought-after speaker and shares the many aspects of God's mercy and grace at women's retreats and conferences independently as well as for Stonecroft Ministries. She's an active member of Advanced Writers and Speakers Association (AWSA) and Word Weavers International where she serves as a mentor for writers. She and her husband Lew live in Central Pennsylvania.

Made in the USA
Middletown, DE
15 August 2020

14496149R00197